COURT OF HONOR

by

Geoff Taylor

SIMON AND SCHUSTER • NEW YORK

PUBLISHED BY SIMON AND SCHUSTER, INC.
ROCKEFELLER CENTER, 630 FIFTH AVENUE
NEW YORK, N.Y. 10020

FIRST PRINTING

LIBRARY OF CONGRESS CATALOG CARD NUMBER: 66-11954
MANUFACTURED IN THE UNITED STATES OF AMERICA
PRINTED BY THE MURRAY PRINTING CO., FORGE VILLAGE, MASS.
BOUND BY BOOK PRESS, NEW YORK, N.Y.
DESIGNED BY EVE METZ

For John and Nico,
who will know why.

AUTHOR'S NOTE

Although this is a novel, some of the main characters—such as Adolf Hitler's personal secretary, the enigmatic and elusive Martin Bormann—are by no means imaginary. Similarly, so far as certain matters of historical fact are concerned, the author gratefully acknowledges the ready assistance of General Emil F. Reinhardt, U.S. Army (Retired), wartime commander of the U.S. 69th Infantry Division. It was this force which, in April, 1945, linked up with Major General Rusakov's 58th Russian Guards Division on the Elbe at Torgau in Saxony, Germany, to effect the first junction of the armies of the East Front and the West Front in Europe.

So far as the Elbe is concerned, the author can only presume that it is still the same noble river which he first came to know during those tumultuous days of liberation and victory in 1945.

—GEOFF TAYLOR

Contents

BOOK ONE

THE COURT CONVENES

I

The Sword and the Noose

THE JUDGE WAS A BLIND MAN, but this in no way seemed to inhibit the air of stiff pride with which he moved confidently in the uniform of a general of the Panzer troops. Nor was it apparent from his proud manner that he could ever have recognized any irony in the circumstance of his being blind and, also, the president of the court. With a gloved hand resting lightly on the shoulder of the boy, he strode quite quickly and confidently into the great cellars. Although he could not see the people seated there, he could not have failed to be aware of their presence, for there was a great scraping of stools and benches on the stone floor as they rose to stand before him. Seating himself in the oaken chair which the boy had placed ready for him, the general took off the slate-gray peaked cap with the silver oak leaves and the swastika-clutching eagle and laid it deliberately and neatly on the Nazi blood banner over the gray army blanket which covered the long trestle table. The cap rested between the naked sword and the noosed rope. Carefully, almost negligently, he peeled off the leather gloves and laid them neatly on the crimson lining of the upturned cap. The people in the dungeon still stood. Some of them coughed. It had been a bitter winter on the Elbe. Their breath was condensing in little puffs of vapor, for the spring sunshine of April 1945 had not yet begun to warm the chilled Saxony earth above the arched roof of the cellars.

As if he were still sighted, the general looked out at the people standing before him. They all seemed awed. Many were ill at ease. One man even nodded respectfully. Foolishly he had forgotten that the general could not see him. In the light of the candles burning and smoking in the great iron sconces on the cellar walls, the general's blinded eyes were strangely compelling, dominating the lean face with the white, puckered scar and the long, thin, scornful nose. Behind the dark glasses, which the general had worn since after Stalingrad, the staring eyes were bulged, expressionless, and the clear, maddening blue of a winter's sky from which long-threatened snow had finally fallen to lie white on the fields under the pale northern sun.

If the general's eyes communicated any emotion at all it was entirely an expression of contempt for those who had not also suffered the pain and the injustice of blindness. They were the eyes of a man who knew little of pity and cared even less.

Without fumbling, the general reached forward over the rough blanket and grasped the hilt of the sword. It was obviously no ordinary blade. The hilt sparkled with precious stones. The general had received the sword from the hands of Adolf Hitler. With the gleaming blade held vertically so that its burnished metal shone in the uncertain light of the candles and torches on the cellar walls, he now struck the table with the hilt.

"Under the authority of the Fehme," he said, "this court is now convened."

"May God preserve our honor," responded the people. Their voices rumbled and echoed against the wet stone walls of the cellars. Then the stools and the benches scraped again as they all sat.

The general laid the sword down so that it pointed toward the vacant bench before the table.

"Let the prisoners be brought in," he said.

When they came, the prisoners were blindfolded and clumsy in their gait. Unlike the general, they shuffled uncertainly as they entered the dungeons. Whenever their shoulders made accidental contact with their escorts they reacted suddenly and nervously. The escorts were silent men who wore civilian clothes but came bearing arms of the Wehrmacht. The weapons were either Luger automatics or Schmeisser machine pistols. The clothing of the escorts was nondescript, but in his lapel, buttonhole or cap, each man wore a blossomed sprig of lilac.

Impassively the general waited until the prisoners had been ranged before him.

"Remove the blindfolds," he said. "Let the charges be made and the accused arraigned and named."

The clerk of the court nodded, imperceptibly clicked his heels and began to read the charges. In a buttonhole of his black civilian leather jacket he also wore a sprig of lilac. His face was ruddy like a farmer's, as if he drank much beer and worked hard at simple tasks in the flat fields of Saxony. It was a kindly face. Just below the hairs of his left armpit a red weal on the white skin was paining him. This was where he had taken a hot poker and tried to erase the serial number which had been tattooed there on his enlistment in the SS. The general could not see this but he knew about it. There was little that the blinded aristocrat in the Panzer uniform did not know about every man and woman in the cellars. The general nodded gently to himself while the clerk read the arraignments. As he listened, the general realized what it was that had been distracting his attention to the affairs of the court. It was the heavy scent of lilac. Even in this spring of defeat, the lilacs of Saxony were blooming. One day they would bloom again in a spring of triumph and victory. Of this he had no doubt and for this he would lay down his life as readily as he had already given his sight.

Not surprisingly, Dietrich von Bluckau, general of the Panzertruppen, former commander of the Panzer Division Elbeland, holder of the Oak Leaves to the Knight's Cross of the Iron Cross with Swords and Diamonds, veteran of the glorious and triumphal thrusts into Poland, Russia, Holland, Belgium and France, tenth Graf von Bluckau and hereditary master of Schloss Galgenstein and all the von Bluckau fields and forests between the Elbe and the Mulde, was unquestionably a patriotic and courageous German. Curiously, he was also an intellectual. His mother, the Gräfin von Bluckau, had seen to this. Herself an intellectual and a descendant of a noble Meissen family which had, for generations, figured prominently in the court circles of the old Saxon monarchy at Dresden, she had zealously and lovingly nurtured the mind, the morals and the manners of Dietrich, her only child. Dietrich had had very little to do with his father, Hasso, the ninth Graf von Bluckau. From 1905, the year of Dietrich's birth, until 1914, the old Graf had been preoccupied with the raising, equipping and training of the Saxon Grenadier regiment, of which, as a von Bluckau, he was the honorary colonel. From the patriotically fervorous days of 1914 until the catastrophic climax of 1918, the Graf Hasso had led a Saxony division through the muddied, bloody Gethsemane of the Western Front. He was a good general. This had not been enough, though. After a sullen mutiny by his disaffected troops in Cologne in December 1918, he had returned silently to Schloss Galgenstein.

The degradation of the German defeat and the ignominy of his division's mutiny had wounded the Graf far more than the gas which had burned his lungs and the shrapnel which had plucked at his lean and straight-backed body. After little more than a winter's brooding at Schloss Galgenstein and some desultory, dispirited hunting of the boars, which during the Great War had begun to overrun the von Bluckau forests, the Graf had vanished, at least so far as young Dietrich had been concerned. Not until the Graf's death during a skirmish on the new Polish borders of a prostrate and defeated Germany, did Dietrich learn that his father had died fighting with the Freikorps Barbarossa, an illegal but fanatically patriotic little army of former officers of the Kaiser who were dedicated to denial of the new frontiers enforced on the fatherland by the infamy of the treaty at Versailles.

For all these reasons and despite the influence of family governesses, schoolteachers in Dresden, university lecturers in Leipzig and military school instructors in Berlin, the all-enveloping influence on Dietrich had been his mother, the Gräfin, and the vast castle of which she became the lonely and embittered mistress. The center of Dietrich's world was Schloss Galgenstein, crouched on its island in the protective marshes from which dank tributaries threaded through the von Bluckau forests and fields to the Elbe and the Mulde.

Inevitably Dietrich came to think of himself, in order of precedence, as a von Bluckau, a Saxon, a German and then a member of the human race. Brooding and dreaming and reading in his study in the great Luther tower of the castle, he inevitably became an intellectual and an idealist. Essentially he was a medievalist and a German medievalist at that. Indisputably he was also a romantic. He always had been. The general had shown this to be so even during the white, frozen horror of the Stalingrad encirclement. After the guns of the massive and horrendous Russian artillery had pinpointed and then pulverized the tanks of his division, he had rallied those of his men who had survived the carnage. Then he had mounted a shivering and frightened white horse which had been abandoned by a supply corps unit with no more supplies to deliver to the fighting troops. With Big Johann, his

Wendish driver and orderly, clinging to a stirrup, he had led the battle-shocked remnants of the Panzer Division Elbeland, stumbling on their bleeding and frozen feet, in a last counterattack. He had galloped ahead toward the Russian positions and then halted to draw the ceremonial sword which his father had carried even in the trenches and shell holes of 1914–18. Before charging the Russian positions, he had turned back to shout encouragement to his men and await their grouping behind him for the desperate assault on the wraithlike Russians in the driving snow. The Red Army artillery had found his men first. Three times, amid gouting snow and flame and clods of black, frozen earth, he saw the bursting shells carelessly toss the same jack-booted leg of one of his men high into the bitter air. Then the Russian gunners had sportively sought out the lone and slightly ridiculous figure of the general, with drawn sword, astride the broken-down horse. The bursting shells flashed in the general's face like summer lightning inexplicably accompanied by drifting curtains of snow and he had wondered if they would ever stop. He was vaguely trying to recall how many shells it had taken to kill each soldier who had died in 1914–18—he had heard the figure when he was a cadet on exercises in the Lüneburger Heide in 1928—when the horse was cut from under him by a splinter of steel as big as a carving knife. The animal screamed and snorted blood as it died. Later, a decimated infantry company from a Panzergrenadier regiment which had long since ceased to exist as an effective fighting force ate the horse. They had been fighting for ten days on a daily issue of one iron ration to every five men. They found the general, unconscious and wounded, still pinned beneath the horse several hours after he had been cut down. The blood warmth of the animal's carcass had kept him alive in the snow. With some amazement, the grenadiers had watched the charge and agreed that it was madness but then so was the tactical situation of the entire German force still fighting at Stalingrad. War itself was only compounded of varying degrees of lunacy. Why else would they be looking forward to eating the general's horse?

General von Bluckau was flown out from Stalingrad that day in a Junkers Ju.52, which landed and took off again during the cover of a blizzard. It was one of the last of the slab-sided, lumbering, three-engined Ju.52 transports to fly a flak-hazarded course into the Stalingrad ring and claw its way out again. The general did not know this at the time, for he was unconscious. Blood from his hastily bandaged wounds had dripped onto the trampled snow as the medical orderlies had waited to put his litter aboard. The blood had looked unexpectedly red, like wine spilled on a dirty, crumpled tablecloth. For several hours after take-off, the Luftwaffe orderly aboard the Ju.52 thought von Bluckau was already dead. The general's gaunt, upturned face was a mask of wet putty. The orderly gave his blanket to a whimpering Bavarian artilleryman who had had both legs amputated at the thigh and lay on his litter looking like a huge-headed dummy discarded by a ventriloquist. The artilleryman died before they landed at Breslau. He suffocated patiently in a pool of his own vomit while the orderly was drinking hot black coffee with the radio operator in the crew compartment. To the gratified surprise of the orderly, the general lived. He was carried out of the aircraft suffering from exposure, frostbite, pneumonia, burns, shock and a number of comparatively superficial though bloody shrapnel wounds, with the Russian metal still jaggedly embedded in them. Some were mildly gangrenous. The von Bluckaus, though, were hardy stock.

There was no questioning the fact that the general could only ever have been unconscious when he was evacuated. Otherwise he would have honored inevitably the Führer's order of the day in which von Paulus and the German Sixth Army at Stalingrad were commanded to fight to the last man and the last round. As might have been expected, von Bluckau fiercely resented the fact of his regaining consciousness in a German hospital far from the front where the last remnants of his Panzer Division Elbeland were dying like whipped and snarling animals in the snow. A week later von Bluckau realized that he was totally and irremediably blind. The thought of it was almost unbearable for him. With no legs or no arms, he could still have commanded troops. There was no place in the Wehrmacht, though, for a general who could not see the enemy. While the general was lying in bed between cool, clean sheets in the quiet convalescent ward of a military hospital in Dresden some time later, an officer of the army legal branch came from Berlin to see him. The visitor interrogated von Bluckau, coldly and without sympathy, about the circumstances of his escape from Stalingrad. Later he returned with a statement which he read formally and carefully to the general and then asked him to sign. The general did so, courteously but stiffly, assuming that this was a preliminary to court-martial proceedings being instituted against him. Something about the tone of his interviewer's voice had confirmed his suspicions. He could tell that the legal officer was too eagerly engaged in writing down the statement to even bother looking up at him. The scribbler, thought the general with resigned contempt, the busy little scribbler. The bedside inquisitor. The Russkis would have had him for breakfast at Stalingrad. By this time, Stalingrad had fallen and Field Marshal von Paulus and the 250,000 men of the battle-tempered Sixth Army lay where they had fallen, buried only by the snow, or had stumbled away into a frozen infinity of captivity. The Führer had publicly denounced the surrender as treachery and the German front fighters at Stalingrad as traitors and cowards. Even in the well-ordered peace of the Dresden hospital and despite the dark isolation of his blindness, von Bluckau had got to know of the arrests, charges, courts-martial, sentences, imprisonments, disgracings and even executions which had swept the ranks of those of the Wehrmacht who had escaped from the caldron at Stalingrad. After making a careful and dispassionate appreciation of his own situation, von Bluckau had been unable to find any reason why he should be spared the due processes of trial, conviction and punishment. The issue was, simply, that he should have died in Stalingrad with the men of his division. The Führer had set a high price on German honor. As a general, thought von Bluckau, he, himself, could expect nothing less than a court-martial, when the SS in the field were busy hanging Wehrmacht deserters and malingerers from the nearest tree or lamppost. The general spoke of this to nobody at the hospital. Nor did anybody speak to him, for he was but a blind man in a cubicle of the silent ward. In the summer of 1943, von Bluckau returned to Schloss Galgenstein to sit in the sun and await his summons to a court-martial. The prospect did not unduly alarm him. Blinded, he was finished anyway as a fighting general. It was not, of course, a happy home-coming, although the war had not yet disturbed so much as a single stone of the old castle or a solitary leaf in the woods. The waterfowl still shrieked and splashed and skittered in the black waters of the Schwarzesee, the marshy lake which surrounded the castle and its terraced lawns. The von

Bluckau lands were heavy with the sun-warmed smell of lilac, cattle, pines, barley, wheat, ripening apples, straw and dung. In other ways, though, the war had left its mark. The ebb and flow of the great European conflict now merely confused his aging mother, the old Gräfin. She talked endlessly of the Wagnerian struggle between the mightiest nations of the world only in terms of the laziness of the British, French, Polish and Russian prisoners who mainly tilled the fields, harvested the crops and tended the forests of the von Bluckau estates grouped around Schloss Galgenstein.

Listening to her conversation, which was now only the blunted edge of a once fine and fierce intellect, von Bluckau realized that she only saw the war as a conspiracy against the traditional establishment of which the von Bluckau family had always been an enduring part. Frequently she forgot he had come home blinded from Stalingrad and railed at him for not making better use of his leave by supervising the affairs of his estates and disciplining the insolent foreign laborers, who did as little work as possible and stole rotting potatoes and turnips to snuffle at like the stupid, illiterate swine they were. Neither to his mother nor even to his wife, Jutte, named for a princess of the old Saxon court to whom her great grandmother had been a pink-cheeked lady-in-waiting, did Dietrich speak of his acceptance of the inevitability of a court-martial. Jutte would only have wept if he had told her about his court-martial fears and the general had had enough of tears, for he had seen holders of the Iron Cross, First Class, weeping before they died in the uniforms which stank of involuntary defecation and were their ragged shrouds. Unlike Jutte, though, they had not usually been drunk when they wept. Jutte was drunk most of the time now. Not in a gross way but almost ethereally, with all the quiet intensity of a nun intoxicated by the beauty and force of her faith. Jutte, he knew, was still beautiful, charming, graceful, intelligent and witty even when she was drunk, but always now there came a point when she wept. There were, he knew, many reasons why she wept, but there had been a time when she laughed as easily as she now wept. That was when they had first met at the university in Leipzig, years before the war. Jutte was then the daughter of a wealthy and notable publisher in Leipzig. She was afire with life then, sparkling with the vivacity and excitement of the world in which she had grown up. As a child, a girl and a young woman, Jutte had traveled widely with her family to where-ever her father's interests had taken him in the pursuit of his career as a publisher of international repute. By the time Dietrich met Jutte, she knew Berlin, Munich, Paris, Brussels, Amsterdam, London and New York as well as he knew Leipzig, Dresden, Chemnitz, Dessau, Wittenberg, Torgau, Meissen and the other provincial cities of his native Saxony. Jutte grew up in her father's world, a lively and stimulating environment peopled by booksellers, publishers, authors, publicists, artists, critics, editors, journalists and academicians. Dietrich knew best the brooding forests and huddled villages and farms of the von Bluckau estates and the big-boned phlegmatic faces of the stolid Saxon peasantry and their ingrained allegiance to the family in the great castle marooned in the marshes between the Elbe and the Mulde. For all his lineage, Dietrich had still felt like a yokel at the family gatherings to which Jutte first began to invite him in her father's elegant house in the old medieval quarter of Leipzig. Often he had despaired of his private hopes for making Jutte a Gräfin von Bluckau. Then had come the harvest ball at Schloss Galgenstein that golden summer night in 1928, a feudal affair for the annual pleasure of the von Bluckau peasantry but not without its bucolic charms which were often the prelude to a busy spring for the sweating midwives in the villages and farms around Schloss Galgenstein.

Dietrich had proposed marriage to Jutte, dark-eyed and slim in a white gown, that night as they leaned over the parapet at the top of the Sprengertor, the castle tower from which a von Bluckau had once leaped into the marshy Schwarzesee below to escape the soldiers of Napoleon. For moments after Dietrich had spoken stiffly and nervously of his love for her, Jutte had leaned against the stone parapet, looking down at the castle courtyard below where the von Bluckau peasants were still dancing and drinking under the colored lanterns between the lime trees. Then she had turned to him, looking up. He was a tall young man. The cool night breeze from the valley of the Elbe, refreshing to faces flushed with wine and young life, had tumbled the dark hair across her eyes. She had brushed it back with a slim white wrist and then taken his hand in hers.

"Dietrich, my love," she said. "How soon?"

They were married that summer in the little Lutheran church in the village of Galgenstein. Dietrich's mother, the old Gräfin, happily blinked back tears in the von Bluckau family pew as Dietrich and the new Gräfin walked together down an aisle hushed and fragrant beneath their feet with the blossoms of the wild lilac of the fields and the hedgerows. In the gold onion steeple of the little church the bells that had first been rung by Martin Luther himself sang sonorously of the marriage. High on the Sprengertor the crested flag of the von Bluckaus flew bravely in the sun.

In their farmhouse kitchens and cottage parlors that night, the tipsy von Bluckau peasants belched happily and spoke solemnly of the marriage as a good match and one worthy of the great castle in the marshes. There was much nodding of heads, that night, much sly winking and a considerable tumbling of giggling wives into beds to which they had first come after the Luther bells had also pealed for them on their own wedding days in Galgenstein. Siegfried, named for the eighth Graf von Bluckau, was born within a year of the marriage of Dietrich and Jutte, and the church bells rang again in Galgenstein, startling the pot-chested white geese from their quiet pleasures in the green slime of the village pond. The peasants and the farmers and the tradesmen within sound of the Luther bells wiped the strong beer from their chins and nodded, happy in their coarse and knowing fashion that the von Bluckau line of succession was assured. It had been a good match up at Schloss Galgenstein. The new little Gräfin had wasted no time foaling a von Bluckau.

For Dietrich, the six years from 1930 to 1936 were the happiest he had known at Galgenstein. Looming like a great barracks above the marshes and the forests, the castle was alive again as it had not been since the Hohenzollern days in the youth of his father.

Over all those feckless, sunny and essentially innocent years of the thirties, far from the sound of marching boots at Nuremberg and the tinkling of broken glass in the windows of Jewish shops, presided the young Gräfin, Jutte, the vivacious and liberal chatelaine of a private court in which the badge of office was the driest martini east of Manhattan and certainly all Germany except, perhaps, the Adlon in Berlin.

In 1936, Jutte's father shot himself. He used a heavy old Webley revolver which he had captured from a British officer during a trench raid in Flanders in 1917. Twice he put the weapon to his head and twice it failed to fire, for it was ill kept and rusted. A persistent man, he tried a third time and it fired. He died immediately.

As a political liberal and an anti-Nazi, a courageous intellectual and a publisher of international distinction, Jutte's father had refused to dismiss Jewish members of his staff, declined to publish an export edition of *Mein Kampf* and had arranged, through his London and New York offices, for the publication in English of an anti-Nazi novel which had been refused publication in Germany. He had then arranged for the author, a Jewish journalist from Hamburg, to be smuggled across the frontier into Switzerland and then to America with consequent immunity from the pressing attentions of the Gestapo. The British revolver, an honorable trophy of war, was one way out for Jutte's father. His more cynical friends deplored the fact of his suicide but privately agreed that it was the most painless and certainly the least degrading alternative to any which might have been offered him by the police apparatus of the Third Reich.

Angrily, because he had loved and respected his father-in-law, a gay and gifted man, Dietrich considered that the true tragedy and pity of his death was that he himself was not a Jew and had chosen to die for nothing more substantial than a principle of philosophy. Seeking desperately to console his wife, he had stated this view to Jutte on their return to Galgenstein from the funeral in Leipzig. Jutte had stared at him for a long time, saying nothing, as if they were strangers but she could recall having met him once at a crowded gathering and was desperately trying to recognize him and recall his name. Her eyes seemed darker than ever, for the sun was going down beyond the Mulde and the only light in the echoed drawing room of the castle came from the open fire with the von Bluckau arms resplendent in their bright ceramic colors on the stone wall above.

"So he was not a Jew?" she said. "Neither was he an Eskimo. Or a Negro. Or a Roman Catholic. Or a Buddhist. He was just a member of the human race. He did not believe in turning his back on humanity."

Dietrich had waited then, confused and ill at ease, standing alone with his anger while Jutte mixed a shaker of dry martinis.

The funeral had been a dreary and vulgar affair, the very opposite of the remembered image of her gay, courageous father, and there was a need for the iced, astringent tang of alcohol to cut the cloying, lingering smell of the luxuriant flowers of death.

Raising his glass thankfully, for he had grown to like this trans-Atlantic innovation of cocktails before dinner, Dietrich awkwardly proposed a toast.

"To your father," he said.

Jutte, though, had forgotten nothing.

"To my father," she said. "To a man who would never have been astute enough to forget that he was a member of the human race."

Slowly, with her head thrown back so that Dietrich could see the pale blue veins tensed on her neck, Jutte drank the martini in one long prolonged action as if it were poison. Then she tapped the fragile glass gently on the oaken mantelpiece high above the fireplace. The glass broke. She let it fall, shattering and ringing, on the stone. She kicked the tiny pieces into the fire where the logs of pine were blazing. Then she wept, leaning with her hands raised to the high mantelpiece and staring down into the flames.

That was the first night Dietrich watched his wife drink until she was drunk. It was not the last. There were many more occasions, more than he could ever have remembered. The day that Siegfried came home, red-faced with pride and excitement, in the uniform of the Hitler youth. The dagger had pleased Siegfried most. He had thrown it up spinning and caught it deftly by the hilt. As is the way of uniforms, Siegfried's had changed him already. "My son," said Jutte. "My only son. A Nazi." It was as if he had been kidnapped or murdered. This was only the beginning for Jutte. There was the announcement of the summary confiscation of her father's publishing enterprise, and all its assets and resources, by the Reich Ministry for Propaganda. The death of her elder brother, Kurt, in a Ju.87 Stuka over the British docks at Southampton. The fall of France. The friends who died. The German friends too frightened to come to Galgenstein any more. The bombing of London. The crippling, for life, of her younger brother, Martin, who jumped into pain, not glory, at Crete. The death, due to heart failure, of Jakob Jakobs, the former works manager of her father's publishing house, who had been with the firm since he had completed his printing apprenticeship in 1910. The old man's heart had failed him in a quarry at the camp at Nordhausen. The death of her mother, suffocated in an RAF terror raid with blockbusters and incendiaries, which had scourged the timbered, medieval heart of the old city in Leipzig. Jutte had wept for her husband, simple and straightforward Dietrich, watching him conform honorably to the iron mold of a system that served only the cause of a madman's dreams of glory. Each time Dietrich came home from the front and each time he left Schloss Galgenstein again, he was a little less her husband and a little more the gaunt-faced, monklike commander of the Panzer Division Elbeland. Strangely, in 1943, she had wept less for his blindness, after Stalingrad, because she thought, at least, in the very fact of his sightlessness he might become her Dietrich again instead of remaining the lean, worried stranger thinking his own thoughts in the uniform of a general of the Panzer troops. She wept for him because she knew he would never see her body again, naked by candlelight in the great bed in their many-windowed room high up in the Sprengertor. She wept because it would be no good now, anyway, for he had come back not only blind from Stalingrad but virtually impotent, too. Aside from all this, she wept because never again would Dietrich be able to sit opposite her at the great dining table of the von Bluckaus, smiling at her and seeing her over a glass of red wine, or ever again share the pleasure of sitting together with a glass of cognac in the drawing room and watching for dragons and knights riding in the flames of the fire roaring below the rich, medieval colors of the von Bluckau arms high on the wall.

Jutte had become an incipient alcoholic. More than that, she had already wondered how much longer she was capable of keeping up the polite pretense of being faithful to Dietrich, for increasingly she had begun to lust drunkenly in her own bed, between wakefulness and sleep, for a man, any man she might have seen that day. It mattered little whom he might have been. A Luftwaffe officer on leave and visiting his home near Galgenstein. A French prisoner raking dung in the stables. Even Siegfried's young Hitler Youth leader cycling with him over the bridge to the castle. The fact of her sexual impulses and the pleasure of their gratification was one of the few constants which had survived the years since disillusionment of life began with her father's suicide in 1936.

Waiting for his court-martial after Stalingrad that summer of

1943, Dietrich had sat day after day under the apple trees on the terrace overlooking the Schwarzesee while Jutte, between drinks or lovers, read to him the books which had enriched and peopled the days and nights of his lonely and patrician boyhood. Jutte read well, even when her voice was drowsy with spent passion or throaty with cognac from the castle cellars, and as he dozed in the warmth of the sunshine beating back from the castle walls, he half listened, half dreamed and saw again the marching medieval figures from a heroic German past whom he had finally followed to Stalingrad and a life of living darkness. Sometimes, if Jutte was not too tired, too restless or too stimulated by alcohol, she would read to him at night, but this was a pleasure too often interrupted and distracted as the RAF terror attacks reached farther out into central Germany in 1943 to set the sirens baying and kindle fires that paled the searchlights wavering and quivering in their frantic cones. On one such night when Leipzig was once more under attack and the quiet Saxony countryside was raucous with the shrilling alarms of provincial fire brigades speeding to the assistance of the besieged and burning city, Jutte had stood weeping at the great west window in the library and watching the sky glow red above the city beyond the Mulde, the city where her young life had flowered in serenity and happiness.

Unable to comfort her, von Blackau had been dismayed by the fact of his own blinded helplessness and the inexorable destiny which awaited a Germany entrapped in the historic nightmare of a two-front war closing in from the east and the west. Assessing the situation, logically and dispassionately, the general knew that he could not see Germany surviving defeat longer than a year after the Anglo-Americans made their long-awaited landings in the west and mounted a second front in Europe. The prospect of Germany's immediate destiny in defeat was an obsession that gnawed at von Bluckau in the quiet desolation of his blindness. Sometimes he spoke of it to Jutte, voicing the doubts and fears that worried at his mind like nervous but persistent rats. Whether Jutte was interested or even listening he often did not know. Often he spoke in a silence relieved only by the clink of a bottle or the ringing of a glass as she fumbled for another drink. These would be the times when she had not been with a man for a while and was restless for another of the furtive couplings with which Dietrich was too proud to accuse her and which he chose, instead, to ignore, like a little boy pretending to himself that the ache in his tooth would go away if he stopped thinking about it. Night after night in the loneliness of the castle's echoing library, von Bluckau spoke to his wife of the fate which awaited a defeated Germany, searching endlessly for a way to buttress the German people against a catastrophe which seemed historically inevitable. They were mournful nights. The blinded aristocrat sitting stiffly, proudly in his chair with the firelight sparkling on the insignia and decorations set against the tailored green cloth of the high-collared Wehrmacht uniform in which he dressed for dinner. The Gräfin Jutte, still beautiful and dark-eyed but with her petite features already coarsened a little by too much wine and too little restraint in her hunger for casual, clandestine lovemaking. Sometimes she swayed as she poured another vintage cognac, but still she achieved a curiously dated elegance in a gown which had become four austere years out of fashion since she had chosen it at a tiny but very expensive boutique in Paris in 1939 while there still had been time. Yet it was the young Gräfin Jutte, for all her aimless, wavering drinking and carnal indiscretions, who opened the door which von Bluckau had been seeking in his thoughts.

Dietrich had been talking of the death of his father as the Freikorpsführer of the Freikorps Barbarossa after 1923 when Jutte said, almost in boredom, "Was he in the Fehme?"

"The Fehme?" von Bluckau said. "The Fehme? I don't know. I've never really thought about it. To be a Freikorps fighter I suppose he was. I seem to have heard some talk as a youngster about the Fehme after 1918."

"They say it was revived after the Kaiser's war," said Jutte. "There was a history lecturer at Leipzig who told us about it. He was most enthusiastic. I read later, much later, that he was doing something cultural in the SS. A contradiction in logic if ever I heard one."

"I know," said von Bluckau. "Now you mention it, I remember him." The fire was roaring in the great chimney. The wind was in an awkward quarter and sometimes a gust over the castle gables sent smoke belching out into the room.

"As a boy I read a lot about it myself," said von Bluckau. "In the old days they were men of honor in the Fehme. Later it was not so good but it still worked. By God, it worked. That was the answer to anarchy then and long before that. I wonder if it could be the answer now? I wonder? How could I ever have not thought of it?"

"You wonder what, Dietrich?" said Jutte. "What have you forgotten?" Unseen by von Bluckau, she was lying with her legs splayed open to the heat of the fire. The Paris frock was pulled back over her thighs. She was thinking of a young Polish prisoner she had seen in the woods by the Elbe that day. He had been chopping logs, stripped to the waist. She could not remember his face, only the flexing muscles of his strong, sweating young back.

"The answer to what, Dietrich?" said Jutte. She was drowsily contented with her thoughts. She could still see the rising, flashing axe of the young foreign woodsman.

"The answer to everything," said von Bluckau, warmed by the first stirrings of a plan for the salvation of a devastated Third Reich from the carnage of anarchy.

"I have the answer to everything, Dietrich," said Jutte. "Our cellars are still full of it. Beautiful wine. Beautiful cognac. Beautiful, beautiful, beautiful." She was slurring her words and soon she would be weeping as she always did when she knew that oblivion was once again nearly upon her. Going to bed alone, for she had not slept with Dietrich since his return from Stalingrad, would be a little like dying. It always was.

"I had almost forgotten," said von Bluckau, and Jutte was surprised by the sudden warmth in his voice. Elated, he rang for a glass and a bottle of one of the sturdy red Galgenstein wines that had been laid down when he was a child. It was the first drink he had taken since he had come home from Stalingrad, but now at last he had something to celebrate. A dream, perhaps, but certainly a plan. As a general of the Wehrmacht he was still not without influence even if he was not a National Socialist party member.

Sitting forward with the heat of the fire leaping at his face, he had raised his glass toward Jutte. "To the Fehme," he said.

The general was glad that his mother, the old Gräfin, had died that winter. These were not the kinds of times she would have cared to share, least of all the circumstances of defeat and dissolution which might justify a national revival of such organizations as the Fehme and the Freikorps. During his lonely boyhood at

Schloss Galgenstein, von Bluckau had read much about the Fehme, for the castle's library was rich in musty, mildewed volumes of German history and legend.

"To the Fehme, then," said Jutte without enthusiasm. "But in God's name, why?"

"Listen to me," said von Bluckau. "I think Germany is going to need something like the Fehme and the summary judicial processes of the old Fehmgerichte. As a plan it is not so silly. Although the historians have tended to prove that the Fehmic courts rarely employed torture, that their meetings were not always secret and that their meeting places were often well known, legend and romance have exaggerated the sinister reputation of the Fehme. There's no doubt that the courts of the Fehme exercised a powerful jurisdiction in Germany, particularly in Westphalia. Nobody disputes the fact that the sessions of the Fehmic courts were often held in secret. The uninitiated were forbidden to join in these sessions on pain of death. When the Fehme whistled, Germans jumped."

"It all sounds most unpleasant," said Jutte.

"Often it was," said von Bluckau. "The courts of honor had the power of life and death in the name of the emperor. We shall need something like that in the hard times that are coming to Germany."

Jutte had sounded incredulous.

"You are not suggesting, my dear Dietrich, a revival of the Fehme? In all seriousness? It was really nothing much more than a German medieval version of the Americans' Ku Klux Klan."

"Why not?" said von Bluckau. "I think there well could be a need. I may be wrong, but so far as I can remember, the Ku Klux Klan has been said to have had its origins as a vigilante force after the anarchy which followed the American Civil War. You were joking, I know, but there could even be an historical precedent there, although the Fehme was in existence centuries before the American Civil War. The Fehme became important after the division of the duchy of Saxony on the fall of Henry the Lion. That was when the Archbishop of Cologne, the Duke of Westphalia from 1180, took over as head of the Fehme as the emperor's representative. After that, the Fehme spread rapidly. Like fire in the woods. Every German freeman born in legal wedlock who had been neither excommunicated nor outlawed was eligible to join.

Princes and noblemen were initiated, even the Emperor Sigismund. In 1429 he became the Freischoff of the Holy Roman Empire. By the middle of the fourteenth century the sworn associates of the Fehme existed in thousands throughout Germany. They were known to one another by secret signs and passwords and all of them were obliged to serve the summonses of the secret courts and to execute their judgments."

Appalled, Jutte stared at her husband's thin, impassive face staring blindly into the fire as he talked. She found it almost impossible to equate his views with the facts of his patrician background and his university education.

"You want to bring this kind of medieval nonsense back to life in Germany?" she said. "Haven't we had enough of this sort of thing under Hitler?"

"The need for it will be forced upon us," said von Bluckau, rubbing the rim of his wine glass so that it made a tiny singing noise. "From what our intelligence people already know, it is obvious that the Anglo-Americans must invade Europe in force in the west during next spring or summer. Within a year of Eisenhower and Montgomery launching their second front in Europe, Germany will be defeated. As it does so often, history will repeat itself. The Third Reich will degenerate into a state of feudal anarchy. Only an organization as ruthless and tough as the old Fehme will be capable of holding us together as a nation."

"I should live to see the day," said Jutte. "Already we have the Gestapo, the political SS, the Waffen SS, the Abwehr, the Sicherheitsdienst, the criminal police, the army's field police, the Hitler Youth and God only knows how many more party organizations. Germany must have more policemen, jailers, spies, pimps, informers, torturers, inquisitors and executioners to the square kilometer than any other country in the Western world outside of Russia. And now you want the Fehme? God, I don't know, Dietrich. Whatever happened to the soul and the mind and the will of the individual? I prefer to put my faith in cognac."

And my lovers, she thought. My lovely, lovely lovers. The young Polish woodcutter, she knew, would be a fierce, thrusting match for her own despairing lust. Unlike so many of the others she had known, he would not be frightened to lie between the yielding thighs of a German woman of quality. She could tell by the way he had looked at her boldly under the pines that he was not even thinking of the penalty which he would risk in profaning the racial laws of the Third Reich. Despising herself, yet excited by the carnal promise of the silent woods beyond the village of Galgenstein, Jutte began to weep, for once again she was drunk. Grimly, von Bluckau had called for Frau Lehmann to put the Gräfin to bed in her own eyrie of a room high in the Sprengertor.

Before he had finished the warm red Galgenstein wine, alone by the fire, von Bluckau had that night formulated his thoughts on a plan for the revival of the Fehme. The general slept well. A soldier's sleep again. It was the first time since Stalingrad. At lunch next day on the terrace by the Schwarzesee, where the wild ducks cruised, idly pushing aside the lily pads, he found to his relief that Jutte's violent reaction to his tentative thoughts about the Fehme had been dispelled by the morning sunshine and what he took to be her pleasure in seeing him emerge at last from the long and brooding lethargy which had possessed him since his return from Stalingrad.

Suddenly, like birds fleeing from the approaching winter, the summer days of 1943 were flying by. Even his own private fears of court-martial were forgotten as he worked with Jutte in the castle library, researching the history of the Fehme and preparing a plan of organization for its renaissance in Germany's hour of defeat and its possible exploitation as an apparatus of resistance in the zones likely to be occupied by the Anglo-Americans and the Russians.

For Jutte, the summer of 1943 was a forester's hut in the pinewoods with the Polish boy's hard young chest pressing against her naked breasts and the distant sound of axes ringing almost like bells while Jan mouthed passionate obscenities in his barbaric Polish, until one day, with the fire of autumn turning the leaves of the birches and the oaks, he was gone. In Galgenstein village the postmistress, a dull and stupid woman who reeked of gin and moth balls, knew only that the Polish Arbeitskommando had been sent to the east, to Silesia, to labor on new airfields for the Luftwaffe. Jutte then had welcomed the distraction of working with von Bluckau on the Fehme plan, although, as a liberal and an intellectual, she detested the means by which such an organization would presumably achieve its ends. On his side, von Bluckau was more than ever convinced of the worth of the Fehme.

"As a general, I would not and could not admit it officially," he told Jutte, "but our enemies in this war have achieved some success with illegal organizations and irregular forces in countries occupied and policed by the armed forces of the Third Reich. The partisans in Russia and the Balkans. The Maquis in France. The White Army in Belgium. The underground resistance movements in Holland, Denmark and Norway. The Fehme, in its own way, could achieve as much for Germany. I have seen enough of these things to know that this is so."

Jutte still could not condone the concept of the Fehme.

"I don't like it, Dietrich. Let us understand each other. I realize now what this thing means to you and I will help you. I still don't have to like it. I think that the last thing Germany needs is the Fehme. We don't need any more secret societies or informers or hanging judges. The institutions we have—the Gestapo and the SS and the rest of them—will be our downfall quickly enough. Why replace them with something no less potentially evil? That's what I believe in my heart. But, in my own fashion, I love you, Dietrich. I like to think you still love me. God knows why you should. I drink too much and I'm a fool with men. Or men are fools with me. I don't know which. It doesn't matter any more. I don't know whether you love me but I do know you love Germany. When, now, she needs you most, and men like you, you are blind and helpless here at Galgenstein. It's been driving me crazy, so I don't know what it's been doing to you. As a German and as a von Bluckau, and a blinded one at that, I can understand you wanting to fight the fatherland's enemies, in the future as in the past. I can understand this even if it doesn't make very much sense to me. To this extent, then, I will help you with the research and the drafting of the Fehme plan, but, for God's sake, don't ask me to have stars in my eyes about it."

For a moment, as he would have done in the old days before the war, von Bluckau took her hand.

"For that," he said, "I thank you. There is much you can do to help me, if you will."

On this basis, then, they had worked well together.

The old Fehme, von Bluckau found, had been elaborate in its organization; not surprisingly, since it had been evolved to cope with a condition of defeat and disintegration, the historical structure of the Fehme was basically applicable to the conditions likely to be confronting soon the Third Reich.

By the autumn of 1943, von Bluckau had completed the draft of his operational plan for the Fehme. Sheet by sheet it had been typed by the Gräfin and locked in the safe in the library. Outside, the trees were shedding their leaves. They crouched, ankle-deep in spent carpets of red and gold. Only the pines, in their soldierly ranks, stood resolute against the bleak, raping winds of the season of the year. Then the Fehme was forgotten for a while when old Zentner, the cackling and dribbling pensioner postman from Galgenstein village, delivered the letter with the Berlin postmark. For the first time, von Bluckau regretted not having warned his wife about the possible outcome of the Stalingrad statement which he had made in the hospital at Dresden. The court-martial summons which she would now have to read him would be just one more bitterness to drive her to the rim of desperation, alcoholism and, perhaps, eventual insanity. Waiting while she ripped open the heavy embossed envelope, he wondered what they would do with him. Then he heard Jutte's gasp and he wondered if he had received the privileged invitation to blow his brains out with his own hand to save face for the men in Berlin. It had been known to happen and to generals, at that.

"It's from the Führer Headquarters," said Jutte. "Signed by the Führer."

My God, von Bluckau had thought to himself. This is really it. Good-bye Galgenstein, Jutte, the wind in the pines, the smell of moss in the Jägerswald, the wine by the fire, the Panzer Division Elbeland, the victories, the defeats, the soft, nuzzling nose of old Meteor, the faithful hunter that still carried him about the estates. Good-bye von Bluckau. He had heard his wife weeping and he had clenched his fist, trying not to betray emotion at the thought of disgrace, demotion and a coward's death before a firing squad if he were to be granted such a military courtesy. Then he had felt his wife's lips caressing his cheek. She had been drinking again.

"Congratulations, Dietrich," she said. "I hate the damned war but I'm proud for you."

He felt foolish and blindly helpless.

"Congratulations for what?"

"You have been awarded the Oak Leaves with Swords and Diamonds to the Knight's Cross of the Iron Cross. Hitler says so himself."

"Read it," said von Bluckau. "I don't believe it."

"Listen," said Jutte. " 'Your unflagging personal zeal, your outstanding skill and courage and the gallant last-ditch attack fought by the men under your command in the Panzer Division Elbeland at Stalingrad have earned the utmost appreciation on the part of the German nation. You and your troops, in a spirit of unexcelled self-sacrifice, have set a noble example of courageous resistance to the last man and to the last round, which is in the highest tradition of our glorious Wehrmacht. In the name of the embattled fighting fronts and a home front besieged by the terror attacks of the Anglo-American air forces, I salute you.' "

"I'll be damned," said von Bluckau.

His hands were shaking, even clenched on the arms of the chair.

"The sun is shining again," said Jutte suddenly. "You should see it. The forest is beautiful."

"We'll drink to that," said von Bluckau and they did. Still drunk that evening, Jutte found one of the French prisoners stealing late tomatoes from the greenhouse behind the stables. She had been riding, and with the whip she had beaten the man to the ground. Then she had stripped naked and fallen upon him, fumbling at his trousers. When they had finished, panting where they lay on the sawdust between the boxes of humid earth and lush green plants, she had threatened to report him to the Gestapo for raping her. That night, while escaping from the Arbeitskommando at Galgenstein, the Frenchman had been shot dead by a railway guard as he boarded a freight train.

When the day came for the award ceremony in Berlin, von Bluckau traveled alone by train. Siegfried had reported for Hitler Youth duty as a runner with a Luftwaffe flak unit near the Leuna oil refineries on the other side of Leipzig. Jutte had again returned to the bottle and her bitter memories and self-accusations.

II

The Banners of Berlin

AMONG HIS PEERS in Berlin, von Bluckau found some pride, mainly for the sake of the men of his division, but no real joy in the occasion. Smarting with disappointment, if only for the sake of his decimated division, in the fact that the Führer was not present to bestow upon him personally the honor he had been awarded, von Bluckau found little compensation in being introduced to Hitler's personal secretary and right-hand man, the engimatic and shadowy Martin Bormann. Over very good coffee —it had been captured from the Americans on the Italian front— their conversation at first was stilted and perfunctory. Bormann, the gutter fighter of the Brownshirt days and now the National Socialist careerist at Hitler's elbow, was obviously unimpressed by his meeting with von Bluckau, the aristocrat and blinded fighting general of the line.

Never a sparkling conversationalist, even at his most relaxed moments, von Bluckau found the meeting hard going until Bormann casually asked him, "Are you any relation to the von Bluckau who died fighting with the Freikorps Barbarossa on the so-called Polish border after 1918?"

Surprised, because his father's death with an illegal force of irregular troops had rarely been discussed either by the von Bluckau family or their landed neighbors who had conservative tastes in warfare, von Bluckau admitted, almost curtly, "He was my father."

"I knew him well," said Bormann. "He was a good German. If you will forgive me, he was somewhat stiff-necked and aloof but a fighting and patriotic German. Was he not Freikorpsführer of the Freikorps Barbarossa?"

"So I believe," said von Bluckau. "I was a youngster when he died." There had been, he recalled to himself, a kind of tacit conspiracy of silence about the Freikorps Barbarossa and the other free corps of the post-1918 era so far as the von Bluckaus and their friends were concerned. The free corps movement, he had gathered, had never been a popular subject for idle drawing-room gossip.

"I was a free corps fighter myself," Bormann continued. His voice, normally flat and cautious, was warmer now. "I was a section leader with the Freikorps Rossbach. There was a fighter for you. Not a gentleman, maybe, but a fighter. I can tell you. There were many of us in those days, skirmishing in the east with the Poles and the new Red Army. They were tough units, all of them. The Freikorps Oberland, the Heinz storm battalions. All very illegal, mind you, like your father's Freikorps Barbarossa, but every one of them was a thorn in the side of the damned Bolsheviks."

Over cigars, and more coffee, as von Bluckau and Bormann had settled to talk in a corner of the reception hall in an annex of the Reich Chancellery, the general had mentioned his research into the historical origins of the Fehme and its possible application as a kind of German resistance organization in what von Bluckau tactfully referred to as the difficult times he saw ahead for Germany. For a moment there was silence, and, nervously, he wondered whether in his even hinting at the faintest possibility of the defeat of German arms to such a dedicated National Socialist party man as Bormann he might have erred on the side of indiscretion if not political heresy. Then he felt Bormann's hand on his knee—a gesture which had repelled him ever since he had had to draw knife against a homosexually perverted fellow cadet at military school—and heard Hitler's party secretary speaking so quietly he was almost whispering.

"My dear von Bluckau," Bormann said, "I must commend you for your patriotic spirit. I must also compliment you on your intelligence, which is an attribute not popularly always associated with the aristocracy nor necessarily a product of simple patriotism. Your blood may be blue, as a Saxony nobleman, but in some ways you can see the way ahead far more clearly and realistically than many others less fortunately placed in our German society. I, for one, do not regard your thoughts about the Fehme as the daydreams of a blinded and frustrated general or the sentimental hobby of an aristocrat with nothing better to do than brood over the past history of our great nation."

Somewhere a band was playing martial airs. The general tapped a finger in time with the catchy march music.

"I want you to know," Bormann said, "that your interest in the Fehme may have given me the key to a problem which has been exercising my mind. If we can believe the reports of our intelligence authorities, it is now certain that the Anglo-Americans will invade western Europe in the spring or summer of 1944, soon after this accursed winter. I agree with you that a two-front war is inevitable. I also agree with you that unless we Germans are vouchsafed some miracle, the military result is also, as you have said, inevitable. As a soldier's general you know these things. As an old front fighter myself I know them, too. Now then, assuming that this state of affairs comes about, how can we preserve German unity, integrity and honor in the face of defeat, surrender and occupation? This has been my worry. Now I am not so worried. You have given me what could be the answer. The Fehme, I feel, could well be the shining sword and the stout shield with which we can guard German honor, come what may. As we both know, it has been before."

Bormann had paused and von Bluckau had listened to the thump of drums and the shrilling of fifes and the roar and dissonance of voices echoing in the great reception hall. The congratulatory voices. The proud voices. The correct voices. The heroic voices. The smug voices. The laughing voices. There had been a rich crop of rewards for courage and ambition and sacrifice this day in the Reich Chancellery.

"I would like to discuss this with you in more detail at a later date and in some privacy," Bormann said softly.

The general smiled, not without irony.

"You can be sure of finding me at Schloss Galgenstein. I'm always at home now. Take either a Dresden or a Leipzig train. There are local connections to Galgenstein. Or I could send my car for you. If the charcoal gas producer is working. It's an old Mercedes but it's comfortable."

"You are too kind, General," said Bormann, "but I will have my own car. Staff privileges, you might say. It will be soon, I assure you. I am not just making polite conversation. I would like to see your documentation on the Fehme plan. I will send a courier for it. I need hardly remind you, of course, my dear von Bluckau, that you are to forget this conversation of ours. Entirely and utterly. As the Führer's personal secretary and confidant, it is essential that I act with all possible discretion. Fortunately, as I have the Führer's ear—I agree even with my enemies on this—I have ways of ensuring that my loyalty to him is unquestioned. You will understand this, my dear General?"

When von Bluckau took his leave to catch the evening train to Leipzig, Bormann gripped his arm tightly.

"We will meet again soon, von Bluckau," he said, almost whispering. "Meanwhile, as I promised, I will send a courier for your papers on the Fehme plan. He will establish his bona fides as my personal representative in this matter by saying that he is looking forward to seeing the lilacs bloom. You will pardon the apparent melodrama, but we live in melodramatic times. In Berlin, anyway."

Loudly, and with great joviality, presumably for the benefit of an SS Sturmbannführer and his wife standing close by, he added, "Once again, General, my congratulations on the honor bestowed upon you, in the name of a grateful nation, by our Führer. Heil Hitler."

Galvanically, almost, von Bluckau had responded. The party salute had not been mandatory in the Panzer Division Elbeland.

"Heil Hitler," said von Bluckau hastily.

For the first time since they had brought him home from Stalingrad, he felt like a soldier again. Waiting for the Chancellory aide whom Bormann had deputed to escort him across Berlin to the Anhalter Bahnhof, he wondered if the new decoration looked well on his immaculate uniform, an old one but still his best and one which, as always, fitted his lean frame like a green glove.

Few passing Berliners, however, noticed the thin, erect figure of the Panzer general with the dark sunglasses and the pink-cheeked young SS officer at his side. They were all too busy hurrying home before the day darkened into night and the air raid sirens began to wail their warnings over the great city on the Spree.

The day after von Bluckau's return to Galgenstein from Berlin, Bormann's courier arrived. They had chatted briefly and inconsequentially about the weather and food-rationing and harvests, by the fire in the library, until the visitor mentioned that he had to catch the afternoon train back to Berlin.

"What a pity the lilacs are not out," he said. "I am looking forward to seeing the lilacs bloom again."

"I can understand that," said von Bluckau and they both laughed at the unintended pun.

After the general had unlocked the safe and handed over the Fehme plan in a package sealed in red wax with the von Bluckau arms on a worn gold ring his father had bequeathed him, he sat by the fire musing upon the workings of a fate that could make him, a provincial landowner and a pensioned-off general, the confidant and collaborator of Hitler's personal secretary and trusted adviser.

"What was all that about?" Jutte asked him when she came in with coffee and some cakes filled with forbidden cream from the castle dairy.

"Just a government man," said von Bluckau. "From Berlin, on official business. Born in Saxony, I'd say, from his accent."

"He certainly was," said Jutte. "Frau Lehmann has just reminded me he was the son of Schrader, the butcher over at Niederleipisch. For a butcher's son he has done very well. A major, or whatever they call them in the Waffen SS, at twenty-six. And decorated like a Christmas tree. Yet he arrives in civilian clothes in a black civil service car looking like the son of a prosperous undertaker. Such unassuming modesty amazed me. I always thought the SS boys slept in their uniforms. For pride, I mean, if for no other reason. I must say he seemed a little embarrassed when Frau Lehmann recognized him. Then I did, too. Good-looking, really, in a sulky sort of way. I remember when he used to deliver sausages in that little DKW truck that was always breaking down. A rather unpleasant young man as I recall him."

"Frau Lehmann should mind her own business," said von Bluckau. "Else she might have it minded for her."

"And so should I?" demanded Jutte. She had been drinking again, straight cognac, and recalling the hot summer day long ago when she had been riding Komet, her big chestnut, on the path through the standing wheat down by the Elbe. Komet had reared suddenly, but before she finished checking him, she had seen the flurry of white, spread-eagled thighs and cupped breasts, strangely white in the sun. It was Helga, one of the village girls in service at the castle. She was with Schrader, the butcher-boy from Niederleipisch.

Scarlet-faced with a conflicting tumult of lust, anger, fear and embarrassment, and clutching awkwardly at his opened trousers, Schrader had stared sullenly up at Jutte, saying nothing. Helga had stood behind him, eyes cast down and frightened, brushing nervously at her crumpled frock.

In her own embarrassment, Jutte had illogically felt anger at the circle of flattened stalks of wheat almost ready for harvesting.

"You're trespassing," she said to Schrader. "Get out of the crop and stay out."

Several months later, Helga's body had been found in the Elbe. She was pregnant. This was less of a scandal than the fact of her suicide. Schrader, who had refused to marry her, joined the SS soon afterward.

Looking now at von Bluckau frowning over his coffee, Jutte laughed.

"Darling, let's be frank for once. There are not many men in whom I am not capable of being at least remotely interested, but your visitor is very definitely one. I have no designs on our former butcher-boy. I'm just femininely curious about whatever you two might conceivably have in common."

The general shrugged his thin shoulders.

"Let's just say you should not worry your pretty little head about it, Jutte. It is purely a routine matter of official army business. At, I might add, a fairly high level. I can tell you this much. They seem to think my ideas on the Fehme have some merit."

Sipping his coffee, which had only too obviously started out as barley, and listening to Jutte fumbling for a cognac bottle in the bookshelves—when she was sober and remorseful she hid bottles from herself in the most unlikely places which, nevertheless, rarely evaded her when she craved a drink again—von Bluckau wondered about the courier from Bormann. Uneasily he wondered to what extent the SS, and its jumped-up butcher boys and street corner louts, was going to meddle in the Fehme plan. In their own way, the Waffen SS had succeeded in serving a useful function on the fighting front, even if you did need a strong stomach to work closely with them in action, but, as an old-guard general with a professional respect for the Geneva Convention on warfare, the less he had to rub shoulders with the Waffen SS the better. Not that there was anything he could do about it now. As the politicians in Berlin were fond of saying over their cognac and cigars, the die was cast. The Fehme plan was now official business in Berlin, if only in a curiously conspiratorial way. Whose business it was, and at what level other than Bormann's, he did not know and did not care to ask. Despondently von Bluckau wondered if he had indeed been wasting his time, a mere dreamer of dreams in a medieval castle among the pines, the potato fields and the marshes of sleepy Saxony.

A month later, von Bluckau knew the answer.

It was January 1944, and the weather was hard. Winter lay upon Saxony like a frozen shroud. Summer, when you thought about it, was like a climatic phenomenon known only to exist on some other planet. It was a bitter winter. In the chilled earth of the fields they had been finding British bomber crews, shot down during terror attacks against Berlin and Leipzig and Chemnitz, with their parachutes unopened, frozen hard, and their fingertips torn and bloody from clawing at the packs. In the shivering forests, the woodcutters' axes rang clear and sharp so that for kilometers you could hear every stroke. From the eaves of the von Bluckau barns, long swords of ice hung down, Damoclean, above the rotting straw. This was the time when Bormann came, climbing stiffly from a black, mud-splashed ministerial Mercedes. He stamped his feet and blew on his fingers and was reluctant to shed his coat, even standing before the roaring fire in the library. "By God," he said, "The British might be keeping us awake in Berlin these nights but at least they're warming the place up with their damned incendiaries." Momentarily von Bluckau had been startled by Bormann's jocular reference to the massive RAF terror attacks which had nightly scourged Berlin even during the appalling weather that had prevailed over the capital during Christmas 1943 and then the new year of 1944.

"Don't look so shocked, my dear von Bluckau," said Bormann.

"Like London, Berlin also thinks it can take it. God knows for how long, though. The raids are no longer a joke. Now we can talk. Alone, if I may be so rude to your charming wife, the Gräfin."

Jutte must be drunk again, von Bluckau thought; she was usually charming then. In the early stages, anyway. At least she was not weeping in maudlin melancholy for days gone by. That would come later.

Over a bowl of hot pea soup by the library fire, Bormann had pounded von Bluckau's knee with a clenched fist.

"You were wasted as a Panzer commander," he declared, blowing noisily on his soup. "I previously congratulated you on being honored by the Führer for your stand at Stalingrad. I now congratulate you a thousand times more on the vision and the patriotic spirit with which you have drawn up the Fehme plan. In Berlin we have, I think, improved upon it or, at least, expanded it. I can tell you in secrecy that it has the Führer's complete approval and that it now has the status of an approved operation which is to be carried out when and as warranted by the circumstances."

Warmed by the fire, the soup and the enthusiasm of his eminent visitor, von Bluckau had reached for a cigar. It was, in a way, like celebrating a birth.

"When?" he said, reflecting sadly that much of the real pleasure in a good cigar had always been in being able to watch with your eyes the luxurious blue swirls of smoke when you exhaled.

"Forthwith," said Bormann. "The first phase, anyway."

The general had choked on the unseen smoke of his cigar.

"That's quick work."

"We need quick work," said Bormann. "The Anglo-Americans will be landing somewhere along the coast of France this spring. Then the two-front war will be a reality for us. Whatever the little doctor boasts in his newspapers and on his radio stations, Germany is going to need not only a resistance movement but a disciplined organization capable of maintaining, by stealth if you like, a system of law and order which will prevent the demoralization of the German population regardless of enemy occupation and foreign ideological persuasion. The Fehme will be the foundation of such a system. Since you have earned, and have been designated, a trusted role in our plans, I consider that the time has come for you to know about them. Are you sure we cannot be overheard? You will pardon my apparent presumption, in your own home, General."

"The door is locked," said von Bluckau. "It is good German oak from our own Jägerswald. Old but strong and thick. You could shoot me and I doubt that anybody would hear."

Bormann laughed, stretching out his boots toward the fire.

"My dear General, I have people to pull my triggers for me. Just as you did in the army. People like my faithful aide, Schrader, sitting behind you at the locked door with a Luger in his lap. I neglected to tell you, we are not entirely alone."

At this, the general also laughed, gently and with quiet assurance.

"I was about to mention that, Herr Bormann. My sense of hearing and smelling have improved in something of an inverse ratio to my loss of sight. I would say that your aide is a young man in his middle twenties, weighs about eighty kilos, smokes cheap cigars, has rubber heels on his shoes, is wearing a leather topcoat, which is dripping on the parquet floor, and visited our stables before entering Schloss Galgenstein without, obviously, having thought to use either the boot scrapers at the top of our steps from the terrace or the mats inside the front door."

"General," said Bormann, "I can see we are going to understand each other. You are a man of unsuspected talents. On behalf of my aide, I apologize. Rudeness I can overlook but stupidity and clumsiness I cannot and will not tolerate. I am sure Major Schrader has just learned a number of useful lessons."

The general, from his chair, raised a hand.

"They were merely casual observations, Herr Bormann."

"The point was taken, just the same," said Bormann. "You are not to be underestimated. Now, I have here the operation order for the Fehme plan, signed by the Führer, and delegating complete authority and responsibility for its execution to me, his personal secretary and adviser. Since the Führer has already made me responsible for the raising of our Volkssturm forces, it is not surprising that he should also entrust me with the creation of the Fehme. There is a difference, though. The Volkssturm is public knowledge. The Fehme is not. The operation order for the Fehme is a highly secret document whose existence and contents are known only to the Führer, to myself, to my personal staff—under pain of death—and to the future members of the Fehme, such as yourself, who will put the plan into operation.

Bormann waited while the general lit another cigar. Then, with the firelight carving clefts of shadow on von Bluckau's thin face, he opened the operation order.

Before Bormann had finished talking quietly but intensely on that snow-besieged night, von Bluckau was to smoke many cigars and drink much coffee laced with vintage cognac, for the operation order as drafted in Berlin made it plain that the Fehme had been planned elaborately, thoroughly and in infinite detail to function not so much as a makeshift resistance organization as a clandestine government capable of efficiently and implacably exercising a covert dictatorship in every square kilometer of German territory occupied by the enemy as and when the armed forces of the Third Reich were forced to yield ground.

Listening to Bormann, von Bluckau realized uneasily that he was about to become linked with what was virtually a shadow government presided over by Bormann in the name of the Führer. No longer did the general have any doubts about the acceptance of his plan. Bormann's briefing was definitive and explicit. The Fehme would be organized in regional jurisdictions throughout the Reich.

Bormann paused, watching von Bluckau's face in the firelight.

"The only punishment which a court of honor of the Fehme can impose is death," he said. "The offences which will come within its competence will normally be acts which the Fehme considers to be injurious to the national honor of Germany, such as collaboration with the occupying powers, cowardice or surrender in the face of the enemy at the fighting front, broaching the security of the Fehme by word or deed or failing to carry out the dictates and directives of the Fehme when ordered to do so."

Between the two men, the flames roared in the great fireplace.

"You will see, my dear von Bluckau," continued Bormann, "that through the Fehme we will continue to prosecute the aims and ideals of National Socialism throughout those German lands occupied by our enemies. The courts of honor will be the cutting edge of our sword of secret justice. With a weapon such as this we will wield a clandestine power long after the battle lines have moved on. In the interests of preserving the unity and honor of the German people, the Fehme will, if necessary, subject them to a reign of terror. If Germany is to be overwhelmed by sheer weight of numbers from the decadent capitalistic west and the Bolshevik barbarians from the east, then we will bide our time, rise up in arms against them from within and liberate the German people. The essential beauty of the Fehme organization, for which I will never cease to be eternally grateful to you, my dear General, is that every step forward into the Third Reich by our enemies will only enlarge the domain of the Fehme, for the Fehme will spring like dragons' teeth from the ground behind them."

"The Fehme will operate throughout the Reich, then?" von Bluckau asked, secretly startled by the scope and the ferocity of Bormann's briefing and the speed with which events had now moved since he had first invoked the legend of the medieval Fehme in the bird-singing peace of Schloss Galgenstein.

"From frontier to frontier," said Bormann. "From the North Sea to the Baltic. From the Rhine to the Oder."

The Fehme, he said, would have a Freistuhle in every historic German state from East Prussia to Westphalia and from Bavaria to Schleswig-Holstein. Contrary to the Gauleiter organization of the German National Socialist Party, each Freistuhle would not necessarily be located in the major city or town which, under all normal circumstances, would be a logical center for regional government and administration.

"We anticipate," said Bormann, "that the occupying forces of our enemies will naturally tend to establish their headquarters in the larger cities and towns of the areas they occupy in Germany."

"If the Anglo-American air forces leave any standing," said von Bluckau.

"Even so," said Bormann, "even in the long run, Germany's larger cities and towns will still be the natural centers of well-established lines of communication by rail, road, canal and river. The enemy headquarters centralized at such places will be alive with security forces, as are the headquarters of the Wehrmacht in Russia or France or Italy or any other of our occupied territories. Such a place, however, is no place for a Freistuhle administering an area of jurisdiction for the Fehme. The security risk will be too great. The enemy, as do we, concentrates at his headquarters all the usual apparatus of military surveillance. For these reasons every Freistuhle will be located in as remote and isolated and unlikely a place as possible. The enemy will not have an unlimited number of security personnel with which to police every square kilometer of the occupied area. In your own Saxony, for instance, Leipzig and Dresden are the most logical centers for military government by an occupying power. As a general who has fought with our victorious armies and worn the invader's boot on his own foot, you must surely agree, von Bluckau."

The general had to concede the point. He had also to admit to himself that Bormann and his staff had taken his plan far more seriously and done much more with it than he would ever have dared to suggest.

"For instance," said Bormann, "I would suggest that in Saxony the Freistuhle of the Fehme should be located right here at Schloss Galgenstein."

The general was startled. He felt that he must have shown his emotion. Bormann was quick to elaborate.

"I should have told you earlier. I have appointed you Freigraf of the Fehme Freistuhle in Saxony."

For von Bluckau, the dark and bitter months of inactivity since Stalingrad seemed never to have happened. He felt a little like the way he had on that autumn dawn in 1939, years before, in Poland when he had first gone forward into action in a tank of the Panzer Division Elbeland. A feeling of being where he was needed, of justifying his existence.

"I had not anticipated that, Herr Bormann," he said quietly.

"Why not?" Bormann answered him. "You have displayed your patriotic German spirit on the field of battle. Far from the front, you have still continued to demonstrate a loyal fighting spirit, despite the affliction of your physical blindness, in the planning which prompted our decision in Berlin to proceed with the Fehme project. As a von Bluckau, you know the local people here in Saxony. What is just as important, they know you and respect you as a traditional leader of their community. They are inherently loyal to you, in their own ways. Even under the National Socialism of our Führer, the old feudal ties have survived in many parts of Germany. Saxony is no exception. You are a logical choice for Freigraf of Saxony. Yet, and forgive me for speaking bluntly, as a blinded and pensioned-off general with no National Socialist political affiliations, you are unlikely to come under anything more than the most cursory military investigation or surveillance by an occupying enemy force. Am I right, so far?"

"Completely," said von Bluckau. Smiling, he leaned forward to warm his hands. "Provided that I and my people here at Galgenstein are such shining knights as you evidently believe us to be."

"I have no doubt of it," said Bormann seriously. "Furthermore, the most careful and, I may add, discreet appraisal of the likely military and political course of the war—I emphasize discreet because the Führer's faith in the heroic destiny of the Third Reich is still unshaken—has led us in Berlin to the conclusion that the conflict of arms will continue until the East Front is joined with the West Front in Germany. There will be no armistice. No gentlemen's agreements. No negotiated peace. This is inevitable, following Stalin's, Churchill's and Roosevelt's agreement on the principle of being satisfied with nothing less than the unconditional surrender of Germany. Their stupidity, of course, is amazing. Had they sat down to confer on the best possible way of prolonging the war, they could not have been more successful. They now have the bayonet at our throat. We have no alternative but to fight to the last, for there will be no honor in our defeat at their hands."

The general closed both hands over his face, closing them like the covers of a book, and then ran them down over his chin to his throat. He was very tired.

"Where are the fronts likely to meet?" he said.

"That's what I'm coming to," said Bormann. "The most objective long-range intelligence appreciations available to us indicate that a junction of the two fronts is likely to have been achieved by the summer of 1945. We know that the Russians and the Anglo-Americans have already agreed on tentative stop lines for the meeting of the fronts in central Germany. In Saxony, the Americans will advance to the Mulde. The Russians will stop on the line of the Elbe. The area between the two rivers will be a no man's land pending the establishment of the link-up and the withdrawal of the respective armies to their agreed zones of occupation. Schloss Galgenstein, it so happens, is located in this no man's land between the Elbe and the Mulde. What better base for the Freistuhle of the Fehme in Saxony?"

"None better," von Bluckau agreed. "It would be impossible for strangers to come within kilometers of the castle without being observed by the tenants of our estates. So far as the castle is concerned, there are underground parts of it which were indeed used for clandestine purposes centuries ago. There is still even an escape tunnel from the old dungeons. It runs out below the Schwarzesee to the woods beyond. The dungeons could be used again either as a headquarters or as the location for sessions of the court of honor. The old armory is ideal for use as a command-post bunker. For maximum security, the entire underground area could be sealed off from normal access."

Bormann sat forward eagerly.

"Are you sure of this, General?"

"I'm positive," said von Bluckau. "I've already evaluated the possibilities. Secret entrances which were used during the Thirty Years' War and later closed could easily be reopened. In fact, there is a family at Galgenstein village who are the descendants of the master stonemason who worked at the castle in the old days. They are still stonemasons. They are also quarry owners, so we would have no trouble getting stone. They lease it from my family, and prisoners of war working in the quarry are quartered in barracks on one of our estates, so a little rebuilding at the castle could be done easily and with a minimum of fuss or curiosity. I consider that in every way Schloss Galgenstein is a logical choice for Fehme headquarters in Saxony."

In his mind's eye, von Bluckau fixed the location of the castle in the triangular area of forests and fields, towns and villages, confined by the confluence of the Elbe and the Mulde near Dessau.

"Excellent," said Bormann. "In the interests of preserving the security of the Fehme, you can make any arrangements you think necessary. After all, you will be the responsible Freigraf. Now, as to the operation of the court of honor itself. I must insist that its procedures follow a standardized and detailed pattern or organization. You will have every opportunity to familiarize yourself with this in your own time, but here is the general outline. Firstly, the court will always meet in secret session. By secret I mean it will be open only to the members of the Fehme in Saxony. Its verdicts and sentences of death, however, can be as open as the sky. In fact, it is essential that they should be, for in this way the reputation of the Fehme will be memorably and ruthlessly established. Once the uninitiated members of the German population are more frightened of the Fehme than of the forces of the occupying powers, then the Fehme will have begun to achieve its objects as a clandestine government of fear."

They were right about Bormann, thought von Bluckau. The man is sinister. He is incapable of not being so.

"The procedure of the Fehme court of honor will be based broadly on that of our ancient German free courts," said Bormann. "While presiding over a session of the court of honor, you will sit at a table with a sword and a noosed rope placed upon it on the flag of the National Socialist Party of Germany, the blood banner with the swastika. The accused will stand or sit before you at the point of the sword. It is important that this and other comparatively simple rituals be observed, for they will become part of the word-of-mouth legend of the Fehme. There will be no need for masks or funny hats or any of that Ku Klux Klan nonsense of the Americans."

Fleetingly von Bluckau noted the coincidence that both Jutte and Bormann should have referred to the Ku Klux Klan in the context of the Fehme.

"The Fehme will only try the guilty," said Bormann, "and, as I have said, the only sentence which the court of honor can normally impose is death. The summons hailing an accused to the court for trial will be issued on your authority as the Freigraf. The summons will be nailed to the accused's door or otherwise placed in a position where he will pass it and see it as he goes about his affairs. That was the old Saxon law and so it shall be now."

The Führer's secretary or not, von Bluckau could not let this pass.

"But this is the twentieth century," he protested.

Sitting by the warmth of his own fire and listening to Bormann's quiet, interminable voice enunciating a policy of terrorization invoked from a dark Germanic past, the general had the illusion that the cigar he was smoking was real but the situation was not.

"You have a comment, General?" said Bormann, his voice surprisingly mild.

"I have," said von Bluckau. "If Saxony is to be occupied, as we fear, then it will be occupied by a modern army. Russian. American. British. It doesn't matter. It will still be a well-organized, well-equipped force. Can we revive the Fehme on the lines you suggest? Will there be either time or opportunity or even need for notes on doors and other ritualistic procedures?"

"That is precisely the point," said Bormann patiently. "Rituals, however simple, will be a necessary part of the propaganda apparatus of the Fehme. It must also be as legalistic as possible. The Fehme could just as easily shoot a German traitor in the back as he passes through the woods or stands in a town square. That, alone, is not good enough for our purposes. It would merely be the criminal act of a Bolshevik partisan or a French resistance terrorist. Justice, in the name of German honor, will only be done by the Fehme. It must also appear to be done. And done by the Fehme, furthermore. Not as murderers but as executioners."

The general held the cigar under his thin nose, sniffing at the aroma of the burning leaf.

"The old Saxon rituals were not designed for blitzkrieg warfare," he said.

"There will still be time to nail a summons on a man's door," said Bormann. "I agree that we cannot hope to recreate literally all the procedures of the medieval Fehmic courts. For instance, six weeks and three days were allowed, according to the ancient Saxon law, and the summons was thrice repeated. Under the conditions of either a Russian or an Anglo-American invasion in force, it would be ridiculous to attempt such a procedure. However, according to the old laws of our ancestors, if the accused were brought before the court, his accuser stated the case and investigation proceeded by the examination of witnesses as in a court of law. The judgment was then put into execution on the spot, if possible. This is one part of the old procedure we can and will follow. The Fehme must strike ruthlessly and without mercy at the betrayers of our German honor."

Outside in the snow-hushed night beyond the storm-shuttered windows of the castle library, a train was whistling mournfully on the Berlin-Dresden line.

"What form will the execution take?" von Bluckau asked.

Bormann was standing now, warming his rump before the fire.

"A good question," he said, "and one to which we have already given much thought. Since we must assume that the Fehme will operate as a clandestine force under the rigors of enemy occupation, the security of the courts of honor must not be hazarded by allowing members of the Fehme to carry military weapons and so risk capture and interrogation. We have studied this question at length. The instrument of execution must be silent and in itself unremarkable and not obviously a weapon. The rope. The knife. The choking scarf. The water pistol. There are many simple everyday objects which, with a little ingenuity and initiative, can be used to take life. I can assure you, my dear General, that the various techniques are laid down in the operations order for the Fehme."

The Graf von Bluckau was tired and he wondered if he had dozed off to sleep and had been dreaming.

"The water pistol?" he said guardedly. "Forgive me, but I have never regarded a water pistol as a lethal weapon."

"Precisely," said Bormann. His voice was animated and alert with enthusiasm. "It is a perfect example of what we have in mind. Water pistols were used by the executioners of the Fehme when the free corps were revived after 1918. It looks innocent enough, I grant you, even when it contains prussic acid. The Fehme of the days after 1918 was not an organization to be laughed at, General. Nor will there be anybody laughing at our new Fehme. Historically, we know it to be a fact that the threat of a squirt of prussic acid in the face was invaluable for ensuring the preservation of both the security and the reputation, sinister if you like, of the Fehme. I personally know all this to be true, General. The weapon was not unknown to us in the days of the old Freikorps Rossbach. It has many tactical advantages. It can be carried without suspicion. It can be wielded without warning. And, I can assure you, there is no arguing after you have had a water pistol full of prussic acid squirted into your face. You suffocate almost instantly. You are lucky if you do. Any delay is most unpleasant."

Warming to his subject, Bormann added jovially, "I can tell you, General, that in the old free corps days there were a lot of guilty Germans who used to carry their umbrellas with them even on the sunniest days."

The summer days, thought von Bluckau. The sunny summer days of peace. Would they ever come to Germany again in his time? Did Germany really need a system under which citizens carried umbrellas as a shield, not against God's rain but the threat of sudden, blinding, choking death by prussic acid spat at them from a toy pistol?

"You seem shocked, General," said Bormann. His voice was politely mannered.

"Not shocked," said von Bluckau, "startled, perhaps. I must admit that as a simple Panzer soldier I am accustomed to more conventional weapons of assault. Flame-throwers, for instance."

The irony escaped Bormann.

"We are living in unconventional times," he said. "We must adapt ourselves in the future as in the past. Now, there are other aspects of the Fehme plan with which you should be familiar at this point. Apart from your responsibilities as Freigraf and president of the Fehmic court of honor in Saxony—the finger of God, as it were—you will also be responsible to me for the carrying out of Operation Lilac in Saxony by the Freikorps Bormann and such Werewolf units as may be available."

The general sat forward so that the fierce glow from the great fireplace beat at his face.

The plan which he had submitted to Bormann had called for a revival of the old Fehmic courts of honor. Nothing more than that. It had not envisaged the formation and employment of irregular fighting troops in action on the field. As the commander of conventional armed forces in the east and in the west, he had seen too many of his troops ambushed and murdered by partisans in Russia and France to be able to overcome an instinctive repugnance toward the activities of underground terrorists. The Fehme, as he had seen it, was to have been a moral force with mainly a judicial function. That Bormann should have expanded the plan into the arena of political action had not really surprised him. This, he realized, was inevitable. Bormann was a politician fighting a politician's war. The general could not complain about this. After all, you needed a long spoon to sup with the devil. The raising of formations of irregular fighting troops, though, offended von Bluckau's sensibilities of pride as a professional soldier and as a member of what the Führer had openly dubbed—and, after such disasters as Stalingrad, with bitter contempt—the Generals' Club.

"What kind of operation will be undertaken by these units?" he asked. Consciously, the general spoke steadily and without emotion. He hoped that his voice was not betraying his doubts of the validity of a plan for recruiting partisans, German or otherwise.

Bormann sat down again, stretching out his boots toward the fire and putting a placating hand on von Bluckau's knee.

"My dear General," he said, "I know what you are thinking. As a soldier from the front you despise the idea of irregular troops fighting for German honor. Quite frankly, I can tell you that since von Paulus surrendered at Stalingrad, the Führer has entertained a similar opinion of many of your exalted colleagues and the troops of the Wehrmacht under their command. For myself, I am not concerned with the past. We no longer have time for the past. The present is hard enough to face, but then I am not particularly concerned with it any more. Time is running out for Germany. I am, however, vitally concerned with the future. The present interests me only in so far as it has any bearing on the bitter future ahead of us. The Fehme is proof of this, surely, but the Fehme plan alone is not enough."

The general stared blindly at the fire. The light of the flames was reflected in the lenses of his dark glasses.

"Don't shake your head, my dear von Bluckau. I am no general. I admit that. But in my own way I fight for Germany as a politician and a bureaucrat. If necessary, and as a soldier this may surprise you, I am ready to die for Germany. I see the Fehme first as a secret judiciary destroying those who would betray the honor of Germany to save their own skins. I see the Fehme secondly as the basis of a clandestine government surviving under the noses of the enemy forces who will occupy and violate Germany. Neither of these roles, however, will be enough for the days of flood and fire to come."

"What is enough?" said the general. "From our own experience as victors in the occupied territories we know that there are limits to what resistance movements can achieve."

"The answer to that question is Operation Lilac," said Bormann. "The world has seen what can be done by the ragged rabble of resistance in Russia and the countries of western Europe despite our sternest measures against them. What the world has not yet seen is what can be done by the application of Teutonic courage, ingenuity and thoroughness to the apparatus of resistance. The Fehme can punish and execute and reign over a considerable section of our population through the manipulation of threat and terror. But this will not be enough. Inevitably the Fehme must fight. It must have its iron fist, its armed forces, clandestine like itself, but forces which will nevertheless play their part in the liberation of the German people."

The general pursed his lips, interested despite his own doubts.

"What kind of operations do you have in mind?"

"Hit-and-run," said Bormann. "To begin with, anyway. Generally the armed forces of the Fehme will carry out defensive and offensive operations according to the military and political situation as it develops on the fighting fronts. Defensive operations will be carried out by the Werewolf organization. The Werewolves will have a limited but invaluable life. They will resist by sabotage the advance of the invaders. They will destroy bridges, dams, power stations, fuel dumps, gas works, power lines, telephones and all facilities likely to be of assistance to the enemy."

With little pride, the general recalled the occasion during the drive into the Ukraine when the Panzer Division Elbeland had supported a Waffen SS infantry formation which had surrounded and then annihilated a town defended by Russian partisans. Sometimes he still thought he could smell the sickly stench of burning human hair.

"You will need a lot of replacements for the Werewolves," he said.

Bormann snapped his fingers confidently.

"I agree. We have foreseen this. The Werewolves, of course, will be expendable. Inevitably they must be. It will be their heroic destiny. But they will establish a tradition of bravery and self-sacrifice which will enrich the legend and the stature of the entire Fehme organization."

"Who will man the Werewolf units?" said von Bluckau.

"The Hitler Youth," said Bormann. "Who else? We will not need them for long but this could be their noblest hour. They are old enough to swear an oath of allegiance to the Fehme and to honor it. They are also young enough to die for it. They are young enough, furthermore, to be able to move freely, if in civilian clothes, throughout their communities without exciting the suspicion of enemy security forces."

The general was thinking of his son. Not the Hitler Youth and the brave banners. Just Siegfried with the straw hair and the summer freckles on his thin von Bluckau nose. The general reflected that in a few words Bormann had said everything that remained to be said about the Hitler Youth and the seduction of an entire generation of young Germans by the pied piper not of Hameln but of Berchtesgaden.

"And the Freikorps Bormann?" said von Bluckau. How curious, he thought, that twenty-five years after his father's death fighting with the Freikorps Barbarossa he should now himself have become involved with yet another manifestation of the German obsession for tilting at windmills.

"Ah," said Bormann. His voice sounded eager. "There will be no boys singing around campfires in the Freikorps Bormann. This will be men's work."

For the first time since he had begun his briefing on the Fehme, Bormann's voice sounded really animated.

"The Freikorps Bormann will be our real shock-troop formation," he said. "It will be an elite organization responsible for carrying out offensive operations on behalf of the Fehme, particularly Operation Lilac. The qualifications for holding even the lowest rank in the Freikorps Bormann will be to have been an officer, an active member of the National Socialist Party, a member of the SS and to have served at the front as an infantry fighter and to have been decorated for bravery in the field."

"A tall order," mused von Bluckau, smiling a little.

"For a division, yes," said Bormann, "but at battalion level, no. In that strength we must and can find them. It is essential that the Freikorps Bormann be an elite unit. It will be the cadre formation for an entire battle order of future Freikorps of the Fehme. Every member of the Freikorps Bormann must have the capability and experience to be a potential leader in other Freikorps to be established later. The FkB must be an eagle's nest of leaders."

On this basis, the general conceded that the planning seemed sound enough.

"I was sure you would see it that way," Bormann said smoothly. "We have the benefit of much good advice from some very experienced people, I can assure you."

The general made a self-deprecatory gesture with one thin hand. The gold ring with the worn von Bluckau crest gleamed in the firelight.

"I can appreciate that, Herr Bormann. You must forgive me. As a general in the line, I became accustomed to looking objectively at plans from the staff."

"And well you might have, my dear von Bluckau," said Bormann. He chuckled maliciously. "The Berlin war communiques of late have certainly been no vote of confidence in much of our general staff planning. There is one more thing I should have mentioned. There is yet another important prerequisite for membership of the Freikorps Bormann."

The general wondered just what further virtues were to be required of the paragons of the Freikorps Bormann.

"With respect," said Bormann, "I doubt if you would ever have guessed just what this prerequisite is. Simply it is this—every volunteer for the Freikorps Bormann must have qualified for prosecution as a war criminal by the enemies of Germany."

The winter wind from the far Baltic had roared louder in the great chimney just then and the general had asked Bormann to repeat his statement.

"This no doubt surprises you," Bormann said. "As an aristocrat and an honored Panzer general on the reserve list, it perhaps shocks you. Just so that you do not misunderstand me, I want you to know that we have been into all this most thoroughly. You can rest assured of that. All potential candidates for membership of the Freikorps Bormann of the Fehme have been rigorously scrutinized. Deliberately adopting the arbitrary standards of our somewhat squeamish and hypocritical enemies, the Anglo-Americans, certain highly qualified legalistic persons in Berlin have carefully and thoroughly examined the service dossiers of all FkB candidates and evaluated their prospects of being charged as war criminals before the tribunals which we already know to have been planned by the Russians, the Americans, the British and the French."

The general was more puzzled than shocked. Since 1939 his finer sensibilities had been atrophied by repeated exposure to human suffering and indignity.

"Why?" he asked. "You must admit, Herr Bormann, that you have set a most unusual standard for membership of an elite fighting unit."

Bormann smiled, watching the thin, worried face of the blinded patrician.

"What you must understand, my dear von Bluckau, is that the Fehme and the Freikorps Bormann and the Werewolves will be fighting a clandestine, underground war behind the very backs of the invaders. It will be no longer a gentleman's war, if it ever was.

"If you care to think about it," Bormann continued, "the reason for the war-crimes qualification is obvious enough. A man who knows he will have to face war-crimes charges if he falls into the avenging hands of our enemies is a man whom you can, beyond any reasonable doubt, expect to leave a battleground either victorious and alive or dead and defeated. Gather together such a group of men and you have a brotherhood with blood on its hands, a conspiracy of death, a society sensitive to betrayal. I, as the Oberstuhlherrführer of the Fehme in all Germany, will hold their dossiers and thus have a lien, as it were, on their loyalty."

"If you will permit me," said the general. "It sounds like blackmail." With a quiet, objective curiosity he wondered just what kind of an outburst this would draw from Bormann. He had not reckoned, however, with the professional cynicism of the only man in Germany who could whisper in the ear of the Führer.

"Blackmail?" said Bormann equably. "My dear von Bluckau, of course it's blackmail. What the sword is to the soldier so blackmail is to the politician. It is our secret weapon, our wonder-worker, our miracle-maker. And throughout history the soldier's sword and the politician's blackmail have been indispensable weapons, together, in the armories of the greatest nations in the world."

Bormann passed von Bluckau a glass of cognac.

"To blackmail," he said.

Carefully, so that he would not spill the vintage spirit, the general raised his glass.

"To the sword," he said.

"To each his own," said Bormann. "Together, though, you and I will achieve the same ends. And speaking of swords, my martial and military friend, I have further news for you. It is no accident that the Freikorps Bormann has been allocated, under your command, to the Fehme in Saxony. The most careful and, again I must add, discreet political, military and economic appreciations available to us have indicated several possibilities. Assuming the first possibility—the Anglo-American invasion of France—what do you think of the second possibility? I mean Germany's chances of survival. Forget politics. Forget the Führer even. Man to man, as a fighting general, what do you think of a long-range situation appraisal which says that Germany could survive defeat in a two-front struggle for no longer than twelve months?"

Often in the past, von Bluckau had discussed this very question. Then, though, it had been with brother generals and fellow officers whom he could trust in any frank exchange of views on questions of tactics and strategy.

"I agree," said the general. "I hate to say it but I must."

"Good," said Bormann. "I would have been disappointed if you had said you would not agree. I would have regarded you as either a liar or a fool and, unless I'm a poor judge, you're neither of these. So the fronts meet, as they must. Where, though? The Russians, we know, don't want the Anglo-Americans on the Oder. The Anglo-Americans don't want the Russians on the Rhine. The most logical geographical location for a meeting of the fronts, then, is somewhere along the line of the Elbe, south and perhaps west of Berlin. Political and military intelligence available to us suggests that the fronts will, indeed, meet in central Germany. If this is what is to happen, then the Fehme forces in Saxony could well have a historic role either in the salvation of the Third Reich or the birth of the Fourth Reich."

"And what about Operation Lilac?" von Bluckau asked.

Bormann chuckled, holding up his glass and staring at the fire through the clear depths of cognac.

"Patience, General, patience. I am coming to Operation Lilac. It will be carried out when and where the fronts meet. That could yet be in East Prussia, Silesia, Saxony or Westphalia. Who really knows? I still think it will be in Saxony. Our intelligence gentlemen are now unanimous in the opinion that the line of the Elbe constitutes a natural geographic demarcation line between the two converging fronts. Which brings me to Operation Lilac. I mentioned that only a miracle can prevent a German defeat. I personally don't believe in miracles. But I do believe that miracles can be made to happen. The Führer, for instance, believes that the Anglo-Americans and the Russians may well fight like jackals over the prostrate body of the German nation. To an extent, too, I also believe this but only in a long-range historical context, when it will all be too late for us. I also believe, however, that such a miracle can be hurried along. I believe it can be provoked. For instance, to be perfectly frank, von Bluckau, both you and I know that the supposed Polish raid on the Gleiwitz radio station in Silesia which helped precipitate our invasion of Poland in 1939 was ingeniously contrived and carried out by our own intelligence people. I believe that even now we can similarly provoke such a situation between the Anglo-Americans and the Russians once the East Front and the West Front begin to come in contact. You see now what I mean?"

Appalled, yet strangely excited, the general nodded, warming to the cognac in the round of his hands.

"I take it," said von Bluckau, "that the object of such a provocation would be to terminate the Second World War in Europe with the commencement of the Third World War—between the Anglo-Americans and the Russians—as and when they meet in Germany?"

"Correct," said Bormann. "Presumably, you find such a plan fantastic and unrealistic?"

"Not necessarily," said the general. "It took only an assassin's pistol at Sarajevo to launch the First World War in 1914. That, also, could just as easily have been deliberately planned."

"Exactly," said Bormann, "and I can tell you that the Fehme staff have planned Operation Lilac on just such a basis."

"Who will carry it out?" said von Bluckau.

"The Freikorps Bormann, of course. Who else?"

"What form will the operation take?"

"Not so fast, my dear von Bluckau," Bormann said. "When you consider the possible outcome of such a provocative action, you will agree on the need for observing the utmost secrecy. All you need know at the moment is that the operation has been planned, the FkB will have the historic role of carrying it out and the battleground may well be here in your own Saxony. You will be briefed progressively as the day comes closer for Operation Lilac."

"Operation Lilac," said the general, savoring the phrase aloud, wondering—as he had often wondered—at the triteness of names which the planning staff bestowed upon plans that called for the breaking of bones, the wounding of flesh and the spilling of blood.

"Remember it well," said Bormann. "If it succeeds, it will launch the third and last world war in history."

"And what of Germany?" said the general. When he said this, he was thinking not only of Germany but also of Saxony and Schloss Galgenstein and the villages, the farms, the forests and the fields that had stood inviolate and peaceful for so long now on the von Bluckau lands.

"A nation gets the destiny it deserves," Bormann said. "You know what the Führer thinks. If he is to burn in final defeat, then it is good enough for Germany to burn with him. Unconditional surrender is unthinkable. If the German people prove to be a nation of straw and surrender the fatherland to the Jewish capitalists and decadents of the west and the Bolshevik barbarians of the east, then they must expect to burn in the fires of war—either this one or the one that I hope will immediately follow it."

"The situation in Germany will be chaotic," said von Bluckau. "It was to police just such a situation that I first planned the Fehme."

Staring into the flames of the fire, Bormann shrugged his shoulders.

"I admit, my dear von Bluckau, that if Operation Lilac goes according to plan and to the Fehme falls the momentous task of provoking a state of armed conflict between the present temporarily allied enemies of the Third Reich, then the immediate result for Germany will indeed be chaos. Frightful and catastrophic chaos. But, like the National Socialist Party which our Führer led to victory out of the chaos of 1918, so will I, with God's help, lead a Fehmic Germany out of the chaos of a year which may yet see our enemies clawing at each other's throats."

The general heard Bormann stand up. Impelled not so much by this as by the formality and intensity of emotion in Bormann's voice, von Bluckau also stood up. The moment had come during this long night of talk by the hearth of his own ancestral home when he had to decide irrevocably between attack and retreat. He could march with the Fehme now or wait in the lonely obscurity of retirement for old age to come to him at Schloss Galgenstein. Unhesitatingly, but with a feeling of utter finality, von Bluckau nodded.

"I am with you, Herr Bormann."

The general felt Bormann's hand gripping his shoulder. There was a suggestion of demoniac possession in the iron grip of the man's fingers.

"And I am with you, General. Will you now take the oath of the Fehme?"

In the echoing silence of the great room, von Bluckau heard the night wind from across the frozen Elbe fumbling at the wooden storm shutters on the windows of the tapestried stone walls. Somewhere beyond the silent, snow-embraced von Bluckau fields outside, a locomotive whistled again, lonely in the waiting night.

"I will," said von Bluckau.

He heard Bormann call his aide.

"Bring the Bible, Schrader," he said.

Under the von Bluckau arms above the fireplace they waited, standing on the skin of the great Russian bear that the general had sent home in 1942.

"Take the Bible in your left hand," said Bormann. "Hold it high and clasp my right hand with your right hand. Now, repeat the words of the oath after me as I pronounce them."

Standing below his family's coat of arms, the general spoke the words carefully and in a firm, ringing voice, for to him an oath was an oath. Like a gun which you never carried unless you were prepared to use it.

"I, Dietrich," he said, "the Graf von Bluckau, hereditary lord of Schloss Galgenstein and master of all the lands pertaining thereto, general of the reserve in the army of the Third Reich and holder of the Knight's Cross, with Oak Leaves, of the Iron Cross, with Swords and Diamonds, being of sound mind, do hereby swear in the name of our Führer, Adolf Hitler, to whom I have already sworn an oath of allegiance, that, in the name of German honor and in the name of our glorious German dead, I now hold myself loyal until death, henceforth and hereafter, to the new German Fehme and to obey the commands, orders and directives of Martin Bormann, the assigned Oberstuhlherrführer of the Fehme. On this Bible, which I now hold, I do so swear."

"With God," said Bormann, "and in the name of our Führer, Adolf Hitler, I am your witness. You are now a sworn member of the Fehme and the assigned Freigraf of the Fehme in Saxony. Fehme, heil!"

"Fehme, heil!" repeated the general. Unobtrusively, he flexed the fingers of his right hand. They had become numbed in Bormann's grip. The ceremony, he thought, had been as disturbing as it had been brief. The von Bluckaus were a traditionally devout Lutheran family. For generations, during the conflict and travail of the religious wars which had ravaged Germany, they had suffered and died in their faith. They revered the Bible even if not every von Bluckau had entirely practiced its precepts. Uncannily, then, it seemed as if Bormann had known what von Bluckau was thinking.

"My dear General," he said, "I know your background, rest assured of that. I, too, am capable of taking the Bible seriously. That Bible on which you just took the oath of loyalty to the Fehme has marched with me ever since I first carried arms for the fatherland."

Bormann left Schloss Galgenstein that night between midnight and dawn. Soft flakes of snow swirled in the beams of the dimmed headlights of his black Mercedes as he waved good-bye, rubbing with gloved hands at the frosted window. Standing on the steps of Schloss Galgenstein, von Bluckau had shivered. The ice and snow upon his face and under his feet had reminded him of the awesome desolation of his division's last nights at Stalingrad.

After that night with Bormann at Galgenstein, though, von Bluckau's work for the Fehme had really begun and he was glad of it, for, since Stalingrad, he had found little joy in his life as a blinded general on the Wehrmacht reserve. The Fehme now became as much a part of his being as had been, once, the decimated Panzer Division Elbeland.

In line with von Bluckau's briefing from Bormann, the organization and establishment tables of the Fehme in Saxony called for the selection of a personal bodyguard, a Freistuhlherr, ten Freischoffen or sheriffs who would act as jurymen, a prosecutor and a minimum of one hundred Freifronen to form the body of the Freistuhl in Saxony and its court of honor. The choice of a bodyguard was not difficult. The general chose his own son, Siegfried, now in his fifteenth year and unlikely to be conscripted for full-time military service before 1946. A strong, tall and intelligent boy, Siegfried knew the forests, the fields, the farms and the marshy waterways of the von Bluckau lands and the surrounding countryside of Saxony as well as he knew the stone-walled world of Schloss Galgenstein itself. The general swore him into the Fehme in January 1944, as the Russians, away in the east, advanced on Leningrad and captured Novgorod.

"You are now my eyes as well as my son," the general told Siegfried. "You and I are comrades in the Fehme. Where I go, you go. What you see, I see. And if and when the Fehme goes into action, there will be troubled times here in Saxony. My life then will largely be in your hands as my bodyguard. You will have to grow up very quickly, Siegfried, but, then, so will all your generation. God help you."

Siegfried had looked at him with troubled eyes.

"Will I carry arms, Father?"

"Of course you will," said von Bluckau. "If there is to be a need for the Fehme, then there will be a need for arms."

Siegfried smiled then and folded his arms, rocking cockily on his heels.

"I will be a good soldier, Father."

"I have no doubts of that," said the general. "After all, you are a von Bluckau. And, God knows, the Hitler Youth has taught you well enough how to fight."

"Even the Panzerfaust," said Siegfried, proudly. "Do you think I will get a chance to knock out a tank?"

"Siegfried," said von Bluckau, "I am sure that when the Anglo-Americans or the Russians get here, there will be no shortage of tank targets for your Panzerfaust."

Children against tanks, thought the general. That we should have come to this. The ultimate idiocy. There was something shameful about the thought of his son, a child, lying behind a hedge and aiming his Panzerfaust weapon at a 50-ton tank, which, if he missed, would first machine-gun him to mangled, bloody pieces of flesh and splintered bone and then grind what was left of him beneath its tracks into the earth of his native Saxony. My God, how we have failed our children, thought the general.

By the end of February, with the Red Army penetrating Estonia and capturing Krivoi Rog, von Bluckau had selected one-legged Heppner, the innkeeper of the Golden Lion in Gross Galgenstein, as his Freistuhlherr and clerk of court. Heppner had been invalided out of the Waffren SS after a band of Russian partisans had trapped his platoon asleep in a Ukrainian barn. The innkeeper's father had been the old Graf von Bluckau's orderly in France and Flanders and had later ridden with him on the covert operations of the Freikorps Barbarossa after 1918. He had brought the Graf's body home in a crude pine coffin from East Prussia to Saxony for burial in the von Bluckau crypt at Schloss Galgenstein. Old Heppner was dead but his son, the one-legged former Feldwebel of the Waffen SS, was the innkeeper at Gross Galgenstein. For him, as for his father, there was no question of anything but loyalty to any cause led by a von Bluckau.

"What if I am called up for service again, General?" Heppner had said just before he took the Fehme oath. "They are talking now about the Volkssturm, a people's army for the home front. They'll even want crocks like me."

The general smiled and gave Heppner the Wilhelmstrasse address in Berlin which Bormann had included in his briefing on the organization of the Fehme.

"All you need do, Herr Heppner, is write to this address and say that I have requested you be assigned to me to work on the estates here at Schloss Galgenstein. Then there will be no call-up for you."

The innkeeper had not seemed surprised. Born and bred within sight of the lofty Sprengertor, the great tower which dominated both Schloss Galgenstein and the low-lying countryside between the Elbe and the Mulde, Heppner was unlikely to be astonished by the amount of influence which the von Bluckau family was capable of wielding, even in 1944.

"You will have enough to do for Germany without marching with the Volkssturm," said von Bluckau. "Your immediate task is to select, quietly and without fuss, twelve Freischoffen to sit as jury in the sessions of the Fehme court of honor in Saxony. Tell them nothing about the Fehme as such. Just say that it is a patriotic duty, in the hard days to come, in which I expect their help. You will select a Freischoffe for each of ten villages within ten kilometers of Schloss Galgenstein. They must be men you know well yourself. Men you could trust with your life. And mine. You must check their party record. Their police record. Their service record. Their race record. Everything you can. I repeat, they must be men whom we can trust with our lives. They must be men who trust us with their lives. Bring them, one by one, to me at Schloss Galgenstein. If I approve your selections, then I will swear them into the Fehme."

"I can think of a hundred such men," said Heppner.

I was right about him, thought von Bluckau. A good family, the Heppners.

"Choose well," he said aloud.

By the end of March, as Berlin suffered its heaviest air attacks of the war so far—the RAF incendiary bombers by night and the American carpet-bombers by day—and as the Russians crossed the Dniester into Bessarabia, von Bluckau had sworn in the ten Freischoffen chosen by the one-legged innkeeper, a sheriff and juryman for each of ten villages that ringed the von Bluckau lands. On taking the oath, each of the Freischoffen in turn was briefed to recruit ten Freifronen, good men and true, to form the cadre force of the rank and file of the Fehme in Saxony.

In April, as American bombers from bases in England were sweeping in daylight right across Saxony to attack targets in Silesia, and the Soviet forces continued their westward advance through the Crimea, von Bluckau had recruited his prosecutor, Krausnick, a lawyer from Leipzig, who had been disbarred during the regime of the old Weimar Republic long before Hitler had come to power. A former Communist, Krausnick had been expelled after he had been charged with supplying the National Socialists in 1933 with lists of members of the German Communist

Party. Krausnick, thought von Bluckau, was no gentleman. He wasn't even a loyal Communist. In Berlin, however, Bormann, as his sponsor, had confirmed the fact that Krausnick's record of service with the National Socialists was impeccable.

"He has all the makings of a hanging judge," said Bormann. "If he has the talent, we have the rope."

By the end of May, as the summer's dust was beginning to powder the lilacs of Saxony, and with Sevastopol fallen to the Russians, von Bluckau had sworn in his hundred Freifronen as members of the Fehme and servants of the court of honor in Saxony.

By June 6, 1944, as the Anglo-American invasion forces stormed ashore on the beaches of Normandy to breach the defenses of the West Wall, von Bluckau was able to report to Bormann that in Saxony the court of honor of the Fehme was now ready to assemble in secret session. Bormann had reacted quickly, driving to Galgenstein from Berlin by car. Rail traffic out of the capital had been dislocated by a heavy American air raid that morning with plummeting target markers leaving great white trails of smoke standing vertically in the blue sky.

"Congratulations," said Bormann when von Bluckau outlined to him every detail of the state of readiness of the Fehme in Saxony. "As I told you last winter, General, what I feared would happen has now begun to happen. With the Anglo-American landings in the west, Germany is now fighting the two-front war we have always dreaded. They are saying we will throw the Anglo-Americans back into the sea. How can we do that if they have already thrown us back onto the fields behind the invasion beaches? Soon, the Russians will start pushing in earnest from the east. Already there are signs of a massive Soviet attack all along the central front in the east. I tell you, General, the hour of destiny for the Fehme will not be long in coming. This autumn will see the last harvest of the Third Reich."

Bormann frowned at the map spread out on the table in von Bluckau's library.

"For God's sake, don't tell anybody I said so," he added.

After this, the months had passed swiftly for von Bluckau as, with Siegfried at his side, he had mingled with the men of the Fehme and with them reconnoitered the countryside around

Schloss Galgenstein, which might soon become the organization's battleground in Saxony.

On the heels of the long-awaited invasion in the west, in June, had come the ugly news of von Stauffenberg's abortive July 20 attempt to kill the Führer with a time bomb in his Wolfsschanze headquarters at Rastenburg in East Prussia. With the wave of arrests, trials and executions that swept Germany after the failure of the July 20 plot had come news, in that dark July, of German defeats at Lublin, Narva, Lvov, Dvinsk, Bialystok, Brest Litovsk, Przemysl and Yaroslav and the smashing of the Mannerheim Line in Finland on the northern front. In August, the Anglo-Americans invaded southern France, and by the end of the month, with the Wehrmacht retreating in Normandy, the Anglo-Americans had captured Orléans, Chartres, Falaise, Cannes, Grasse, Rouen and Paris.

On September 11, as Anglo-American forces in the west crossed into Third Reich territory to fight for the first time on German soil, von Bluckau had received the telegram for which he had been waiting. The schoolgirl daughter of the postmaster at Galgenstein had delivered it, wobbling into the courtyard of the castle on her bicycle. Siegfried read the telegram to him: "The guests have arrived." It was signed "Rossbach," the code name which Bormann had chosen for the Fehme alert in honor of the old Fehme Freikorps Rossbach in which he had himself fought during the troubled years after 1918. The telegram was the prearranged signal alerting the Fehme throughout Germany that enemy forces were now fighting on German land and that the days of invasion and occupation were at hand. Far away in the west, behind the American lines, the new German Fehme had been born.

As 1945 dawned in the ground-frozen depths of that last bleak winter of the war in Germany, von Bluckau knew that, as Bormann had prophesied, the testing time for every patriotic German could not be long delayed. He was glad at least that the Fehme in Saxony was ready.

From the east and from the west, the two great fronts were closing on Germany like the pincers of a blacksmith of the gods.

In January, the Russians captured Warsaw, Cracow, Gumbinnen and Tannenberg. Their armored columns clattered and roared on their way into Pomerania and Silesia and East Prussia.

Saxony's turn was coming. Returning excitedly from the battlements at the top of the Sprengertor on a day when the east wind was blowing, Siegfried declared he had heard the distant rumble of artillery.

In the west, the Americans crossed the Ruhr River. By March 1 they had captured München-Gladbach and by March 2 they had reached the Rhine. By the end of March the Anglo-Americans had swept across the Rhine in a gigantic assault, and Cologne, Mainz, Worms and Kaiserslautern had fallen.

Now, in this month of April as the lilacs bloomed again, the fury of the war had swept closer, encompassing Saxony on all sides so that the old state crouched, marooned like an island in a rising tide of encircling fire, steel, confusion and panic. In the west, the Anglo-Americans had encircled the Ruhr, captured Essen, Hannover, Brunswick, Weimar and Celle and, by April 11, were within 70 miles of Berlin. In the implacable east, catastrophe had followed catastrophe as the Russians swept westward, occupying Stettin and driving on to surround Berlin.

On this blackest day yet, April 25, the Russians and the Americans had met on the Elbe, little more than ten kilometers from Schloss Galgenstein.

For von Bluckau, the heroic dream of the Fehme was no longer an academic abstraction on winter nights beside the crackling fire in the great open hearth in his library. The Fehme was now a desperate reality, a conspiracy hidden deep in the dungeons of his own Schloss Galgenstein. Quartered in the von Bluckau forests, farms and villages was the Freikorps Bormann, a furtive but determined force of a thousand tough, silent men, with each of the hundred Freifronen of the Fehme sheltering and victualing ten of the waiting FkB fighters. Located in Schloss Galgenstein itself was Schrader, the operational Freikorpsführer himself; Schrader, the sulky, good-looking butcher-boy turned SS officer; Schrader, who had been Bormann's personal choice; Schrader, who had succeeded brilliantly in assembling the troops of the Freikorps Bormann at Galgenstein before the Russians had closed the encircling ring of fire around besieged Berlin and the clandestine national headquarters of the Fehme.

The general, though, no longer thought of Schrader as the one-time butcher-boy from Niederleipisch, one of the local villages, but as the limping priest, for this was how Jutte had sardonically described him on his arrival at Schloss Galgenstein with the news that a thousand men of the FkB had come with him and, overnight, had been dispersed and hidden on the von Bluckau estates. A flaxen-haired young man with staring, thyroidal blue eyes, Schrader was wearing the uniform of a chaplain of the United States Army as he limped up the worn stone steps that climbed to the great oaken door of the castle. He had introduced himself formally with a punctilious clicking of heels. The general was mildly amused by this presumption of Prussian etiquette.

"Sturmbannführer Schrader, Waffen SS," said the FkB leader, apparently unaware of the incongruity of his American uniform and chaplain's insignia. Less curtly he added, "The lilacs are blooming."

"They will soon fall," said the general, completing the agreed security check and feeling slightly ridiculous.

"Operation Lilac?" he said.

"Yes, General. I am here to report to you and to carry out the operation, as and when ordered. I am also here to acquaint you with the relevant details."

"Come inside, then, Major," said the general, deliberately using the regular army equivalent of the SS rank of Sturmbannführer. He found it difficult to quell a growing sense of irritation. For a young man of minor rank, Schrader seemed very sure of himself.

"It will be warmer in the library. And we will be undisturbed."

III

The Lilacs of April

OVER THE ERSATZ COFFEE, the general listened to Major Schrader's description of the orders for the operation which he was to carry out.

"Briefly," said Schrader, "the object of Operation Lilac is to provoke a state of armed conflict between the Russian and American forces—now advancing toward each other to consolidate their meeting on the line of the Elbe—and to create a political situation capable of exploitation by the Fehme in the interests of German unity and honor."

My God, thought von Bluckau, Bormann really meant what he said.

"The thousand men of the Freikorps Bormann will take part in what is essentially an agent provocateur action," Schrader was saying. "The operation has been planned down to the last detail. My own uniform, for instance. We have brought with us Russian and American uniforms, Russian and American weapons, Russian and American vehicles, Russian and American documentation. A special Fehme unit has for months been assembling this equipment at Wehrmacht salvage dumps of captured enemy war materiel."

"What about communications?" said the general.

"We will have adequate facilities," said Schrader. "We have a radio link between Fehme headquarters in Berlin and a mobile radio station, Werewolfsender, which has been set up on the bombed-out and abandoned Luftwaffe base at Falkewitz, a few kilometers from here, east of the Elbe. From Werewolfsender, there will be a radio link with my own Freikorps Bormann headquarters, which will be located here in Schloss Galgenstein. From FkB headquarters we will have tactical field radio links with each of the ten FkB companies. I am instructed by Oberstuhlherrführer Bormann to tell you that immediately the Russians and the Americans have completed the military occupation of Saxony, east and west of the Elbe, the Fehme is to inaugurate a reign of terror, if necessary, to ensure the complete co-operation of the local German civilian population with the Fehme and the FkB regardless of the severity of the enemy occupation. Once the Russo-American link-up is consolidated in force and the Third Reich is cut in half, we can conclude that Germany has lost the conventional military war. Under these circumstances, Werewolfsender will be our major link with the civilian population of Saxony. The main instruments of terror and discipline will, of course, be the sessions of the court of honor over which you will preside as court president and Freigraf of the Fehme Freistuhl in Saxony."

Marveling at the boundless self-confidence of youth, the general listened to the young SS Sturmbannführer pacing back and forth by the fireplace, his boot heels ringing on the parquet floor.

"Oberstuhlherrführer Bormann has asked me to repeat to you his orders," said Schrader. "Your court of honor will hunt down, arrest, try and execute any German guilty of collaboration, cowardice or treason and also take into protective custody any other nationality, prisoner or forced laborer, who endangers the security of the Fehme and prejudices the success of Operation Lilac. If necessary, the accused can be tried and convicted in their absence. Their execution can be ordered and delegated for action by any sworn member of the Fehme. Preferably, of course, an accused should be charged in your court and sentenced then and there to death."

"Naturally," said von Bluckau, not without irony.

"The execution should be carried out immediately," Schrader continued, "or as soon as possible thereafter."

Pouring coffee for the general, he added, "Herr Bormann says that the Fehme must strike like lightning. The arrests, convictions, sentences and executions of accused persons arraigned as collaborators, traitors and informers before the court of honor will be promulgated as radio broadcasts by Werewolfsender to ensure the widest possible recognition of the power and ruthlessness of the Fehme. With the Fehme in clandestine control of the wills of our people in Saxony, then the FkB can proceed with Operation Lilac."

Listening to Schrader, the general had to concede that, although its conception was fantastic, there was no practical reason why it could not be carried out. Once having been launched, there was more than a passing chance that Operation Lilac would achieve its objective of provoking a conflict of arms between the probing front-line spearheads of the converging Russo-American forces. With this much achieved, the rest of it, as was so often the case in war, would be in the lap of the gods. He said as much to the young Sturmbannführer from the SS, but Schrader barely listened.

General the Freiherr von Bluckau only knew the half of it, Schrader thought contemptuously. The blinded blueblood and his precious court of honor were just pawns in a much bigger game. What the country gentleman of a general did not know was that Operation Lilac was merely the key to a master plan, itself to be triggered into action by Adolf Hitler's death, after which Bormann would take over as Führer of the Fourth Reich and Reichsführer of the Fehme Front Party of Germany. Schrader could still recall the shiver of excitement with which in Berlin, following his taking of the oath of loyalty both to the Fehme and to Bormann, he had listened to Bormann's briefing on the real reasons for Operation Lilac.

"Militarily and logistically this war is already lost," Bormann had told him, raising his voice a little above the thundering of Berlin flak guns that night. "The Führer will stay here in Berlin and die here in Berlin. I know him well enough to say this. The deathwish is now his creed. If there is to be no German victory, then he will seek death. It may come to him in any one of a number of ways. A British or American bomb. A Russian grenade or shell. An assassin's bullet. Or by his own hand. Death will be his last victory. He is obsessed with death. He cannot resist it. When it happens, the Third Reich will have lost the war politically. This will be the greater tragedy. Without Adolf Hitler, the National Socialist Party will collapse like the bridge from which the keystone of its arch is taken. What Germany will need then is a new party and a new Führer. That new political organization will be the Fehme Front Party of Germany."

The muzzle flashes of the nearest guns, flung back by the low cloud over Berlin, had lit Bormann's face satanically in the darkened room.

"I will be the leader of the Fehme Front," he said. "Historically, the time will be right. Now, as in the past, the Fehme can and will unite Germans to shield them from the anarchy that must follow defeat and disintegration. Operation Lilac already has the status and legality of a plan officially approved by the Führer himself. This was achieved by presenting Operation Lilac to him as a secret counterrevolutionary action, an operation designed to forestall any repetition of the July twentieth plot against the Führer's life and the government of the Third Reich. I need hardly add, my dear Schrader, that it is fundamentally important that the Führer should not know that the fact of his death will be the signal for the commencement of an operation which will enable me to take over as his successor. The only reason I am entrusting you with this information—which could hang us both—is that as the designated leader of the Freikorps Bormann you will automatically become the Reichsleiter of the Fehme Korps, the new SS of the new Germany. You will also command the elite formation which will guard me as the new Führer—the Leibstandarte Bormann, which will be hand picked from the FkB and the new Fehme Korps."

Despite himself, Schrader had been unable to stop flinching as a jettisoned British bomb load erupted with flame and violence less than a block away, kilometers from where the scarlet and green flares of the enemy pathfinders hung in the sky over the Anhalter Bahnhof.

"What about General von Bluckau?" he said.

Bormann smiled, unmoved by the blast wave that beat suddenly at his windows.

"You are also an extremely ambitious young officer, Sturmbannfhürer. I like this. You, Schrader, have a lot to live for, a lot to fight for. Unlike General the Freiherr von Bluckau, you have everything to gain by your utmost loyalty to me. People like von Bluckau can serve our purpose only for so long. So far, we have been able to use their ideas and exploit their ideals. In the long run, though, a man like von Bluckau is expendable. The trouble with him is that he is a gentleman. After the July twentieth plot against the life of the Führer and the security of Germany, we arrested and tried and hanged and shot thousands of Germans like von Bluckau—aristocrats, industrialists, intellectuals, clerics, writers, academicians and so-called patriots. Nearly all of them were too idealistic to be practical. I despised them less for what they tried to do, frankly, than for what they failed to do. They were dreamers and bunglers. General von Bluckau could just as easily have been one of them. They were his kind and his class. Like them, von Bluckau is an old-fashioned German gentleman who would die for his patriotic ideals. If he could only decide what his ideals were. What the Fehme wants is men who will stay alive and pull the trigger for their ideals."

Outside in the fire-reddened night, the streets of Berlin were strident with the urgent warnings of ambulances and fire brigades.

"Use General von Bluckau, Sturmbannführer," said Bormann. "Use him well. Tactically he is important to us in Saxony. Strategically he is expendable. But, in the interests of achieving the real objectives of Operation Lilac, with which he is not to be made familiar, do not hesitate to put him up against the nearest wall. Only a totality of method will ensure a totality of success for Operation Lilac. Never forget that, Schrader."

Nor had Schrader forgotten Bormann's words. Indeed, the memory of them gave him an exquisite, almost carnal, sensation of pleasure while he was delivering the limited and tactical briefing on Operation Lilac to von Bluckau, the distinguished Panzer commander, the stiff-necked nobleman and the oblivious husband of the woman who had at one and the same time both humiliated and excited Schrader that day long ago in the wheatfield with Helga.

Regardless of his personal feelings, however, Schrader now made it clear to von Bluckau that Operation Lilac was to be no mere haphazard skirmish by bands of patriotic but ill-prepared guerrilla forces.

"The order of battle is already defined," he told the general. "It calls for the Freikorps Bormann to operate in two battalions, each of five hundred men—Battalion Ost and Battalion West. There are five companies in each battalion—A, B, C, D and E. Each company has a strength of one hundred men."

Schrader resumed his nervous pacing back and forth.

"On the executive signal for Operation Lilac, from Bormann in Berlin, relayed via the Werewolfsender radio station at Falkewitz airfield, the FkB will go into action. The signal will be in plain language—'The lilacs will fall.' This will be followed by the date and the hour. The plan is that Battalion Ost will move east to the Elbe in American uniforms and with American arms in American jeeps. Simultaneously Battalion West will move out west to the Mulde in Russian uniforms and with Russian weapons in Russian trucks. The captured enemy uniforms, arms and vehicles to be used by both battalions have all been brought into the Galgenstein area here at night from Berlin and are now dispersed and hidden by the Freifronen of the Fehme in barns, garages and woods near their homes."

The thought of the Galgenstein lands being turned into an illicit armed camp depressed von Bluckau, but he was committed now and there was nothing he could say or do.

Schrader clearly had no such doubts, for this was the operation which he was to command in action.

"During the daylight hours before the actual night of Operation Lilac," he continued, "each FkB company will recapture one liberated prisoner of war in Russian or American uniform, according to the assumed enemy nationality of each FkB battalion. In American uniforms, the troops of Battalion Ost will attack the pontoon bridge thrown across the Elbe at Torgau by the Russians. Simultaneously the men of Battalion West, in Russian uniforms, will attack the divisional headquarters of the U.S. Sixty-ninth Division at Naunhof, west of the Mulde."

"Why the recaptured prisoners of war?" asked von Bluckau. It was a tactic that puzzled him.

"For a very good reason," said Schrader. "During the course of both actions the recaptured prisoners of war will be shot and left behind by the FkB as tangible evidence to support any charges likely to be exchanged between the Russians and the Americans.

"Every one of the ten Americans shot and left at Torgau will be in possession of forged orders for an American OSS attack on the bridge at Torgau. Every one of the ten dead Russians at Naunhof will be in possession of forged papers linking them with a fictional Russian-armed German division recruited from the ranks of the German prisoners captured at Stalingrad."

A dirty business, thought von Bluckau, and an insult to the men who fought at Stalingrad but, then, desperate times had always called for desperate measures.

"What about the Werewolf forces?" he asked, thinking of Siegfried's friends in the Hitler Youth.

Schrader was emphatic about this aspect of Operation Lilac.

"Simultaneously with the two FkB attacks," he said, "the Werewolf organization will carry out its last defensive action and distract enemy forces by widespread sabotage. This will cover the withdrawal of the two FkB battalions, who will disperse to control points in former prison camps where Werewolf units have collected cast-off British, American and Russian clothing left in the stalags by departing prisoners. When the situation created by Operation Lilac has stabilized sufficiently, the FkB will be progressively recalled by radio to the Galgenstein area and will stand by for orders."

Listening to Schrader, von Bluckau found it difficult to equate the implications of Operation Lilac with his own thoughts of a Fehme revival, thoughts which had stimulated him for so long in the privacy of this very same room in Schloss Galgenstein.

"Meanwhile," Schrader continued, "the Werewolfsender radio station will be exacerbating any discord between the Russians and the Americans by calling on the people of Saxony to rise with the Fehme, the Freikorps Bormann and the Werewolves and to take up arms against both the Russians and the Americans. Prior to the launching of Operation Lilac, the security challenge for all personnel involved is 'The lilacs are blooming,' and the response is 'They will soon fall.' Once the operation has been launched in its final shooting phase, the challenge will be 'The lilacs have fallen,' with the response, 'They will bloom again.' Sprigs of lilac will be worn in the lapels, buttonholes or on the hats of all members of the Fehme, the FkB and the Werewolves. As part of the Fehme's role in disciplining the civilian population, sprigs of lilac will also be left on the bodies of those accused and executed by order of the court of honor as a sign that they have been formally tried, sentenced and executed and not just haphazardly murdered."

The coffee in the silver pot engraved with the von Bluckau crest was cold by the time Schrader had finished briefing the general on Operation Lilac.

"Have you any questions, sir?" he asked.

The general shook his head. The briefing had been explicit and to the point. Very much so.

To this, then, had come General the Freiherr Dietrich von Bluckau as the lilacs bloomed in Saxony during that spring of German defeat in 1945. The killing season had begun. Silently and stealthily, the first of those Germans found guilty before the first sessions of the court of honor at Schloss Galgenstein, or in their absence and on the evidence of Fehme informers, had been put to death with the historic weapons of the old Fehme. The rope or the water pistol filled with prussic acid. Weapons that were easy to conceal, easy to use and easy to abandon. The one broke the victim's neck as he dangled, twitching and kicking, from a tree in his own back garden, from a rafter in his own barn or from a rusted hook on the dungeon walls of Schloss Galgenstein. The other was a swift and unsuspected splash of liquid in the face, a shout of shock or annoyance, a gasping inhalation, the paralysis of the central nervous system, the suffocation of life in an unbruised body and a sickly smell of almonds.

For forty-eight hours now the court of honor had been sitting in the cellars below the castle whose great walls had withstood the casual cannon fire of passing American fighter-bombers and the careless ricochets of shells from Russian tanks and artillery searching for the weary Wehrmacht infantry battalion which had made a futile last-ditch stand in the village at Galgenstein. At the height of the brief, confused little battle for possession of the village, Jutte von Bluckau had vanished without apparent reason or explanation, but after the Russians had straggled northward along the Elbe to join the divisions sweeping toward the southern outskirts of Berlin, von Bluckau, his son, his household servants, Major Schrader and his adjutant, his staff, the Freischoffen and the Freifronen of the Fehme had emerged unscathed from the concealed headquarters in the old dungeons and the armory below the castle. The work of the Fehme had begun. The ropes were noosed and the water pistols carefully charged with prussic acid. Hidden in their bunkers and foxholes in the great forests of Galgenstein, the thousand fighting men of the FkB still waited patiently in their Russian and American uniforms for the signal that would launch them into Operation Lilac.

Now, on this day of April 26, as von Bluckau sat waiting for the arraignment of more prisoners before yet another session of the court of honor at Schloss Galgenstein, the Russians of the 58th Guards Division and the Americans of the U.S. 69th Division had met with ceremony, jubilation and some suspicion on the banks of the Elbe at nearby Torgau. With a single handshake, the Russian General Rusakov and the American General Reinhardt had joined the two great fronts which now sundered the Third Reich.

As the fronts closed, south of Berlin and north of Dresden, the preliminary alert signal for Operation Lilac had come from Berlin via the Werewolfsender station in the debris of the Falkewitz air base and had then been flashed to FkB headquarters in Schloss Galgenstein. From there it had been repeated by tactical field radio to the battalion commanders and company commanders of Battalion Ost and Battalion West, crouched in the deep, dank, sod-covered bunkers in the cover of the Galgenstein forests.

The details of Operation Lilac, though, were not in von Bluckau's mind as he waited impassively, for the arraignment of these new accused, listening to their names and trying to picture their faces and the expressions in their eyes.

With the assistance of the court's interpreter, a schoolteacher from Torgau, the one-legged Heppner, as the Freistuhlherr and court clerk, was reading the names of the accused. They had, as usual, been indicted by Krausnick, but von Bluckau knew even less about them than usual, for on this day he had risked a visit to Major Schrader's FkB field headquarters in the Galgenstein forest so that he could go over detailed plans for the starting of Operation Lilac.

Originally, the general had merely despised, but had been prepared to use, the lawyer Krausnick as a political turncoat now zealously converted to the ideals and ethics of National Socialism. Latterly, though, presiding over sessions of the court of honor, von Bluckau had almost begun to fear Krausnick as the kind of fanatic who would stop at nothing in the interests not so much of Germany as of a militant neo-Nazism. There was a shuffling of feet as the accused people, in turn, stood to answer the arraignment.

"Major Bruno von Kleist-Schulenhorst, officer of the Luftwaffe," called Heppner.

A good Silesian family, thought von Bluckau. Landowners and leaders. What was a von Kleist-Schulenhorst doing before such a tribunal as this?

The charge was treason. Had it not been for the July 20 plot less than a year before, von Bluckau would have been astounded.

"How do you plead?" asked Heppner.

By his voice, the Luftwaffe major sounded uncowed.

"Not guilty. Least of all before this court. It has no jurisdiction."

"So far as I am concerned, as president, it has every jurisdiction," said von Bluckau sharply. "Your plea is noted. Proceed with the next accused, Freistuhlherr."

"Technical Sergeant George Abraham Kowalski, soldier, United States Army."

The charge was rape.

"Rape?" said the American. "That's crazy. I never raped anybody. The Russkis did maybe. Me, never. I was too stoned. The Russkis could have raped me for all I knew."

Somebody, one of the Freifronen, sniggered and Heppner called angrily for order.

"I don't know who you people are," said the American. "I don't know what this place is or what kind of a court this is, but I don't plead guilty to anything. What's more I want to get out of here. You can put the court where the monkey puts his nuts."

The general's thin face flushed so that the scar on his jaw looked like a white chalk mark.

"You will sit down and keep quiet," he said. Just the same, he felt uneasy. He had been right, after all. Krausnick could be mad. It was one thing for the Fehme to try German citizens, but it was another matter to sit in judgment on members of the armed services of the enemy. There was a Geneva Convention relating to the status and treatment of prisoners of war to which Germany had been a signatory. Damn Krausnick, thought the general.

"Otto Schillinger, Lutheran pastor, of the village of Kotzdorf," said Heppner.

The charge against the cleric was sedition.

"How do you plead?"

"Guilty," said Schillinger. "Guilty of being a German."

"Pastor," said von Bluckau, "this is neither the time nor the place for pulpit polemics. Please just answer the charge. Now, how do you plead?"

The pastor's voice was calm and resonant.

"If speaking the truth about the antichrist forces of National Socialism in Germany be sedition, then I plead guilty."

"Proceed, Freistuhlherr," said von Bluckau.

"Dermott Duncan," said Heppner. "American national, author and formerly a civilian internee at Oflag VIII G, Kreuzenberg."

Another non-German national, thought von Bluckau, and also probably subject to the protection of the Geneva Convention on treatment of prisoners. What was Krausnick doing?

The charge against the American Prominente prisoner was espionage.

A bellow of wild laughter startled von Bluckau.

"Espionage?" boomed the American. "I have been a prisoner since 1943, as the records of the German government will show. How then could I have even had the opportunity to engage in espionage? It would be ridiculous for me to plead either guilty or not guilty. I refuse to do so. I am a writer not a spy."

Krausnick interposed, his voice sibilant.

"Freigraf," he said to von Bluckau, "I think that you, as president of this court, should know that, as prosecutor for this jurisdiction of the Fehme in Saxony, I intend to prove that the prisoner Dermott Duncan has abused the privilege of prisoner-of-war mail allowed him under the terms of the Geneva Convention. I will show that Wehrmacht censors and cryptographers of the Sicherheitsdienst, during a routine check of prisoner-of-war mail from Oflag VIII G at Kreuzenberg, clearly established that the accused attempted to use a clumsy code to inform British intelligence authorities, via his London publisher, of the alleged circumstances under which a group of British, French and Polish officers were shot during an attempt to escape from Oflag VIII G."

"They were murdered," said the American.

"You are here to answer charges," said von Bluckau, "not to make them. To the charge of espionage, how do you plead?"

"If it will help terminate my appearance before this drumhead court-martial, I plead not guilty," said Duncan.

"Proceed with the next accused," said von Bluckau.

Heppner cleared his throat, wishing that he could spit.

"Horst Graber, Burgermeister of Lutzin!"

The charge against the Burgermeister was sabotage, in that, at Lutzin, on April 19, he had attempted to prevent the demolition of the Siebenjahrenbrucke bridge across the Neisse by seeking to remove explosive charges placed there by Wehrmacht engineers during the planned withdrawal from the Oder-Neisse line. Graber was also charged with cowardice in that he had endeavored to surrender the town to advancing Soviet army units.

"I plead guilty to trying to save the bridge," said Graber. He sounded frightened yet defiant. "I do not plead guilty to the charge of sabotage. That is an indictment to be answered by the madmen of Berlin who would destroy all the villages and all the towns of Germany for the sake of a war and a cause that is already lost."

"We need no patriotic addresses from you, Burgermeister," said von Bluckau. "Save your breath for your defense as a betrayer of German honor."

"Ulrike Engelhöffer, of Elsterwalde," said Heppner, arraigning the next accused, "you are charged with treason, in that prior to July twentieth, 1944, you, with your late husband, Wilhelm Engelhöffer, publisher and editor, were an accessory to a conspiracy to assassinate the Führer, Adolf Hitler, and overthrow the National Socialist Government of the Third Reich. How do you plead?"

The woman's voice was low but clear.

"I plead guilty," she said, "and if my husband had not been murdered by the servants of this mockery of a court, he too would be proud to plead guilty to such a charge."

"I am touched by the accused's solicitude, Mr. President," Krausnick interposed smoothly. "She evidently wishes to expedite these proceedings at least so far as her own case is concerned. May we proceed to the next arraignment?"

"You may," said von Bluckau, "and with more speed and less speechmaking from the remaining accused. This is a court of honor not a debating society."

"Roland Stolzer," intoned Heppner, "officer of the SS. You are charged with treason, in that, near Herzberg, Saxony, on April twenty-third, you sought to surrender yourself to a unit of the American armed forces, as you believed it to be, and tendered names, ranks and numbers of SS personnel at Auschwitz-Birkenau in a sub-camp of which you had served as an officer and an anthropologist on special duties. How do you plead?"

"Not guilty," said Stolzer. "It is all a mistake. I can explain everything."

"You will be quiet," said von Bluckau. "You will have your opportunity to explain."

The general frowned as he heard the next accused arraigned.

"Warrant Officer Thomas Albert Dart, Royal Air Force. You are charged with the theft, on April twenty-third, of a loaf of bread from the house of Herr Zentner in the village of Kotzdorf. How do you plead?"

"I have nothing to say," the English airman told the interpreter. "Under the Geneva Convention I need only state my name, rank and regimental number. My name is—"

The general shifted restlessly in his chair before the table with its noose and sword.

"That will be enough," he interrupted. "We know your name, rank and number, Warrant Officer. The question now is—to the charge of stealing, do you plead guilty or not guilty?"

Waiting while the interpreter put the question to the English airman, von Bluckau puzzled over the reason for the charge.

"He pleads not guilty, Mr. President," said the schoolmaster interpreter.

A loaf of bread, thought von Bluckau. Why the charge?

"Mr. Prosecutor," he said, "I must confess—I do not understand the charge. Why does the larceny of a loaf of bread constitute a reason for bringing this accused before the court?"

"I can appreciate your concern, Mr. President," said Krausnick. "I propose to show, however, that the accused did, in fact, steal a loaf of bread. It was an act of looting. He was intercepted in the village of Kotzdorf by men of the Fehme. Certainly, it was only a loaf of bread. However, the accused was but one of thousands of British, American, French, Polish, Italian and Russian prisoners of war released from Stalag IV J at Hohenleipisch who not only stole bread but looted and pillaged German homes in every village within a day's march of the camp. The accused was the British, and senior, man-of-confidence at Stalag IV J, accredited by the detaining power, Germany, and the protecting power, Switzerland. It is our contention that the accused betrayed the trust so reposed in him as camp representative of the International Red Cross, failed to maintain discipline and order among the prisoners for whom he was responsible and, in the interests of the defenseless German civilian population now being terrorized by bands of liberated prisoners and foreign workers, should stand trial before this court of honor as an example to be remembered."

"Proceed, Mr. Prosecutor," said von Bluckau. "The charge stands. Arraign the next accused."

"Private Johann Schwemma," said Heppner, "you are charged with desertion from the Wehrmacht in the face of the enemy. How do you plead?"

The soldier spoke slowly but with firm deliberation.

"I was going home to my farm," he said. "I was worried about my family."

"A lot of other Germans are also worried about their farms and their families," said von Bluckau. "To the charge of desertion, how do you plead?"

"Not guilty, sir," said Schwemma. "I was also trying to find my regiment. Any regiment, if it came to that."

For no good reason that he could readily define, von Bluckau felt at ease with Schwemma. He supposed that it was because the only real difference between a fighting general and a fighting soldier was their difference in rank and responsibility. Despite this normally insuperable barrier, they had much in common. Both of us, thought von Bluckau, have known the terrors, the discomforts and the excitements of combat. Both of us have now become entangled in something far more complex than the simple, elemental acts of fighting or dying. The traditionalists of the old German officer corps were correct. Politics was no pastime for soldiers.

There was also a familiar ring to the soldier's name, thought von Bluckau, and a memorable quality in his voice. This could be a soldier he had known, but he had commanded so many and now most of them were dead. Before the general could search his memory, not as good now as it had been before Stalingrad, the next accused had been arraigned.

"Caroline Brookwood, English national and journalist," said Heppner, "you are charged with espionage. How do you plead?"

The woman spoke with an air of amused surprise, a note of cool contempt in her voice. She sounded young yet poised.

"Not guilty, of course."

I had not bargained for this, thought von Bluckau. Not only the men of other nations but their women, too. I hope Bormann knows what he is doing. We could all swing by the neck for this kind of thing.

Brooding over the Frankensteinian legalistic possibilities likely to be created by Bormann's version of the Fehme and uneasily concerned by his own implication in whatever was to come in the wake of Operation Lilac and the courts of honor, von Bluckau at first did not recognize the familiar name and title of the next and last accused arraigned before him in the dungeons of Schloss Galgenstein.

For the first time, Heppner's voice had sounded diffident and uncertain.

"Jutte, Gräfin von Bluckau."

There was utter silence in the body of the court. There was no coughing. No scraping of benches. No dragging of boots on the stone floor. No whispering. Just the sound of people waiting and looking and listening. The general could hear them breathing.

"To the charge of collaboration in a scandalous and immoral way with the enemies of the Third Reich, how do you plead?"

"Before the bench of this court," said Jutte, "I plead not guilty. Before God, perhaps, I would plead guilty."

It really is her, thought von Bluckau. It's her voice. The breath of her body is in her voice. What are they doing to me? I did not even know she was back at Galgenstein. Where has she been? Either this is a nightmare or I have gone mad. Yet that really was her voice. I can't just sit here. I can't just pretend it is not happening.

"Mr. Prosecutor," he said suddenly, "I take it that you do, in fact, have a case to present to the court in relation to this accused?"

"I have, Mr. President," said Krausnick. The voice was smooth and without emotion.

"You realize, of course, that the accused is my wife," said von Bluckau. "The question now arises—can I or must I sit in judgment on my own wife?"

"Mr. President," said Krausnick, "it is a strange circumstance, I grant you, but these are strange times and this is no ordinary court. So far as the Fehme is concerned, it has been laid down that there can be no exceptions in the arraignment of accused persons and no flinching by the officers and servants of the court of honor, including yourself. The whole structure of the Fehme and its associated organizations is based upon this principle. I hesitate to remind you, sir, of the terms of the Fehme oath."

"You need not remind me," said von Bluckau tersely. "I am entirely familiar with the terms of the Fehme oath. More so than most people here today."

Sick at heart, the general deliberated briefly in his own mind, but he knew there could only be one decision.

"Proceed, Mr. Prosecutor," he said.

"As the court pleases, Mr. President," said Krausnick. "I will proceed with the case against Major Bruno von Kleist-Schulenhorst."

As Krausnick began the case against the Luftwaffe major, there was compassion and admiration in the faces of the men with the Fehme lilac in their lapels as they stared, almost with embarrassment, at the blinded general; a von Bluckau and a German hero, sitting stiff-backed in his immaculate uniform before the robe and the sword on the simple, soldierly table which now separated him from his wife.

In a corner of the crowded dungeon, still dank with the winter's chill of frozen earth, only one man smiled discreetly to himself.

Major Schrader was an exemplary product of the leadership schools of the SS.

He felt no pity because he knew no pity.

BOOK TWO

THE COURT SITS

I
The Traitor Major

MAJOR BRUNO VON KLEIST-SCHULENHORST was under no illusions as to the dangers of the situation in which he now found himself placed as an accused arraigned before the court of honor at Schloss Galgenstein. He knew what to expect. With little, if any, recourse to the basic principles of justice, he would be prosecuted, convicted, sentenced and executed. This, he knew, was the function of the court of honor. For Bruno it had all begun with the thesis which he had written at Leipzig University in 1939 just before the war. Originally, the subject of his paper had been the apparatus of the ancient Teutonic local courts, but before he had completed very much research in that field, he had become fascinated with the enigma of the Fehmic courts of the Middle Ages and the very real jurisdiction and influence which they had wielded in Germany, particularly in Westphalia. Probing deeper into the subject with all the dedicated fervor of an idealistic university scholar, Bruno inevitably came face to face with the fact of the Fehme's revival in Germany during the period of defeat, disillusionment and despair which had followed the collapse of Hohenzollern Germany in 1918. As the God-fearing son of a Lutheran lawyer from Dessau in Saxony, Bruno had warmed to his subject and completed a thesis in which he set out an indictment proving that the Fehmic courts were bad in law, evil in intent, inimical of justice and a dark and murderous page in the history of jurisprudence in Germany.

The thesis was not accepted. More than that, it was curtly and contemptuously rejected.

Chagrined and angry, Bruno had spoken to his friend and tutor, Dr. Felix Eppling, a member of the university staff and a lecturer in political science.

"Why?" said Bruno. "I researched the subject backwards and forwards. I tried to be objective, but the facts themselves dictated the conclusions that I had to accept. The Fehme and the Freikorps were rotten. Rotten to the core. On the evidence, I honestly believed this. I still do. I'm not a politician. I'm not even a National Socialist. I'm a graduate of one of the oldest and greatest universities in all Germany. Is the truth a dirty word, even at Leipzig University?"

"Bruno," said Dr. Eppling with an air of tired but patient tolerance, "I have read your paper. I know all about it. In any political climate other than that of Communist Russia, Fascist Italy or Spain or Nazi Germany, the thesis would have earned you an honors degree in law. As your tutor in political science, I congratulate you. But I want you to refresh my memory. Particularly about Gerhardt Rossbach. What did you have to say about that hero of our Nazi colleagues' conception of the new German mystique?"

"Gladly," said Bruno. "Rossbach was a murderer, a sadist and a homosexual deviate. According to his own statements, he perverted Ernst Roehm. He was a member of the post-1918 Fehme in Germany. On behalf of the illegal courts of honor of the Fehme he carried out many executions. Less politely, and more legalistically, they should be termed murders or assassinations. He founded and commanded the Rossbach Freikorps in the Ruhr, the Baltic states and Silesia. He figured prominently with his Freikorps during the irregular German actions against the Red Army in the east after 1918. Admittedly, he displayed great qualities of animal courage and leadership when he led the Rossbach Freikorps from Berlin to Thorensberg on the Baltic and rescued Bischoff's Iron Division. Is that enough?"

"Not quite, my fiery young friend," said Eppling. "And please keep your voice down, damn it. Remember the proximity of my Nazi neighbor with the big ears. What your thesis did not mention and what you evidently did not realize is that one of the section leaders in the Rossbach Freikorps, and a participant in many Fehme murders, became adjutant to Captain von Pfeffer in the first organization of the SA, was a member of the Reichstag in 1936 and is today personal secretary and aide to the Führer. I speak of Martin Bormann."

Bruno was genuinely shocked.

"Bormann? I did not realize that."

"No doubt," said Dr. Eppling, "but some National Socialist members of the faculty at Leipzig did. They did not appreciate your somewhat unflattering profile of such a perfect German hero, on National Socialist standards, as Rossbach. Nor did they care for the implications to be drawn from his long association with Bormann and other Nazi dignitaries. Unless you are particularly craving martyrdom—or are prepared to spend the best years of your life carrying rocks in a quarry at one of Herr Himmler's camps for political nonconformists—I would suggest you forget you ever wrote your thesis. With a little luck, the National Socialists on the faculty at Leipzig University might also forget."

Bruno was not sorry when the war came later that year. Within a few months of leaving the university at Leipzig he had realized that the German legal profession was no place for a newly graduated young lawyer who put his professional scruples and ideals before the pagan principles of the Nazi Party. The week that he heard Dr. Eppling had been arrested and taken under what was euphemistically termed protective custody in a camp at a place called Dachau, Bruno became a pragmatist. He joined the Luftwaffe. For a man who loved his country and cherished his ideals but no longer cared to try to equate them with the new Nazi philosophy that the ends entirely justified the means, there was no better place than the Luftwaffe· The issues of life in the Luftwaffe were, at least, clear-cut and not complicated by questions of conscience, philosophy or political expediency. You flew badly or well. You became a pilot or not. You killed or you were killed. Like generations of Germans before him, Bruno von Kleist-Schulenhorst had been able to retreat, into a uniform, from the political realities of his time. Orders were orders and politics were for the politicians.

By the spring of 1942 Bruno had shot down his quota of tubby, obsolete little Rata fighters and a whole string of the laughable PO-2 biplanes, which the Russkis had expended as prodigally as trucks wherever they were needed on the front. On flight after flight in that summer of 1942 he had strafed horses, cattle, trains, carts, marching men, orchards, forests, bridges, hospitals, artillery, trucks and tanks in the Tolstoian immensity of the Russian campaign. Always, though, there had been more targets to strafe on the planetary infinity of Russian earth that lay below the black and yellow stripes on the airscrew spinner of his Me.109. God, he thought, how many of them do we have to kill?

As the first snows of yet another, and no longer victorious, Russian winter began to drift over the crude earthen strips used by the wing, Bruno realized that the exultant mood of that first triumphal summer had gone, leaving only the dimming memories of the faces of friends who had died, by attrition, in the course of combat with the wing. Tired beyond any mere recourse to sleep, Bruno had flown back to Germany just before Christmas of 1942 for home leave in Dessau and a posting, in the new year, to a fighter leader's school at Jocken, near Osnabrück.

Fresh from a long and myopic tactical isolation amongst the dust, the mud, the fleas, the flies, the lice and the endless horizons of the primitive vastness of the East Front, Bruno recognized at Jocken, no longer living from flight to flight, that Germany's war, viewed strategically, had reached a new and significant phase.

During his first week amid the order and comfort of the big base at Jocken, in the heart of the Third Reich, the air raid sirens kept him awake every night as RAF bomber streams rumbled overhead on their way to targets in central Germany. During the once-inviolate daylight hours over Germany, the sirens had moaned again as the first deep-penetration American heavy bomber formations began to add their weight to the stepped-up tempo of the nightly British terror bombers. With the memory of Germany's increasingly desperate commitment in the east still raw in his mind, Bruno had recognized the changing nature of the air war in the west as a portent of things to come. The "Christmas tree" target-marker flares of the RAF, hanging in the night sky and the inexorable sweep of the American B-17 and B-24 vapor trails by day were the outriders of the old German nightmare, the two-front war, for the air armadas of the Anglo-Americans were like the leaves blown before the approaching storm. One night in March, while Bruno was in the very act of admiring the color of a glass of red Rhine wine at a formal mess dinner to celebrate the conclusion of his fighter leaders' course, a Halifax which had been attacked and damaged by nightfighters on its way to Kassel had jettisoned its bomb load on the dimmed-out lights of the airfield at Jocken. The last bomb in the stick had hit the officers' mess building. When Bruno regained consciousness, he was in the hospital. A piano had crashed through the ceiling of the mess and broken both his legs.

Bruno had done his best to seem downcast when he was told that he would not be taking up his appointment as a fighter squadron commander on the East Front. Privately, he enjoyed every month of his recovery and convalescence during the summer of 1943. In the autumn, when he was declared fit for flying, the air war in Europe had reached yet another significant phase. Operational flying at night was new to Bruno, but he did well that autumn and winter of 1943–44. By the spring of 1944 he had shot down five Lancasters and eleven Halifaxes at night. The victories had been absurdly easy. The main worry was avoiding collisions with the hundreds of aircraft that swarmed in the great bomber streams, their slipstreams buffeting his heavy, twin-engined Ju.88. That and the difficulties of getting down on the ground again after combat, for the RAF flew in appalling weather. Then, on the night of March 30–31, 1944, had come the time of the great Nuremberg massacre. For once the weather had favored the nightfighters. With a rising moon, the forecast cloud cover had vanished and the British bombers had flown naked under the sky, weaving their contrails behind them in the moonlight. Within ten minutes that night Bruno had blown the wing off one Halifax and ignited the indendiary bomb load of another so that it disintegrated before the crew had time to bail out. Twenty minutes later, following the course of the British main-force bomber stream by the fires of shot-down RAF aircraft burning on the ground far below, Bruno had stalked a Lancaster, whose crew saw him before he could close for the kill. The Lancaster had lost a lot of altitude and by the time Bruno had pursued it out over the French coast east of Le Havre, both aircraft were down to under a thousand feet. In a sea mist which cloaked the moon and swathed the horizon in dark obscurity, the Lancaster began to steep-turn, round and round, over the sea. Out of ammunition, thought Bruno. Dead gunners, maybe. God, I could run out of fuel before he does if he wants to keep this up. Grimly then, he began to steep-turn also inside the Lancaster until a quick burst from the bomber's rear turret drummed into one wing of the Ju.88. The bomber and the nightfighter kept turning.

The Lancaster hit the sea first, exploding in a great white gout of flame and spray. The British altimeters, Bruno remembered, were only barometric, and accurate within no more than thirty meters, more or less. Low flying over the sea at night called for something better than that. While Bruno was still thinking about this, his port motor, on the inside of his steep turn, had cut abruptly and the Ju.88 had flicked suddenly on its back, and suddenly the dark waters of the channel had grabbed at his own wing tip. The rest of it had been just a nightmare of pain, the shock of immersion in icy water, broken teeth in his mouth, blood in his nostrils and the wet, rubbery, salty smell of his lifejacket. When the Kriegsmarine E-boat picked him up early next morning, returning to Le Havre from a night patrol, he was delirious, for when his seat harness had broken under the impact of the crash into the sea, he had been thrown clear through the cockpit canopy, fracturing his skull under the torn and bloody helmet. He never saw his Ju.88 crew again. Like the Lancaster crew which they had chased to the coast from Stuttgart, southwest of Nuremberg, they were also feeding the herring in the cold, gray waters of the English Channel. When Bruno came out of the Luftwaffe hospital near Dresden, he found that he was grounded. The head injury had left him seeing double whenever he was tired or under stress. That was when they sent him to Dulag Luft, Frankfurt-on-Main as an interrogation officer. The English which he had learned to speak at Leipzig University improved rapidly at Frankfurt. As a law graduate, he frankly enjoyed the thrust and parry of intelligence interrogation, the evaluation of the reactions of the shot-down airmen whose discipline, loyalty and steadfastness he had to probe and shake. The strong, the craven, the friendly, the arrogant, the sullen, the quiet, the noisy, the calm and the scared. As an airman himself, he pitied them. So often he had nearly been in their shoes. Not that many of them wore shoes. Mostly they shuffled into his office in wooden clogs, for, by then, flying jackets and fleece-lined flying boots were being confiscated for winter use by the shivering German ground troops on the East Front.

Dirty, unshaven and hungry, the enemy airmen had been plucked like rag dolls from the sky, soon to be discarded like unwanted human trash in their unlovely prison camps. Better them than me, Bruno had thought. He had found the work rewarding, in the fascination of putting together the jig-saw puzzle pieces of information which added up to a picture of the enemy air forces, until he began to recognize a curiously unpleasant pattern emerging from his interrogations—a pattern of systematic beating-up of Anglo-American aircrews by German civilians. He had shrugged his shoulders when he had first heard of Himmler's order to the German criminal police that they were not to interfere with civilians attacking shot-down enemy fliers. What did the enemy airmen expect? Coffee and cakes? It had been different at Frankfurt, though, when he first became convinced that he had in fact recognized a technique of agent-provocateurs whipping up the emotions of civilians not only in the bombed cities and industrial areas but also in the unthreatened countryside. Individual and seemingly casual questioning of enemy air force prisoners had established the pattern or, rather, the pattern had established itself, and cautious, unofficial questioning of escorting German guards had confirmed it.

Beyond any reasonable doubt, Bruno was able to establish that in a score of target cities in western and central Germany, a systematic procedure of carefully provoked lynch law was summarily executing Anglo-American airmen before they could be claimed by the Luftwaffe and taken to Frankfurt for interrogation. It was by a Luftwaffe corporal at Dulag Luft who had escorted hundreds of enemy air force prisoners to Frankfurt that Bruno first heard the name of the Fehme mentioned. Before he had been able to follow up the lead, mainly out of personal curiosity, the corporal had been posted to the East Front. By the time Bruno had finished his tour of duty at Dulag Luft he was convinced that Anglo-American fliers were being beaten to death and hung from lamp posts at the instigation of an organization reputed to call itself the Fehme. Since, if it did exist, the Fehme had no official status, no uniforms and no face, then there was nothing he could prove even if this had been his intention. Bruno was also convinced of one other thing and found it ironical that the convincing of him should have been done unwittingly by the bedraggled and defeated airmen he had interrogated day after day, night after night. Germany, he was now convinced, could only ever lose the war. Air power would win it and the Anglo-Americans had more than enough of air power. A tall, shambling American bombardier, only survivor of a B-17 Flying Fortress which had exploded over Regensburg, had said it all when Bruno had asked him if he thought America and England and Russia would win the war. "I don't rightly know, sir," the bombardier had drawled without arrogance. "All I know is our brass never ever looked like running out of B-17s or bombardiers. No matter how hard I sometimes wished they would."

Bruno was still thinking about the American bombardier lieutenant from Great Falls, Montana, and the flood of Anglo-American airmen prisoners at Dulag Luft and the suspected but unproven activities of the Fehme in German Target areas while he was convalescing at a Luftwaffe hospital near Wiesbaden. They had operated on his head in an attempt to correct his tendency toward double vision, as the malfunction had begun to worry him again under the strain of long hours of interrogation duties at Frankfurt. The surgeon was a girl, Elise Gehrter, whom he had known as a brilliant medical student at Leipzig. Her family had since died during an RAF attack on Leipzig, from which city they had obstinately refused to be evacuated, and she was alone and lonely. They talked a great deal together about old times whenever she came to see him on her rounds. When he was discharged from the hospital, with a week's leave, Bruno took Elise with him to an inn, deep in the Harz Mountains. It was as if there had never been a war and they were back at the university again. Desperately they had clung to their memories as they had clung to each other's naked bodies in the rough, warm blankets with the wind whining in the pines outside their window. Afterward, they would lie there in the dark talking, and one night when Bruno had told Elise about the Fehme thesis he had written and his suspicions that somebody was reviving the Fehme again, she had said he should join the Kreisau Circle.

"Who are they?" he had said, "and why should I join?"

"They represent the other Germany," Elise said, "the non-National Socialist Germany. Your Germany. My Germany."

"You know who they are?" said Bruno.

"Of course," said Elise. "I'm one of them. In a small way."

"You realize," said Bruno, "that if I'm a Nazi after all, then you've just put a rope around this lovely warm neck of yours?"

"I do," said Elise softly, running her fingertips down his naked back. "But I know you're not a National Socialist. So do the Kreisau Circle. They told me. They know you. They know all about that thesis on the Fehme. Dr. Eppling read it to them before he was arrested and executed."

"He was executed?" said Bruno. "I did not know that."

For a moment he had lain there, his thigh hairy against the soft, naked warmth of Elise.

"How do I get in touch with the Kreisau Circle?"

"I'll tell you," she said. "Not just now, though. Afterward."

Before he had returned to duty at Frankfurt, Bruno had made contact with the Kreisau Circle, the movement founded by Helmut Graf von Moltke, Silesian landowner, jurist and descendant of the great field marshal. Although he was an adviser on international and military law to the high command of the Wehrmacht, von Moltke was a freethinker and a God-fearing Christian who had gathered around him an influential group of distinguished representatives of schools of thought concerned with German resistance to the National Socialist regime of Adolf Hitler. Bruno never visited the von Moltke estate at Kreisau in Silesia nor did he ever meet von Moltke, who had already been arrested in January 1944, but with Elise as an intermediary he was assigned to investigation of the clandestine Kreisau Circle's own suspicions that moves were being made in Germany to re-establish the medieval Fehme as a neo-Nazi party to seize power during the chaos which would follow the inevitable defeat of Germany. Arising from its contacts in high places in Berlin, the Kreisau Circle also had reason to believe that the Fehme was planning some kind of politico-military action designed to provoke friction between the Soviet and the Western allies. However successful this coup might be, on the irresponsible standards of such an organization as the Fehme, the results of renewed conflict in Europe could only be disastrous for the German people. Somehow, the facts had to be established and the Anglo-Americans and the Russians forewarned.

Following the arrest of von Moltke in January and during the early months of that summer of 1944, Bruno had been able to do little about investigating the Fehme rumors, restricted as he was by his interrogation duties at Frankfurt. Then had come his carefully arranged transfer, as station intelligence officer, to the Luftwaffe base at Falkewitz in Saxony, a land he knew well as a Dessauer. On the basis of information known to the Kreisau Circle, Saxony was a center of clandestine Fehme activity. Under the guise of maintaining and checking Luftwaffe security in the local area of the airfield, Bruno was able to move freely about Saxony, quietly gathering together a dossier of threats, hints, indiscretions and apparently unrelated and curious events, which, put together, had soon begun to form the sinister outline of such a clandestine organization as the Fehme.

By July 1944, with the Anglo-American invasion forces consolidating their landings in strength on the Normandy coast, Bruno had satisfied himself that whatever Fehme activity was being organized in Saxony was centered on the von Bluckau estates at Galgenstein, between the Elbe and the Mulde—a conclusion on which he was instructed to report to von Moltke's deputy near the Kreisau estates in Silesia. Bruno had burned the innocuous but coded postcard ordering him to Kreisau and had watched the ashes sift into the fire. How typical, he had thought. Always the struggle for power between the robber barons of Germany, though, at least, von Moltke's motives could not be impugned on grounds of self-interest.

Then had come July 20 and Colonel Klaus Graf Schenk von Stauffenberg's attempt to assassinate Adolf Hitler.

The reverberations of the attaché-case bomb which exploded abortively in the Wolfsschanze were heard far beyond the barbed wire, the bunkers and the pinewoods that surrounded the Führer's headquarters in the sandy fields of Rastenburg in East Prussia.

Overnight the conspirators and plotters of the idealistic but loosely knit forces of resistance against National Socialism became the hunted and desperate victims of all the agents of the merciless, vengeful and badly frightened police state which the Nazis had made of Germany. No longer just Jews or Catholics or Communists of subjugated territories, but now German nationals of intellect, rank, position, wealth, privilege and racial purity waited throughout the Third Reich for the knock on the door, the Gestapo summons, the rabid indictment before the macabre circus of the People's Court in Berlin and the jerking, strangling neck in the noose on the butcher's hook on the wall of a drab room in the Berlin-Plötzensee prison. With every hanging, shooting, suicide or concentration camp committal during the Nazi blood purge which followed the failure and exposure of the July 20 plot, the flame of resistance throughout Germany flickered and died.

Only the darkness of doubt and fear was left.

Hundreds of freethinking Germans had been arrested, tried and executed, but thousands more, all linked in some way with the July 20 plot, waited in hiding and in hope that the war would end before the Gestapo came for them.

Bruno had waited, too, fearfully wondering to what extent he had been committed or linked with the Kreisau Circle, praying that they had not listed or mentioned his name, for he could see little purpose in dying for a lost and decimated cause. The shadow of the noose had hung over him all the rest of that year and even until the last months of the war in 1945, for, to the end, the inquisitors and the hangmen of the Gestapo and the SS had continued to ply their trade, hunting down the men and the women who had dared plot against the person of the Führer and the political apparatus of National Socialism. Almost it had seemed like a merciful portent, an avenging act of God Himself, when Dr. Roland Freisler, the merciless and paranoiac president of the People's Court, was crushed by a falling roof beam of his court during an air raid on Berlin. As if to point the moral, the deaconess who nursed him before he died in hospital was a sister of Graf Albrecht von Bernstorff, whom Freisler had already sentenced to death as a convicted July 20 conspirator. But the black, grim course of National Socialist vengeance had not been stayed. On January 23, 1945, von Moltke himself was executed at Berlin-Plötzensee and Bruno wondered when his own turn would come. Not until that last night at Falkewitz, with the base being hurriedly evacuated only hours before the arrival of the first of Konev's tanks from the east, had he learned why he had been spared. A ragged Lutheran pastor from Kotzdorf, a link in the chain of communications of the remnants of the Kreisau Circle, had told him that Elise had died in Ravensbrueck concentration camp for women after Gestapo interrogators had failed to get her to name any of the Kreisau conspirators whom she had known. Then it was that he knew what he had to do.

That night, while the wing's column of retreating transport was taking shelter during yet another RAF attack on Leipzig, he deserted. Driving his own staff car, he sped through the streets of Leipzig, blasting the horn at fire fighters, salvage parties and policemen. Clear of the target area where the city was burning and exploding in the green and crimson glare of the British pathfinders' flares, Bruno headed west along the dark sweep of the autobahn between Leipzig and Halle.

Seventy-two hours later he had cautiously surrendered to an American infantry patrol and was being questioned by a bored and incredulous intelligence officer.

"Let me get this straight, Major," the American captain said. "You're telling me that in the immediate vicinity of this castle at Galgenstein, between the Elbe and the Mulde, there's this underground Fehme outfit that's going to stage some kind of fake action to stir up all hell when we get to link up with the Russkis. Is that what you're telling me?"

"Briefly," said Bruno, "that's about it."

The American captain shook his head.

"You Krauts might be nutty but not that nutty. Major, you're going back to the divisional cage like any other PW while we check this out."

Bruno was still in the American division's stockade for prisoners of war at Halle when he was abruptly marched out to the commanding officer's quarters beyond the wire. Waiting for him with a jeep, was Captain Sperry, the intelligence officer who had first interrogated him after he had surrendered to the infantry patrol.

The American threw him a black civilian leather jacket.

"Shove this over your Luftwaffe tunic. You're coming with me."

Out on the autobahn again and heading back east to Leipzig, Sperry told him that the U.S. 69th Division had captured Leipzig and had advanced to the line of the Mulde. Forward patrols had linked up with Russian forces on the line of the Elbe, beyond the Mulde.

"Tomorrow morning," said the American, "General Reinhardt of the Sixty-ninth Division is going to meet with General Rusakov, of the Russian Fifty-eighth Guards Division at Torgau on the Elbe. You know, hands across the river and east meets west in allied comradeship. Deutschland kaputt and all that crap. You remember that statement of yours about the Fehme? I mentioned it at a security briefing for tomorrow. I should keep my big mouth shut. Now I've got to take you and an infantry patrol to go look in the woods to see if there are any nasty Werewolves there. You'd better not make a monkey out of me, Major. The top brass are interested in this little excursion."

"I'm not playing games, Captain," Bruno said. "You'll see."

And see they did.

At Sperry's corps headquarters, Bruno was subjected to an icily detached interrogation by a thin and preoccupied American colonel who was the assistant chief of staff, G-2. When he had asked his last question, the colonel sat back frowning at a map of the Torgau area. Then he looked up at Sperry.

"Do you think there is anything in this German officer's story, Captain?"

"Enough to want to check it out, sir," said Sperry.

"I agree," said the colonel. "We have enough problems linking up with the Russians without the Germans getting into the act with a heap of medieval melodrama. I'll contact the Sixty-ninth Division and have them assign you a company of infantry to search the woods at Galgenstein. If you find anything that's too big for you to handle, the infantrymen will have radio. They can call battalion and regiment. I suggest you get right on the ball. We want this report checked out today. We'll all hang by the thumbs if anything goes wrong with the big meeting between General Reinhardt and the Russki general at Torgau tomorrow."

The crow's feet radiating from the tired eyes above the dark pouched bags crinkled a little as the colonel smiled austerely.

"*Life* and *Time* and the rest of the press camp would never forgive us," he said.

Outside, Sperry shook his head and whistled in mournful consternation.

"I get all the breaks," he said. "If there's no Fehme and no Werewolves I get laughed out of the intelligence corps of the U.S. Army. If there is, and we find them, I get my foolish head shot off. If we don't find them and they start lousing up Russo-American relationships at divisional command level, I get court-martialed and ten years in Leavenworth. You better be on the ball,

Major. Unless you want to spend the rest of your life in the stockade."

Two hours later, on that sharp and sunny spring day, they had picked up the escort company at the 69th Division's headquarters at Naunhof and were moving out, in a long line of jeeps, between hedgerows of fragrant-blooming lilac on the road to Torgau. Past the acres of shell-blasted rubble that had so recently been Eilenburg before American artillery had poured 10,000 rounds of high explosive and incendiary shells into the town in 48 hours, they turned off north toward Galgenstein.

Soon they could see the medieval bulk of Schloss Galgenstein far across the undulating fields, towering above the distant pines and silent farms.

"That would have made a good flak tower," said Sperry, staring at the proud profile of the great castle.

"We thought of that," said Bruno, "when your fighter-bombers started strafing the barges on the Elbe here. It was too far from the river, though. Out of range most of the time."

"Just as well, maybe," said Sperry benevolently. "You'd only have finished up with one castle down."

Musing over the contradictory complexities of colloquial English, Bruno nudged Sperry as the jeep patrol rolled into Gross Galgenstein village. A burned-out Tiger tank was canted awkwardly in a ditch. Flies swarmed over the open hatch. The smell of charred and corrupted flesh hung heavily on the sun-warmed air. A liberated Italian prisoner of war was standing in the open doorway of a deserted house. He had just disemboweled a stolen chicken and was leisurely wiping his bloodied hands on a curtain ripped from a window. Farther down the street, German children were playing some kind of game with a flak gun mounted on a Wehrmacht truck which had crashed into a shop window.

"I hope that damned thing's not loaded," said Sperry.

Bruno shrugged. It was hot in the leather jacket.

"What isn't?" he said.

Apart from the children, and God only knew where their parents were, the village seemed deserted, yet Sperry could not escape the feeling that the patrol was being watched. He had had the same sensation often since he had first crossed the Rhine months ago.

They came to a corner where a dead horse lay on its back. The legs were stiff and wooden but the belly was swollen and distended like a huge rubber beach toy.

"We turn off here," said Bruno. "This is the road to the Jägerswald forest and Schloss Galgenstein."

If Sperry was glad to be out of the silent, sullen village, he was even less happy in the Jägerswald. The infantry can have their job and their citations, he thought. Me, I love intelligence work and the comfortable feeling of having a desk between me and the shooting. What the hell am I doing out here, anyway? I don't like this one little bit.

When the patrol halted, Bruno went over the map with the escorting infantry captain, who seemed bored with the entire proceedings. Sperry admired the infantry officer his professional detachment and soldierly aplomb but hoped that he knew what he was doing. Evidently he did, for, quite quickly and without fuss, he had halved his company and stationed one element on the eastern border of the forest and the other on the western edge. Then, after talking quietly and briefly on his radio, he had got both halves of his company of infantrymen moving toward each other through the undergrowth and between the trees.

The search took longer than it might normally have done that afternoon, for the Jägerswald was not a tidy and typical German forest. Sperry had known many where the trees were planted with such mathematical exactitude that if you stood one way in the center, you could see the tiny figure of a man half a mile away in the open sunshine, and if you stood facing slightly differently, he just disappeared. It was not like this in the Jägerswald. Birches struggled with pines and oaks to claw their way out of rank, tangled undergrowth to reach toward the sun and the sky. Sometimes, for no apparent reason, there would be a clearing that seemed swept clean of everything except moss and fallen pine needles, springy like a cushion underfoot; or a narrow beaten path would writhe its way from darkness to darkness in the shadows of the forest.

By the time the two halves of the company met again in the depths of the Jägerswald they had covered the ground and found two elderly German civilians cutting wood, some twenty boar, a dozen deer, a limping red fox, some squirrels and what could have otherwise been a good day's bag of rabbits.

"Nice hunting country," said the young patrol commander, "but no Werewolves."

Just an easy afternoon's stroll in the woods, thought Sperry. I wish I could have been that calm about it. Let's get the hell out of here. Give me the New York subway any day.

The patrol commander yawned and looked at his watch.

"Well," he said, "I guess that just about does it?"

"Thanks a lot," said Sperry apologetically. "I'm sorry there wasn't a little more action for you."

"Don't be sorry," said the infantry officer, suddenly curt. He no longer seemed quite so young. "Be glad. Be like us. It'll be dark soon. I'll move the men out if it's OK with you. They could use some sleep. They've had plenty of this. With action."

"Sure," said Sperry, feeling like a civilian. He turned to Bruno.

"What about you, Major?"

"I'd like to talk to those two woodcutters again," said Bruno, frowning. He seemed puzzled. "I don't know why, but I would."

"OK," said Sperry. "Then we would have checked everything out."

"You want help?" said the infantry officer. His eyes were still on the trees of the Jägerswald.

I don't want help, thought Sperry. I want out. Just the same, he managed an appropriately casual smile.

"No, thanks. Not with two old civilian Krauts."

"What about your prisoner?"

Bruno smiled, turning up the collar of his leather jacket. It was getting colder now as the sun got lower and the shadows longer.

"I'm not going anywhere. There's no place I want to go except west."

The patrol commander stared at Sperry. He seemed dubious.

"Just the same, Captain," he said, "don't stick around these woods too long. They're no place to be on your own if it gets dark."

It was very still and quiet in the Jägerswald after the German and the American had heard the last of the patrol's jeeps start up and whine toward the Torgau road.

"Like he said, it'll be dark soon," said Sperry. "Let's go find those woodcutters."

They found them where they had left them, in a sudden and surprised clearing, but they were not still sawing wood. They were talking together near a little shack which the patrol had searched, and when Bruno and Sperry came upon them, they looked up quickly and self-consciously the way people do in a room when you know they've been talking about you.

Bruno suddenly stopped walking.

"That's it," he said. "I knew there was something."

"What's on your mind?" said Sperry.

"Just offer them a cigarette," said Bruno.

"This war may be great for the American tobacco industry," said Sperry irritably, "but, as an American officer, I'm getting pissed off keeping my country's enemies in cigarettes. I'm supposed to be a soldier not a goddam social worker."

"Just offer them a cigarette," said Bruno urgently.

After a brief exchange of greetings, the two middle-aged civilians had declined Sperry's offer of a cigarette.

"That's it," said Bruno.

"That's what?"

It was sunset already and Sperry was remembering what the patrol commander had said about the forests after dark.

"The first time we spoke to them, when we had the patrol with us, they weren't smoking," said Bruno. "But when I went into their shack where they kept their dry clothes and their food for the day, I could smell fresh cigar smoke. I forgot about it, but it stuck in my mind until we were on our way back to the jeeps and then I remembered it."

"So?" said Sperry. "As one intelligence officer to another, just tell me."

"So there's somebody around here somewhere smoking cigars and he's not a woodcutter," said Bruno.

"You could be right, Major," Sperry said. "I think I have some interrogation to do."

"I think so, too," said Bruno. "But it would be quicker my way."

"Your way?"

Bruno explained. They would put the two civilians back to back.

They would then march each one away from the other. Sperry would interrogate one of them. If his man did not talk, Sperry would fire his revolver once. Into the ground. Not into the body of the civilian. Just into the ground. The chances were that the other civilian being interrogated by Bruno would assume that his friend had been shot for not talking. He himself would then talk. Very quickly.

"It could work," said Sperry. There was also a good chance he would put a .45 slug into his own foot.

"It will work," said Bruno. "The National Socialists have conditioned us Germans to acceptance of the inevitable logic and persuasive power of the gun. It will work."

Sperry had to admit that, in fact, it did work. Before he could have fired a second shot, the thin-faced, unshaven, middle-aged German with the scrubby little Hitler mustache was pleading with Bruno for his life.

"The Fehme?" Bruno was shouting, "the Fehme? Where is the Fehme?" when the door of the shack behind him opened slowly, rasping protestingly on the rusted hinges like the door of any dilapidated woodsman's shack in a forest, and a voice spoke gently.

"Right behind you, my friend," said the voice. It was the voice of the man whom he was later to know as Schrader. He was smiling as he cradled the U.S. Army Tommy gun which he was pointing at Bruno's stomach as the Luftwaffe major spun around.

"I suggest you do nothing rash," said Schrader, "or you and the American will be cut down by the fire of half a dozen excellent American Tommy guns."

On Schrader's shouted command, another five men were suddenly standing around the clearing. Like Schrader, they also were each armed with an American Tommy gun and were wearing civilian clothes with sprigs of lilac in their lapels. They seemed to have stepped right up out of the mossy, bramble-guarded earth between the pines, the birches and the oaks. Beside each of the men was a strong, square wooden lid on which the natural grass of the undergrowth between the trees had been carefully grown. Each lid, perfectly camouflaged and heavy with earth, had been lifted from a timbered shaft which was the entrance to an underground bunker.

"The revolver trick was a mistake," said Schrader pleasantly. "We heard it down below. We always have sentries watching and listening. You should have quietly taken our faithful Freifronen, Hans and Georg, with you and those heavy-footed soldiers of yours. Now I will ask some questions of my own. Not here. In the bunker."

Inside the shack, the two elderly woodsmen bent over a small stove. It was bolted to a slab of concrete. Grunting, they swung it back on its hinges. In the shaft below, steps descended.

Schrader gestured with the Tommy gun.

"Down there," he said.

The bunker was unexpectedly big. There were more men there. Silent, watchful men in civilian clothes with sprigs of lilac in their lapels. There were rough wooden bunks, a radio setup, tables, chairs and a big wallboard with large maps of Saxony pinned to it. Like bomb-twisted plumbing, the roots of the trees above writhed down behind the timber beams that braced the sandy soil of the walls and ceilings. The robber barons, thought Bruno. The robber barons are taking over again in their caves.

Lighting a cigar, Schrader noticed that both Sperry and Bruno looked at it involuntarily.

"Ah," said Schrader, "the cigar smoke. The ventilator shaft. That was careless of me. And clever of you."

Carefully, so as not to mash it up irreparably, he butted the cigar.

"Now," he said, "I have some questions for you."

He began with Sperry. What was the disposition of the U.S. 69th Division? Where were the last-known locations of the regiments, the battalions and the companies? What were their radio call signals? What were the recognition challenges and the responses? What was a Luftwaffe major doing escorting an American infantry patrol searching for patriotic Germans?

Leaving one of the Fehme men standing with a Luger pushed into the back of Sperry's neck, Schrader had then begun to question Bruno. Although he knew that he was not essentially a brave man, Bruno had refused to answer Schrader's questions. He was surprised that he had had this much resolve. He had always known that flying an Me.109, on day interceptions, or a Ju.88 on night penetrations of the British bomber streams, had not necessarily demanded the highest level of courage. There was courage, certainly, but there was usually a way out. You had the initiative of attack. If it got too tough, you could always break, rolling over and down and then come back on your own terms when you judged that the tactical relationship between you and the enemy aircraft was such that you could shoot him down. And survive. The function of a fighter pilot, day or night, was not only to kill and maul but to survive. There were always plenty more enemy bombers where the one you didn't get came from. This business of being held at the point of a gun in a silly hole in the ground in your own native Saxony by a fellow German was different. This posed moral and philosophic issues. Tracer, floating and then streaking pyrotechnically in the night from the rear turret of a black, weaving Lancaster or Halifax, was one thing. A Luger, squat and ugly, in the hand of a man so close you could see the hairs in his nostrils was another thing again. It was immediate. It was instant. It was now. It was death with a breath that stank of cigar smoke and garlic sausage. Bruno was not concerned for Sperry's safety. Even the Fehme would hesitate before they murdered an American officer in an American divisional area. Bruno thought of Elise, the woman surgeon who could replace double vision with normal vision; Elise, the subject of Gestapo interrogations; Elise, the warm and vibrant body he had once caressed but which now lay bruised and broken and corrupting in quicklime in a mass grave at Ravensbrueck.

"I have nothing to tell you," said Bruno.

"That's a shame," said Schrader. He sighed regretfully.

Then he turned toward the Fehme man standing with the Luger pressed into the back of Sperry's neck.

"Fire!" he said. Even as he said it, Bruno thought it was an absurd thing to say. Schrader sounded like the commander of an artillery battery. The blast of the Luger firing roared like a major explosion in the confines of the bunker, and Bruno blinked involuntarily. When he opened his eyes, the American was lying where the impact of the bullet had thrown him, face down. As Sperry died, he half-turned, writhing, and Bruno saw that his face was gone. Only an obscene open wound was left below the still recognizable hairline of the forehead. The gunpowder smell that Bruno had known from his own guns in Me.109s and Ju.88s was there again, but this time it was compounded with the smell of stale cigar smoke, the garlic sausage and the fresh, lovely fragrance of sprigs of lilac.

"Strip him," said Schrader. "We can use the uniform if we wash the blood out."

He turned back to Bruno.

"Well, my gallant and treacherous Luftwaffe Major," he said, "You will not die yet. The American is the man we wanted to talk. You cannot know what we want to know. You will keep. Your flying days are over but you are a very special person. A German officer and a traitor. You will not die so quickly. The Fehme has a court of honor for people like you."

That night the Fehme men lifted Sperry's naked, faceless body, wrapped in a blood-wet blanket, carried it out of the underground bunker in the Jägerswald, loaded it aboard his own jeep, drove cautiously across a field of plowed barley stubble in the moonlight with guns ready against the intervention of the Russians, who were also patrolling the area, and came to the banks of the Elbe. There they rolled the body down some stone ferry steps into the dark river, swollen and resurgent with the floods of spring.

"Next stop, Hamburg," said Schrader. "He's off our doorstep."

"The American patrol will come back looking for him," said Bruno. He spoke quietly and with conviction.

In the darkness, Schrader chuckled.

"They found nothing today. What will they find tomorrow? Some more wild boar in the Jägerswald?"

Schrader and the two Fehme men who had come with him had then driven the jeep back to a farm on the von Bluckau estate, jacked it up, put it on blocks and hidden the wheels until they would be needed again.

With Schrader walking softly behind him, Bruno had come to Schloss Galgenstein, his footsteps ringing on the oaken planks of the stone-arched bridge across the moat of the Schwarzesee. Up the stone steps they had gone into the dark, deserted great hall of the empty castle. The air inside was dank and heavy with the reek of cold ashes, and broken glass had crunched and splintered beneath his boots. They had come to a vast fireplace then, and Schrader had stepped into it, so high it was, and pushed at the wall against which so many fires had warmed generations of von

Bluckaus and their guests. The wall, in part, had swung back and behind it there was a spiral iron staircase.

"The Schraubetreppe," said Schrader conversationally. "They built it after one of the von Bluckaus had to jump into the Schwarzesee from the top of the Sprengertor, escaping from the soldiers of Napoleon. The present Graf von Bluckau has had the foresight to open it up again for the Fehme. It serves each floor of the castle, fireplace by fireplace, from the battlements down to the old dungeons. The aristocracy always did have a way out."

So Bruno had come to the cell in the old dungeons of Schloss Galgenstein and the furtive medieval rituals of the court of honor.

The fact that he found himself sharing an illegal captivity with, among others, a combat-status American soldier, a liberated British air force prisoner of war, a Prominente American civilian internee and an English woman journalist only confirmed Bruno's fears, if they needed any confirmation after the casual killing of Sperry, that he did not have very much longer to live. To bag these kinds of birds, thought Bruno, the men of the Fehme must be madmen, and when madmen went armed, death was a ready recruit.

As a law graduate, and remembering his original student-days thesis on the medieval Fehme and its more modern, twentieth-century perversions of the civilized principles of justice, he had been detachedly fascinated by the ritual and procedures of his arraignment with his fellow prisoners from the other cells below the great hall of Schloss Galgenstein.

Strangely, he had only felt a kind of pity for the lonely, immaculate figure of General Graf von Bluckau, sitting with blinded eyes before the crude symbols of Fehme justice, the noose and the sword. So much for five hundred years of noble pride and privilege, he thought; so much for the reputation of a noble name.

Convinced of the futility of making any kind of a defense before the court of honor, Bruno had met Krausnick's prosecution with curt and almost bored answers, impatient to have done with the whole macabre farce.

Now the jury of Freischoffen was standing and von Bluckau was putting to them the question which, in any decent community or society of men, was the cornerstone of justice.

"Have you considered your verdict, Mr. Foreman?"

"We have, sir."

You have not, thought Bruno. You have sat there and nodded like sleepy owls at the prosecutor's cross-examination and the evidence of Schrader and now you have not even left the court, yet you say you have considered your verdict.

"On the charge of treason," said von Bluckau, "are you agreed upon a verdict?"

"We are, sir."

"What is your verdict?"

"Guilty, sir."

The general looked up. The dark glasses were like great scales over the black sockets in his lean face. Standing before him and facing him across the table with its noose and sword, Bruno studied the decorations that glowed in a martial spectrum of red, white and black on the green whipcord cloth of von Bluckau's tunic. Several of the decorations and campaign medals Bruno had won and worn himself until the Fehme men had stripped them from his yellow-piped Luftwaffe jacket before the trial.

"Major Bruno von Kleist-Schulenhorst," said von Bluckau, "have you anything to say before I pronounce sentence upon you?"

"Yes," said Bruno. "I refuse to accept any conviction or any sentence imposed upon me by this court. It has no legality, no status and no jurisdiction."

The general's face was without expression, undisturbed by even the merest flicker of emotion. His voice was cold and clipped and his words measured.

"This is a court of honor," he said. "It has many precedents in our German history. It is a law unto itself."

There is nothing more to be said, thought Bruno. Even though he looks sane, von Bluckau is as mad as the rest of them.

"You have been found guilty of treason," said von Bluckau. "Under the terms of reference of this court of honor, the penalty for treason is death."

Reaching, without fumbling, for the sword before him he held it by the hilt, the blade pointing to the arched stone roof of the great cellars.

"I sentence you to death and may God have mercy on your soul."

The general laid the sword down again on the table so that the burnished tip pointed across the army blanket toward Bruno.

"Remove the prisoner," said von Bluckau.

In the gloom of the cellar, a single figure had arisen and was standing to attention. It was Schrader.

"Mr. President, sir," he said.

The general frowned. He resented having to ask. Only a blind man would have to ask.

"Who is it?"

"Sturmbannführer Schrader, sir."

"What is it, Major?"

The stuffy bastard, thought Schrader. He'll recognize SS ranks soon enough.

"Permission to address you, sir," said Schrader, "on a matter of importance."

"You have my permission, Major. Please be specific. There is much business before the court."

"Speaking specifically, sir," said Schrader with honeyed sarcasm, "three companies of American infantrymen are searching the local area of Galgenstein for an intelligence officer whom we had to execute in the interests of Fehme security. Although I understand that death sentences imposed by this court are customarily carried out, if not immediately, then as soon as possible thereafter, I suggest that the sentence just imposed, and any others likely to be so, should be delayed until the rising of the court. With American army units policing the Schloss Galgenstein area, I respectfully submit that, in the security interests not only of this court and the Fehme but also of Operation Lilac, any executions arising from these proceedings should be delayed until the Americans quit the immediate area."

The general rubbed thoughtfully at the long white scar where a fragment of shrapnel had seared the flesh of his jaw at Stalingrad. Invariably it began to itch during moments of nervous tension.

"So be it, Major. Thank you. The Freistuhlherr will see to it that maximum security is kept upon all prisoners awaiting execution under death sentences imposed by this court. Call the next accused."

Heppner passed the typed list of accused persons to the interpreter.

"Technical Sergeant George Abraham Kowalski," said the interpreter eagerly, preening in the focus of attention of the court.

"The charge," Krausnick began suavely, "is one of rape. Sergeant Kowalski, you are an enlisted soldier serving with the United States Army?"

A tall, gaunt man, who seemed to be perpetually slouched out of an innate and courteous deference to people shorter than he, Kowalski stared angrily at Krausnick.

"You bet," he said. "You bet I am, sir. And I don't need any interpreter. I can speak Polish and German good. When I have to."

Kowalski was hungry, tired, scared, would have given a month's pay for a cigarette and felt as if he had lived all his life in the greasy slicker, torn shirt, crumpled pants and muddy combat boots in which he had gone out with the patrol to the big meeting on the Elbe, but he wanted no doubts about which army he belonged to.

"Damn right I am," he said. "I'm an American soldier."

"Then you would agree," said Krausnick, "that the government of the Third Reich is entitled to take a serious view of your raping a defenseless German woman?"

"No, I wouldn't agree, sir," said Kowalski. "I don't believe this boy scout group of yours represents the German government or any other government. And I didn't rape any German woman. I already told you. I got stoned with some Russkis, maybe, but rape, no. It's crazy. Just plain crazy."

Krausnick turned toward von Bluckau.

"Mr. President, the prosecution intends to prove that the accused, Kowalski did, in fact, rape a German woman civilian in company with soldiers of a Russian army unit."

They're nuts, thought Kowalski. The whole goddam nation. Grandpa Kowalski was right about the Germans. They're spooky. Look at that crazy general sitting there like a dummy in the waxworks. How come this had to happen to me?

II
The Wayward GI

For Kowalski, it had all begun only forty-eight hours earlier as he sat on the green grass in the warm spring sunshine on the east bank of the Elbe at Torgau, trying not to vomit. Somehow, it seemed important that he should not. History was being made at Torgau that smiling day as the generals shook hands and the East Front met the West Front, and here he was sitting right in the middle of it and trying miserably not to throw up. Suddenly he was glad of the fact that he was just a U.S. Army sergeant and not a diplomat or a four-star general with protocol to be observed and manners to be minded. No wonder the Russians had broken the back of the German army at Stalingrad. A nation that drank like the Russkis did just had to be tough, otherwise it would have died out long ago.

Not that Kowalski didn't have his own problems of protocol.

The flat-faced, grinning young Russian soldier sitting beside Kowalski slapped him on the back and raised a dented pannikin of German schnapps.

Kowalski, gagging with nausea, raised his own pannikin.

"Roosevelt!" said the Russian.

"Stalin!" said the American. He felt too sick to be bothered explaining that Roosevelt was dead.

Together they drank the raw, oily spirit. The Russian with the burp gun, the broad and beaming face, the buckshot scars of smallpox, the stench of sweat and cheap perfume. The American with the unbuttoned GI raincoat, the M-1 carbine and the muddy, blunt-toed combat boots.

Kowalski coughed cautiously, hoping that he would disgrace neither the Premier of the Union of Soviet Socialist Republics nor the President of the United States of America. With the sleeve of his raincoat, Kowalski wiped at his eyes. They streamed tears as the schnapps burned at his throat.

"Churchill!" said the cheerful and indefatigable Russian. Kowalski heard himself groan. It was almost a whimper. Winston Churchill would love this, he thought. The old boy would drink this happy Russian rube right into the river. Me, I've had it. Tall and gangling, even sitting down, the American held out his pannikin while the young Russian, stocky and bow-legged, slopped out more schnapps from a bottle with a label from Breslau. "Churchill!" said the Russian. "Churchill!" said the American with quiet desperation. Together they toasted the British war leader while across the wide and surging waters of the Elbe rang the faint shouts of the American and Russian patrols hailing each other from the opposite and distant banks. When the Churchill toast was done, the Russian was waiting again with the Breslau bottle of schnapps. Hell, thought Kowalski. He was fresh out of the names of Russian notables to toast. With any luck, his indestructible, iron-gutted Russian buddy with the bottles would soon be the same way. Faintly, he clutched at sudden, bemused inspiration. This could be the final toast. Then he could pass out with dignity. "Hitler!" Kowalski cried. "Hitler kaputt!" Quickly, to short-circuit and reduce the possibility of any further toasting in this particular area of triumphal celebration, he added, "Deutschland kaputt! Krieg kaputt! Alles kaputt!"

The Russian was delighted. He filled the pannikins again until they spilled over onto the German grass.

"Deutschland kaputt!" he responded. "Krieg kaputt! Alles kaputt!"

Kowalski kaputt, too, thought the American. Fighting against waves of nausea, Kowalski drank the toast, trying to smile as he carefully set the emptied pannikin down beside him. Crazy, he thought. Momma would never believe it. George Abraham Kowalski from Flatbush, sitting on the east bank of the Elbe at Torgau in the middle of Germany, plumb between two of the biggest armies in the world, getting stoned with a Russian soldier and toasting all the big shots from Eisenhower to Adolf Hitler. This was a patrol to remember. He wished he was back in Flatbush.

The young Russian picked up the empty schanpps bottle and tossed it out into the river, far from where they were sitting on the bank of the feathered reeds where plump, stilt-legged little birds were worrying at the mud. Like a hand grenade, thought Kowalski giddily. A Molotov grenade. No, a Molotov cocktail. Whatever it was. The Russians raised Kowalski's M-1 and sighted on the drifting, bobbing bottle. The first shot raised a gout of wind-whipped spray a few feet upstream. The next shot exploded the bottle like a glass bomb. Kowalski grinned. "You're OK, soldier." He felt uneasy though. You just didn't fool around with weapons while you were all liquored up. Not in the U.S. Army. Not on a patrol and in an area within range of a farmhouse stiff with American and Russian brass and war correspondents and photographers. It was crazy. Court-martial crazy. The Russian tossed another empty bottle out into the Elbe. No wonder I want to throw up, thought Kowalski. That's one bottle each already. Straight, too. Even the thought of it brought the salty, slippery saliva welling up around his tongue. The Russki handed Kowalski his own automatic rifle and pointed out toward the bottle that rolled and spun in a tortuous eddy of the river.

"Schnapps kaputt!" the Russian said and grinned, winking and sweating in the glare of the sun.

"I'm an interpreter," said Kowalski. "My grandfather came from Minsk. My grandmother came from Galicia. I was born in Silesia and raised in America. I speak German, Polish and English good and some Russian but I don't shoot so good."

The Russian shook his head, shaven close to the round skull, and thumped Kowalski companionably on the shoulders.

"We are good soldiers," he said. "We win the war. You shoot good. The bottle! Kaputt!"

Stuff the bottle, thought Kowalski, and he reached for the burp gun, marveling at the way of a war with men. Until they had flown him into Germany in a hurry to join the 69th Division as an interpreter in time for the U.S. First Army offensive toward the Elbe and the Russians, around the Harz Mountains, the last time he had handled any kind of military weapon had been way back in boot camp in New Jersey. He had not even needed to qualify as a sharpshooter to be a translator in Russian and Polish at a backwater SHAEF intelligence unit marooned in a stately, echoing town mansion in the West End of London. The main hazard on that particular assignment had been venereal disease.

The Russian slapped the butt of the burp gun.

"The bottle," he said. "Kaputt!"

"OK," said Kowalski, wearily. He might as well get it over with. "How do you fire the goddam thing?"

The Russian nearly toppled over as he leaned forward.

"You could use a shower, old buddy," Kowalski muttered, his queasy gut rebelling at the rank smell of sweat, stale perfume and sour schnapps.

"I just pull this little old trigger?" he said, relieved. Just as it seemed important not to vomit between comradely toasts to the Allied great, so it also seemed important to know how to handle the Russian's burp gun.

"Quick," said the Russian and pointed a stubby, black-nailed finger. The bottle which he had tossed into the river for Kowalski, upstream from where they sat, was spinning out into midstream on the sweep of current.

"Kaputt!" said Kowalski. His voice was thick and slurred. The effort of concentrating his sight on the drifting target was making him feel sick again. Impatient to be done with the crazy game, he cut loose savagely on the trigger, forgetting to pack his shoulder in behind the butt.

The stuttering burst of fire chopped the bottle into a white froth of glass splinters. The recoil also jumped the butt back into his face. Shocked by the anguish and pain of the blow, Kowalski neither knew nor cared where the kicking, crackling burst of fire zipped and buzzed as he dropped the weapon. Somewhere, back up on the riverbank meadow near the pines, he could hear Russians singing as they danced and jigged to an accordion while American GIs roared and whistled and clapped to the tempo of the wild music of the steppes.

"You shoot good," said the Russian, leaning over Kowalski as he writhed on the grass clutching at his jaw. It felt like it was broken. The American could see the sweat in the pores of the looming face.

"You've got a soldier's chin," said the Russian. You stupid, dumb bastard, Kowalski thought. The Russian passed him a pannikin of schnapps. "Drink this, you'll feel better. Dr. Schnapps, the soldier's friend."

For the first time since he had crossed the Elbe that morning with the patrol that covered the arrival of the big wheels from division, Kowalski felt like taking a good slug of the raw rotgut stuff. Rockets of pain were exploding slowly and continuously inside his head. He tossed the schnapps down the way the Russians did. Then, blessedly, a black wave of unconsciousness engulfed him, drowning the pain of having to think.

When Kowalski woke again, it was in a time of darkness with somebody kicking him. A lantern was shining in his face. He was lying on a warm, crumpled mess of straw in what smelled like a barn.

Behind the yellow, glaring eye of the lantern a man was speaking in German.

"Is that him?"

"He was with them," a woman's voice whispered, also in German. "He is an American but he was with the Russians. He speaks German."

"So, Mr. American," said the man's voice, "this is how you win the war? Raping German women in barns? This is how you liberate Europe?"

In the light of the lantern, Kowalski could see that the German was wearing civilian clothes. In his lapel was a sprig of lilac. There were two other men with him, also in civilian clothes and wearing little sprigs of lilac.

"On your feet, American," said the man with the lantern and began kicking Kowalski in the ribs. He was wearing heavy boots.

The barn, thought Kowalski, getting to his feet. Now I remember. The Russkis carrying me here. There was a woman with them, somehow. Then they began to drink again and I could hear the woman laughing and screaming, but then I passed out like a light.

"I had nothing to do with any woman," said Kowalski. "I was too drunk. I've been asleep all night. If there was a woman here, you'd better talk to the Russkis."

"The Russkis are in the Elbe," said the man with the lantern. "They got lost in the dark and had a most regrettable accident."

In the rustling gloom of the barn beyond the glow of light held up to Kowalski's face, the two other German civilians with the sprigs of lilac in their lapels exchanged low, throaty snickers of amusement.

Kowalski heard the sharp, oiled click of a gun being cocked.

"No, Sergeant," said the man with the lantern. "We want to talk to you. We have a special court for gentlemen like you. You are going to appear before this court on charges of rape. Now, march."

In the light of the lantern, the man was holding a water pistol.

"Do not try anything silly," he said. "This toy is filled with prussic acid. It is very quick, very quiet and very effective. We gave some of these toys to the son of the lady you say you did not rape in the barn. The boy, on our instructions, gave them to the Russkis. They were very drunk and very happy. They had had their fun with the lady in the barn. Then they had more fun squirting each other's faces with the pistols. Only for a very short time. They were dead long before we put their bodies in the Elbe. We stripped them and kept their uniforms. You can carry the uniforms. March, Sergeant, march."

So Kowalski had come in the night to Schloss Galgenstein, and a cell in the old dungeons below the castle, hurried on through the dark woods by the silent men with the water pistols and the sprigs of lilac in their lapels. The Russian uniforms were heavy and smelled faintly of almonds.

Lying in his cell in the darkness, Kowalski had wondered what kind of court it was that would try him and what sort of a trial he would get. The French and the Dutch and the Belgians had played it rough in the underground resistance against the Krauts. What could he expect from a German resistance group against the Allied armies?

Now he knew. It hadn't been a trial. More like the start of a lynching than anything else. The moment they brought in the drab, frightened little German hausfrau he knew that he was running out of time. Somebody just had to swing. He could tell by the way the Fehme men growled and nodded and shifted on their feet as she described how the Russians had dragged her into the barn and held her down and taken it in turns while her son had run screaming and whimpering across the dark fields to the village where the Fehme found him.

"And the accused, the American, Sergeant Kowalski, was there?" said Krausnick. "He was in the barn. With the Russians. While you were being attacked?"

"Yes." She was weeping as she whispered the word. You dumb, ugly, scared little bitch, thought Kowalski. I'm even sorry for you, but I wouldn't have wanted to rape you in a million years. But you're going to get me killed. For not touching you. For passing out cold while I was with those crazy Russkis.

"Did the accused attack you?" asked Krausnick.

"I don't know. It was too dark. There were too many of them. I can remember seeing the American. They kept lifting him onto me. He was very drunk. He kept rolling off."

That's what I've said all along, thought Kowalski. I was too stoned to do anything about it if I'd wanted to. They've got to let me go.

"Did the accused try to prevent the Russians attacking you?" said Krausnick.

"No. It was dark and they were holding me down. I don't know anything. I don't want to talk about it any more."

The woman was weeping then, looking down at the great squares of stone on the uneven floor of the dungeons.

"Thank you," said Krausnick. "You and your son will be in good hands now with the Fehme."

The verdict of guilty was the foregone conclusion that Kowalski had known it would be, but the sentence of death had shocked him because it had been pronounced by a presumably sane German officer of rank and distinction; shocked him because he was entirely innocent of the charge; shocked him because he now knew that he was helpless and alone and about to die at the hands of lunatics. Suddenly his apathy was gone and he began shouting at the general, storming at the heroic and immaculate figure with the medals and the dark glasses.

"I demand my rights as a prisoner of war," Kowalski raged. "I am a soldier of the United States Army. You can't get away with this."

Swiftly, two Fehme men had pinioned him, one with a hooked arm gagging his mouth.

"You are a prisoner of the Fehme," said von Bluckau. "The Fehme is not a signatory to the Geneva Convention. You have no rights before this court."

To the Fehme guards, von Bluckau had nodded curtly.

"Remove the prisoner. The court will proceed with the next case."

Curiously enough, Warrant Officer Thomas Dart, Royal Air

Force, felt no fear as the ferret-faced prosecutor, the man they called Krausnick, began to call against him the evidence of the Fehme men who had burst into the farmhouse that night at Kotzdorf.

As a regular airman of the Royal Air Force and a professional man-at-arms, Tommy Dart felt only an angry contempt for the raffish tribunal before which he now stood accused on a ridiculous charge of looting, pillaging or otherwise stealing a loaf of bread. He felt anger, too, at himself for having abandoned his declared principles as man-of-confidence at Stalag IV J. If he had stayed in the camp as he had urged prisoners in all compounds to do ever since that windy, cloud-scattered April morning when the Russian cavalry patrol had machine-gunned the hinges from the gates of the stalag, he would not now be being buggered about by what seemed to be a shower of Nazi war criminals.

III

The Man-of-Confidence

Strangely, the realization that the war was over for Stalag IV J, Hohenleipisch, had proved to be the time of ultimate personal frustration for Tommy Dart; a period of disillusionment culminating in that climactically frustrating interview with Colonel Kravchenkov, the stolid Russian who had taken over command of the camp after the big T-34 tanks and endless Soviet truck convoys had rolled past the camp to set up command posts and headquarters in Hohenleipisch, Niederleipisch and other towns along the line of the Elbe.

Like all the others that had gone before it, this interview with the Russian had been an exercise in futility, for with the liberation by the heedless, inexorable Red Army had vanished not only the German commandant, staff and guards but all the values, ethics and disciplines with which the prisoners of war at Stalag IV J had preserved their sanity and self-respect in a world of captivity.

Standing in front of Kravchenkov's desk, irresolute and angry, Tommy had abstractedly watched the main gate of the camp through the office windows as he had so often done in the days when a German commandant had sat at the same desk.

High above the pine-log observation tower over the stalag gate from which the proud, predatory German eagle and claw-clutched swastika had long since been jubilantly wrenched, the flags of the United Nations fluttered in a bright consort of celebration.

No longer did the bowed, helmet-heavy heads and rifle-slung shoulders of bored German guards pace back and forth on their perch above the rusted barbed wire of the main gate.

The Germans had been gone nearly ten days now, swept away in that night of dark, confused, agonized waiting when the East Front had infiltrated past Stalag IV J with an eerie crackle of small arms fire in the uneasy night beyond the wire, a night flickering and alive with the greedy, leaping flames of burning villages and farms, the rolling boom of artillery, the slam of tank guns and the sustained, tumbling roaring of German demolition explosions.

The slow, labored creaking of Kravchenkov's chair brought Tommy Dart's attention back to the camp commandant as the Russian swiveled around to face the desk. A fly, sluggish in the torporous heat engendered by the tinkling, glowing stove and the morning sunshine on the dusty windows, was crawling speculatively over Kravchenkov's round, shaven head but the Russian made no move to brush it away. Time is no object, thought Tommy irritably. Twenty thousand liberated prisoners of war of a dozen different nationalities with no food except what they can loot beyond the wire, and the Russian commandant is too tired even to brush a fly from his pink, bull-necked head. God, I don't know, thought Tommy. Three years of battling with the Germans as British man-of-confidence and now I have to deal with the Russians. If I had any gumption I'd just look after myself and get the hell out of here. I'm a warrant officer, not a wing commander. The war is over for Stalag IV J. And for Warrant Officer Dart. Deutschland kaputt. Alles kaputt. Up you, Jack, I'm aboard.

As if sensing the thin little Englishman's thoughts, Kravchenkov suddenly sat forward at the desk, his pudgy fingers splayed out like sausages on the pad of green blotting paper.

The Russian's neck, sweating a little, bulged over the high, tight collar of his brown whipcord tunic.

"No," he said. "Your men must not go farther than five kilometers from the camp. They can forage all the food they want in the farms and the villages. They are not babies."

"There's no food left within five kilos of the camp," said Tommy. "The whole stalag has been at it for over a week."

Kravchenkov finally brushed irritably at the fly, staring impassively at it when it fell stunned onto the blotting pad. In the oppressive silence of the room, Tommy heard the tiny sound of the impact.

The Russian flicked the fly aside with a forefinger encircled by a heavy, elaborate gold ring, which until quite recently had graced the hand of a Silesian butcher who had also been the belligerently patriotic Burgermeister of his village.

"I have my orders," said Kravchenkov, almost sadly. "So have my field police."

"But Russian and American forces made contact on the Elbe, only yesterday," objected the little Englishman. "You just told me so yourself. I think you said the divisional commanders will be meeting any day now at Torgau. The Russian. The American. Why can't I take the men from the British compound across the Elbe at Torgau now that there's been a link-up and the area is free of German forces? We don't want transport. We don't expect it. We'll walk there. All we want to do is cross the Elbe at Torgau and go home."

"Home?" said Kravchenkov, his tobacco-stained teeth gleaming in a sudden wide smile. "We would all like to go home, Warrant Officer Dart."

"Until the war ends," said Tommy, "and so long as the situation remains the way it is now at Stalag IV J, I am still the British man-of-confidence under the terms of the Geneva Convention. As such, I am still responsible for the welfare of ten thousand prisoners of war in the British compounds of this camp. I am not so much concerned with getting them home as getting them across the Elbe into the American zone of occupation, where food, medical aid and transportation will be provided by either the British or the Americans. With respect, Colonel, none of these facilities appear to be available on this side of the Elbe. I appreciate the fact that the Russian forces are still fighting north and south along the east bank of the Elbe and, as liberated prisoners, we must expect to have to take care of ourselves for a bit. There are limits, though, to the amount of food that can be looted in any area. I submit that we have now reached those limits so far as living off the land is concerned."

Tommy forbore from adding that, as front-line troops, Konev's forces in the area were naturally getting the lion's share of the looted food, for they, too, seemed to be living off the land in Saxony.

"I just have to take my men out across the bridge at Torgau," said Tommy.

Patiently, like a schoolmaster repeating an all too familiar lesson, Kravchenkov sighed.

"The bridge at Torgau is down," he said. "So is the railway viaduct. The Germans blew them up. They always blow them up. They always did. In the Ukraine. On the Don. In Poland. In

Silesia. Now in Saxony. They must be the world's greatest bridge demolishers. It is always the same. Every time I come to a bridge, they have blown it up. We win the war but we lose the bridges."

Kravchenkov smiled, gently patting the belly which strained at the buttons of his khaki-colored tunic.

"If we were to start drinking a tiny glass of vodka for every time I have seen the Germans blow up a bridge in this war, we would soon be very happy, you and I. It is so at Torgau. The road bridge and the railway bridge. They are both on the bottom of the river. Blown up. Kaputt. The Americans will be crossing the Elbe by boat to meet General Rusakov on our side of the river. You will have to do what I have had to do ever since Stalingrad, Warrant Officer Dart. You will have to wait until the engineers build a pontoon bridge across the river."

The wide, plastic Slavonic features creased again in a smile.

"Unless you British can walk upon the water?" he added.

"We can't walk upon the water," said Tommy without humor. "Nor can we wait. There is a danger of typhus in the camp. Already many of my men are starving and they are sick with dysentery."

"They will have to wait," said Kravchenkov. "Those who are not fighting must always wait."

He tapped a file of messages with the paper tube of his rank black Polish cigarette.

"I have my orders, Warrant Officer Dart."

The Englishman nodded sadly.

Looking down at the dull black sheen of the toecaps of his carefully dubbined boots—despite his impatience with red tape, Tommy was still a regular airman at heart—he was aware of the faded purple-and-white ribbon of the Distinguished Flying Medal below his gunner's wing. Heartened, inexplicably, by the memories which the ribbon evoked, Dart stared patronizingly at the Russian colonel still slumped behind his desk. You'd crap your pants and fill your boots in a rear turret over the Ruhr, he thought. You potbellied, frightened, red-tape Russian army bastard.

"That is final?" he asked. "Orders are orders?"

Kravchenkov nodded heavily, the scarlet and silver of his stiff shoulder epaulets glinting. Behind him, the morning sun glinted on motes of dust swirling through a window shattered by a stone pitched by some exuberant prisoner the morning the stalag awoke to find that the Germans had gone.

"You and your men may have been liberated," said the Russian, "but for us Russians this is still a fighting area. For the Germans, too. Tell your men to wait and to keep out of the woods. When the Germans go to ground, the woods are not a good place to be. Even if you have a gun."

The Russian tapped his thigh with the edge of a steel rule. Tommy was entirely unprepared for the hollow, metallic ring.

"I left this leg in a forest on the Vistula last summer," said Kravchenkov. "I would be the last man to suggest that the Germans can't shoot straight. Even on the run."

Tommy stared reflectively at the Russian, suddenly glad that he had not voiced his contemptuous thought about armchair warriors.

"Orders are orders, then?" he said, more briskly.

"*Befehl ist Befehl*," said Kravchenkov in jocular, thickly accented German.

"Right," said Tommy and saluted. Smartly. Up-one-two-three-away. A double stamp of the heels. A crisp, regimental regular RAF salute. A parade-ground job.

The Russian smiled, this time to himself, as the gray-faced little Englishman, straight-backed in his tidy, patched battle dress, marched out of the office.

Tommy Dart walked on slowly into the camp, delaying his return to Barrack 1A.

They would be waiting for him there, the British camp leader and his British compound leaders; waiting for him to come back from his interview with Kravchenkov as they had so often awaited his return from meetings with Lehmann, the German commandant.

As the Vertrauensmann—literally, in German, man-of-trust or, as the League of Nations had translated it in English, man-of-confidence—Tommy had been recognized by both the Detaining Power, Germany, and the Protecting Power, Switzerland, as the sole negotiator on behalf of the British prisoners at Stalag IV J. Tommy had tasted to the full the bitterness of years of pleading lost and futile causes with the Germans, yet always he had been able to rationalize his failures and frustrations with a private philosophical acceptance of the fact that he was only a pawn in a game of international legality played according to the German rules enforced by the Germans to best suit the Germans.

With our own bloody allies you'd think I'd be able to get somewhere, thought Tommy. Just for once I'd like to get something done for the lads. Kravchenkov had still been hung-over from the night before, of course. He was the same every morning. The loss of a leg had evidently not curbed his love of liquor.

Tommy could hear the muttering of the radio as he slammed back the counter top in the cramped bunkroom from which, day and night, for three years he had administered the destinies of a largely transient population of 10,000 British prisoners. The radio was the once-clandestine apparatus, retrieved from its hiding place in the latrine of Barrack 45A, which had been miraculously put together by a moody genius of an RAF radar navigator from tinny scraps of rubbish and smuggled or stolen components.

How bloody silly, thought Tommy. Liberated for nearly ten days and here we are, still sitting around in Stalag IV J waiting for the BBC news from London.

As usual, they were perched on his carefully made-up bunk with a brew of ersatz German barley coffee bubbling and steaming in the battered Italian dixie on the stove. On the table, a modified packing case, a small can of looted German condensed milk stood ceremoniously by each waiting jam-tin mug. There had been a sudden abundance of condensed milk since a week before the camp's liberation. Workers of Russian Arbeitskommandos had made a killing on the camp's black market after a gaggle of scarlet-nosed P-51 Mustangs, their Perspex canopies glinting in the sun, had strafed the big Elbe barge and it had gone aground on the east bank of the river near Uhlsteinwalde. The Germans had seen very little of the cargo of Wehrmacht condensed milk after it had been salvaged by the Russian working parties which had been marched down to the riverbank from Stalag IV J.

Regimental Sergeant Major Tremarthen, the dark and saturnine British camp leader, got up to pour the brew as Tommy came into the bunkroom.

"Any luck?" he inquired, concentrating more on pouring the coffee than listening for any anticipated answer from the man-of-confidence. Captured at Crete after a truck had overturned and pinned him down until the arrival of German paratroopers, Tremarthen had learned to expect the minimum of good fortune.

"No go," said Tommy.

"Just what I bloody well expected," said Hughes. A gloomy soul who had been taken prisoner at Tobruk, RSM Hughes, British army compound leader, already regarded the liberation as a bad joke. The last mail to get through to Hohenleipisch, before the bombing had got really bad in central Germany, had brought him an anonymous "Dear John" letter confiding that his wife was sleeping with a Polish naval officer.

"That's bloody funny," Hughes had said entirely without humor. "If it hadn't been for Poland I wouldn't have been here in the first place."

Now, as they stirred their coffee and spooned greedily at the sweet sustenance of the condensed milk, he stared belligerently at Tommy.

"No go?" he repeated. It sounded like an accusation.

"No go," said Tommy, licking his spoon clean of condensed milk.

"I told you we should have got the hell out of here the day the Russkis arrived," said van Mieren, the RAF compound leader. A big, olive-skinned South African who had worked his way to England as a ship's steward to join the RAF, van Mieren was a constant source of irritation to Tommy. The South African had been a cattle auctioneer and had an appropriately bull-like voice and manner. He represented a new RAF which had grown up, vast and cosmopolitan, in the years since Tommy had been shot down in a Mk.3 Wellington—a gigantic force now, with a Bomber Command of four-engined Lancasters and Halifaxes, skippered and crewed by the floodtide of the Empire Air Training Scheme; youngsters who graduated from mass-produced courses with commissions or three stripes to match their wings; kids who would not believe Tommy when he told them he had flown his first tour as an air gunner with the rank of leading aircraftsman. If you could call it a rank. A lance corporal in the army was probably senior. So much, Tommy had always thought, for the glory of being a regular airman who had remustered to air crew at the start of the war.

For no other reasons than these, Tommy Dart had always cherished an illogical resentment of Van Mieren and the new generation of bomber crews who in later years had begun to crowd the prison camps of Germany; the young and cocky men, survivors of operations in which main forces of up to a thousand Lancasters and Halifaxes nightly bombed with implacable ferocity on the beautiful target indicator flares showered down with eerie, scientific accuracy by the Pathfinder Force.

"Where do we go from here?" asked van Mieren.

"Where do we go?" echoed Tommy. "We go nowhere."

"You're kidding," said the South African. Anger darkened his brown Boer eyes.

Wearily Tommy shook his head.

"We may be liberated, but the Russkis are still pushing troops over the Elbe, south to Prague and north to Berlin. And both the Yanks and the Russkis are still chasing Jerry troops up and down the corridor between the Elbe and the Mulde and between Berlin and Dresden. We're right in the middle of it."

"Not just ordinary Jerry footsloggers, either," said Hughes with sour relish. "They're mostly SS. They're all around the twist, of course. More so now that they know they've had it. I've never seen an SS man yet who had ever heard about the Geneva Convention for POWs like us. I've seen the bastards in action. I'll wait."

Tremarthen poured more barley coffee into the tin mugs.

"Maybe," he said, "but I'd still take my chances with the SS. Outside the wire, I mean. Things are a little more even now. You can pick up guns easy enough, they tell me. It's a long time since I sighted up on something, but it'd be a pleasure."

"Balls to that," said van Mieren with the airman's inherent distrust of ground fighting. "We should have gotten off our asses and moved out of here quick, like the Poles and the Yanks."

"Should we?" said Tommy. Thoughtfully he stirred condensed milk into his barley coffee. "The Yanks weren't so bloody clever. They walked into the middle of a tank battle between Russki T-34s and German Tigers. They lost some GIs and when the Russkis got it all sorted out, they put the Yanks under guard in the nearest village for their own safety. They're probably still there. Let's face it, POWs are just a bloody nuisance around here. They are in any combat area. I say we stay put. Until I hand over the British personnel of this camp to the commanding officer of a British or American unit I'm still the man-of-confidence."

"You won't be for much longer if we don't start getting the boys out of here pretty damned soon," said van Mieren."

"I know," said Tommy wearily, "but there's a right way to do it."

"With the help of that Russian commandant out there?" said van Mieren derisively. "Let's just go."

Tommy sighed. Day by day, he liked van Mieren less.

"If you'd use your bloody brains," he said, "you'd realize that there's still a war going on outside the wire, all along the Elbe. The Jerries are still holding some of the bridges. We don't know which ones. Torgau's our best bet, but the Jerries blew all the bridges there before the Russkis arrived. Now the Russkis are building a pontoon bridge. When it's finished, they'll want to get their troops and their vehicles across. They don't want a lot of foreign-speaking POWs and displaced persons and slave workers and God knows what cluttering up the bridge."

"That's according to Kravchenkov?" said Hughes, blowing impatiently at his brew. Always it was too hot or too cold.

Tommy nodded. He felt tired. Tired of everything.

"Go and ask him yourself if you don't believe me."

There was a dispirited silence that lasted until Hughes stood up quickly.

"The news," he said. "We'll miss it."

"Big deal," said van Mieren. "So we've been liberated."

Reverentially, though, as had long been their furtive custom, the four British camp administrators listened to the suave, pontifical voice of the BBC.

In the silence which descended upon the creaking, wind-haunted wooden barracks in Saxony after Tommy had switched off the radio, they could hear a looted hen excitedly proclaiming the miracle of a newly laid egg.

"They didn't say anything about the link-up at Torgau," said Hughes. His tone of voice suggested that the BBC was suspect as a news organization.

The South African yawned.

"What do you say, Tommy? This place is getting like a city garbage dump. I tell you, the RAF compound will be empty in a week. They're starting to take off on their own. Regardless of you, me, General Eisenhower, the BBC, the Russkis and the SS in the woods. We've got to do something."

He leaned forward, brandishing a spoon.

"I'm telling you, Tommy, we've had it here. We've got to get the boys out. What about it?"

"What about it?" said Tommy suddenly. "I'll tell you what about it. I'm going to Torgau. Alone."

The South African pilot sat up, brushing the straw of Tommy's paillasse from the thick, gray-blue material of his RAF battle dress.

"Alone?" he said. "What about us?"

"You stay here," said Tommy. "If we all go, the boys will think it's a walk-out. They'll take off, too.

"Another thing," said Tommy, patting the pocket of his battle dress, which, unlike van Mieren's, was old, faded, patched and threadbare. "You wouldn't get far without a travel pass. I've got the only one that Kravchenkov's prepared to issue just now."

The South African was scornful.

"Travel pass!" he said. "You'd have to find a Russki soldier capable of reading it first."

"We're not dealing with the average Russki footslogger here now," said Tommy. "Kravchenkov's got a company of Red Army military policeman patrolling the stalag area. The combat troops couldn't care less, I admit. Just now, though, you wouldn't get past the first village beyond five kilometers without a travel pass signed by Kravchenkov."

Tommy chewed at his empty pipe.

"You know how trigger-happy the Russkis are, even in broad daylight. Once you start creeping around in the woods and making like an escaper, you're really asking for it. They're still fighting a war, remember."

Despondently van Mieren shrugged his big shoulders. He was built like a bullock.

"I guess you're right, Tommy. It would be kind of stupid to get shot by the Russkis."

"OK," said the little Englishman. "That's the way it is then.

You boys stand by here while I go see the local Russian commander at Torgau."

Nobody was at the main gate to farewell Tommy when he walked out of Stalag IV J that day and he was glad, for he was excited, like a child, by the prospect of going free far beyond the gate of the camp, free to turn left or right at the end of the dusty white spur road that linked the stalag with the highway between Elsterwalde and Falkewitz. If he wanted to, he could walk right around the outside of the fences of the camp on the track beaten smooth by the boots of patrolling guards and the paws of their leashed dogs. He could strike out across the open fields beyond. For years he had wondered what it would be like to stroll across the countryside and climb up inside the gleaming Byzantine onion dome of the little village church you could see from the compounds and look back over the furrows toward the deserted watch towers and the dismal, wired squalor of the camp. Yet, now, he was sad, too, because he knew he would not bother to do it. It would surely be an anticlimax to achieve, in an hour, an ambition which he had cherished for three years.

Tommy also realized that he was scared. What kind of a world would he find waiting for him out there?

Now, at the main gate of the camp, the vastness of a free world in which he was no longer a military factor, however small, overpowered him with a terrifying sense of loneliness and inadequacy. Almost he seemed reluctant to walk away from the gate and the once-hated status of prisoner.

Then he saw Kravchenkov. The Russian was talking to other Red Army officers in a captured DKW staff car. As Tommy stepped out along the road toward the Kommandantur offices, Kravchenkov gave the low roof of the camouflage-painted little car a comradely thump with the flat of his hand. Then he stood back, swinging his tin leg awkwardly, and saluted farewell to his visitors. He was grinning and the gold fillings of his teeth gleamed in the sunshine.

The dust from the departed DKW hung like a dry, white mist in the air as Tommy came opposite the Russian and, in passing, saluted. The act of saluting had never worried Tommy. Only the absence of it. If the RAF had made him an officer he would have expected to have been saluted.

"The meeting at Torgau is official," said the Russian as proudly as if the 1st Ukrainian Army had just taken Berlin instead of linking up with the U.S. First Army on the Elbe.

"Those men in the car," he said, "they are from my old regiment. They just told me about Torgau. Tonight we celebrate. It has been a long march to the Elbe. For everyone."

"Good show," said Tommy without enthusiasm. Kravchenkov had been celebrating every night since he had taken over command of Stalag IV J. The shouts and shrieks which had always signaled another Kravchenkov party at the Kommandantur officers' mess had invariably been heard inside the stalag long after the last grease candles had been snuffed out and the barracks were silent with the tired thoughts of men wondering when they would cross the Elbe.

"Can you come, Comrade Dart?" said Kravchenkov, solemnly attentive to this small matter of protocol.

Tommy smiled. It was the first time since before he had been shot down that he had been invited to a party. A real party with wine and women and food.

"No, thank you, Colonel," he said. "With your approval, and the authority of your pass, I'm going to Torgau to see the local Russian commander there."

Kravchenkov pursed his lips like a disappointed father musing over the hopes and follies of a wayward son. Then he smiled and shrugged his shoulders, rounded and burly beneath the stiff scarlet-and-silver epaulets.

"He will have his orders, too," said the Russian. "The war is not yet over. Not for the fighting soldier." Inwardly Tommy winced at the unwitting reminder of his noncombatant status as a liberated prisoner.

"Good luck, anyway," said Kravchenkov. "And just remember, if there's one thing better than a dead German it's a live fräulein."

"Thank you, Colonel," said Tommy, stepping back and saluting. "I'll probably need all the luck I can get."

Kravchenkov winked, wagging an admonitory finger at him.

"Only with the Amerikanski," he said. "They are the sly ones."

"Don't you believe it, Colonel," said Tommy firmly.

"One thing more," said Kravchenkov, his moonface serious

again. "They probably don't teach you these things in the air force. Never open a German door the way you do at home. Kick it open and jump away. German engineers do clever things with mines and grenades."

He slapped his artificial leg.

"I should lend you Iron Joseph, eh? Good-bye, Comrade. You may only have been a flier, but we could still make a good soldier of you in the Red Army."

Tommy walked carefully that day like a child trespassing in a strange and deserted garden. Saxony, beyond the wire, was not how he had always thought it would be. The open fields about him had seemed wider and emptier than he would have expected, defenseless beneath the benign, blue domain of the spring sky. The villages cowered like immobile herds of cattle, frightened and with heads averted. Only children were about in the streets, playing with the uneasy air of children whose parents were late coming home after leaving them all day until the shadows fell. Adults, when Tommy saw them, appeared as if flushed from cover, retreating from him with faces of fear or suspicion. Invariably they were old people, mainly stoop-shouldered women. Tommy wondered just what had happened to the armed forces of Germany. Only a few weeks earlier, thousands of German soldiers had been fighting a rear-guard action over this same countryside, retreating grimly to the Elbe. It was as if they had all fallen backwards into the great river, firing as they fell.

The forests worried Tommy most of all. Once, when the road passed through the Jägerswald, a dark forest of whispering pines and tangled, overgrown copses of birches, he could feel physically an immediate drop in air temperature. The chill of winter was still there, imprisoned by the black pines, and he could not escape the conviction that he was being watched. He had wanted to run toward the open fields. It had been like that all day. Eager in his loneliness for a friendly face, a wave or a shout, Tommy had been haunted by a brooding air of desolation which was heightened rather than relieved by the clear, shrill calls of wild birds.

Kravchenkov had been the last human being to whom he had spoken that long, melancholy day on the road to Torgau until late in the afternoon. Then it was that, with the scent from the lilac hedges deepening in the dusk, he had had to jump for the ditch to avoid being run down by, of all unexpected things, a motor hearse that came lurching wildly around the corner of a white-washed wall in the village street of Kotzdorf.

Skidding violently, the hearse bounded over the ditch and rammed the three-pointed Mercedes star on its vintage radiator into the stone wall. Steaming, rusty water flooded down onto the grass.

"I guess it's a while since I last drove an automobile," said a loud and cheerful voice.

Gingerly the driver climbed out into the mud of the ditch. He was wearing a faded red British Airborne beret and a camouflaged jump jacket. Tommy recognized him and was glad, for it was getting dark, and after so long in the crowded confusion of a stalag barracks, he had been starting to feel desperately lonely on the German road at sunset. Tommy knew him as Jean Lebrac, a French-Canadian paratrooper sergeant who had been captured at Arnhem and had never got used to the idea. A psychopathically obsessed escaper, he had spent more time in the cooler at Stalag IV J than any other five men in the British or American compounds. Not surprisingly, he had been the first man back inside the wire with looted food after the Russians had liberated the camp.

He grinned when he saw Tommy.

"Hi!" he said. "Look who's here. The man-of-confidence! You're not deserting the sinking ship, Tommy?"

"I'm on my way to see the Russian commandant at Torgau," said Tommy, annoyed by the light-hearted assumption that he was walking out on his responsibilities.

A long, thin figure in RAF battle-dress jacket and looted blue German football shorts was climbing awkwardly out of the back of the hearse. Tommy recognized the pink-cheeked, almost effeminate good looks of Malmesbury, another of his charges from the camp at Hohenleipisch. Malmesbury had been captured shortly after D-Day when the Mosquito he was navigating had abruptly disintegrated after his pilot had pulled out a little late from a strafing run on a German munitions train between Paris and Orléans.

At Hohenleipisch, Malmesbury had partnered Lebrac in many of his more suicidal attempts to escape.

There was a splash and then a stream of obscenities in a languid, English public-school accent as Malmesbury stepped backwards into the green-slimed water and glutinous mud of the ditch.

"You dumb French-Canadian bastard," he said. "You nearly killed me. Honest to Christ, if it was raining harlots, I'd get hit by a queer."

"You were asking for it, anyway, you sacrilegious Protestant," said Lebrac. "Stretched out like the lord of the manor in the back of the hearse while I did all the driving."

"All the damage, you mean," said Malmesbury, mournfully surveying the damaged radiator.

"No panic," said Lebrac. "We'll just run her into that farmyard down the road a piece. There'll be something in the barn to fix the radiator. Let's get her out of here first."

By the time they had maneuvered the hearse out of the ditch and cautiously driven it, steaming and creaking ominously, into the farmyard it was nearly dark.

"Looks like we stay the night," said Lebrac. "I'll take a look around the barn first, though. Could be there's some pitch or cement in there."

"Good Lord!" said Malmesbury. With an air of patrician distaste he had been wiping dung and the mud of the ditch from his bare, knobbly knees. Now he was washing his hands at the farmyard pump.

"Look at that!" he said.

If it had been a Wehrmacht steel helmet, they wouldn't have given it a second glance, but it was a long time since any of them had seen a Homburg hat. A sleek, black, expensive Homburg it was, its silk lining gleaming in the last light of sunset. It lay there negligently on the manure-stained cobblestones, looking as if its owner had dropped it dashing for a train and hadn't had time to pick it up. But the nearest railway station to Kotzdorf was at Falkewitz, ten kilometers away, where trains no longer pounded along the blue-steel rails of the Berlin-Dresden line.

The French Canadian picked up the hat. There was a name inscribed in gilt on the leather band. Wilhelm Engelhöffer.

"Just what we needed," he said. "It'll go well with the hearse.

Real class." Tucking the paratrooper beret into his jump jacket, he tipped the Homburg over one eye.

"How do I look?"

"Ridiculous," said Malmesbury.

"You look like a looter," said Tommy. Now, as always, he disapproved of looting. He was haunted still by the prospect of what would happen if the Germans counterattacked against the Russians and returned to the farms and villages which had been stripped by the prisoners of Hohenleipisch.

"What else?" said Lebrac. "This living off the land is the deal. Don't criticize it. It beats work. I think I just heard some chickens in the barn. Let's fix ourselves something to eat. Unless you know a good diner on the road between here and Berlin."

Inside the barn, the Canadian stepped back quickly.

"I knew it," he said. "Every time we get to a farm that's not lousy with ex-PWs or drunken Russkis there's something else wrong with it. Take a look at that."

It was evidently the owner of the Homburg. A big, well-dressed man in a black leather topcoat, he was sprawled face down on the blood-soaked straw. He was dead. Jean Lebrac knelt by the body.

"Booby trap," said Malmesbury nervously.

"Booby trap, my ass," said the French Canadian. "You'd have been a big help in the army. Just the same, I want to see Montreal again."

Bulky in his paratrooper jacket, he moved with a lithe, catlike grace. He might have been wearing gym shoes not steel-studded army boots. Grasping the dead German's heels, he spoke over his shoulder.

"Hit the deck. Just in case."

Tumbling into the straw, Tommy and Malmesbury waited.

The French Canadian gave the German's heels a sudden, brutal tug and threw himself onto his back.

No bang, thought Malmesbury. Jolly good. No wicked zip of hurtling, fragmented steel like the time Jean had taken a pine branch and cautiously opened the door of a Luftwaffe tanker truck abandoned in the woods near Elsterwerda. He'd been deaf for days after that lot went up.

"Just a stiff," said the Canadian. Casually he crossed himself. Somewhere outside behind the barn a dog yelped. In the cool of the evening there was a fragrance of lilac where a bush stood by the barn door.

"He don't look like any farmer to me," said Lebrac. "What's he doing here, anyway?"

"Minding his own business," said Tommy. "Like we should be."

Death in the air was an operational risk he had once been prepared to accept, but now, with the chaos and uncertainty of liberation all about him, he wanted no part of death in a barn with its face in the straw where the flies crawled, black and gorged.

Lebrac was less inhibited. Blooded in combat as a paratrooper, he tended to evaluate sudden and violent forms of death with all the appraising, clinical interest of the trained professional. Rolling the body over, he searched the pockets of the clothing dispassionately and quickly.

"Goddam!" he said suddenly. His hand had gone to one outflung wrist. Turning back a pigskin glove, it had revealed a gold watch with an expensive band of gold links. Clutched in the other hand was a sprig of lilac.

Lebrac stripped the watch from the dead man's wrist and held it to his ear under the brim of the jauntily raked Homburg.

"Doesn't even need winding," he said. "Going like a charm."

He held it out, the gold a dull gleam in the callused cushion of his palm.

"Some ticker. Finders keepers. He don't need to know the time any more."

Lebrac slipped the watch into the bulged pocket of his jump jacket.

"I'd be crazy to wear it. The way these Russkis are about watches."

Malmesbury nodded thoughtfully.

"That's what puzzles me. It's jolly odd."

"What's odd?"

"Herr Engelhöffer," said Malmesbury. "He has no wallet. No papers. Nothing at all to identify him. It's not like the Russkis to lift his papers and leave his watch. Particularly a watch like that."

Lebrac was frowning and seemed to be listening for something, but there was nothing to be heard in the barn except their voices and the sound of their feet shuffling the dry straw as they talked.

"I'll tell you something else," said the French Canadian. "He was knifed and not very long ago. He's still warm and that's fresh lilac in his right hand."

"It's all very odd," said Malmesbury. "I wonder who did it?"

"Who cares?" said Lebrac. "So he's kaputt. If it wasn't the Russkis, maybe it was the pixies or Jack the Giant Killer. So what? The way things are going, Germany's just a nuthouse anyway. Anybody could have done it."

He walked back to the doorway of the barn.

Outside, the red-tiled farm buildings that made an enclosed square of the yard were throwing dark shadows across the cobblestones. High overhead, in the last of the sunset, a pink fleece of cirrus cloud was idling north toward the Baltic in a tranquil, deserted sky that ten days before had been streaked and smudged with the speeding contrails and hanging flak-bursts that had signaled the final phase of the Anglo-American air assault on Berlin and on the cities and towns of central Germany between the converging fronts.

Looking up at the high windows of the farmhouse, Tommy thought they looked like blind eyes in a dead face. He started as the evening wind plucked playfully at a curtain and he began to wonder if there was somebody up there watching them.

"Let's get out of here," said Tommy.

"Not without those eggs," said the Canadian. "There's a hen around here somewheres. We could have that, too. I'd like some chicken for supper."

"OK," said Malmesbury, "but do we have to stay the night? There was a buzz in the camp this morning that the Jerries have counterattacked back up this side of the Elbe from Dresden. If they get this far, they'll take a dim view of three Kriegsgefangenen living in a German farmhouse with a dead German civilian in the barn. I'd hate to have to explain it to some spooky SS creature in the middle of the night. Let's go back to the stalag."

Lebrac was incredulous.

"Hike twelve kilometers back to that lousy dump?"

"Why not?" said Tommy. "There may not be any food there, but it's where we should be if the Jerries do put in a counter-attack."

Lebrac tipped the Homburg over his eyes and scratched angrily at the back of his head.

"Look, we grab ourselves some eggs, a chicken, a good night's sleep. I'm beat. In the morning we fix the radiator. Then we get the hell out of here. There's no sign of a German counterattack and by now the Russkis will have drunk all the liquor and raped all the women in this lousy little village. Let's have a quiet night here. How about it?"

A rifle had cracked then, flighting the birds in the rustling birch trees that lined the village street beyond the farmyard.

"Christ, here we go again," said Malmesbury. Involuntarily he had ducked as something shattered a tile on the farmhouse roof and whined away into the evening sky.

Lebrac had gone. Running quickly but bent forward as if he had been kicked in the groin or was looking for something on the ground, Lebrac reached the farmyard wall. From behind a stack of pine logs he peered over into the street. He stood back, relaxed, and waved to Tommy and Malmesbury.

"Just a GI Russki," he said, "and very, very high. Don't they do anything else but get stoned in the Red Army? If they fight like they drink, they must be tigers."

Even as they watched, the Russian soldier toppled off his bicycle with a slow inevitability but still holding his rifle high by the butt as if it were a gilded lance and he a knight, dehorsed in ancient joust.

The white, dusty perspective of the village street with its green-budding birch trees was deserted except for the Russian, cursing and shouting as he struggled to regain his feet.

Behind a shuttered cottage window, an old woman's voice shrilled in harsh German, like an indignant parrot. A door banged. The sound of children's voices stopped abruptly as if hands had been clapped over their mouths. There was a great silence in Kotzdorf.

The rifle cracked again and somewhere a pane of window glass shattered, tinkling musically.

"He's off again," said Lebrac. "Boy, is he loaded! I'm glad he doesn't have any grenades. I hope."

"What's he shooting at, old boy?" said Malmesbury. "This sort of thing always makes me nervous."

"I don't think even he knows," said the Canadian.

"That's it, then," said Malmesbury firmly, "I'm not moving while he's still in the village."

"Fair enough," said Lebrac. "I knew you'd see it my way. Let's get some chow organized."

An hour later, after they had run down a squawking fowl in a flurry of straw and feathers behind the barn and plucked it ready for the pot, fresh uproar broke out in the village street of Kotzdorf. This time, reported the ever-curious Lebrac, it was a Russian provost motorcycle outfit rounding up the bellicose private.

Tommy thought of the narrow road that led back to the Hohenleipisch stalag between the black, watchful pines; the pines where he had seen a young deer halted like a life-sized piece of Meissen porcelain; the pines that, even in the sunny sanity of high noon, had echoed to the sudden cackle of automatic weapons as Cossack cavalry and hunted Wehrmacht men played a desperate game of hide and seek; the pines of the shadowy forest called Jägerswald-Galgenstein.

In the chill of falling night, Malmesbury shivered. The ogres of the medieval Germanic legends were abroad again amid the forests of Saxony and, like the peasants of past centuries, wise men had learned anew to keep to the trodden ways and the sunlit hours.

"Let's stay, then," said Tommy.

"Amen," said Malmesbury.

"Now you're talking," said the Canadian. "One thing about four walls. You can always get your back to one of them."

Whistling tunelessly and dangling the plucked, naked bird by its horny legs, he kicked open a door of the farmhouse. It was empty of course. They usually were. Doors open. Windows open. A shipwrecked farm left high and dry on the German plains by the flood tide of a storm of retribution that had sprung from Moscow and Voronezh, Stalingrad and Grozny, the Ukraine and the Pripet Marshes. There was a special quality of emptiness about the farmhouse which was unusually oppressive. A brooding and watchful silence like a desecrated church or a pillaged vault.

"Nice farm," said Lebrac. "Some setup."

"Farmers always live well, old boy," said Malmesbury. "I knew a girl whose father had this farm in Norfolk just near our squadron."

"OK, lover-boy," said Lebrac, "never mind the memoirs. Let's just check this joint out first. In case."

"In case of what?" said Malmesbury.

"In case somebody cuts our throats while we're asleep," said the French Canadian patiently. "You were always a sharp map reader to escape with, but you'd have made a hell of a soldier. How the heck you ever thought fast enough to navigate a Mosquito I'll never know. Now, let's go."

"You first," said Malmesbury. "You have a talent for this sort of thing, old boy."

Lebrac smiled sourly.

"Flattery will get you nowhere."

Room by room, they did the rounds of the silent, deserted old farmhouse. Plainly, others had been there before them but not just to cook a fowl casually stolen from the barnyard or to sleep a transient night. Books and linen, clothes and cutlery, even jars of preserved fruit from past harvests had been tipped onto the floors of the abandoned rooms and kicked and trampled in the hunt for loot. Tommy was glad that none of the women of the household had stayed in the farmhouse. The senseless vandalism would have broken their hearts. Any women's hearts.

"Pretty stupid, isn't it?" Tommy said to Malmesbury.

The young navigator, lanky-legged as a colt in the blue German shorts, nodded.

"Not my idea of fun," he said.

The Kotzdorf farm, its looted and pillaged cupboards and drawers agape, was utterly deserted that evening. Or so it seemed by the time that Lebrac declared himself satisfied with his search.

Although it was against all his declared principles as the British man-of-confidence at Stalag IV J, Tommy had to admit that it was almost like being home again as the French Canadian quickly got a fire roaring in the stove, with much solemn sniffing at the fowl bubbling and simmering in the black iron pot without which he never traveled a single kilometer. In the flickering light of a candle wedged in a bottle, Malmesbury was humming contentedly as he laid big clean plates and shining cutlery on the kitchen table. Tommy noticed that the door leading to the empty, pillaged rooms upstairs was still open and he closed it.

"Jolly good idea," said Malmsbury. "I don't like dining with ghosts."

Lebrac kicked shut the door to the barnyard.

"Nor that guy outside in the barn."

"You know," said Tommy, "we should do something about him."

"Like what?" said the Canadian, irritably. "So there's a dead Kraut in the barn. There's dead Krauts, dead Russkis, dead Limeys, dead Canucks, dead Yanks lying around all over Germany. Not just Germany, either. All over. You name it, Europe's got it. That's the way a war goes. Jesus, I don't know. You wild-blue-yonder boys of the air force should never have left home. You want to do something for that poor slob in the barn, you go find yourself a shovel."

After they had eaten—with due appreciation by Malmesbury and Tommy of the miracles which the French Canadian had wrought with a tough old barnyard hen, some herbs, an onion and some greenish potatoes—Lebrac settled back in a creaking chair with his heels on the stove top, belching contentedly to himself. While Malmesbury was washing up and carefully stowing the plates and the knives and the forks back in the big dresser, Tommy went out to get some more firewood. After the cozy firelight of the kitchen, it was dark in the silent square of the barnyard. Tommy avoided the black open door of the barn where the dead German civilian lay spread-eagled in the straw. Beyond the barn and the stables, there was an orchard with trees holding bare, supplicant arms out against the northern sky where, like summer lightning, the fires and explosions of the massed Russian artillery were flickering and glowing above the dark cheek of the horizon. South, where Konev's divisions were swarming along the Elbe toward Czechoslovakia, a glow of fires on the underbelly of the overcast marked the uneasy battle line which had swept over and liberated Stalag IV J at Hohenleipisch. West, between the Kotzdorf farm and a distant England, where the snug and friendly pubs would have opened for another night of warm beer and crowded companionship, lay the twilight zone bounded by the Elbe and the Mulde, the cautious meeting ground of Russians and Americans as the two great fronts in Europe rumbled closer together. A pleasantly pastoral land by day, it was a corridor of stealthy fear at night as a desperate, two-way traffic of fighting or fleeing German troops ran the gantlet of Russian patrols while the Wehrmacht hurried north to the relief of besieged Berlin or retreated south toward the mountain fastnesses of the Erz Gebirge. In the east, behind the high stone wall of the Kotzdorf farm, beyond the silent, cowering village and thousands more like it in Saxony and Silesia, was the tide of plodding, grimy, dusty, dirty, cheerful, friendly or sullen Russians still surging westward to the Elbe.

Kotzdorf, thought Tommy, was a place he never wanted to see again after this night.

With a load of pickets ripped from a fence, Tommy started back to the farmhouse. Even in April, the nights were still cold in Saxony once the sun had gone down, and he was eager for the warmth of the fire. For no other reason than that he anticipated that the Canadian might be expecting him to do it, Tommy walked into the barn on his way back to the kitchen. He thought at first that his eyes were taking longer than he had expected to adjust to the darkness inside, but after he had held a lighted match high above his head, he could no longer deny the truth of what he could see. Or could not see. The dead German was no longer there. The body was gone.

The kitchen, when Tommy pushed open the door and dropped the pickets by the stove, was a haven of cozy security. Lebrac was pragmatically undisturbed by Tommy's announcement that the body in the barn had vanished.

"The local folk must have done the right thing by him," he said. "There's a graveyard right by the church, farther down the village street. That's where he'd be now."

"The body in the barn," said Malmesbury. "It sounds like one of those appalling plays we used to do at school. Just the same, I didn't hear anybody moving around out there in the yard."

"One thing's for sure," said Lebrac. "Herr Engelhöffer wouldn't have been making too much noise. How's that coffee coming?"

Malmesbury, who had been fussing at the stove, filled the cups with an ersatz but fairly palatable brew of barley coffee.

Critically the Canadian sipped at it.

"You could have used a little more salt, old buddy."

They were silent for a while, watching the fire glowing in the stove. The kitchen windows rattled gently to the distant rumbling of the guns in Berlin. Once, from somewhere in the direction of the Jägerswald forest, near Galgenstein, an automatic weapon cackled insanely and then silenced.

"Schmeisser," said Lebrac, carefully rolling tobacco in a tiny square of paper from an old issue of the North German edition of the *Völkischer Beobachter* which had served them as a tablecloth. "Bloody good weapon, the Schmeisser. And the Krauts know how to use it."

A single shot cracked, ringing like a bell in the frosty night.

"Russki carbine," said the Canadian, cocking his head toward the window. "And just as well, too. I'd sure as hell hate for an SS patrol to walk in here right now."

They were sitting back puffing cautiously at the evil-smelling cigarettes rolled by Lebrac when they heard the piano. Somewhere in the farmhouse somebody was playing a piano.

Lebrac brought his boots down from the stove with a thud that rattled the cups on their hooks in the cupboard.

"That's coming from upstairs."

The Canadian reached for the axe with which he had split the wooden pickets for the stove.

"Hang on," said Malmesbury, listening to the music and humming to himself. Then he nodded.

"It's a Nazi marching song," he said. "I forget the name."

Tommy recognized it, too. He'd first heard it sung by shirt-sleeved, sunburned German panzer troops riding lightheartedly on a westbound freight train with their Tiger tanks lashed down to the rocking flatcars.

A chair bounced and clattered on the tiled floor of the kitchen as Lebrac lurched onto his feet.

"Let's go," he said. "This is crazy. A Russki combat area and there's some nut upstairs playing Nazi marching songs!"

With the handle of the axe tucked into his gut like the butt of a Tommy gun, he was suddenly gone from the kitchen and mounting the staircase in great silent leaps long before Malmesbury and Tommy caught up with him, the melody of the German marching song drowning any noise they made.

The piano was in what had been, before looters had slashed the chintz cushions and scuffed muddy boots on the deep carpet, a pleasant living room with a view that looked out over the farm and the village toward the feudal, unfenced strips of the von Bluckau fields of Kotzdorf and the dark and distant ramparts of the tangled Jägerswald.

In the gloom of the upstairs landing, Tommy and Malmesbury waited as Lebrac reached for the porcelain knob of the closed door. The music was loud and impassioned with the arrogance of its composer. If they're SS men in there, thought Tommy, the Canadian had better be bloody quick with the axe.

With explosive violence, Lebrac suddenly kicked open the door, jumping into the room with the axe swung back over his shoulder.

"*Stille!*" he roared and then stopped in his tracks, the axe still poised.

"Well, what do you know," he said wonderingly. "Jack and Jill!"

Looking past him from the doorway, Tommy saw first the yellow light of a hurricane lamp and then the children, a boy and a girl, sitting at the piano. The music had not stopped. The children were still playing, straight-backed and looking stiffly in front of them. A duet of defiance with an undertone of madness. They did not look up, even as the three men walked toward them. The two ash-blond heads, the boy's cropped short, did not move. They had no sheets of music, but they played the pompous marching tune very well, ennobling it almost with a kind of desperate pride.

In careful German, Tommy spoke slowly to the boy, raising his voice against the crash of chords.

"Why are you playing that march?"

The boy, about ten, and the girl, a little younger, might both have been deaf. Like two puppets they played on. The room was cold. In the shadows where the lamp could not shine, broken glass from a window splintered under the boots of the three men.

"What are your names?" Tommy said with gentle persistence. "Do you live here?"

On and on went the tune, over and over again, maddening in its repetition. Patiently Tommy questioned the children, but they would not or could not answer.

Irresolute, for once, in the face of a situation that could not be resolved by force of arms or bold enterprise, Lebrac stood embarrassed, fumbling with the axe.

"Put that bloody thing down," said Malmesbury. "They're probably scared stiff and I don't blame them. You look like you just jumped out of a cave."

"What's with them?" said Lebrac, leaning the axe against a brocaded chair. "Maybe they're in shock? Bomb-happy?"

"Could be," said Tommy. "The poor little devils."

He turned to the boy again.

"You'll have the Russkis in here if you keep on playing that," he said.

The reaction was disconcerting but effective. Two pairs of lithe young hands smashed down on the keys in a jangle of discord. The two blond heads turned toward the shattered window where flowered curtains and muslin stirred in the night breeze.

"I think you got through to them," said Lebrac. "You just said the magic word—Russkis."

In the silence of the old farmhouse, deeper than ever now that the children were no longer playing their piano, something creaked downstairs; then there was a crash and the skelter of running feet.

"It's in the kitchen," said Malmesbury, but the Canadian was gone, grabbing the axe as he sprinted out across the landing and back down the dark stairs. While Malmesbury and Tommy followed him, the children started on the piano again; faster and louder this time but still the maddening repetition of the same tune. The kitchen, when they got there, was empty. On the floor, to one side of the table, though, a trap door had been flung back, overturning a chair. The door to the yard was wide open. Lebrac had disappeared.

"There we were," said Malmesbury, "sitting around eating the farmer's chicken and worrying about the SS, and all the time there was somebody under the damned floor." Nervously he added, "What's happened to Lebrac?"

They found the Canadian outside in the yard. He was talking in halting German to a slim, womanly figure in slacks. She was speaking softly, almost whispering, as the Canadian walked her back to the kitchen.

"She was heading for the cellar," Lebrac explained. He sat her down by the red glow of the stove and for a long while she wept quietly while the men waited. Like most German women during the war, she was wearing no lipstick or make-up but there was a quality of beauty about the broad brow, the high cheekbones and the wind-browned skin. Even under the stress of the emotions which were racking her, there was a generosity of mouth and a serenity in the wide blue eyes.

The woman sobbed quietly, one hand clenched in the pocket of a zippered ski jacket and the other brushing at mud caked on her corduroy slacks. There was more mud, wet and shining, on her heavy ski boots and Tommy wondered what she had been doing.

Gratefully she drank the coffee which Malmesbury with grave courtesy had poured for her. Lebrac held a match for her after he had produced a hoarded Lucky from his baggy jump jacket.

To reassure her, Tommy tried a few words in his halting, half-learned German.

"We are British," he said. "There are no Russkis here in the house."

"I knew that," she said. "Thank God."

Surprised both by her English and her ready recognition of their nationality, the men stared at her with interest."

"My husband was a journalist," she said. "We lived in London once. Years ago, before the Nazis."

"So you speak good English," said Lebrac. He nodded toward the yard door of the kitchen.

"What were you doing out there?"

The woman looked at him, at the Homburg hat hanging on a peg by the calendar of a Torgau baker. Then she stared at the fire that Malmesbury was stoking into new life.

"I was burying my husband," she said.

The fire roared exuberantly in response to Malmesbury's coaxing. Out in the dark fields somewhere a lost and unmilked cow bellowed in forlorn protest. Upstairs, Tommy noticed, the children were no longer playing the piano.

"That was him in the barn?" said Lebrac.

The woman nodded, still staring at the fire. Then she looked up again.

"That's his hat, isn't it?"

The Canadian took a long drag at his cigarette, plucking a shred of tobacco irritably from his lip.

"I guess it is, ma'am. And I'm sorry. Real sorry. Not just about the hat. About your husband, I mean."

Looking a little like a boy caught stealing apples, he reached into his jump jacket. He held up the watch, peering at the engraved inscription on the back of it as it swung, glinting in the firelight.

"'Willi Engelhöffer'" he said slowly. "Your husband's, too?"

"Yes," said the woman. "I'm Ulrike Engelhöffer."

"I guess it's yours then," said Lebrac.

"Thank you," said Ulrike. "I'd like it for my son."

She listened to the watch, holding it to her ear. The gold of its metal was only a little brighter than the bun of blond hair drawn back from her brow.

"It's still going," she said. The serene blue eyes widened, but she did not weep.

"I hope you understand, ma'am," said Lebrac. Already there was a diffidence about him now that neither Malmesbury nor Tommy had ever known before. "I never knew your husband. If it hadn't been me with his watch, it would have been the Russkis. But they've got plenty of watches already. In fact, one's got mine, right now. The Cossack son of a bitch. Pardon me, ma'am. That's a fine watch."

"I know," said Ulrike. "I gave it to him as a wedding present."

Lebrac grinned. The ugly, irrepressible grin that Malmesbury and Tommy knew best.

"I'm glad you got it back," he said.

Passing her more coffee and another precious Lucky Strike, the Canadian sat forward. The big raw hands grasped the tight, threadbare knees of his battle-dress trousers.

"Suppose you just tell us what's going on around here?"

"We're liberated prisoners of war," Tommy added quietly. "Now we just want to get home. We get a little jumpy when people start popping in and out of cellars."

Ulrike smiled for the first time since they had brought her into the kitchen.

"I can understand that. I'm on the run myself."

"With the Russkis," said Tommy. "I can't blame you. They even scare us."

"Not the Russkis," said Ulrike. She was no longer smiling. "You lose a war, you must expect hard times for a while. Until things get back to normal. It wasn't the Russkis we were running from."

The Canadian's chair creaked. He was an impatient man and he had an instinct for trouble.

"Who the hell were you on the run from, then, ma'am?"

"Germans," said the woman. "Just Germans."

"SS?" said Lebrac quickly. Although it would have surprised him to know it, the paratrooper had a compulsive neurosis about the SS. Memories of the men with the cabalistic death's-head insignia grinning on their caps and uniform lapels crowded his mind blackly whenever he thought about what had happened to the rest of his platoon after they had been captured at Arnhem.

"Not the SS," said Ulrike. "The Fehme."

"That's a new one," said Malmesbury gloomily. Already he was eager for the dawn and the return of sanity with the rising of the sun.

"That's just about what it is," said Ulrike. "A new SS. An underground SS. A kind of Nazi resistance movement."

Malmesbury groaned, moodily stirring the barley coffee bubbling in its pot.

"If I ever get home again after this, I'll never complain about a wet English Sunday afternoon. A new SS? You must be kidding."

"Suppose," said Lebrac, "suppose you start right in at the beginning and tell us just what goes on, ma'am. But, first of all, how come you knew we were British before we came after you down here?"

"The children," said Ulrike. "I had an arrangement with the children."

Lebrac looked surprised. Also a little embarrassed. It's just not my day, he thought.

"Not those two upstairs? They're yours?"

Ulrike nodded, almost smiling.

"Günther and Gerda, bless them."

"I guess we may have scared them," said the Canadian apologetically. "We didn't mean to. We went up there to stop whoever it was playing that tune on the piano. We didn't want the Russkis joining the party. They don't like German marching songs. Anyway, we busted in. I had an axe."

He reached for the pot of coffee.

"You never know, these days."

"I wouldn't worry about it too much," said Ulrike. "The children have seen worse than that these past weeks. They were playing that tune for a reason. It was 'Wir Fahren gegen England' –'We Are Marching against England.' It was the signal to me that we had British visitors. Children can come and go without questions, even in times like these, and they were my lookouts, my sentries if you like. It was like a kind of game for them. They have had to play some strange games since we left home."

"This is not your home, then?" said Tommy.

"No, we came from Elsterwalde, farther east."

"I still don't understand," said Lebrac slowly. "Suppose Frau Engelhöffer starts right in at the beginning. I know you've had a rough day, ma'am, but if there's going to be any more trouble, I'd like to know just what kind."

"I don't mind," said Ulrike. "It's something to be able to talk to somebody sane like yourselves. You're like people from another world. I suppose it all began with the July twentieth plot."

"The officer plot?" said Malmesbury.

"It was bigger than that," said Ulrike.

Lebrac was suddenly interested.

"You mean the Germans who tried to knock off Hitler?"

The woman was puzzled.

"Pardon?"

"He means the people who tried to assassinate Hitler," Tommy explained.

Ulrike nodded, smiling faintly at the Canadian's unfamiliar idiom.

"Were you and your husband conspirators?" said Lebrac. Since the liberation of the camp at Hohenleipisch, he had listened skeptically to many German civilians protesting their hatred of the Nazi regime.

"No," said Ulrike. "Not really. We were sympathizers but not active conspirators. Sympathetic enough to conspire to hide Willi's brother with us when he was on the run from the Gestapo. Even if we had turned him away when he came to Elsterwalde, it would have made no difference. They were very ingenious in Berlin. They brought in a new law. Sippenhaft. Family guilt. Any relative, close or distant, of an accused convicted by the People's Court was considered to share his guilt and was therefore liable to arrest and prosecution."

"That makes it kind of tough," said Lebrac. "Were you arrested?"

"The police and the local National Socialist officials had cleared out by then," said Ulrike. "They weren't waiting for the Russkis. We thought we were safe so long as I could hide, at least until after the Russian assault troops had moved on out of the town. We had heard what they were like. Then we got the Fehme warning. A sprig of lilac and a note nailed to our door. It said that Willi was a July twentieth conspirator and in the absence of the normal judicial processes of the government of the Third Reich, he would be arrested and tried before a court of honor by the Fehme. So we took the children that night and ran."

"You'll pardon me saying this, ma'am," said the Canadian, more bewildered than suspicious, "but I can't believe you. I know there's a lot of crazy Germans, but they can't be this crazy."

Ulrike shrugged her shoulders, crouched by the stove.

"They followed us," she said. "Day after day, village after village. Today the Fehme men with the sprigs of lilac came to Kotzdorf and they saw Willi walking in the street. He had gone to find bread for the children. They chased him back into the farm here. My God, you don't believe me? Who was that, then, I buried tonight? Without a priest to bless him. Even the priest is dead, the priest who refused to betray Willi's brother's confession after he became a Catholic convert. The priest we came to for help. The Gestapo had even taken him."

With a sudden violence of grief, Ulrike buried her face in her hands, sobbing distractedly while the stove's warm glow dried the mud on her ski boots, the mud of her husband's grave behind the barn.

"Frau Engelhöffer," said Lebrac, "when we take off out of here in the morning, you and the children had better come with us. It sounds like a lousy joke, but we've got a hearse out there with enough gas to get to Torgau on the Elbe. Once I've fixed the radiator."

Ulrike was smiling when she looked up.

"You gentlemen are very kind," she said. "For Günther's and Gerda's sakes I will accept your offer. Hearse or no hearse. Your company on the journey will be more than enough. Even the Fehme would surely hesitate to make trouble for British soldiers."

"I hope you're right," said Malmesbury. "We'll get cracking at dawn. This place gives me the creeps. Where will you and the children sleep?"

"Upstairs. If there is any trouble during the night, there is a way out for them through the window and over the downstairs roof to the orchard. They know what to do if I cannot go with them. We have friends in the village who will take care of them."

"Fair enough," said Lebrac. "If we keep the front door bolted and barricaded, the only way in is through the kitchen here, which is where we'll be. Folks who come visiting will have to get past us first. That way you'll get some warning."

The French Canadian yawned, stretching back with his hands gripped together behind his neck. He yawned and pleasurably wriggled his toes inside the Yank combat boots for which he had traded half a loaf of black bread during the famine months before the camp at Hohenleipisch was liberated. The situation at last seemed to be under control and that was the way he liked it.

"Let's hit the sack," he said. "We got a busy morning coming up. How about it, Frau Engelhöffer? Let's round up those kids of yours."

"They're here," said Ulrike. "Right behind you."

The three men had been sitting in a half-circle facing Ulrike in a rocking chair by the stove. When they turned around, the children were standing at the door that led upstairs. Like two stark-eyed, white-faced little apparitions they were waiting in the shadows. As they moved forward, the fire's glow glinted on Gerda's hair. It was as golden fair as her mother's but plaited and ribboned. In his right hand, Günther was gripping what looked like a chocolate Easter egg.

For the first time since Arnhem, the French Canadian felt the sudden thrill and nausea that danger at arm's length always gave him, an almost physical sensation of being punched in the gut.

"The kid's got a grenade," he said.

Now that Tommy looked harder, he could see it was a Wehrmacht grenade in Günther's hand. With the collapse of organized German resistance in the area, jettisoned grenades were as common as pine cones along some of the roads of westward retreat.

"This is ridiculous," said Malmesbury. "I knew the Volkssturm was recruiting them young, but this is absolutely ridiculous."

"Just shut up," said Lebrac. "This isn't funny. How long have they been standing there, ma'am?"

"About ten minutes," said Ulrike. "I must apologize. It is just a precaution. Günther has had to grow up quickly in the last few weeks."

"You can say that again," said Lebrac. "Now, ma'am, would you tell Günther we're all one big happy family here and for him to be a good kid and hand over that grenade. In a stone room like this it could kill the lot of us."

Ulrike spoke to the children and they came shyly closer until they were standing by her near the stove. Hollow-eyed and shivering a little, they listened as she spoke to them in soft German until, with a curiously stiff little bow, Günther handed the grenade to the French Canadian.

"That's better," said Lebrac, gently tossing the grenade up and down, hefting the weight in the palm of his hand.

"This just could be right handy," he said and slipped it into his jump-jacket pocket.

"I'm glad we got that sorted out," said Tommy. He would have liked to be back at Hohenleipisch.

"I'll get the children up to bed," said Ulrike. "But before I go, I know I can trust you. There's a bottle of cognac down in the cellar, hidden in the potato bin. Why leave it for the Russkis? Pleasant dreams, gentlemen, and many thanks. My husband would shake your hands."

Solemnly and with extravagant courtesy, the children said good night and then they were gone with their mother, chattering happily as she led them upstairs by candlelight. Watching them go, Tommy felt lonelier than he had ever felt before. Less than three months had passed since he had endured the shock and the anguish which followed the notification, by the International Red Cross, that his wife and children had died during the V-2 bombardment of London. In a totally unexpected way the hardships, the frustrations and the responsibilities of his status as man-of-confidence at Stalag IV J had somehow shielded him against the full emotional impact of the realization of his loss. The sight of Ulrike and her children going up to bed, though, brought home to him, as no other circumstance had done before, a sudden and utter awareness that there was absolutely nothing left of his former life. He wondered if this explained his preoccupation with the welfare of the liberated prisoners marooned in the camp at Hohenleipisch. They were all a part of the past to which he was still clinging, a past interred in half an acre of burned and broken bricks in London. For this reason, he realized, it was important that he should finish what he had begun when he had started his lonely walk to Torgau. Tommy slowly shook his head as he watched the German woman and her children going upstairs to bed.

"And we thought we had troubles," he said.

The French Canadian put an arm around his shoulder. Although he knew Tommy's family had died, he had never commented on the news and Tommy had never sought his or anybody's sympathy.

"Let's go, old buddy," said Lebrac. "Where's that cognac?"

After they had stoked up the stove for the night they settled back, relishing the fire and the strength of the cognac and prolonging the pleasure of it with cup after cup of hot, black ersatz coffee sweetened with rough, sticky beet sugar, also from the cellar. Lebrac had found a guitar in a village earlier that day, and as they drank with their boots drying against the stove, the paratrooper began to hum, then sing, the haunting, nostalgic French-Canadian ballads which he had learned as a country boy in Quebec.

"Jolly good," said Malmesbury, almost asleep in his chair. "No wonder you never forget them. They're very good. Don't you think so, Tommy?"

Tommy didn't trust himself to speak, for, in the firelight which was their only link with home in the uneasy isolation of the German farm, he had found the folk songs, born of farms and cabins in distant Canada, evocative of all the things he would never know now that his wife and children were dead.

Lebrac plucked restlessly at the guitar, selecting and discarding fragments of tunes remembered and days gone by.

"There's one I haven't played for you yet," he said. "It's my own. I call it 'Liberation Blues.' I've been working at it ever since the Russkis opened the gates. Could you stand it?"

Malmesbury reached for the cognac, noting with satisfaction that the bottle was far from empty.

"Fire away, old boy. On this stuff I could stand anything. Don't wake them upstairs, though. You've scared those kids once already."

"Drop dead," said Lebrac amiably. "I'll keep it down."

In the light of the stove fire, his hand cast a giant, cavorting shadow on the wall as he strummed a curiously plaintive and repetitive melody like a Negro spititual with an underlying beat of marching feet.

"This is the refrain," the French Canadian said and began to sing, staring into the fire:

"The River Elbe flows fast and wide,
How do we get to the other side?
There's one more river to cross, boys,
Just one more river to cross."

Then, drawing the thoughts of the other two men, he sang the verses:

"All the way to the cold North Sea;
Far from the folks we want to see,
Fräulein, Fräulein, tell me please,
Who's that hanging in the tall pine trees?

"Please don't shoot me, I'm just free;
I served my time in the infantry.
The Führer's had it, so have I;
Over the river I must fly.

"The German bread is stiff and black,
So is the body on the long road back.
The crops are green and the fields are mined;
The tears that fall are the German kind.

"The generals make their speeches still;
How's the view from the top of the hill?
Soldier, soldier, dead in the ditch,
German? Russki? Which is which?

"Achtung! Achtung! No planes fly;
Gone are the bombers, gone from the sky.
Who's that screaming like a sow?
The Russians are drunk on the road to Torgau."

Lebrac paused long enough to swig down a cracked cup of cognac.

"Want to hear the rest?"

"It's no lullaby," said Malmesbury. "I'm glad you didn't sing it to Frau Engelhöffer's kids."

"It's a lament," said Lebrac, "not a lullaby."

Almost as if it were alive, the guitar twanged when the French Canadian picked it up again.

"Here we go," he said, pinching out a cigarette before he began to strum and sing again.

"The wire's down and the stalag's free,
What's going to happen to such as we?
Got me a gal in my old town
But Torgau Bridge is blown and down.

"Berlin's burning and the lilac's out;
See how the Cossacks run down a Kraut.
I don't want no Purple Heart,
All I want is a good head start.

"Down by the riverbank, bullets fly;
Back at the stalag, dead guards lie.
Dawn till dark, the prisoners prowl;
All on their own, the farm dogs howl.

"Shake the hand of GI Joe,
East I came but West I'll go;
Down on my knees or any how,
I'll cross the bridge at old Torgau.

"Alles kaputt und alles verboten,
Here on the east bank Russian is spoken.
Don't drink the water, there's a body in the well;
Now the war is over you can all go to hell.

"The River Elbe flows fast and wide,
How do we get to the other side?
There's one more river to cross, boys,
Just one more river to cross."

Lebrac finished with a sudden bravura of jangled chords.

"That's it," he said. " 'The Liberation Blues.' "

"Bloody morbid," said Malmesbury, "but I like it. Another brandy for the troubador?"

The sound of clapping behind them brought Lebrac to his feet, brandy flying from the cup in his hand.

A U.S. Army officer, the brass of a padre's insignia glinting on his lapels, was standing in the kitchen doorway. With him was a sergeant and a PFC. They were carrying Tommy guns.

"Yanks!" said Malmesbury. "Thank Christ. I'm sorry, Reverend, but we've been waiting for the good old U.S. Army to cross the Elbe for days."

"I'm sorry," said the officer in the padre's uniform with the sprig of lilac in one buttonhole. "I must disillusion you. We are not from the good old U.S. Army. We are not Yanks. There are no Amis in the area. I am not a padre. My name is Schrader and I am a Sturmbannführer in the Waffen SS. I regret to interrupt your little concert, to which we listened with much interest, but you are all under arrest."

"Arrest?" said Lebrac. "What for? Who's arresting who?"

"The Fehme," said the SS officer. "You may not have heard, yet, of the Fehme, but you and many other people in Saxony are soon going to hear a lot about the Fehme."

"I've heard plenty, already," said Lebrac, thinking of Ulrike Engelhöffer, "and what I've heard I don't like."

Here we go again, thought Malmesbury. I knew this place was the kiss of death.

Tommy Dart stepped forward smartly as if he were back on parade in the RAF.

"Sturmbannführer,'" he said, "I am Warrant Officer Dart, Royal Air Force. I am the British man-of-confidence at Stalag IV J, Hohenleipisch, and as such I am accredited by the prisoners-of-war administration of the armed forces of the German Government, the Swiss Government and the International Red Cross. I protest against this high-handed and illegal action you propose to take in violation of the terms of the Geneva Convention. I also demand to know for what reason you are arresting us, if that is the appropriate term. Kidnaping would be more to the point."

Schrader smiled, warming his hands at the stove.

"My dear Warrant Officer, you are the very man we particularly wanted to meet. I never dreamed we would ever have the good fortune to come face to face with you. Now, you want reasons. I see that you gentlemen had bread with your supper tonight. Did you pay for that bread? I doubt it. A million Reichmarks would not buy a single loaf of bread in Saxony today. You stole the bread, I suggest."

It had to happen, thought Tommy. The very thing I kept warning the boys about in camp.

"We found the bread," he said. "We went into a bakery with the roof blown off and there was a stale loaf of bread on the floor and we were hungry and we took it and we ate it. Is that stealing?"

Whether or not this was the truth no longer mattered.

"The Fehme regards it as stealing," said Schrader. "Or, more specifically, looting. The three of you will be charged with stealing bread which could have fed a German woman and her children. You have compromised your legal status as military prisoners of war. You are under arrest. You will be tried and sentenced and punished as an example to the disgusting rabble of liberated prisoners of war now terrorizing Saxony. Quickly, now, where is the woman?"

"What woman?" said Lebrac. "You want to start a brothel too, Reverend?"

Without a change of facial expression, the smiling Schrader kicked Lebrac in the groin. The French Canadian fell doubled-up to the floor, groaning and clutching at his testicles.

"I presume she's upstairs," said Schrader. "I have no time to waste."

Quietly and commandingly, he spoke in German to the Fehme man in the uniform of an American PFC, who left them, taking the stairs three at a time. Soon he was clattering back down again but only with the woman, Ulrike.

By then, Tommy and Malmesbury had got Lebrac up onto his feet. The swarthy-complexioned French Canadian was still swearing and cursing with pain, but he was able to stand between the two Englishmen when the Fehme man in the U.S. sergeant's uniform lined them up against the wall. More than anything, Lebrac's grenade worried Tommy. He felt the hard shape of it against his hip as Lebrac shifted painfully on his feet. The Fehme guard was far enough away, at the stove, for them to talk.

"If they search us and find that grenade, we'll be in a lot of trouble," whispered Tommy.

Lebrac, though, was unimpressed.

"What kind of trouble you think we got already?" he said softly. "We're dealing with SS men, old buddy. Not officers and gentlemen. We've got to get out of here before they start getting really rough. I'm going to make a break. Malmesbury's coming. You'd better come, too. I've got it figured out. When I say the word, you just follow me and stay with me. We'll risk the radiator on the hearse. It'll get us far enough away."

"We could be making things a lot worse," said Tommy.

"You make up your own mind, old buddy," whispered Lebrac. "If you want to come, you're welcome."

Worried by the prospect of just what kind of violent action the French Canadian might be planning to let loose, Tommy watched and listened while Frau Engelhöffer talked with Schrader. The children had evidently got away safely, out of the window and over the roof, but the Englishman was puzzled both by Ulrike's quiescent, unemotional attitude and the fact that she also had not escaped.

"You are required to appear before a court of honor," Schrader was saying to her now. "You will be charged with having been an accessory to your husband's complicity in the July twentieth plot against the life of the Führer and the government of the Third Reich."

"I see that I have no alternative," said Ulrike.

Her voice was steady and the gaze of the wide, blue eyes was level and unafraid.

"It is a pity that you could not have extended such a legalistic courtesy to my late husband before your Fehme men murdered him today with their knives."

"These are pressing times, Frau Engelhöffer," said Schrader. "Your husband was tried, convicted and sentenced, in absentia, by the Fehme court of honor. The men with the knives were not murderers. They were sworn members of the Fehme carrying out the sentence of the court of honor."

"Then why bother bringing me before the court?" Ulrike asked. "Was I not also tried in absentia?"

Schrader nodded, fingering the lilac in a buttonhole of his American padre's uniform.

"We were not concerned with you then. We are now. As the British jurists have it, justice shall not only be done but shall also be seen to have been done."

"You mean," said Ulrike, "the court wishes to make an example of me?"

"You could put it that way," said Schrader. "This is surely the function of most trial proceedings, particularly courts of honor in the old Germanic tradition?"

"So be it, then, Sturmbannführer," said Ulrike. "Could you oblige me with the courtesy of a cigarette?"

Tommy found himself astounded by the woman's attitude toward Schrader. Not so much her calmness as her shrugged acquiescence with the demand that she be tried by the peers of the men who had stabbed her husband to death. Tears he would have expected. Or rage. Hysteria certainly, but not this casual compliance with the inevitable. Maybe, he thought, it was to this sickeningly abject state that a decade of Nazi government and indoctrination was capable of reducing intelligent people. Watching the blond, boyish, petulant-faced young SS officer holding a match for Ulrike's cigarette, Tommy puzzled over the enigma of the German race. They look like us, he thought, but they don't think or act like us or anybody else on earth. What makes them tick?

Tommy had no more time for mentally debating the question so often discussed in the camp at Hohenleipisch, for Lebrac was whispering urgently.

"Tell them there's coffee in the big iron pot on the stove," he said.

Uneasily, for he knew that the explosively belligerent French Canadian would just as soon have emptied the scalding contents of the pot over his captors' heads, Tommy spoke to the nearest German guard who nodded and grinned. Slowly he set out three cups on the table and walked to the stove.

"That's it, old buddy," whispered Lebrac, watching the Fehme man. "Just keep going like that."

Instinctively Tommy braced himself but for what he did not know nor did he like to think.

"Lift it off, you dumb Kraut bastard," the French Canadian whispered, lips barely moving. Tommy could feel him tensing, shifting imperceptibly on his feet.

As the guard lifted the pot of steaming coffee, Tommy noticed the round, red glow of the fire where they had earlier taken out the circular, cast-iron stove lid.

Beside him, he could feel Lebrac's elbow moving as he held his hands behind his back.

Suddenly then the French Canadian was holding the German grenade out in front of him with his right hand. In the left hand, between thumb and forefinger, he was holding the pin.

The Fehme men stood stock-still like open-mouthed statues.

"Granate!" shouted Lebrac. "Achtung!"

Lunging forward, he tossed the grenade toward the glowing hole in the top of the stove. It fell with a metallic clang, into the heart of the coals.

"Let's go!" screamed the French Canadian. With Malmesbury, he sprang for the kitchen door and the open yard in the darkness beyond. Turning to follow Lebrac, Tommy felt his boots slip clumsily from beneath him. As he fell, rolling desperately toward the open cellar trap, he saw that Ulrike, Schrader and one of the Fehme guards were already cannoning down the steps ahead of him. Only the guard with the pot of coffee was still standing, gaping foolishly at the stove.

From the cellar, the sound of the grenade exploding in the confined space of the stone-walled kitchen was more like the wicked, booming crack of an artillery shell. Crouched in the cellar, Tommy listened to shards of metal buzzing like infuriated wasps and ringing against the stone walls. A blazing brand of wood flailed down into the cellar. In a brief, shocked moment of lucidity Tommy recognized it as one of the pickets he had wrenched from the orchard fence and later fed to the fire.

Schrader got to his feet. He was holding a Luger. Tommy stared at its ugly snout. I knew it would come to this, he thought. After all those years behind the wire it has to be like this.

"Upstairs," said Schrader. "Quick. Or I kill you now."

Stumbling through the smoke and the flames, Schrader and the surviving Fehme man herded Tommy and Ulrike out into the yard in time to see the hearse backing wildly out of the stable, headlights blazing. Tommy recognized the crouched silhouette of Lebrac, burly at the wheel. Malmesbury was beside him. Lebrac braked and then violently accelerated, tires screeching and skidding as he wrenched the hearse around in a half-circle. Then Schrader cut loose with the Fehme man's Tommy gun. The shots went wild as Lebrac roared toward the gate and the village road beyond. Even without water, thc engine should get them as far as the woods, thought Tommy. Once they were in the Jägerswald they had a chance. Then a man was standing squarely in the gateway in the glare of the headlights from the oncoming hearse. He was holding what looked like a great big club.

"Feuer!" Schrader shouted. "Feuer!"

As the man knelt, raising the weapon to his shoulder, Tommy recognized it as a Panzerfaust, the German infantry weapon which, handled expertly and calmly, could stop and kill even a Russian T-34 tank.

"Down," said Schrader, shouldering Tommy and Ulrike to the cobblestones. Crouched against the farmhouse wall, Tommy heard a giant, hissing sigh as the Panzerfaust warhead rocketed straight at the radiator of the oncoming hearse. The blast of the explosion jerked him against the wall and smashed every window overlooking the farmyard. Out of the night a strange rain of metallic objects rattled haphazardly on the cobblestones. A wheel landed near him and then went bounding grotesquely away in the darkness. When he looked up again all that was left of the hearse was what seemed like an untidy ring of old iron and rubbish smoldering in the light of the burning, twisted fuel tank. The flames illuminated what Tommy took to be a heap of clothing until it jerked spasmodically and he recognized the camouflage pattern of Lebrac's jump jacket. It was burning as was the hair on his head.

The man who had fired the Panzerfaust walked slowly forward into the circle of light. Carefully he inspected what lay there.

"Kaputt," he called. "Alles fertig."

Schrader stood up, brushing mud from the knees of his American uniform.

"Your foolish friends are dead," he said to Tommy. "Turn around."

He pushed the Tommy gun gently against the back of the Englishman's head. The snout of steel was still warm from firing.

"I could take your head off like a rotten pumpkin," Schrader said. "Just remember that. The Fehme is not to be confused with the German Red Cross. Now you will bury our comrade."

After Tommy had dug the grave and they had buried the flash-burned, ash-blackened Fehme corpse from the kitchen, Schrader had looked at his watch and nodded.

"Now we go to Galgenstein," he said. "The court of honor must not be kept waiting."

They walked out into the fields then in single file, the flames of the burning farmhouse at Kotzdorf throwing their shadows before them across the soggy furrows and the rotting, frost-blackened stubble. Before dawn they had come to the Elbe and crossed its dark waters by a river skiff hidden in the reeds, and so Warrant Officer Thomas Dart, Royal Air Force, had come, with Ulrike Engelhöffer of Elsterwalde, to the cellars of Schloss Galgenstein.

Now the solemn mockery of trial was over and the court president with the immaculate uniform of the German army, the sightless eyes and the proud, intelligent face was asking him if he had anything to say before sentence was passed on him.

Krausnick, the disbarred lawyer and turncoat Communist now become an advocate for neo-Nazi terror and blackmail, had prosecuted the case against Tommy with a fanaticism born of fear, flecks of spittle coagulating at the corners of his narrow mouth as he led his witnesses through their evidence. The plundered farms. The pillaged cottages. The looted shops. The raped and frantic women. The wandering children, fighting for the crusts they found in gutters. A waking nightmare of anarchy in a countryside through which the liberated prisoners of the stalag at Hohenleipisch prowled like jackals in the wake of the Red Army after it had invaded Saxony and freed them. Climaxing his denunciation, Krausnick had pointed at Tommy, shouting his hatred until the dark cellars rang with the echoes of his voice. Then he had spoken almost in a whisper.

"The accused," he said, "is not only one of these brigands who were so recently prisoners of war of the Third Reich. He was one of their leaders, responsible for their correct and honorable conduct. As the man-of-confidence at Stalag IV J, Hohenleipisch, he accepted a position of trust under the terms of the Geneva Convention. Every one of us here needs only to go back to what is left of our homes and possessions to see how negligently and cynically this so-called man-of-confidence has failed the trust reposed in him. I submit to you, gentlemen of the Fehme and to the jury of this court of honor, that this accused is guilty of the charge on which he stands arraigned. In the interests of German honor and as an example to those who would defile it, I urge you to find the accused guilty as charged."

The twelve Freischoffen of the jury had needed little urging. Each man, with his family, had suffered the shock of invasion and endured the chaos of defeat in a once-familiar countryside where the German word was no longer law and where, in fact, there was no law at all but the law of survival. They had found Tommy guilty, hanging around his neck the burden of responsibility for acts of haphazard violence committed upon the community of Saxony by the outriders of a vast and truculent host of prisoners precipitately released from camps, farms, mines, quarries, mills and factories.

So now, thought Tommy, he was being asked if he had anything to say, as if he had been indeed the subject of an inquiry by a fair and constitutional process of law.

For a moment, the habitual apathy of spirit engendered by years of confinement behind the rusted wire of Hohenleipisch almost submerged his will to resist. Then he thought of Lebrac and Malmesbury and the stupid, senseless way they had had to die after their first few days of freedom.

"The court is waiting," said von Bluckau.

"I do have something to say," said Tommy. "I am a regular airman in the service of the Royal Air Force. I was captured in action during the course of my duties as an air gunner. As man-of-confidence at Stalag IV J, Hohenleipisch, I faithfully discharged my responsibilities until the day the camp was liberated by Russian forces. After that it was a practical impossibility for me to control or discipline the prisoners in the camp. With the departure of the German commandant and his staff and the arrival of a Russian commander, I no longer had any jurisdiction of any kind. The solution, as I saw it, was for me to see the Russian authorities at Torgau and arrange for transportation of prisoners from Stalag IV J across the Elbe and into the American lines. This was where I was going until I was arrested by the Fehme, if you could call it arrest. The court has alleged I was a party to the stealing of a loaf of bread at Kotzdorf. This I admit. Having endured starvation inside Stalag IV J as a prisoner of war, I certainly did not intend to starve outside the camp as a free man. I believe this court, however, to be illegal and I intend so to report at the earliest possible opportunity to the senior officer of the first British or American unit to which I report after leaving here."

Patiently von Bluckau heard the Englishman out. The air was heavy with the fragrance of the sprigs of lilac in the lapels of the Fehme men who crowded the cellar. Lilacs and the spring, thought von Bluckau. Lilacs and the Fehme. What a difference a winter could make.

"Warrant Officer Dart," said von Bluckau, speaking slowly for the benefit of the interpreter, "I have listened carefully to your statement. You should know that I, too, am a professional soldier. I am, until this war ends, a general of the German army. You spoke, and reasoned, with military correctness. This I recognize and appreciate. However, in Germany today and more particularly in Saxony, the time for military correctness is past. This has been conclusively demonstrated by both the Russians and many of your liberated comrades. An example must be made and the making of examples is a function of this court of honor and the Fehme which it represents. With the authority vested in me as President of this court and as a Freigraf of the Fehme, I order that you be not put to death as would a German looter but detained as a hostage in the custody of the Fehme. This sentence will be promulgated by word of mouth, by printed pamphlet and by public broadcast on transmissions of the Fehme radio station in Saxony, Werewolfsender."

The general sat back, shoulders squared, aloof in the lonely world behind his dark glasses.

"Remove the prisoner. Proceed with the next case, Mr. Prosecutor."

Krausnick bowed, fingering the sprig of lilac in his lapel.

"Frau Ulrike Engelhöffer," he said.

The name echoed and re-echoed as it was called and iron keys jangled as a Fehme guard hurried to her cell.

IV
The Editor's Widow

Among the waiting ranks of Fehme men there was an undertone of comment and a leaning forward of heads as the indictment of Ulrike Engelhöffer began, for the wife of the Elsterwalde newspaper editor had not been unknown in the Galgenstein district.

There was some surprise, even disappointment, that the woman showed neither fear before the court nor any sorrow arising from the Fehme's execution of her husband, a circumstance which had already been broadcast by Werewolfsender and passed on by word of mouth.

Ulrike sensed this feeling of the court as Krausnick began to outline the case against her, and she found some satisfaction in her knowledge of the reaction she had aroused. These play-acting potato diggers, she thought. If only they knew how she welcomed every second of her arraignment before the court, remembering every face and mentally noting every name she could. Collectively they had murdered her husband and now there they were, in their smug ranks, all ready for identification.

For Willi's sake, and for the children's, this could be a time of trial well spent. It had been a dark and terrible road to it, though, beginning with the night that Heinrich, Willi's brother, had come silently to them in the old home overlooking the river at Elsterwalde.

Talented and quick-witted, Heini enjoyed an impeccable National Socialist record, which had smoothed the course of his career as a journalist with the Ministry of Propaganda. By 1939 he was one of Dr. Goebbels' bright young men. With the war came new laurels to adorn his reputation and prestige, for during the blitzkrieg that smashed through Belgium and Holland into France and, later, in Russia, Heini had been decorated for heroism and devotion to duty while serving with front-line Propaganda Korps units recording the triumphs of German arms.

"Not bad for a typewriter trooper!" he had declared, visiting them in Elsterwalde with yet another medal from the hand of the Führer and new orders returning him from the East Front to an administrative post in the ministry offices at Berlin.

It was during that summer of 1944 that Ulrike and Willi had noticed the change in Heini. It was no transient mood. Nor was it due simply to his being back in civilian clothes with more work and more responsibility. He visited them less at Elsterwalde and when he came, there was less laughter than in the old days. Once, when Willi had jestingly asked him who was the little lady who must have been taking up all his time in Berlin between infrequent visits to Elsterwalde, Heini had flushed and angrily told his brother to mind his own business. He had apologized, of course, with a flash of his old charm and spirit, but then had fallen silent again until it was time to take the local train that connected at Falkenberg with the express from Dresden to Berlin. Willi had been quiet, too, for the two brothers had always been close to each other but now, beyond doubt, their relationship was strained.

"Something's wrong with Heini," he had said to Ulrike after the express had sped away, dwindling between a long perspective of marching pines as it ran the gantlet of the American and British fighter-bombers that had begun to prowl the Reichsbahn system in central Germany.

"I wonder what it is?" said Ulrike. "Something's worrying him."

Willi had run a finger around the inside of his collar. It had been a long hot summer's day in Saxony. A day for drowsing in the shade of the pines.

"I hate to think," he had said.

They had not had to wait long, for soon it was July 20 and there were the blazoned headlines in the Leipzig newspapers offering a million marks for information leading to the arrest of Goerdeler, a former mayor of Leipzig and now, suddenly, a hunted conspirator in the plot which had abortively sought to assassinate Adolf Hitler and seize power from the National Socialist government of the Third Reich. Soon after that, Heini had visited them again and they had been disturbed by his appearance. Overnight, it seemed, he was older, thinner and more than ever nervously preoccupied with unspoken thoughts that kept him pacing his bedroom until the early hours of the morning. During the day he slumped in a chair, listening interminably to the radio and starting up quickly whenever the telephone shrilled, which was often, since he was in the home of a provincial newspaper proprietor and editor.

"My God, it's terrible in Berlin," he said one evening, pushing aside the thick pea soup which Ulrike had made, knowing how much he had always enjoyed it.

"You mean the air raids?" said Willi.

"No, I don't mean the air raids," said Heini. Irritably, he added, "Forget it."

Only after Heini had returned to Berlin, reluctantly and with none of his former obvious pleasure in his work, did Ulrike find the discarded Leipzig daily with little crosses penciled alongside the names of July 20 conspirators who had been convicted of treason by the People's Court in Berlin and sentenced to death by the implacable Judge Freisler.

"Did you mark these?" Ulrike asked Willi when he came home from the office that night, grumbling about the quality of the rationed newsprint he was getting for his presses.

"No," he said. "That's Heini's writing."

They had looked at each other then, saying nothing, and she had silently brought him his coffee.

Going to bed, she had found no sleep and shortly before dawn, troubled by her fears that Heini was implicated in the July 20 plot, she had found that Willi also was awake.

"Sorry," she whispered. "Did I wake you?"

"I haven't been asleep," he said.

Ulrike turned toward him, trying to see his face in the dark. "Heini's mixed up in it, isn't he?"

"I think so."

"Will they get him?"

The bed creaked as Willi put his arm about her, a good strong arm.

"We are not children, you and I. What else can we think? Why should Heini be any luckier than the rest of them?"

She had wept then and Willi had caressed her, gently and constantly, until her nightgown had slipped above her thighs and then their flesh was hot together in a sudden passion of being two together, alone in a dark world of silent and fearful night, and after it was over, Willi had chuckled suddenly.

"At least that's not illegal," he said. "Not even under a Nazi government."

Lighting a cigarette, he had gone to the window overlooking the river meadows beyond the town and drawn the blackout curtain. For a while he stood there watching the predatory groping of distant searchlights on the western horizon. It looked like Leipzig's turn again that night. By the time he got back into the warm and rumpled bed, Ulrike was asleep and he was glad, for he had known she was worrying, and well she might have been. If Heini had been tilting at windmills and was in danger, then so was all the family.

The day brought no news, good or bad. Only the pleasing, familiar smell of fresh-brewed coffee and the excited cries of Günther and Gerda trying out a new kite in the meadow beyond the orchard at the back of the house. Maybe, thought Ulrike, Heini had only owed money or had got one of the Berlin blitz girls into trouble. As the days passed peacefully enough, both Willi and Ulrike relaxed.

Summer slipped into autumn and the apples were red and sweet and then came the winter nights by the great tiled stove with the moonlight sharp and clear on the snow outside. Soon it would be Christmas, of a kind, and there might be a small oasis of warmth and love and security in the grim calendar of all the years of the war. Christmas came, assuredly, and there was the magic of its being to sparkle in the eyes of Günther and his sister. Before the new year of 1945 was a week old, though, on a night of terrible cold with a wind that seared the lungs of late travelers, while ice jams groaned under the bridge across the Elster, Heini came unannounced; not tugging cheerfully at the bell on the front door as had always been his custom but tapping furtively, almost scratching, at a back window.

He barely spoke as they bustled him through the house to stand shivering in the warmth of the stove and then it was just to apologize for the wet earth on his boots.

"What have you been doing?" Ulrike asked. "You're as muddy as a soldier. Have you been on maneuvers?"

Heini looked older than ever and exhausted. It was hard to realize he was Willi's younger brother, by five years. He had not shaved that day and he had the look of a man who had been sleeping in his clothes.

"You could say it was maneuvers," he said and laughed harshly, as a man does at one of life's bad jokes. "I walked across the fields from the station on the main line. I did not want anybody to know I was coming here."

Then it was that Ulrike had known that what she had feared for Heini and Willi and the children was beginning to happen and there could be no end to it all but death.

"There is a warrant out for my arrest," said Heini. "The Gestapo are looking for me. I tried to keep you all out of it but it's too late now. They got someone to talk under interrogation and they know I was in the July twentieth conspiracy. God help us. And God forgive me for what I'm doing to you all."

He had cried then, tears of utter despair, with the snow and the frozen mud of the fields melting on the bright carpet in the room where they all had known so much of life and its happiness.

"I'm sorry," said Heini, "but I've been on the run for days. I welcomed the air raids. It distracted them and made it tougher to pick me up in the shelters and in the underground stations. Then I ran out of money and ration cards and now I'm sick. God, I had to go somewhere. If you could just put me up for a couple of nights."

Willi had put an arm about his shoulder then and Ulrike had knelt to untie the laces of his sodden boots.

"You stay as long as you need," said Willi. "What kind of a brother do you think I am?"

"We can hide you," said Ulrike. "Nobody need know. Nobody could have seen you come to the house."

They had had to tell Günther and Gerda, of course, and they did so that very night, making a kind of game of it as the children giggled and snuggled, wide-eyed, into their pillows, promising to keep the secret of Uncle Heini.

As the days and the nights went by, it seemed that, incredibly, they were succeeding and that Heini would continue to evade arrest until he could get away to Stettin, where arrangements were being made for him to stow away aboard an ore freighter returning to Sweden.

The end, when it came, was such a bitter turn of fate that Ulrike had wondered if God, too, was in league with the Gestapo.

Strong again, if a little pale after weeks of furtive days and nights in his old hiking tent under the gabled roof behind the guest room in the attic, Heini had finally left Elsterwalde with his former high spirits partially restored. He had a rail ticket to Stettin which Willi had quietly bought for him at Falkenberg on the main line. Papers identifying Heini as a Swedish seaman, which had arrived mysteriously in a ministry press release addressed to Willi at his newspaper office, were obviously good enough to get Heini past the train checks en route to the Baltic coast. After the forged identity papers, had come a postcard from an entirely fictitious Aunt Augustina in Stettin, inviting Heini to be present at his equally fictitious cousin's forthcoming wedding in Stettin.

"That's the ship," said Heini. "The *Augustina.* That's the day she sails. They've fixed it for me to get aboard. Once I'm in Stockholm you can all relax."

He had laughed then with a flash of his old gaiety.

"When you get a card from Sweden signed Adolf, you can stop worrying about knocks on the door."

After the best supper that Ulrike could provide from the meager German rations of early 1945, she had packed him more food for his rucksack so that he would not have to risk entering a station restaurant.

Heini had gone that night, as he had come, trudging across the fields and slipping through the woods. By dawn he was in Falkenberg and a few hours later he was waiting for the Berlin express to be signaled in from Dresden.

Out of a blue and smiling summer morning's sky, then, malign fate had intervened in the shape of a small group of fifty American bombers, narrow-winged and double-tailed Liberators, which had been detached from a heavy attack on the Leuna refineries, near Leipzig, to make a diversionary strike on the marshaling yard and rail junction at provincial Falkenberg.

Crouched between the blue-steeled rails which could so easily have carried him on to the port of Stettin and final asylum in neutral Sweden, Heini had been trapped in the pattern of exploding bombs which had gouted inexorably across the peaceful complex of platforms, main lines, sidings, yards, trucks, roundhouses, signal boxes and railwaymen's cottages. Lying wounded and unconscious in a civilian casualty clearing station after the all-clear had gone, Heini was recognized by an air raid warden who had once lived in Elsterwalde before moving to a National Socialist administrative post in Falkenberg. The Gestapo came for Heini that night, and after the gangs of Russian and Polish prisoners had got the main line back into running order, he left for Berlin, under arrest, on the very train for which he had waited so desperately in the morning. The end came quickly after that, for the People's Court was still out for blood. Still lying wounded in a stretcher, he was tried, harangued and convicted. Wounded, he was sentenced to death by the virulent Judge Freisler in his black judicial robes. Wounded, he was lifted in a noose of wire and hanged by the neck from a butcher's hook on a steel rail on the wall of a drab room in the Berlin-Plötzensee jail. His drumming heels kicked much plaster from the wall before his agony ended in death. They came to Elsterwalde then for Willi, and the interrogations at the police office overlooking the pleasant town square where the lilacs were budding had continued long into the night. There was no sleep for Willi when he was questioned by relays of interrogators, fresh with zeal and fired with the anger of the July 20 purge. The truth of the matter was that, despite his brother's implication, Willi had never been involved in the conspiracy which had exploded that July day in the Führer's Wolfsschantze headquarters at Rastenburg. For once the Gestapo had been unable to circumvent the truth of a suspect's statement, to twist it to the lies with which they would confront and condemn him before the People's Court.

It had been like the end of a long nightmare when they released Willi from further questioning and he came home to sit for hours, exhausted, by the stove while Ulrike hushed the children or sent them out to play in the orchard where the first courageous apple blossoms were already putting their faith in the promise of yet another spring. Ulrike had hoped that Willi's release was not just the beginning of some unimaginable new nightmare, for the Gestapo was like some contagious disease, befouling and destroying all that it chanced to touch. The days had passed, though, and the only shock had been the promulgation of the Sippenhaft laws, bearing home to the innocent families of convicted July 20 conspirators the guilt of their blood. There was talk of Sippenhaft camps being established in the Erz Gebirge by the SS, but there was also ominous news from the East Front which could also be a disguised blessing. The Russians, they were saying, would be rolling through the Erz Gebirge long before the Gestapo could fill the camps in the once-joyous mountains south of Dresden. Willi, imperturbable as ever and even more dedicated to his craft as a newspaperman than he had been before, merely shrugged his shoulders and worried happily about getting out the next issue of the *Elsterwalder Kreisblatt.*

The printing presses of Elsterwalde's newspaper, brought from Nuremberg by Willi's grandfather, had first put ink to paper early in the nineteenth century.

Founded in 1817 and later incorporating the *Elsterwalder Zeitung,* the *Falkenberger Nachrichten,* the *Zaundorfer Tageblatt* and the *Galgensteiner Anzeiger,* the once-admired *Elsterwalder Kreisblatt* was, by April 1945, reduced to four tightly set pages in which the true tidings of German despair could only be read between the lines of traditional Gothic type which recorded the daily doctrine according to the latest press releases from the propaganda ministry in Berlin.

Yet, to Willi, it was still his, and the Engelhöffer family's, newspaper; one day, God willing, it would be able to speak with a free and clear voice. Until that day its wheezing but faithful presses would continue to roll and beat, putting the ink to the type and the type to the paper.

Only a matter of days before the American 69th Division battered its way into Leipzig and the Russians stormed across the Oder and the Neisse, the *Elsterwalder Kreisblatt* was published as usual in early April for its readers in Elsterwalde, Falkenberg, Zaundorf, Galgenstein and all the villages between.

On that bright, gin-clear morning of spring, Elsterwalde's district newspaper made grim reading, and if you were a loyal German or even a dedicated National Socialist, the war news was hardly worth the ten pfennigs it cost to buy the *Elsterwalder Kreisblatt.*

There was one remarkable feature of this issue, though. The editorial. Willi had written it the previous night with Ulrike at his side, for, by then, with most of the remaining staff called up for service in the Volkssturm, Ulrike had become his copy boy, reporter, sub-editor and proofreader, while a neighbor's daughter minded the children.

Willi had sat back, taken off his horn-rimmed glasses, rubbed his reddened eyes and swung to and fro in the swivel chair where his father and his grandfather had sat awhile every night after they had put the day's paper to bed; a tired man in shirt sleeves with a good day's work done.

"The Russians have broken through on the Neisse," he said. "They will probably be here tomorrow night. God help Saxony."

"Better them than the Gestapo," Ulrike had said angrily. "To this we Germans are reduced. Safe in the arms of the invader. So long as I can hide until the front troops move on we will be all right."

Willi nodded. Better than Ulrike he knew the pattern of Russian invasion. The captured town flung open to the mercy of the fighting troops who captured it. The pillaging, the looting, the drinking, the raping. In that sequence. Then the order to the infantry to move on and the arrival of the military police, the commissars and, finally, the military government authorities.

"I agree," said Willi, "but just the same, it will be our last issue. After nearly a hundred years. I think I will write an editorial. A real editorial. Like the old days before 1933. Not a party handout from Berlin."

Ulrike frowned, fiddling with the keys of her typewriter.

"Do you think you should, Willi? Even now?"

"Why not? With the Russkis so close, there's not a Gestapo man for miles. Not one capable of running, anyway. The police office has closed down except for that old fool Schmulze. Evacuation of civilians has been officially ordered as from dawn tomorrow. If we stay, we will be living in a ghost town by tomorrow night. There will be nobody left to arrest us."

"I still don't like it," said Ulrike. "But I know what the paper has meant to you and always will mean to you. If you must, you must."

"I must," said Willi. "It's not often that a newspaperman can simultaneously announce the death of his country and the death of his newspaper. This is one leader I must write. We should all have written leaders like it years ago. I'll call it 'The Last Issue.' It's not clever but it's appropriate and you certainly couldn't say that it's not topical. The last issue of a newspaper that's served its readers for a century. The last issue facing every German. To die with National Socialism because a crazy psychopath in Berlin says so or to live for another day, another Germany?"

Afraid as she was, Ulrike could only feel pride for Willi, but it was too late for brave words and she said so because she loved him.

"I know," said Willi. "We all surrendered long ago. And the National Socialists never let us forget it. But is it ever too late for the truth? Was it too late for Christ when they nailed Him to the cross?"

"You know it's never too late," said Ulrike. "That's why I married you. That's why you're the man I love. That's why I'm glad you're the father of my children."

"Let's start, then," said Willi. "It may be the last issue, but that's no reason why it should go to press late."

Pushing aside the litter of galley pulls and page proofs, damp and heavy with the fresh, black ink, he had pulled the typewriter toward him.

"THE LAST ISSUE," he typed and sat there looking at it. A simple heading but a satisfying one.

"I like that," he said.

That night, Ulrike knew, Willi wrote the finest leader, the finest anything, that he had ever written. Pounding at the typewriter in a haze of tobacco smoke and taking as his theme the last issue confronting not just a provincial newspaper editor in Saxony but every German living amid the wreckage of a defeated and dishonored Third Reich, he said everything that he knew he and every other freethinking editor in Germany should have said long before, when there was still time and opportunity to speak in defense of liberty and democracy. It was a sermon in the angry Wittenberg traditions of Martin Luther, the founder of Willi's family faith. It was a call to arms which could once have aroused freedom-loving Germans to stand and fight, to defeat and disband the National Socialists when they still had been only brown-shirted louts fighting on street corners. It was an indictment of himself and every other living German, not for having lost the fight for freedom, but for never having begun it. It was a challenge to every German not to die for Adolf Hitler in a war already lost but to live for a free new Germany built on the ashes of the old.

Sensing, even then, that no good would come of it, yet proud of what was being done, Ulrike read the leader slowly, remembering every word.

When she put it down, Willi was peering intently at her over the tops of his glasses as he had always done as a young reporter when he was anxious for her girlish approval of everything he wrote.

"Well?" he said.

"I'm glad you wrote it," she said simply. "I'm glad you're going to print it. I think it's the best thing you've ever done."

Willi had put his name to it then, carefully printed and with the type face marked so that old Spillmann, the only remaining compositor on the staff, would set it right and true for all to see and read.

"It's little enough to do and it's too late," he said, "but at least it's an act of faith. It might even save some lives."

"Where will you run it?" Ulrike asked.

Willi reached for a page proof.

"Right here," he said, "on page one. Where the ministry people wanted me to run those ridiculous diagrams showing children how to assemble, load and fire Panzerfaust weapons at Russian tanks. Now I think of it, I will open the leader with that. That's what it needs to bring it down to earth."

He reached for the typewriter again and typing with angry speed revised the opening paragraph of the leader.

Punctually, for the last time, the presses rolled that night.

Standing there by the machines in the harsh electric light with the tang of ink and paper all about them, Willi plucked at the first copy to come edging down between the wires of the conveyor. He opened out the front page and there it was, "THE LAST ISSUE," invested with the quality of living significance which print gives to words.

They read it, heads close together.

"I never thought I'd ever see it again in a German newspaper," said Ulrike. "The naked, unashamed, uncompromised truth. I'm awestruck."

Willi nodded, folding the newspaper and slipping it under his arm.

"The best thing I ever wrote. Make that my epitaph."

Ulrike smiled, linking her arm with his.

"That's every newspaperman's epitaph. Let's go home now. I think I'll sleep tonight."

"So will I," said Willi. "Regardless of the Russians. Or the Gestapo. Even if they did come back, which they won't, I've said it at last. In my own way and in my own newspaper."

They went home and they slept and in the morning the village and the countryside beyond were strangely quiet and still, for panic and fear, the scouts of war, had come to every door in Elsterwalde as the Russian guns boomed louder in the east. Many houses were already empty and, as the day wore on with the lilac fragrant and sweet-flowered in the sun, many more homes were left deserted as the Elsterwalders trekked out of town to join the westward migration of refugees to the Elbe. A silent and unhappy convoy, it moved slowly, with a squeaking of oxcart wheels and a rattling of barrows and perambulators loaded with food, clothing, bedding and such household possessions as could be moved. When the people were not looking at the ground, treading the familiar road they might never see again, they were watching the sky, waiting for the Anglo-American fighters which had for weeks laid a trail of crackling, smoking destruction along the line of the Elbe and all the roads leading to it. No fighter-bombers came from the west this day, though, and they knew then that not far behind them, in the silent countryside to the east, the Russians were pressing forward, and the children began to cry as their elders hurried them faster toward the west.

From the window of the attic room, behind which they had hidden Heini with his sleeping bag in the absurd tent under the roof, Ulrike and Willi had watched the people leaving Elsterwalde.

"Now we can hide," said Willi. "The Russians will be here tonight. They must be close when the Anglo-American airmen won't risk hitting them by mistake. I think we can start settling the children down now."

While Heini had still been hiding with them up in the roof, and using the catastrophic Anglo-American fire raids on Dresden on February 13 and 14 as an excuse, Willi had excavated and fitted out an air raid shelter deep under the greenhouse, where in happier summers he had raised tomatoes that had been the pride and envy of Elsterwalde. Now, with an entrance camouflaged by a compost heap, the underground shelter was ready for use as a family retreat during the initial Genghis Khan phase of the typical Russian occupation of a captured village or town such as Elsterwalde. The bunker had ample food, clothing, bedding, medical supplies, books and even games and toys for Günther and Gerda. The family could emerge in their own good time when it would be safe to do so after the Russian fighting troops had gone and the occupation bureaucrats had taken over Elsterwalde.

Ulrike took Willi's arm as they walked down the stairs.

"You know," she said, "the children are being very good about it. I even think they might enjoy it. It could be just a picnic for them."

"A Nazi picnic," said Willi. "Underground. How appropriate."

They went out into the front garden to call the children, where they had been playing in the long grass beyond the lilac hedge, and they did not notice the note pinned to the front door until after they had seen the sprig of lilac also pinned there.

Willi laughed, settling his glasses on his nose as he read the note.

"The children must have a new game."

Then Ulrike had watched his face stiffen. Slowly, almost sadly, he shook his head. Then he took Ulrike's hand.

"We've got to go, darling. Just as soon as it's dark."

"Go where, Willi? What's the matter?"

"The note," he said. "Read the note."

It was typed and short and to the point.

Headed simply "THE FEHME," it read: "The subject of this summons, Wilhelm Harald Engelhöffer, editor and publisher, of Elsterwalde, is to appear before the court of honor of the Fehme in Saxony on charges of complicity in the July 20 plot against the person of our Führer, Adolf Hitler, and the Government of the Third Reich, and on a further charge of sedition arising out of publication of an article, 'The Last Issue,' in this day's issue of the *Elsterwalder Kreisblatt*. The said Wilhelm Engelhöffer, with members of his family, is to remain under house arrest until the arrival of a Fehme escort.

"Fehme, heil!"

Ulrike struggled to control her emotions and to speak quietly, for she could hear the children's voices as they ran back laughing toward the house. They had found some spring mushrooms.

"What does it mean, Willi? Is it a practical joke in the worst of taste?"

Willi spoke quietly. Suddenly he seemed very tired.

"It's no joke, darling. The lilac is the badge of an organization called the Fehme. It means that the rumors I've heard are true. I did not mention them to you because I could not believe them to be true and I did not want to alarm you needlessly. The Fehme, as I heard it, is a kind of Nazi resistance movement, an underground activity to carry on the fight when Germany and the National Socialist government are finished. It is a terrorist organization in the worst sense. A police superintendent from Breslau spoke to me about it just before he was killed in a railway accident. At least they said it was an accident. He fell from a train. We've got to get out of here, darling. We've got to go. Obviously they have some Elsterwalde people in the Fehme or they could not have done this so quickly. Being locals, they would probably know about the shelter and inevitably they would find us there."

"Where can we go?" said Ulrike, waving to Günther and Gerda as the children took a shortcut, giggling, through the lilacs.

"We can't go east," said Willi. "Not through the front. Not with the kids. Anyway, the army field police would pick us up."

"Then we go west," she said.

"West it is," agreed Willi. "Tonight, as soon as it's dark."

The children hadn't liked it, of course. They had been looking forward to the long picnic in the shelter. The dark woods were different, even in the company of their parents. They were nothing like the green and pleasant groves they had known on summer outings, all patterned with shifting sunlight, with berries and mushrooms to find and birds to sing to them. The woods at night were like the bad places in the fairy tales with branches to claw your face and tall pines standing around you like giant soldiers in the dark.

Whenever they could, Ulrike and Willi had ridden their bicycles, rucksacks heavy on their backs and the children clinging to their waists so they would not fall from their seats on the carriers over the rear wheels.

That was how they had left Elsterwalde, fleeing the faceless threat of something called the Fehme. A sprig of lilac and a curt note pinned arrogantly to the door of their home. Behind them lay everything they had ever known and loved. Their home, their garden, their books, their friends, their livelihood. Ahead, somewhere beyond the dark, rustling forests and the lonely fields and the panic-stricken villages, lay the years they might be lucky enough to live.

If Ulrike had ever thought that she had endured a living nightmare before Heini's arrest and execution, the furtive westward journey of flight from Elsterwalde and the Fehme was enough to convince her that, perhaps, the worst was yet to come.

Once, on a chilled dawn, after they had slept exhausted and uninvited in a farmer's barn, she had happened to stir awake, roused by voices, and had looked down into the yard outside to see two civilians just below with sprigs of lilac in their lapels. They were questioning the sleepy and unwitting farmer. She had been devoutly thankful then that the family had taken shelter, not asked for it, and on her knees in the straw, while Willi and the children, still slept, she had prayed to God with gratitude and asked that they might be delivered from the forces of evil that pursued them. Perhaps He had heard her, for, finally, they had come safely to Kotzdorf, their immediate destination near the Elbe. The friends with whom they sought brief sanctuary in Kotzdorf were still there in the village, but they were too late to see Father Josephus, a Catholic priest whom Heini had told them to contact if ever they found themselves endangered because of his implication in the July 20 conspiracy. The priest was a member of von Moltke's Kreisau Circle and had links with an influential group of Germans whose common cause was the eventual overthrow of the National Socialist regime. Ulrike and Willi, though, had come too late to Kotzdorf. Under Gestapo interrogation, the village priest had earlier refused to reveal details of the confession which he had heard from a July 20 conspirator prior to his arrest and subsequent imprisonment. Father Josephus, too, had been arrested. On the eve of Christmas 1944, he had died for his faith with a wire noose around his neck in a shabby back room of the prison at Berlin-Plötzensee.

To spare their Kotzdorf friends the consequences of any involvement with the Fehme, Willi had insisted on moving his family into the abandoned and pillaged farmhouse near the open fields at the end of the village street. Here they had rested and planned their next move.

"Their is only one hope," said Willi. "We must get across the Elbe at Torgau. Somehow, we must get to the Americans, front or no front. If there is too much fighting, we will just have to go to earth and wait. It shouldn't be for long. The Americans must be over the Mulde and advancing toward the Elbe by now."

"We will need food, at least for the children," said Ulrike. "If only there were some bread."

Then she had remembered their friends in the village.

"Just a couple of loaves would do," she said.

Willi had nodded and picked up his rucksack.

"Not now," she said. "Leave it till after dark. The Fehme knows you but you don't know the Fehme."

Willi shook aside her hand.

"We can't waste time," he said. "We must be on the way as soon as it is dark. I'll go for the bread now."

He had kissed her then and the children, too, and often later she wondered if he had had a presentiment of death. It would have been like him to go, just the same, for he had always nourished a contempt for death and an impatience with fear and doubt.

That was the last time she had seen him until he had come running back up the village street just before sunset. Turning in through the gate of the farmyard, he had run into the barn opposite the farmhouse. Too late, Ulrike realized that his best Homburg hat, relic of days of editorial pride, had fallen from his head and lay, incongruously and obviously, on the cobblestones of the yard. The two men in civilian clothes who also came running up the village street saw the hat as they passed the gate and swerved back on their tracks, like hunting dogs. These men, too, wore lilac in their lapels, but in their hands they held knives, the naked blades flashing and glinting in the late afternoon sunshine. Unhesitatingly they made for the barn. When they came out again not long after, one of them paused to wipe the blade of his knife on his boot. He had said something to his companion and they had laughed together. After they had gone, Ulrike found Willi lying sprawled in a mess of his own blood on the tumbled straw where he had fought with his attackers. He was dead. Soon after that, even as Ulrike was still weeping over Willi's body, she had heard the low-gear whine of an approaching car. Running back into the farmhouse she had told the children what to do while she returned to hide in the hayloft above the barn.

There had been no need to make a game of it with the children, for already Günther was beginning to think like a grown man.

It was the British prisoners who had arrived, cursing the steaming, laboring motor hearse they had driven into the yard, talking quietly in the barn over Willi's body and then joking and rattling dishes as they cooked and ate their meal in the kitchen while she had dug the shallow grave behind the barn and buried Willi with only the stars as witnesses but thankful for God's small mercy that her children had not seen the manner of their father's death. When Günther and Gerda had diverted the Britishers' attention with "Wir Fahren gegen England" played on the piano upstairs, she had returned to the suddenly deserted kitchen. While she was lifting the trap leading to the cellar stairs, it had slipped from her hands and the Britisher in the paratrooper jacket had come bounding down the stairs to see her and pursue her into the yard. As things turned out, the British prisoners had probably saved her sanity. They had at least been the symbols of something decent to which she could cling, dazed by her grief and sickened with fear for herself and the children. By the time she had finished talking with the Britishers and had led Günther and Gerda up to bed, she had taken herself sufficiently in hand to tell her son and daughter that their father had gone away and one day soon they would see him again and that they were always to remember that he was a good, brave and loving man. Perhaps because they had wanted to do so, the children had believed the lie and they had, miraculously, gone quickly to sleep.

While they slept, Ulrike had paced back and forth, pausing only to look out over the silent village street, and before long she had made her decision. If the Fehme came for her, the children could climb out the window of the bedroom, cross the roof below, drop down into the orchard beyond and make their way back to the friends in the village who had, Ulrike remembered, already volunteered to care for the children until after Willi and Ulrike had gone on ahead and reached the American lines. Günther would look after Gerda and get her safely to the friendly house, probably making a game of it for her, for he was wise now, far beyond his years. The boy would be like his father when he grew up, a kindly and quietly courageous man. After the children were safe, Ulrike reasoned, she would be free to go with the Fehme to their court of honor so that she could sear the faces of Willi's murderers into her memory and burn their names into her mind. One day, somehow, justice would call them to account and she would have been the instrument of retribution. It was a risk, but, for Willi's sake, it had to be taken.

So it was, as she had watched Schrader and his two men walking quietly in the moonlight along the deserted village street and into the farmyard, that she had wakened the children, wrapped them up warmly, told them what to do, kissed them and bundled them out onto the roof. After a while, when they had gone, the Fehme man in the American sergeant's uniform with the sprig of lilac in his lapel had come upstairs for her and she had gone down to the kitchen where the British prisoners from Hohenleipisch were standing against the wall. The one in the paratrooper jacket looked sick, whereas earlier he had seemed so strong, and she wondered what the Fehme had been doing to him. Then, seeing the look in his eyes, Ulrike had speculated on what he in turn planned to do to the Fehme men and even while she was listening to Schrader telling her that she was to appear before the court of honor, Ulrike had been watching the paratrooper, tensing herself as she waited for something to happen. When, suddenly, she saw him hold out the grenade, shout and then toss it into the fiery hole in the top of the stove, she had dived for the open trap door above the cellar steps. After the thunderous shock of the explosion she had waited, wondering whether Schrader and the Fehme man with him in the cellar would take her and the remaining Britisher, the air gunner, and finish them off with the Tommy guns and leave them to burn with the farm. Instead had come the long, stumbling walk across the fields and the cautious approach to the banks of the Elbe, where the skiff lay moored amid the whispering reeds.

Then had come the passage across the broad, dark waters of the river, flowing faster than she would have imagined, in a silence broken only by the slow, soft splash of oars and the creak of oarlocks. After the landing on the far bank, where a line of willows hung their heads in the river, came the long, cautious trek to Galgenstein village with the many-towered bulk of the von Bluckau castle looming dizzily against the frosted stars. Stone steps then; a great hall reeking of burned timber; a fireplace you could stand upright in and, behind it, an iron-backed stone door pushed open with more steps, iron now, spiraling down into an echoing underground chamber all shadowed and restless with the light of torches burning in rusted iron sconces on the damp walls. Ulrike had come to the court of honor and she was glad to be there.

So it was that, now, with the travesty of the proceedings against her completed, she stood convicted but without fear, to hear the sentence which was to be imposed upon her by the general with the noble name which, as a local Elsterwalder, she had for so long respected. So much now for the von Bluckaus, she thought; so much for all the generations of aristocratic breeding and pride. This was the face of murder. A thin, disdainful face. A pallor that accentuated the darkness of the glasses protecting the sightless eyes. A clipped accent. A peremptory manner. A general's uniform all bright and splendid with the ribbons and honors of the military caste. A cellar crowded with thugs and fools and dreamers. A court of honor, they had said. She almost laughed out loud.

"Ulrike Engelhöffer," von Bluckau said, "you have been found guilty of the charge brought against you by this court of honor. As Freigraf of the Saxony Freistuhle of the Fehme and as president of this court, it is within my power to impose upon you the supreme penalty—death."

Behind her, Ulrike sensed, the men of the Fehme were leaning forward eagerly so that they might hear every word.

"Such, however, is not my intention," von Bluckau continued. "Instead, I propose to impose upon you a lesser sentence. This is in no way to be construed as an act of clemency arising from the fact that the execution of your husband has already been carried out by sworn members of the Fehme. Certainly, though, that circumstance has been taken into consideration. As a result, I feel that, being the widow of a dead traitor executed by the Fehme, you will be of more service to our cause as a living testimony to the power of jurisdiction of the Fehme."

Shoulders squared, the general sat as if at attention.

"I order, therefore, that you be released from arrest on the rising of this court and that you be banished from within the borders of Saxony, forbidden to return on pain of death and with the further injunction that any attempt by you to return to Saxony or, in any way, to compromise the security of the Fehme organization, will bring down upon you the consequences of the arrest, by the Fehme, of your children, wherever you may be in Germany. I would remind you, Frau Engelhöffer, that the jurisdiction of the Fehme, enemy occupation or not, is bounded only by the ancient frontiers of Germany herself."

While the clerk of the court recorded the sentence, von Bluckau paused, then looked up, sightless but no less commanding in his manner.

"Has the prisoner anything to say?" said von Bluckau.

The fool, Ulrike thought. The blind fool. The proud, blue-blooded fool. Men like this lost the struggle of July 20. To him, a woman is of no account, least of all a woman of common stock, so he is letting me go. God, how they will all regret this day, for now I am going to live and I will never forget the names and the faces of the men who murdered my husband. We know now who they are, Willi. Ulrike clenched her hands with the strain of not betraying her emotions.

"I have nothing to say," she said. "Thank you."

"Remove the prisoner to the cells," said von Bluckau. He

spoke curtly, almost impatiently, for he was tiring. This was no business for a soldier and already he knew it.

"Mr. Prosecutor, we will proceed with the next case. Which is it?"

"An American national" said Krausnick, "Herr Dermott Duncan."

Another one of them, thought von Bluckau. Another foreigner to haunt his professional soldier's conscience. German against German was one thing. It was the history of Germany. Exercising a clandestine jurisdiction, illegal even in Germany, over nationals of other countries was something else again. It smacked of the SS. We all could swing for this one day, he thought. I hope to God that Bormann and the rest of us know what we are doing.

"Proceed," said von Bluckau and sat back, waiting for the voices to begin again.

The scent of lilacs, he thought, would never smell sweet again.

V
The Well of Death

Dermott Duncan, the big man in the shabby civilian suit with the khaki shirt and the garish tartan tie, pulled thoughtfully at the red beard which had pugnaciously dominated the jackets of a dozen New York and London best sellers during the decade before the war had begun in 1939. An American national, thought Dermott. That's what they called me. What a bunch of barbarians. Obviously they've never heard of me. To them I'm just an American national. My publisher would choke on his martini. My agent would take up knitting. Not a bad title for a book, though. *An American National–The Decline and Fall of Dermott Duncan, Journalist, Foreign Correspondent, Author, Prominente Internee, Displaced Person, Fugitive and Prisoner of the Fehme.* The Fleet Street boys would love it. A lot of them had always hated his successful American guts. That big, fat, loud-mouthed, best-selling, swashbuckling trans-Atlantic Scot, Dermott Duncan, they'd say. The poor man's John Gunther. Not sticking his neck out again for another of those "I Was There" potboilers? That's Dermott, they'd say. That's Dermott's form. But espionage? Not in a million years! He wouldn't have the brains for it! And they'd be right, too. At least about this damn-fool espionage nonsense. He was a writer, not a cloak-and-dagger man. The fatcats of the SHAEF press camp, living it up at the Scribe in Paris, would hate him even more if he got away with this and lived to tell the tale. Charged with espionage by a clandestine German court of no known status that sat in secret in a cellar below a castle owned by a Kraut general as crazy as Ludwig of Bavaria! If he ever saw Times Square or Piccadilly again, he'd sizzle their socks with *The Well of Death.*

If it never sold a nickel's worth, this was the book that was going to justify his existence as a writer; the book that was going to be the pay-off for the years he had sweated out as an ambitious young reporter in the Midwest, as an ulcerated rewrite man on a tough desk in New York City, as a *Time* correspondent in London and as a free-wheeling global free lance with a string of hit-and-git best sellers to his name; the book that had put him right where he was now, in peril of his life; the book that might never get published if this court of neo-Nazi psychopaths had their way.

Dermott's road to the court of honor at Galgenstein had started in 1943 with the boredom, depression and frustration of that first summer as a Prominente prisoner at Oflag VIII G in the great medieval fortress of Kreuzenberg on the Nogat River south of Danzig in Prussia. If he had not been in such a hurry to get to North Africa to cover the death of the Afrika Korps for Associated Press, he would never have bullied and finagled his way into the VIP Sunderland bound for Tunis. Nor, within a few hours of take-off from the RAF base at Plymouth, would he have been sitting in a rubber dinghy in the Bay of Biscay with the few passengers and crew members who had survived the shock and violence of the ditching.

As the German trawler had nudged alongside just before dawn to pick them up and land them at Cherbourg, his only consolation had been that, without even having really meant to, he had grabbed and saved his portable typewriter.

Jill, the English girl who was his second wife, by then was contentedly married to a Norwich solicitor doing something important but dull at the Admiralty. She would have been vastly amused. Long before they had started to think about a divorce, just after Dieppe, Jill had hated the battered little Remington.

"It's bloody silly to be jealous of a typewriter," she said during his last leave in London, "but I am. It means more to you than I ever will. It's all your ego and energy as a writer locked up in a neat little case with scruffy foreign labels stuck all over it. God, how I wish it were only a woman. I could do something about her. But a career like yours, my darling, is something I can't fight. Something I don't want to fight. Not any more. I've had it, my sweet."

They had gone home to the flat, then, and Dermott had found a flask of Chianti he had brought home from Libya and they had made love, lying across the bed still dressed, with Dermott lifting her skirts up over her thighs as he might have a woman he had picked up in Regent Street after dinner at his club. Even as his hands had grasped at the naked flesh of her buttocks he knew that it was all no good any more, that he was grossly lusting after the image which had kept him awake on the long nights in the Mediterranean aboard the Liberty ship plugging home to the Clyde. They made their love with a kind of sad, desperate intensity and when it was over, Jill had pushed him away and smoothed her dress down and lain there, staring at the ceiling and smoking one of the Chesterfields from the carton he had brought home from the ship.

There was no anger in her voice when she finally spoke, only weariness and sadness.

"It's no good any more, Dermott. We both know that."

It had not been an indictment or an accusation but a sad acceptance of the inevitable truth.

"I know," said Dermott. "I'm sorry, Jill. Something's gone wrong. It's me, I suppose."

"I think it is," she said. "You or me, though, what's the difference? It just hasn't worked out. Even without the war, it would have been the same. The war only made it worse quicker. There's just nothing there any more."

"If we'd had children–" said Dermott, wondering if there was another bottle of Chianti in the bulging parachute bag.

"Thank God we didn't," said Jill. "It would only have complicated the inevitable result."

"You're probably right," said Dermott.

He raised his glass and caught his own reflection in the dressing-table mirror. He was looking older. One of his letters from Libya was stuck in a corner of the mirror. He stared at his reflection owlishly. Bright, china-blue eyes set too close together. Sandy hair. Freckles. A fox-red beard. The great author and war correspondent, thought Dermott. The big by-line man. The lousy lover. The hopeless husband.

"Arivederci!" he said.

In the morning, over tea and toast and marmalade, Dermott had made some mildly self-conscious jokes about the condemned man eating a hearty meal. Then he had put his hand on Jill's.

"You still feel the same?" he said.

Outside, somewhere in the street, a dog was barking excitedly. It sounded as if it had a cat treed.

"I do, Dermott," said Jill. "I'm sorry, but I do. I want to go through with a divorce."

Except for some rather prim meetings at a solicitor's office and then the inevitably dreary court proceedings, Dermott had seen little of Jill other than for casual encounters at restaurants and faintly embarrassed chance meetings at a party or two.

After the divorce had come through, he had taken Jill to dinner by candlelight in the little Soho restaurant where they had gone so often after they had first met as lovers. The occasion had fallen flat, so far as Dermott was concerned, when he found himself becoming jealously resentful of the happiness which Jill had obviously been able to find without him.

"Anybody else on the horizon?" he asked, aware of the forced casualness with which he voiced the thought which had been itching at his mind, even over the black-market duck from Norfolk and the prewar Burgundy, which was worth every penny of the ransom he knew would be extorted from him.

"Perhaps," said Jill, "there is somebody else now, but so far we're just good friends."

With mischievous intent she had changed the subject.

"This is a terribly good Burgundy, Dermott. I always did say you had an impeccable taste in wines."

"That makes me feel a whole lot better," said Dermott. "At least I had one redeeming feature."

It was then that he had announced that he would be going back to the Middle East soon to cover the last days of the Afrika Korps before Rommel was driven back across the Mediterranean, but Jill had not been visibly impressed by the implication that this might be her last chance to say farewell to a man going to the wars again.

"Dermott," she said severely, "you just made that up to impress me."

He had had to laugh then, for Jill's accusation was almost correct.

When he admitted this, Jill leaned forward and kissed him on the cheek.

"You old fox," she said. "You don't change. Bless your heart. Just the same, if it'll make you happy, I hope you get the trip."

It was mainly so that he could write to Jill and tell her that he had not been faking and playing on her sympathy that he had blustered his way aboard the Sunderland.

Later, on his way to internment in Germany after the ditching in the Bay of Biscay, he had reflected that maybe his colleagues, critics and rivals were not too far wide of the mark when they charged him with making a profession of shooting his big mouth off.

The reaction of the German authorities, however, had been flattering for his ego. Since he had been captured after having been shot down in an airplane, he accompanied the surviving members of the Sunderland crew to Frankfurt-am-Main for routine examination by intelligence officers at Dulag Luft, the Luftwaffe transit and interrogation camp. Once they had established the fact that he was Dermott Duncan, the war correspondent and author, the rough and ready treatment which had first been accorded him as just another Allied flier was hastily replaced by the speculative suavity reserved for the Prominente, such notable prisoners and internees as fell into German hands.

In Berlin, the somewhat clumsy efforts of a series of Ministry of Propaganda officials to subvert him as a turncoat writer for the greater glory of the Third Reich at first amused him. As the process continued, at the cocktails and canapé level, he found himself bored and then, finally, angered by what he could only describe as an insult to his intelligence if not his patriotism. Having voiced this sentiment with all the explosive vigor of his highland Scots ancestry and American frankness, Dermott had quickly found himself squatting on the straw-littered floor of a cattle truck with a party of inveterate officer escapers and reputedly bound for the fortress camp at Kreuzenberg.

"If only I'd kept my big mouth shut," he complained to the officer he found jammed against him by the crush of bodies, "I'd still be drinking brandy and smoking cigars with the Jerry propaganda boys in Berlin."

"I wouldn't worry, old boy," said the officer, intently studying a tiny compass which he had unclipped from a fly-button in his battle-dress pants. "You'd have looked pretty bloody silly trying to smoke a cigar while you were dangling by the neck with Lord Haw-Haw after the war."

"You have a point there," conceded Dermott. "If the damned war ever ends. Where are we going, anyway?"

"The compass heading is northeast," said the officer, a Long Range Desert Group major who had been taken prisoner during a raid on a Luftwaffe airfield 278 miles behind the German lines in Libya.

"It looks like Kreuzenberg, all right," he said. "Particularly with you on board. They keep Prominente prisoners like you there as well as bad boys like us. It's supposed to be escape-proof."

On his arrival at Kreuzenberg, as forecast by the knowledgeable officer with the escape compass, Dermott found himself, for the first time in fifteen years as a journalist and author, with nothing to do but sit and think. He found it unutterably boring. Not that there was a lack of excitement. Since, like Colditz on the Mulde, in Saxony, Kreuzenberg was virtually an establishment dedicated to the pursuit of higher studies in advanced escaping technologies for recalcitrant Allied officers who had already graduated as escapers from conventional oflags, the fortress on the Nogat was continually astir with escaping plans and attempts. The proximity of the Baltic, to the north, with the tantalizing prospect of a neutral Sweden not far away below the misted sea horizon, constituted a challenge and a stimulus rather than a natural water barrier. For Dermott, though, these pleasures were entirely vicarious. Apart from the fact that he freely admitted that he was neither physically nor psychologically qualified for walking all the way across Europe to get shot at trying to cross the frontiers of Spain or Switzerland, he knew that his status as a Prominente civilian internee was likely to be compromised by any attempt to escape.

"Put it like this, old boy," said the Senior British Officer at Kreuzenberg, an RAF group captain. "Escape by all means but make sure you get clean away. If they caught you, there's a chance you might find yourself strictly on your own. As a civilian internee you'd be largely out of my jurisdiction, such as it is. You could finish up in worse places than Kreuzenberg."

Dermott had not doubted this for a moment. Not entirely reluctantly, he had taken the group captain's advice and abandoned any ideas of escaping. Instead, he had turned to writing, and the writing of history at that. Not history in the raw as he had covered it so often in Manchuria, Abyssinia, Spain, Austria, the Saar, the Sudetenland and all the other areas of conflict which had been his restless, book-of-the-month hunting grounds before 1939. The events which so preoccupied him at Kreuzenberg were those which had occurred, centuries before, in and around the old Prussian fortress itself. A chance remark by a Canadian commando captain about the depth and the thickness of the foundations of Schloss Kreuzenberg and the abandonment of a tunneling project had first aroused Dermott's interest.

"You wouldn't believe it," the Canadian had complained bitterly. "The place is more than 800 years old, but the only way to get through those foundations is with gelignite and a jack hammer. I'll pay the Order of Teutonic Knights. When they built a castle, they built it for keeps."

Thinking of all the other prisoners who, over the centuries, must have endured just such a captivity as that shared by himself and his companions behind the walls of Kreuzenberg, Dermott had gone to sleep that night with his mind pleasantly active with plans for a new book. Not a quick-and-the-dead book. Not a war correspondent's book, pounded out between foreign assignments. Not a book, probably, that would spin him fat royalties, yet a book, perhaps, that might outlive him; a scholarly and painstaking novel based on the history of Schloss Kreuzenberg. A single thread in the tapestry of German history. Just the life story of a medieval castle set in the context of a novel illumined by the passing years. Nothing clever in the way of titles, he thought. *Kreuzenberg* he'd call it. That and nothing more. He suspected that when he took it home after the war, his publisher and his agent would be aghast at his change of pace as a writer and argue with him over interminable lunches (how welcome those meals would have been at grim, austere Kreuzenberg), trying to convince him that he was stepping out of character, a Falstaff trying to play Hamlet. Just the same he'd do it. He had nothing to lose. Not even time. He had all the time in the world; too much time. He had to do something or he would go crazy. Either it was a project like the book or else some half-baked escaping venture with a good chance of getting a bullet smack in the middle of his spine. No, not that, he thought. Not a cripple getting old in a wheel chair. *Kreuzenberg* could be the book he had always been going to write and which he had never got down to doing. A narrative in depth. He slept happily that night, barely stirring on the paillasse of straw and the rough boards of his bunk.

The next morning, early, he spoke to Bauer, the camp's Sonderführer, a German officer whose specialist duties included the unenviable task of seeking to convince the prisoners of Kreuzenberg of the superior virtues of life in Germany under the rule of the Third Reich.

Middle-aged, earnest and fundamentally ineffective, Bauer was neither unintelligent nor naïve. Trained as a political indoctrination and propaganda officer, Bauer had been a newspaperman in Munich before the war. Venturing upon the freemasonry of the press, he had gone to some trouble to ingratiate himself with Dermott after flattering allusions to his international reputation both as a journalist and as an author. Assuming that Bauer had been instructed by his superior officers in Berlin to keep working at his defection, Dermott had basked in the notoriety with which he had found himself invested by the German authorities but had given Bauer no grounds for assuming that he was getting anywhere. Nor had he ever had any intention of doing so.

When, though, he awoke that first morning, still excited by his plans for a historical novel based on Schloss Kreuzenberg, he realized that Bauer would be the man to help him.

On the pretext of discussing an East Front dispatch in that day's issue of the *Deutsche Allgemeine Zeitung*, written by a Berlin journalist he had once known, Dermott allowed the conversation to be steered around, as he knew it inevitably would be, to the subject of whether he was doing any writing.

"Oddly enough, I am thinking of doing something," Dermott said. "What I had in mind was a novel based on Kreuzenberg. They tell me the place has quite a history."

Bauer's reaction had been enthusiastic, eyes blinking excitedly behind the thick lenses of his rimless glasses.

"Indeed it has, Herr Duncan. Nearly eight hundred years of history. I think the idea is excellent. If I can help in any way, I will be happy to do so. You will need paper, of course."

He laughed excitedly, the morning sunlight flashing on a gold-capped tooth.

"A first requisite for an author, eh? Paper to write on!"

I've made his day, thought Dermott. He thinks he's got me hooked. Two can play that game, though.

"Thank you," said Dermott. "I'll need paper, of course, but I'll also need access to research material. Books about the castle and the district. History books and local historical records, all that sort of thing."

Bauer was transparently eager to help.

"Leave it to me. I can get you those. You speak good German, so I take it you can read our language, too?"

"Well enough," said Dermott.

"Just leave it to me," said Bauer. "I will arrange everything." He had bustled away then, almost dancing on his toes. Now he'll call Berlin to say he's landed me, thought Dermott. They'll tell him to give me as much rope as he thinks I'll need to hang myself. This should be interesting. I'd better square it away with the Senior British Officer.

The group captain had approved the project, with a mildly phrased qualification.

"You've been around, Dermott, so I shouldn't have to tell you. The German, in my experience, is at his most charming when he think he's getting you where he wants you. Don't let them get you over a barrel."

"I know what you mean, sir," said Dermott. "As a journalist I covered a few of their big Nuremberg party rallies. I'd never underestimate them. As somebody said once, they're either at your feet or at your throat."

Bauer, as it transpired, was mainly at Dermott's feet. Not only were books, records and documented archives delivered for his appraisal and use as research material, but he was also allowed out of the fortress, on parole and escorted by Bauer, so that he could study the archives and historical records in the vaults of the town hall of Kreuzenberg, down by the river. Bauer was pathetically eager to please him and although Dermott knew that the German's motives were, no doubt, aligned with those of his superiors in the Berlin offices of the Ministry of Propaganda, he had to admit that he was dealing with a man who did his job well, kept his promises and, as a Nazi propagandist, was probably the helpless victim of political circumstances beyond his power to control. Getting to know Bauer, as their association of mutual convenience prospered, Dermott realized that at heart the German officer, like many newspapermen, was an internationalist and a humanist. As a German officer, though, and necessarily a National Socialist, he would never dare admit it. Nor did Dermott press him to do so. With Bauer, he wanted neither friendship nor enmity, just a professional relationship based on a mutual respect and poised on the razor's edge of expediency. Before the winter of 1943 was over, and with the industrious Bauer's assistance, Dermott had completed his basic research into the history of Schloss Kreuzenberg. Bauer, he found, had not been exaggerating when he had enthused about the historical background of the old fortress. It had been built nearly 800 years before by the Knights of the Teutonic Order. Founded in 1191, the order had, in 1230, under the fiery leadership of its Grand Master, Hermann von Salza, begun to undertake the conquest and conversion to Christianity of the barbarian Prussians. As the God-fearing crusader knights, bearing a sword in one hand and a Bible in the other, conquered Prussia, they protected their hard-won domains with great castles and peopled the new Teutonic territories with stolid colonists from Germany. So as the praying knights rode east, the fortress of Krauzenberg had been built in 1275.

Impregnable for so long, and so often, against siege from beyond the massive walls that dominated the green heights of the hill above the banks of the Nogat, Schloss Kreuzenberg was now as impregnable to escape from within. During the long hard winter of 1943, escape after escape had been mounted and had failed, while Dermott completed the research for his novel, completely absorbed in the task which he had set himself and genially oblivious to the good-natured gibes of his military comrades to whom Schloss Kreuzenberg was still only a prison whose walls could, and must, be breached.

In the spring of 1944, as the winds of East Prussia mellowed with the fragrance of lilac and the sweet warmth of ripening crops, it was not the walls of Kreuzenberg but the well in the big quadrangle of the Mittelschloss which finally brought Dermott face to face with the reality of the fact that at Kreuzenberg, as at scores of other prison camps in Germany, another escaping season had begun.

Bauer, ironically enough, was the instrument of Dermott's involvement with Wing Commander Lees, the leader of the escape committee at Kreuzenberg. Dermott had never liked Lees. Further than that, and it privately shocked him to have to admit it to himself, he did not even trust him. The wing commander was a slightly built young man whose coltish good looks, at first glance, made him seem much younger than his twenty-five years. Only the eyes gave him away. Deep-blue and dark-ringed, they were the sullen, brooding eyes of a delinquent, a man who would not hesitate to kill or be killed. They were the eyes of a man who, as a fighter pilot, had survived the Battle of France and the Battle of Britain to emerge in 1941 as one of the youngest, most highly decorated and most ruthlessly efficient wing leaders in Fighter Command.

Arrogantly lonely in the knowledge that he had a knack for making enemies quicker than friends, yet supremely capable of being indifferent to either, Lees had found in the challenge of escape from German captivity much of the fierce, elemental excitement which had for so long driven him to high achievement and honored recognition as a fighter leader. In the oflags of Germany, as in the squadrons of the Royal Air Force, Lees found not friendship but the grudging respect of the loyal team for the ruthless but efficient leader.

In Germany, as in England, the price of loyalty to his leadership was often high. In the last three escapes which Lees had planned and led before being sent to Kreuzenberg, four men had died. Nobody, including Dermott, doubted Lees's courage but there were many, and Dermott was one of them, who wondered how many more men were yet to die under the spell of Lees's obsession with his own personal compulsion to escape and return to duty as a fighter pilot. This was why, Dermott thought, he disliked and distrusted Lees. Under pressure, the man was capable of going it alone, leaving the devil to take care of the hindmost. He had the smell of death about him. He would, in fact, have made an excellent SS officer.

To Lees's credit, he had never questioned Dermott's decision not to risk compromising his Prominente internment status by making inevitably abortive attempts to escape. Cynically, the author had attributed Lees's tolerance on this issue to the fact that he probably preferred to see escaping preserved as a sport for officers and gentlemen. Dermott's unsought confrontation with Lees, in the wing commander's capacity as escape leader, had begun soon after the earnest Bauer had triumphantly produced what he described to Dermott as the trump card in the program of research for the Kreuzenberg novel. It was a set of photostatic copies of the original specifications and construction plans of the fortress which had been drawn up, with meticulous accuracy, prior to its restoration in the early nineteenth century. Studying the plans overnight—Bauer had insisted on their return within twenty-four hours—Dermott had been fascinated by the role played in the history of the Kreuzenberg fortress by the bricked-over well, which, with its low encircling stone wall and gabled windlass shelter, had long been a familiar loitering point for prisoners in the great quadrangle of the Mittelschloss. Sunk during the fifteenth century as a precaution against the travails of siege, the well was shown to reach 500 feet down to the mean water level of the Nogat River as it swept past the green bluff on which the fortress stood. In its time, the well had faithfully served the embattled Knights of the Teutonic Order. Not only had it slaked the thirsty throats of the besieged defenders of Schloss Kreuzenberg. On one occasion, when a Polish siege had briefly breached the walls, the well had successfully hidden a distinguished knight of the order until the invaders had been driven out. Another knight, more portly and less fortunate, had died in its dark and echoing depths when the windlass rope broke, allegedly shredded by the sword of a fellow knight whose wife he had taken to bed. Time and again, too, the well of Schloss Kreuzenberg had been the deep hiding place for the treasures and archives of the order. The loyal and law-abiding Kreuzenbergers of the town never doubted the truth of the legend that there was more gold and silver than water at the bottom of the well in the fortress on the hill.

Enriched, somehow, by this knowledge, Dermott had been standing looking at the well-head that evening before curfew when Lees hailed him. The wing commander, thought Dermott, was the kind of man who always kept bobbing up everywhere. Particularly when he was not welcome. Still intrigued by the story of the well, Dermott had mentioned it to Lees, who had nodded quietly as he listened and then, with sudden interest, reached forward to tap a stick on the bricked dome.

"Why not?" he had said to himself rather than to Dermott. "Why not, indeed?" Then he had questioned Dermott about the overflow tunnel which had been driven at right angles to the well, at the 250-foot level, far under the foundations of the fortress, emerging on the hillside above the river and below the fortress walls.

"Why did they need that?" he asked.

"Something to do with the springs that feed the well," said Dermott. "At certain times of the year in certain years the springs rise. A local phenomenon. Something to do with the levels of the Nogat and the tides in the Baltic. If they didn't spill the water off, the well would flood the quadrangle here."

Lees stared at him, the sullen eyes almost lively.

"Is the overflow tunnel still in existence?"

Still unsuspecting, Dermott had nodded.

Then the ethical implications of what Lees obviously had in mind suddenly troubled Dermott.

"You can't do that," he said.

"We can," said the wing commander amiably, "and, by God, we will. It'll need a little work and a lot of luck but it's a piece of cake. Congratulations, Dermott."

"Congratulations, nothing," exploded Dermott, staring at Lees, who was slapping the stick he always carried like a cane against the sharply pressed trousers of his blue-gray RAF battle dress. The dapper little bastard, thought Dermott. Patiently, and trying not to lose his temper, he outlined the situation. The castle plans and specifications had been supplied to him by Bauer without the knowledge of the German camp commandant or the town authorities in Kreuzenberg. Bauer trusted him to use the information for the specified purpose of literary research. If Dermott made the information available to the escape committee and an escape was based upon it, any subsequent German investigation would almost certainly trace the breach of security back to Bauer.

"Tough luck for Bauer," said Lees. "As an officer he acted stupidly in the first place, giving you the information. If I were his commanding officer, I would not hesitate to court-martial him for criminal negligence."

"There's the minor point of ethical principle that he trusted me personally," said Dermott. "I may not be an officer in the armed forces, but that doesn't mean I can go around breaking my word and betraying sources of privileged information even to a German. I never did it in newspaper work and I don't intend to start now."

"A pleasing sentiment, old boy," said Lees, "and it pleases me. However, you should have thought of that before you started playing parole games with the Germans."

Dermott felt his chest tighten with suppressed rage. The little prig, he thought. The holy little hero.

"Now, just a minute Lees. I've got what I wanted from them. They've got nothing from me. Nor will they. Ever. Don't you start waving the bloody Union Jack at me. My hobby's writing. Your's is escaping. Let's keep it that."

"OK, old boy," Lees said hastily. "Don't flap. I didn't mean there was any question of your loyalty. But let's face it. It's my job to organize escaping activities in this oflag and you're obstructing me. We're just not getting anywhere like this."

"You can say that again," Dermott agreed. "Absolutely nowhere. And don't start again on this business of the well. You do your own dirty work."

Lees, then, had stared at Dermott, amazed.

"I really believe you are genuine, Dermott. Worried about some damned silly principle of parole. My God, old boy, this isn't the Battle of Waterloo. It's the Second World War. They bomb and strafe our women and kids. We bomb and strafe theirs. It's a dirty business but the ends justify the means and that includes escaping. Dermott, I'm going to take this up with the Senior British Officer."

"By all means," said Dermott, his equanimity restored, "and I'll have great pleasure in telling him, too."

It had been no good, though. Lees even had the group captain mesmerized. He had been no help to Dermott. Nor was Dermott surprised. Like the wing commander, Group Captain Grace was a professional airman, a regular officer of the RAF. Linked by the camaraderie and traditions of their service and sharing the freemasonry of their years as operational pilots and leaders, they were members of a politely undefined club to which Dermott Duncan, the civilian and the scribbler, could never belong. More than that, Dermott was convinced that Grace trod carefully with his junior, the wing commander.

Dermott had even wondered whether Grace was cautiously mindful of the fact that the thrusting, sullen-eyed young wing commander was rumored, and with good reason, to maintain a secret black book in which he noted the names of officers he considered eligible for postwar arraignment on the grounds of their having obstructed, or put in hazard, escapes which he had planned and led.

Whatever the reasons, the conference with the group captain went Lees's way.

"It is an officer's duty to escape," Grace had summed up. "Wing Commander Lees has been apprised of a way of escape. If the escape method is feasible and can be assessed as having an acceptable degree of risk, then I can see no reason why I should not approve it and delegate responsibility for its execution to the escape committee. Here and now."

"Thank you, sir," said Lees, standing up briskly.

Three bags full, sir, thought Dermott. May I lead the charge, sir? The honor of the regiment is at stake. Lees is the name, sir. Lees for death and glory. The little prick.

"OK," said Dermott, "but for the record, it's your decision, Group Captain. Your decision entirely, not mine. And I think it stinks."

There had been nothing more, though, that Dermott could say or do.

To Dermott's surprise, Lees insisted on keeping him fully informed as to the preparations for the "Big Choir," as the escape down the well had been coded for conversational security reasons. Sourly, and with no illusions, Dermott concluded that this unsought privilege was extended to him either because he was regarded as a security risk who could be trapped into passing on planted false information to the German authorities or merely that Lees wished to compromise him in the event of Bauer's implication in any subsequent German investigation.

Despite his frank dislike for Lees and his forebodings about the way the whole thing had got started, Dermott had had to admit that the man's ability justified his reputation as a courageous and grimly efficient escape leader. Within a week, Lees had organized a genuine choir of officers. Daily they practiced their repertoire, grouped around a conductor whose podium was the wellhead. Within another week, once the bored guards on the battlemented walls of the quadrangle had become accustomed to this latest foible of the mad British officers, a curved section of the bricked-in dome had been deftly removed and replaced by another, previously fabricated in readiness. The transposition was effected with uncanny ease, since the gabled roof over the wellhead screened the work from the guards on the battlements above. On the few tense occasions when a German officer or guard had entered the quadrangle while the manhole cover was being installed in the brick dome over the well, they were jestingly persuaded into joining the choir's rendition of familiar and sentimental German airs. When the German visitors had moved on again, the work had been resumed. Meanwhile, rope for a ladder to drop from the windlass to the overflow tunnel at the 250-foot level was woven and spliced with cord stolen and salvaged from the incinerators behind the barracks store in the German Kommandantur area. Discreet questioning of the cadaverous, unshaven Russians manning the creaking latrine wagons, aided by some furtive bribery with cigarettes, established that the exit of the overflow tunnel from the well, below the apple orchard which flowered and fruited farther down the hill beneath the fortress walls, was barricaded by an ancient iron gate whose rusted bars should quickly yield to some industrious filing from inside. With the approval of the German camp authorities, a crude stage was built around the well, ostensibly for a series of open-air summer concerts which would crown the efforts of what had been dubbed the Kreuzenberg Choristers. By the end of March 1944, the Big Choir was also ready. This was the party of twenty-six officers which Lees had calculated could be hidden under the stage before roll call on the evening before the day of the breakout.

Once the last man down the well had signaled that he was entering the tunnel, the rope ladder and signal line would be retrieved and the manhole cover replaced by a volunteer who would remain hidden under the stage until after the next morning's Appell and the resumption of the Kreuzenberg Choristers' daily practice. The major factor of uncertainty was whether or not the overflow tunnel was clear and had not been blocked either by debris or cave-ins. Since the plans provided by the guileless Bauer had indicated that the tunnel was solidly lined with brick, this had not seemed likely. Lees and the escape committee were further reassured by the discovery that when the springs had last risen the well, four years earlier, the overflow had spilled out down the hillside.

Various plans for diverting the attention of the guards had been put forward and debated. The short-circuiting of the camp's electrical lighting system. A fire in one of the barrack rooms. A spoof escape elsewhere in the fortress. They were all rejected on the basis they would only result in a dislocation of the fortress security routine and an unpredictable flurry of German surveillance measures. Instead, it was decided to invite the commandant and his staff to attend an indoor dress rehearsal, after evening Appell, of the first of the concerts allegedly to be held in the quadrangle during the high summer months still to come.

"Put a lot of German songs on the program and get them to join," said Lees. "You know what a maudlin lot they are. The louder they sing the less they'll hear. Far better to have them inside with the boys than snooping around outside."

On the night of the escape, the old stable used as a primitive theater was crowded not only with Allied officer prisoners but also an impressive retinue of the German Kommandantur staff in their best uniforms and on their best behavior.

By the time that Colonel Stahle, the camp commandant at Kreuzenberg, had arrived, greeted with due military courtesy by Group Captain Grace, and the Kreuzenberg Choristers had swung into their first song, Schubert's "The Erlking," Dermott found it hard to believe that outside in the deserted quadrangle

Lees and his party were already committed not just to a plan but to imminent action which could gain some of them liberty and honor or a bullet in the back.

After the concert rehearsal had ended, with Stahle and Grace exchanging military courtesies once more, the rear-guard volunteer hidden under the stage had made the cautious, prearranged signal confirming the success of the breakout. Neither that night, nor next day, did Dermott share in the jubilation which enthused the barrack rooms of Oflag VIII G at Schloss Kreuzenberg. If anything, he was mainly conscious of an air of impending doom. He could not pin it down to any single significant reason. It was a combination of factors which conspired to make him uneasy. There had been such times before, during his days as a war correspondent in Spain and Manchuria, and each time his intuition had saved his life. It was the same again at Kreuzenberg. There were so many straws in the rising wind. There was the business about Bauer and the exploitation by Lees of information supplied, however unofficially, under conditions of parole and privilege. There had been rumors that Himmler had issued an order that escaping British or American officers, on recapture, were to be held in military or civilian prisons pending a decision by the German High Command as to whether or not they were to be handed over into the jurisdiction of the Gestapo. There had been further rumors, only a few days before the breakout by the Big Choir, about a mass escape by tunnel from Stalag Luft III, the big Luftwaffe prison camp at Sagan in Silesia, after which an ominously high proportion of officers had allegedly been shot while evading capture. Almost on the eve of the Big Choir escape, Colonel Stahle had addressed the Kreuzenberg prisoners on parade in the quadrangle. Neither confirming nor denying the Sagan rumors, he had warned them that the German authorities were now taking a harsher view of escaping and said that he felt it was his duty and responsibility to warn them that escaping could no longer be regarded as a sport.

"I know it is your duty as officers to attempt to escape and return to duty," Stahle said. "This being so, I must impress upon you that in honoring your obligations of duty you are now also risking the supreme penalty. Think it over, gentlemen."

Stahle had looked worried, even ill, and Dermott wondered

if, for once, the facts of the Sagan affair outstripped the rumors.

Even though Grace had agreed that the Big Choir escape should go ahead as planned, Dermott knew that he, too, was worried. This also he found disturbing. As a Falstaffian extrovert he had always disliked being worried.

Long before roll call that evening, when the absence of at least some of the twenty-five escapers could no longer have been concealed, the storm had broken. During the afternoon a German Unteroffizier interpreter from Schloss Kreuzenberg, traveling on leave by train to Danzig, had recognized two of his singularly uncommunicative fellow passengers as British officers from Oflag VIII G. With their arrest, and a quick check at the fortress which revealed that twenty-five officer prisoners were missing, it was only a matter of hours before anxious German search parties at the Kreuzenberg fortress had discovered the manhole in the brick dome over the well, the rope ladder and the breached iron gate at the mouth of the overflow tunnel on the hill below the walls.

Amusement at the discomfiture of the German camp authorities, traditionally one of the vicarious delights of any successful breakout, was short-lived in the barracks of Kreuzenberg that night when a scared Wehrmacht orderly room clerk from the Kommandantur informed Group Captain Grace that Oberst Stahle had been relieved of his duties. Further, Stahle had already left the fortress, under escort, pending his appearance before a court-martial, not at the local military district headquarters but in Berlin. By midnight, a contingent of Gestapo men had arrived by bus from Danzig. By dawn, after the officer prisoners had spent a dreary, uneasy night on parade in the quadrangle, the Gestapo had completed a remorselessly methodical, inch-by-inch search of the camp. When they had gone, taking with them a sergeant, a corporal and six privates of the garrison guard, also to face court-martial, the British and Allied officers were allowed to return to the wreckage of their quarters. There was little complaint, though, for an air of uneasy speculation lay over Kreuzenberg, which was only briefly relieved by the arrival of Scheuriger, the new commandant. Although he was not, as had been dismally forecast, an SS man, he was clearly a harsher breed of German army officer than his predecessor. Unlike the presumably disgraced Stahle, Scheuriger was barely in his thirties, fresh from combat duties on the East Front, wore decorations awarded only since 1939 and was clearly indoctrinated with all the single-minded, unsmiling zeal of the dedicated National Socialist.

Grace's reactions were uncompromisingly gloomy.

"I don't like the smell of this. We asked for it, I suppose, and, by God, I think we're going to get it."

"Not we," said Dermott savagely. "You. And Lees. Just remember I begged you to forget about the well. Have they caught up with Bauer yet?"

Despairingly, Grace had shrugged his shoulders.

"Not yet. He's still around. That's all we need now. Subversion of a German officer and a breach of parole."

Within a week, all twenty-five of the escapers had been recaptured and returned to Kreuzenberg. They had been luckier than the air force men who had broken out of the camp at Sagan. Last to return was Lees, who, as might have been expected, had done well. He had reached Tuttlingen, within thirty miles of the Swiss frontier, before he was arrested, with some loss of dignity, in a lavatory at the railway station.

"I had a minute or two with him before they put him in the cooler," said Grace. "He's as cocky as ever."

"I'm glad somebody is," said Dermott. Although the initial uproar and confusion caused by the German reaction to the escape had died down, he had still been unable to shake off the feeling of imminent disaster which had plagued him for so long.

The following day, all officer prisoners at Kreuzenberg other than the escapers held in solitary confinement in the Kommandantur cells were summarily ordered to parade with their gear and rations. Complainingly they assembled and awaited the arrival of Scheuriger. When he came, the new commandant wasted no words.

"You are all being moved to a new camp," he said, "effective as of now. Group Captain Grace, I hold you personally responsible for the safe conduct of your officers. There will be no escaping foolishness. The guards have my explicit orders to shoot to kill."

Despite the groans with which the prisoners had greeted the announcement of their sudden and immediate departure, the prospect of a journey to another camp with a change of scenery and routine was viewed lightheartedly enough. The march out of the fortress, down the hill and across the fields to the railway yards at Kreuzenberg was almost a holiday occasion, with the sun warm on their backs and the spring fragrance of lilac and apple blossom sweetening the air of a brief, illusory freedom. Even the fact that no train waited for them in the yards, and no train came, called for little more than jocular comment. By late afternoon, though, as shadows began to lengthen and still they waited in a cold wind that had begun to sing in the telegraph wires of the yards, the prisoners were tired and hungry and restless, eager to be gone to wherever they were going. Then, just before a forlorn sunset, had come the announcement that they were returning to Schloss Kreuzenberg. Dispirited, they had straggled back across the fields at dusk, laboring up the same hill down which Lees and his men had so recently fled from the fortress, eager for the freedom which was almost in their grasp.

Returning from the Kommandantur that evening, after reporting to Oberst Scheuriger, Group Captain Grace reported that the day's march down to Kreuzenberg station had apparently only been a security measure to clear the camp while the twenty-five recaptured escapers of the Big Choir made the real move of the day, by army truck, for detention and trial at another camp.

Exhausted by their march and the day's frustrating events, the prisoners of Kreuzenberg went to sleep early that night, almost grateful to be back behind the rusted wire and stone walls of the fortress which most of them had known for so long. Dermott, though, was one who did not sleep easily. Nagging at his conscience was the escape committee's exploitation of Lees's knowledge of the fortress plans entrusted to him by Bauer.

The German officer, as such, meant nothing to him personally. What did matter to Dermott was that he had unwittingly betrayed a source of privileged information. Several times, as a working journalist before the war, he had had pressure put upon him by a worried editor or newspaper proprietor to reveal his sources of information for a story which caused a stir at Cabinet level in London or in Washington, but he always refused. Now, though, it was not his professional reputation as a trusted and respected writer that was at stake. In Bauer's case, exposure of the role which the German officer had accidentally played in the escape through the well could cost Bauer his life. For these reasons, Dermott had been relieved to see Bauer still going about his official duties in the fortress the following day. To ease his own troubled mind, Dermott had decided that the least he could do would be to warn Bauer of the possibility of his implication in the escape. The quadrangle compound had been comparatively deserted, so he had been able to speak freely.

"Bauer," he said, speaking quickly before they could be interrupted, "I have something on my conscience."

"So?" said Bauer. "Even after twenty year as a journalist?"

In his ponderous, heavy-handed way, Bauer had always managed to derive some amusement, as had Dermott, from an occasional exchange of ironies and sarcasms at each other's expense.

"I'm serious," said Dermott. "This could cost you your neck. Those castle plans you let me have. They were the reason for the escape. I can't tell you who used them, but I want you to know that it was against my will. I was careless, if you like, but at no time was it my intention to break faith with you behind your back. I'm sorry about it and I apologize. You could be in real trouble, Bauer."

Bauer had looked at him sadly then, like a father with a wayward son.

"Herr Duncan," he said, "I am not as stupid as your gallant and foolhardy young officers might assume me to be. When I first heard about the escape, my immediate assumption was, in fact, that the fortress plans had gone astray. My next assumption was that if the plans had indeed been used for the escape, this was not because of any deliberate intent on your part. I have always thought you to be an honorable man. Because of what you have just told me I still consider you to be an honorable man. I thank you for the warning and I gladly accept your apologies."

"It's the least I could do," said Dermott. "Are the Gestapo still in charge of the investigation?"

Bauer shifted his briefcase to the other hand.

"I fear so."

"Can they trace anything back to you?"

Removing his glasses, Bauer squinted his nearsighted eyes in the morning sunshine as he polished the lenses against the lapel of his uniform with quick, fussy precision.

"I have never made the mistake of underrating the efficiency of the Gestapo," he said. "There is every reason to suppose they might question the old town archivist in Kreuzenberg from whom I borrowed the photostats of the plans."

That's bad, thought Dermott. Real bad.

"I hope like hell they don't," he said.

Bauer readjusted his glasses.

"I would not implicate you, Herr Duncan. There is enough trouble here already."

"I wasn't worried about that," said Dermott.

"Just the same," said Bauer, "you needn't let it worry you. Nor will I worry. There are other things to be considered. You see, I, too, have something on my conscience."

"Such as?" said Dermott.

Bauer had looked at him, suddenly ill at ease, and then had looked away quickly, as if he had not cared to meet Dermott's eyes.

"It is nothing I have done," he said. "One day, perhaps, I will tell you."

As the days went by, with no further Gestapo action, Dermott relaxed, as did the rest of the prisoners and internees at Kreuzenberg, for whom the dreary, familiar routine of captivity had at least returned to normal. Then, in May 1944 had come the BBC news from London via the camp's illegal radio that fifty of the fifty-three officers who had escaped from Stalag Luft III at Sagan in Silesia had been summarily executed, in secret, and without trial.

Group Captain Grace, more than any other prisoner at Kreuzenberg, had been shocked by the news. As Senior British Officer at Oflag VIII G, he had approved the Big Choir escape within a few weeks of the rumored breakout at Sagan.

"I hope to God that Lees and his boys don't get into the wrong hands," he said to Dermott. "Colonel Scheuriger won't tell me a damned thing about their whereabouts or what is happening to them."

"Nothing?" said Dermott. "Nothing at all?"

"Nothing," said Grace. "He won't even tell me where they've gone. He just keeps saying it's a matter for higher authority now. I don't mind telling you, Dermott, I'm worried. I don't like it one little bit."

Nor does anybody else, thought Dermott.

A few hours later Dermott had intercepted Bauer, who since the escape had only made rare appearances in the quadrangle compound. On these few occasions, Dermott had found him withdrawn and uncommunicative. Assuming that the German officer had been worrying, and with considerable justification, about the likelihood of Gestapo investigators linking the escape with his indiscretion over the castle plans, Dermott had shrugged aside the man's changed personality.

"No wonder you don't underestimate the Gestapo," he said. "After Sagan, neither do we."

"A bad business," said Bauer. "I don't like it any more than you do."

Bauer then had done something which Dermott was quick to notice as being quite out of character. Always before, Bauer's behavior as a German officer had been correct and exemplary. Now, in uniform and on duty in broad daylight in the prisoners' compound, he offered Dermott a cigarette and leisurely lit one himself.

"Thanks," said Dermott, relishing even the flavor of the cheap French brand which he had always regarded as being the bottom of the barrel. "What's worrying us now is what might be happening to Lees and the rest of the escapers from here. Christ only knows what the Gestapo could have done to them. The commandant won't say where they are. Do you know?"

"Yes," said Bauer, "I know where they are. I have always known. Keep looking at me and I will tell you."

"Keep looking at you?"

"Yes, keep looking at me."

Bauer's fingers were trembling so much Dermott wondered if he was going to drop the cigarette.

"They are in the well," said Bauer. "Wing Commander Lees and the other officers who escaped with him. All dead. Don't look, Herr Duncan. Don't look at the well. I think I am under observation. Be casual."

Either he's crazy or I'm crazy, thought Duncan. Twenty-five dead officers in a well and I've got to look casual.

"It happened the day you were all marched down to the railway station in the town," Bauer was saying. "The commandant paraded us all when you were gone. The whole garrison. The British officers were brought out of their cells in the cooler. The commandant read an order from Berlin. Then a squad of plainclothes detectives from the Gestapo and Kripo offices in Danzig shot the British officers, one by one. In the back of the neck. The Gestapo men took it in turn. Then they dumped the bodies down the well, threw down some hand grenades just in case anyone was still alive and had the bricks put back in the dome over the well. Even the bricklayer was a Gestapo man. They were gone by the time you all came back in the evening."

For a moment, Dermott didn't know whether it was angry bile or the rank French tobacco that suddenly gave him a bitter taste in his mouth. For several minutes he was too stunned to speak.

"I like the humanitarian touch with the grenades," he said. "As you say, it surely does not pay to underestimate the Gestapo."

A sardonic thought occurred to him and he laughed aloud, quite without humor.

"No wonder the commandant told Group Captain Grace that the case of Wing Commander Lees and the other escapers with him was now a matter for higher authority."

"Please," said Bauer. "I am not laughing. I told you I had something on my conscience. I said I would tell you about it one day. I just have. I could do nothing to stop it, but now, at least, I have done this much."

The German officer was obviously distressed, but Dermott had still been puzzled by the fact of Bauer having risked telling him about the executions.

"This is a war crime," said Dermott quietly. "You must know that. I have to report it to Grace."

"If you take my advice," said Bauer, "you will not report it to anybody till you get home again. The Nazis are tearing up the book of rules. Report this while you are still a prisoner, and you will achieve nothing except perhaps your own death at the hands of the Gestapo. Wait till it all ends and you are back in England or America."

"You could be right," said Dermott. "But why are you telling me all this? Aren't you taking a big chance?"

High up on the fortress walls a guard was coughing endlessly, and with indifference, as if just to pass the time.

"A friend of mine in the town just telephoned me," said Bauer. "The Gestapo are back in Kreuzenberg. They will be questioning the archives staff tomorrow. I don't have too much time left. Do you want some names for a dossier?"

Dermott knew what he had to do now. Bauer had just said the word. That's what he needed. A dossier. The documented story of a small massacre. The years at Kreuzenberg would not have been wasted if he could achieve this much.

He stared at Bauer.

"The Gestapo. I want all their names. And the Kripo boys, too. And if you don't know any names, then I want the names of people elsewhere who can tell me now or later. The events, too, and the times. I want to reconstruct the whole thing as it happened. There's a day coming for people like the Gestapo and the rest of them. We can't talk out here, though. Where can we? And when? As you said, Bauer, you might not have much time left."

"I know," said Bauer. "That's why I spoke to you."

Carefully he took off his glasses and put them in a pocket of his tunic.

"Knock me down," he said.

Open-mouthed, Dermott looked at him.

"I am still a German officer," said Bauer. "Knock me down and you'll get time in the cooler. Right away. Punitive solitary. Later tonight we can talk in your cell when I visit you to point out the error of your pigheaded American ways. You can take notes. I will hand the notes over to Group Captain Grace in a sealed envelope for you to claim when you come out of the cooler. Now quick. Schnell! Knock me down!"

"I hate to do this," said Dermott.

For the first time that morning, Bauer smiled, briefly.

"So long as you don't break my glasses."

More because he was unskilled at unarmed combat than because he was a big man, Dermott hit Bauer far harder than he had intended.

The consequences, as predicted by Bauer, were immediate. Within a few minutes of Bauer having been knocked down, bellowing for a guard, Dermott was on his way to the Kommandantur to face a charge of having struck a German officer.

Prevailed upon to apologize to Bauer by a puzzled and nervous Group Captain Grace, who had hurriedly sought to intervene, Dermott was sentenced to fourteen days' solitary confinement.

Bauer came to the cell that night. For three hours Dermott questioned him, detailing the answers in the notebook which would be returned, as confiscated property, to Grace for repossession by Dermott on his release. When they had finished, Dermott had the basis of a dossier, not only on the Gestapo men, but also the criminal policemen from Kripo headquarters in Danzig who had helped carry out the killings at the well. Where Bauer had not known a name he had supplied names of officials in Kreuzenberg, Danzig and Berlin who had authorized, planned or administered the policy of execution at Schloss Kreuzenberg.

"That's enough for a start," said Dermott. "Later on I'll get the names of all the garrison staff who were paraded. They were witnesses. I'll need them."

Bauer stood up, buttoning his greatcoat.

"I didn't have time to get those," he said. "And I don't think I'll have time tomorrow."

"You've done enough," said Dermott. "If you make out OK tomorrow after the Gestapo get through asking awkward questions in town, I'd like to know."

"It will be a pleasure," said the German officer.

They had shaken hands then, and after Bauer had gone, Dermott had lain awake for a long time, nourishing thoughts of the retribution he was desperately resolved to bring down upon the heads of the Gestapo men and their Kripo colleagues from Danzig.

The next night it was not Bauer but Group Captain Grace who visited him in the cell.

"Did Bauer give you a sealed envelope?" Dermott asked immediately.

"He did," said Grace. "It's stowed away. No worries."

"Where's Bauer?" asked Dermott.

"That's why I'm here," said the group captain. "Bauer is dead. He shot himself this afternoon. The Kreuzenberg archivist talked this morning after they broke his arm. He told the Gestapo about Bauer borrowing the photostats of the fortress plans. Somebody tipped Bauer off they were coming up here for him, so he took the quick way out. Can't say I blame him, either. By the way, you're in the clear. He left a note for the commandant saying he left his brief case in one of the barrack latrines and that somebody must have opened it and had a look at the plans. Not a bad little chap for a Jerry, that Bauer. At least we're all off the hook on that parole business."

As soon as he came out of solitary, Dermott began transcribing his shorthand notes for the Kreuzenberg dossier. Slowly and patiently, exploiting his position as editor of the official, hand-lettered camp news-sheet, which he had founded for the express purpose of being able to make regular contact with German personnel in the Kommandantur offices, Dermott completed the dossier with the names, ranks and numbers of every member of the fortress garrison who had paraded in the quadrangle compound for the executions at the well. During casual conversations with Kommandantur staff associated with the censoring of the camp's news-sheet, Dermott also checked the names of Gestapo and Kripo men implicated in the executions. Employing the interrogative and deductive skills which had served him so well for so long as a foreign correspondent and author before and during the war, Dermott achieved his objective without arousing either suspicion or interest. By the autumn of 1944, the dossier, as it stood, was already an indictment in itself, even without further recourse to further investigation by Allied intelligence or police authorities. During the winter of 1944–45, Dermott completed the task of transposing the dossier into the typescript of *Kreuzenberg*, his novel, as a lengthy and documented chapter, "The Well of Death," which was superficially the description of a seventeenth-century day of execution at Schloss Kreuzenberg.

With the names, ranks, numbers and other details of the actual 1944 executions carefully garbled in a simple code, only a Gestapo investigator schooled in the long history of Schloss Kreuzenberg would have been able to recognize "The Well of Death" chapter as a cover story for an incriminating and contemporary dossier.

By December 1944, Dermott had typed three copies of the entire manuscript. One he gave into Group Captain Grace's care and one he entrusted to the camp's padre, a Welsh minister captured at Crete, jestingly promising them both invitations to the publisher's party for the launching of the book.

Remembering Bauer's warning about the Gestapo, Dermott had not disclosed to anybody the true facts of the disappearance of Lees and his men, other than to stipulate that in the event of his death the manuscripts should be handed over to Allied intelligence authorities.

The third copy of the book Dermott stowed with his little portable typewriter in a rucksack, ready for the obviously imminent move westward away from the approaching Russian forces as they rolled inexorably through East Prussia and Pomerania toward the Baltic coast.

When it came, the move out of the camp was panic-stricken and ill-organized. Russian penetrations had been reported on the coast west of Kreuzenberg, between Danzig and Stettin, and the Germans of the fortress garrison were plainly scared.

On a bitter night shrouded by snow and speared with ice, the prisoners of Schloss Kreuzenberg had turned their shivering backs on the hilltop fortress, too chilled and dispirited even to look over their shoulders at the flame and smoke of the thunderous demolition charges which Oberst Scheuriger had ordered set. For Dermott, as for every man in the forced evacuation of Oflag VIII G, January and February 1945 were not so much months on a calendar as infinities of frozen despair during which they thought no longer of freedom but prayed only for survival as they trekked westward into Silesia and, finally, Saxony.

After a day's march on snow-trampled roads, even a night's shivering rest on sodden straw in a ramshackle barn became something to be treasured, a few hours' respite from blizzards, trigger-happy guards and the risk of strafing and rocketing by British or American fighter-bombers. Early in April 1945, the survivors of the trek from Kreuzenberg had come to rest in the cheerful squalor of an overcrowded stalag for British army prisoners in

Saxony. Free at last from the exhaustion, the terror and the peril of the snow-cursed refugee roads of eastern Germany, the men from Kreuzenberg had slept thankfully enough under leaking canvas in the mud of the open compounds of their new camp. Three weeks later, the stalag had been liberated by a Russian infantry division as Konev's forces swarmed westward to the line of the Elbe. Through it all, Dermott had clung to the manuscript of *Kreuzenberg* with its coded chapter detailing the circumstances of the executions at the well. Neither Group Captain Grace nor the perpetually and irritatingly jolly padre were with him at the camp in Saxony. They had fallen out sick during the long nightmare of the trek from Kreuzenberg. Not knowing what might have happened to them, Dermott was more anxious than ever before to cross the Elbe and reach London with "The Well of Death," the story that he sensed would finally justify his existence as a writer.

Within forty-eight hours of the stalag's liberation, Dermott was on his way again, wandering westward to the Elbe, where it was rumored the Russian cavalry had already linked up with the American patrols probing eastward from the Mulde.

Less than five miles from Torgau, scene of the rumored junction of the fronts, Dermott had stopped the jeep with the youthful-looking American padre in the smartly pressed uniform of an officer of the United States Army. In a buttonhole of his battle-dress jacket he was wearing a jaunty sprig of lilac. To the padre and the three strangely silent American enlisted men with him, Dermott had outlined the circumstances of the small massacre at Kreuzenberg. He had mentioned earlier attempts to make coded reference to the shootings by POW mail to London but had not referred to the dossier in his manuscript. Then he had demanded immediate transportation back to and beyond the American lines.

"It mightn't sound very Christian, padre," he said, "but I want like hell to see these Gestapo men swing. And the commandant at Oflag VIII G, Scheuriger."

"Not very Christian at all," the padre had agreed, smiling amiably. "Just the same, you can certainly ride along with us, Herr Duncan."

The padre had been Schrader, the Fehme Freikorps leader, and

Dermott once again had found himself a Prominente prisoner, this time at Schloss Galgenstein.

You've never really got it made in this life, Dermott thought. Just when you've got things going for you, the world blows up in your face. One thing, though, the Fehme don't know there's a complete dossier in "The Well of Death." At least I gave myself that much of a break even if I did open my great big mouth too wide and too soon.

The subsequent proceedings of the court of honor at Schloss Galgenstein had fascinated Dermott almost as much as they had alarmed him. They were a macabre jest in jurisprudence, a process for legalizing kidnaping and murder, and as such, merely reflected the ultimate policies and practices of the Third Reich itself. Dermott had in no way been surprised. What had sustained him as he listened to Schrader and Krausnick building their distorted charges of espionage against him was the knowledge that he was witnessing the birth of the Fehme, a neo-Nazi movement already waiting to raise again the burning flag of militant German nationalism after it had fallen from the palsied hands of the madmen in Berlin. With the Fehme story and "The Well of Death," he could write his own ticket back in London and New York. Move over, Quentin Reynolds. Move over, John Gunther. Dermott Duncan is back in town. If only these fools in their cellar knew what I could do to them, thought Duncan. The gilded general. The SS bastard in the padre's uniform. The dumb Saxon farmers and the play-acting soldiers with lilac in their lapels. They'd shoot me on the spot if they had half a chance.

The jury of Freischoffen had solemnly found him guilty, of course. In the eyes of the court of honor he was a Spion, an agent of traitorous intent, not a freed captive seeking retribution for the silent men in the black leather topcoats and narrow-brimmed felt hats who had shot twenty-five British officers in the back of the neck and dumped their bodies down a well. Now the prosecutor, the paranoiac one they called Krausnick, was bowing to the judge, the blinded general with the dark glasses.

"You speak German?" von Bluckau said.

"I speak fluent German, Italian, French, Spanish and passable English," said Dermott.

The thin face above the high, tight military collar was disdainful as von Bluckau nodded.

"You have been found guilty of espionage by this sworn court of honor of the Fehme. Have you anything to say before I pass sentence?"

Dermott thought of the dossier. "The Well of Death." The twenty-five bodies rotting in the dank depths of the old well far below the cobblestones of the quadrangle of the burned-out shell of Schloss Kreuzenberg. Somehow, he had to get out of this alive. The big thing was to get to London with the evidence. If he achieved this much, his time as a prisoner would not have been entirely wasted. He would gain nothing by shooting his mouth off and saying what he wanted to say. He must bide his time. For once, he would shut up.

Feeling absurd, he inclined his head slightly in what he hoped might be construed as a mark of respect to von Bluckau and the court over which he presided.

"I have nothing to say except that I am not guilty of the charge, regardless of the court's finding."

At this, von Bluckau had sat back, relaxed, almost as if he had been anticipating a tirade of abuse from the big American in the crumpled, untidy civilian clothes. Then he sat forward again, speaking with slow deliberation.

"In view of the status previously accorded you as a Prominente prisoner by the government of the Third Reich, the order of this court is that you shall be kept in custody as a hostage pending a ruling from the leadership of the Fehme.

The general nodded peremptorily.

"Remove the prisoner."

Dermott went back to the dark and chilled cells of Schloss Galgenstein exulting in his good fortune. He was still a prisoner but he was also still alive and "The Well of Death" dossier was still in his rucksack.

Listening as Dermott was returned to his cell, von Bluckau wondered about the next prisoner, a German national and, of all things, a hairdresser from Torgau. Idly, von Bluckau sought to remember just what squalid offense had been committed by this entirely undistinguished defamer of the ideals of German honor.

VI
The Burgermeister Who Surrendered

HORST GRABER WAS neither merely a hairdresser nor was he, in fact, a citizen of Torgau. Until April 1945, Graber had for three years been the Burgermeister of Lutzin, a small market town on the west bank of the Neisse in Silesia. Born in Lutzin, Graber had never left the town, except for holiday visits to Dresden or Berlin or the Baltic coast, until he was conscripted for army service in 1939. His career as a soldier of the Third Reich was as brief as it was indifferent. In France, during the Wehrmacht's victorious blitzkrieg summer of 1940, he had been the only survivor of a minor incident of German arms when the supply truck on which he was riding toward encircled and burning Dunkirk was ambushed by a lonely dug-in British antitank-gun manned by Tommies committed to a desperate rear-guard action. Their fire was as effective as their hopes were forlorn. The unsuspecting truck on the country road was a plump target and they did not miss. Running from the flaming wreckage of the capsized truck, Graber had been mistakenly cut down by machine-gun fire from the confused crew of a passing German tank. Graber went home to Lutzin in a hospital train with one arm less but an inward contentment in the thought that he was returning from the front to the little town on the west bank of the unhurried Neisse. The son of a passionately left-wing father for whom Germany's last hope of national salvation had been the Weimar Republic, Horst Graber had never agreed that the holocaust of another war was the proper and rational course for a National Socialist Germany.

Surviving front-line duty with one arm and an Iron Cross, Second Class, he had been happy enough just to come home from France to his wife, his friends and his tobacconist's shop and hairdressing business in Lutzin's oak-shaded Bismarckplatz. Superficially, he saw little that had changed. The Wehrmacht's triumphant blitzkrieg in the west was a long, long way from Silesia. In Lutzin, the houses, the shops and, beyond the town, the farms and the fields were exactly as Graber had always remembered them during his time as a soldier. There were the missing faces, of course, and the funeral notices solemnly recording the fact that yet another son of Lutzin had died a hero's death at the front, but the Neisse still flowed serenely below the graceful spans of the Siebenjahrenbrucke, Lutzin's only bridge and traditionally the pride of the town's burghers. Seven years it had taken to build after Napoleon's soldiers, retreating from Moscow, had blown up its predecessor. Seven long years of sweat and skill and sacrifice, so the town's archives said. One sweeping arch of stone for each year of constructon. To Graber, as to most people of Lutzin, the Siebenjahrenbrucke was as much an enduring monument to the courage and determination of their Silesian forebears as it was a way to cross the river. It was over a town council issue on the Seven Years' Bridge that Graber, soon after his return from France in 1940, had become Burgermeister.

As a member of the town council of Lutzin, Horst had been instrumental in defeating a move for the demolition of the Seven Years' Bridge and its replacement by a modern steel viaduct capable also of carrying rail traffic across the Neisse. In the uproar which followed the vote in the council chamber of the old Rathaus, the Burgermeister had resigned. Induced by friends to stand for the office, Graber found himself elected. On his first day, standing at a window of the Burgermeister's office in the fifteenth-century Rathaus, Graber had looked across the gabled roofs and chimney pots of Lutzin and smiled down at the Seven Years' Bridge, still spanning the Neisse with seven arches of good Silesian stone.

"Good morning, old friend," he had whispered to the bridge. "Stand fast, stand fast. I'll see to it that you do."

There had been no more talk of railway viaducts after that, though, for as the course of the war thundered on, year after year, the Third Reich and the Reichsbahn had had more urgent uses for Ruhr steel and Silesian iron than a new bridge for Lutzin.

The final threat, when it came, was voiced by a tired, unsmiling lieutenant of engineers on the morning of April 17, 1945.

The scout car in which he had arrived in the Bismarckplatz was one of the last of a long column of German army vehicles which all night had been rumbling across the Seven Years' Bridge to the west bank of the Neisse.

Warming his hands on the radiator of the scout car's overheated engine and shouting above the roar of tanks and trucks jamming the once quiet streets of Lutzin, the engineer lieutenant had warned Graber that the Russians were less than fifteen miles east of the river. They had launched a major offensive, he said, all along the line of the Oder and the Neisse. Wehrmacht forces were regrouping west of the rivers.

"I've got orders to blow the bridge," he shouted. "The town must be evacuated. Tell your people to get out. They can go west if they keep off the main roads."

"Why blow the bridge?" Graber shouted back. "The Russians will only assume you're going to defend the town. They'll smash it to bits. They'll shell it till there's nothing left. Then they'll cross the river in boats and have a pontoon bridge working in twenty-four hours. What's the use of it all now? Lieutenant, I'm going to surrender the town. And the bridge."

The engineer had reached for the Luger in its holster on his hip and then desisted, shrugging his shoulders.

"You'll hang if you do, Burgermeister. I have my orders. I'm still going to blow the bridge."

Tires squealing, the scout car had wheeled around in the square and disappeared toward the river, nudging its way impatiently past the oncoming columns of retreating tanks and trucks.

On the flagpole of the clock tower of the Rathaus, where the blood-red swastika banner of the Third Reich had flown for so long, Graber had hoisted a white tablecloth.

To Graber's surprise, the ensign of surrender had brought no angry burst of fire from the retreating Wehrmacht formations crowding the square and the streets below, no shouted abuse from the people of Lutzin as they struggled to load carts, wheelbarrows and perambulators for the trek west to Saxony and the Elbe.

By mid-afternoon, when the town was cleared of army vehicles which had already fanned out westward into the open country and no more convoys came lurching furiously across the Seven

Years' Bridge, Graber walked slowly east to the Neisse. His own wife had already left for the Elbe, sharing a plodding oxcart with old friends and neighbors.

For a town under imminent threat of enemy attack, Lutzin was strangely quiet, even more peaceful and quiet now than he had ever known it. Past the deserted homes with the flimsy doors and windows hopefully locked against the Russians in their millions, Graber had strolled almost leisurely toward the river and the bridge.

In a bunker by the approach road across the meadows to the bridge, the engineer lieutenant and his sappers were waiting by the plungers wired to the demolition charges that, in one convulsive second, would destroy forever the graceful, time-hallowed arches of the Siebenjahrenbrucke.

Unshaven and with dust and sweat congealing on his sunburned neck, the lieutenant held a slice of dry, black bread in one hand and his Luger in the other.

"Burgermeister," he said, "take one step past this bunker toward those wires and for you the war is over."

Suddenly tired, Graber had simply nodded.

The lieutenant cut himself a slice of salami, all greasy in the sun.

"It's over anyway, Burgermeister. For all of us. Ever since Stalingrad I've been walking backwards and blowing up bridges."

"Why blow this one?" said Graber. "Particularly now."

"I'm just a lieutenant of engineers, that's why. It would be all the same if I was the general."

"I'm just a Burgermeister," said Graber. "But I've just surrendered my town."

The lieutenant belched gently and lit a cigarette. Garlic always gave him hell these days.

"I saw the white flag," he said, staring distastefully at the nicotine stains on his fingers. "They'll hang you for that. Why did you do it?"

Horst looked back critically at the clock tower of the Rathaus. Amazing how a tablecloth from a distance could look like a real white flag. He turned away, staring at the green roof of the boathouse down on the river bank. They had had some fine regattas there in the old days.

"I thought it might save a few lives," he said. "Maybe it might even save their homes for them. When they come back. And the bridge. When's it to be, by the way?"

The lieutenant grunted, reaching into a tunic pocket for his watch.

"Damned strap broke," he said.

Thoughtfully he looked at the watch in his hand.

"Ten minutes," he said. "Kaputt!"

For a few moments, Graber thought of making a dash for the bridge and the demolition charges, but he knew he would never make it. The engineer lieutenant was weary and discouraged, but he was still a good soldier. Too good not to shoot. Too good to miss.

The ten minutes passed slowly. A pair of finches sang and twittered peaceably in the pines behind the bunker. Across the river, cattle grazed on the familiar meadow farms that would soon be an area of Russian occupation. Once, behind the rising ground in the heat haze on the far bank of the Neisse, there was the faint metallic chatter of automatic weapons. Then silence.

"Stragglers?" said Graber, the onetime soldier.

The lieutenant nodded, getting out his watch again.

"Poor bastards," he said. "They've got two minutes to get to the bridge."

Long before any retreating German troops could have reached the bridge from the high ground to the east, the engineer had clenched his fingers over the watch.

"Now," he said, nodding to a sergeant waiting by the plunger in the squat, gray steel box. "Keep your heads down."

There was not one explosion but a series in sequence, crackling like a prolonged strike of lightning across the length of the bridge, gouting seven bursts of smoke and debris high into the air. Then, as wreckage falling from the sky lashed the river into foam, the entire structure writhed, twisted, lurched and, quite suddenly, slid roaring into the depths of the Neisse.

Where the Siebenjahrenbrucke had stood for centuries only an unspanned river flowed, still muddy and swirling with the forces of destruction.

"Good-bye, old friend," said Graber.

Overhead there was a sudden shrieking in the sky like express trains pounding through a tunnel.

"Good-bye is right," said the lieutenant. "That's the Russki artillery. I can take you as far as the town, Burgermeister, but no farther. The field police don't like civilians riding on Wehrmacht transport."

"No, thanks," said Graber. "I'll walk."

The engineer officer swung himself up into the scout car, wincing as the first of the shells cracked and roared in Lutzin.

"As you wish," he said. "If a Russki shell doesn't get you, a rope will. Good luck, Burgermeister. Sorry about your bridge."

Coughing a little in the trail of dust left by the speeding scout car, Graber had walked back into the town, utterly indifferent to the falling shells and crashing walls. In the Bismarckplatz, where incendiary shells had set some of the old oaks alight, Graber stood watching the Rathaus burn. When the clock tower fell down, grotesquely and slowly, taking with it the white flag of surrender, he had walked on out of the town, not caring whether he lived or died but consumed with a fierce hatred for the madness which had broken the bridge and was burning the town. Near the railway station, bright with fire in a cloud of red brick dust raised by the shells that were still falling, Graber had passed the overturned scout car and the bodies that hung untidily from it. The engineer lieutenant had blown his last bridge for the great retreat. Graber walked on alone.

With a cousin in Torgau on the Elbe a footsore and weary week later, Graber had found shelter and also news of total sorrow, for it was then that the final blow had come. The crowded local train on which his wife, with other refugees from the east, had been shuttling back east again to Torgau from embattled Leipzig had been strafed by American fighter-bombers between Riesa and Wurzen. She was dead before the burning train had even stopped, and by nightfall she had been buried in a mass grave hurriedly dug in a field alongside the railway line. Too shocked to speak after he had been told the news by his cousin, Graber had walked out onto the castle bridge at Torgau knowing only that he wanted nothing more but to leap deep down into the waiting waters of the Elbe.

It was the scout car which had changed Graber's mind about suicide. Not the scout car which had carried the stolid, tired lieutenant of engineers and his demolition charges to Lutzin and the Siebenjahrenbrucke. That scout car, he knew, was a flame-blistered wreck lying on its back in an acrid-smelling shellhole outside Lutzin and the engineer officer was dead. The scout car on Torgau Bridge was just one more anonymous, hurrying German Army vehicle like any other, crowded with exhausted and dispirited German soldiery retreating to the west. It was simply the evocative thought aroused by the sight of the scout car that had changed Graber's mind about self-destruction, the thought that maybe he could at least try to save the bridge at Torgau. Clearly the time was coming for its inevitable destruction by the demolition engineers of the Wehrmacht.

It was April 23, 1945, the day that Graber did not throw himself into the Elbe, and the people of Torgau were already whispering that Cottbus, Senftenberg, Elsterwerda, Grossenhain, Königsbruck and many other neighborly towns to the east had been captured by the Russkis as they drove implacably on from the Neisse toward the Elbe. Even Falkenberg, less than fifteen miles east of Torgau and previously reduced to blackened rubble by a wild-goose formation of USAAF Marauder bombers, had been occupied by the Russians. Few Torgauers questioned the order by the garrison commander that the entire civilian population was to evacuate the city while there was still time to get out. Brooding and apathetic, Graber had wandered the streets of Torgau and watched the citizens of the old city packing such possessions as they could carry and hastily preparing for the enforced trek to Klitzschen, thirty miles southwest of Torgau and just south of the road to Eilenburg, a town already decimated by American artillery which had advanced past Leipzig from the west.

Horst Graber recognized the recurring pattern of impending disaster. The Russians by then were not far away. It was while Torgau held its breath and waited that Graber made up his mind. He would save the bridge at Torgau. Whether he died or not in the attempt no longer mattered. There was nothing to live for any more. His dying in this way might achieve something, make some kind of sense, in all the nightmare destruction that had already taken from him his wife, his home, his town and his bridge.

The moment of final decision came for Graber at 1 P.M. on April 23, when Torgau's sirens howled a warning, not of air attacks from a sky suddenly deserted by American fighters and bombers. Instead, it was a tank alarm. Soon, from across the wide and flooding Elbe, Russian tanks and field guns were shelling Torgau. The East Front had reached the line of the Elbe.

Moving furtively around the town all that day and into the night, while the bombardment from the east bank boomed on until 11 P.M., Graber, crazed with an exultant excitement, completed his plans to save the bridge at Torgau.

The key to the success which Graber now sought with reckless and unreasoning obsession lay with an engineer battalion transiently quartered in Torgau's deserted high school in the Schloss-strasse. Among the ranks of the unit, Graber had happened upon two soldiers who were old friends and neighbors from Lutzin. Heartened by this providential contact, Graber had confided to them his hopes for saving Torgau's bridge. Embittered and disillusioned by the swath of useless destruction which had swept behind them on the retreat across Germany to the Elbe, they had already heard word-of-mouth rumors of Graber's attempts to save the Siebenjahrenbrucke on the Neisse and to preserve Lutzin by the surrender of the town. As battle-wearied soldiers who knew that Germany's defeat was already absolute, they endorsed Graber's stand at Lutzin but grimly predicted that he would yet swing by the neck for his convictions. They, too, though, had had enough of insensate destruction and of their own part in it. Risking with Graber the certainty of summary execution if they were detected, they had shown the little Burgermeister where to cut most effectively the electrical connections to the packs of explosives already clamped in position on both the castle bridge and the railway viaduct at Torgau. They also agreed to warn him when it was time to slash the wires, for to do it too soon would give the unit time to make them good again. By 11 P.M. on April 23, as the Russian bombardment stopped, Graber sensed that this was when he had to act. In the eerie silence which followed the cessation of shelling from across the river, he moved cautiously down the brick-strewn Schloss-strasse toward the schoolhouse billets of the engineer battalion and his friends from Lutzin.

Lit only by the careless flames of burning buildings, the city crouched below the dark bulk of Schloss Hartenfels like a trapped beast awaiting the hunter who would come with the dawn. For Torgau, Graber knew, the end of it all was only hours away. Keeping to the shadows, he came furtively and carefully to the high school to find that he was too late. The engineers had gone. They could only have moved up to the bridge, Graber reasoned. They would never have retreated west toward the Mulde while the bridges still spanned the Elbe. No longer cautious of interception by the field police, for time was now his enemy, Graber had turned and run desperately back along the city streets toward the bridge, broken glass from shattered windows crunching like ice under his boots and the garbage-incinerator smell of burning buildings heavy in his nostrils.

It was nearly 3:30 A.M. on April 24, with yet another day of retreat, chaos and death soon to dawn for Germany, as Graber ran onto the approaches to the bridge at Torgau, seeking the cables he had to cut. An exhausted, balding little man, he ran with a pair of heavy wire cutters cradled to his chest like a Tommy gun. Gasping for breath, he spurned the shouted warnings from startled engineer troops waiting by their plungers in the roadside bunkers and fled the pursuing shots that whined and buzzed as they ricocheted past him toward the towering structure of the bridge. One bullet, at random and nearly spent, clanged into the metal hand of his artificial arm, wrenching him around so that he spun on his feet and fell to the ground. Struggling to stand up, he was knocked down again by a sudden blossoming of heat, blast, flame and searing light. Before the brilliant flash of the explosion briefly blinded him to everything except a dizzy spectrum of all colors, Graber saw the silhouetted spans of the great bridge buckle and writhe like a living thing in pain and then thunder down into the dark, tumultuous waters of the Elbe.

Once again, nearly a thousand years after the first time in the recorded history of the old Elbeside town, the bridge at Torgau was down.

Broken masonry, splintered timber and twisted steelwork were still thudding down out of the dark and echoing sky when the field police arrested Graber.

Back in Torgau, the streets fogged by acrid smoke from the bombarded and burning buildings, the big men in the steel helmets nodded as he showed his papers.

"Graber?" said a field police lieutenant, briskly arrogant in the knowledge of the summary powers that gave him the right to arrest a general if necessary. "Horst Graber? The Burgermeister of Lutzin? The man who surrendered the town?"

"I tried to save the town," said Graber conscious only of the fact that he had failed again. "And to save our Siebenjahrenbrucke. And to save the bridge here at Torgau."

"Save your breath, Burgermeister," said the lieutenant. "You'll need it. You're under arrest. We've been watching for you."

Not long, though, was Graber in the cell where they had thrust him to lie distraught and shaken in the lonely darkness, nauseated by the stench of stale urine and excreta. Within a few hours, after day had dawned, the door had swung open. Expecting either a field police escort to a noose swinging from the nearest Torgau lamppost or else a burst of fire from a marauding Russian infantry patrol, Graber had been surprised to see that his visitors were merely two surly Germans in civilian clothes.

"Graber?" said the civilian, guardedly holding the door open.

The little Burgermeister nodded, wondering why they should be wearing celebratory sprigs of lilac in the lapels of their leather jackets.

"You're coming with us, Burgermeister," said the civilian at the door. The other one, Graber was puzzled to see, was holding what looked like a toy water pistol.

"Where?" said Graber. But neither man had spoken and he had gone silently with them.

So Horst Graber, lately the Burgermeister of Lutzin, lover of fine bridges, formerly a soldier of the Wehrmacht, holder of the Iron Cross, Second Class, with a jagged bullet hole in the hand of his artificial arm, had journeyed through the silent forests to Schloss Galgenstein and his arraignment at the court of honor of the Fehme in Saxony.

The case against Graber had been conducted on the basis of presumed and already proven guilt. The cross-examination of him by Krausnick had degenerated into a shouted tirade of invective and abuse until the seated general, whom Graber was startled to recognize as the aristocratic Graf von Bluckau of Galgenstein, had halted the proceedings.

"Mr. Prosecutor," said von Bluckau, "the court does not have unlimited time at its disposal. I suggest that if you have completed the case against the accused, it be now put to the Freischoffen of the jury."

The corners of his mouth foamed with spittle, Krausnick had nodded, breathing heavily still with the fury of the emotions which had stirred his rabid denunciations of Graber.

To a man, the Freischoffen were unanimous. The accused, Horst Graber, was guilty.

A proper decision, thought von Bluckau. Sound, even on conventional military grounds. Only a madman or a traitor would seek to prevent the demolition of a major bridge behind a hard-pressed German army or even consider surrendering a German town and its people to the untender mercies of waves of Bolshevik barbarians from out of the east. There was no doubting what penalty this conviction demanded.

"Do you have anything to say before I pronounce sentence?" von Bluckau asked, his voice curt with contempt.

"The bridges!" Graber shouted, his voice ringing out suddenly. "Let the bridges speak!"

A tiny muscle began jumping on the thin, scarred jaw of the general.

"You will be quiet," said von Bluckau.

"Let the bridges speak!" raved Graber. "You are the people who should be on trial. The leaders of despair. The field marshals of folly. The generals of chaos. The breakers of bridges and the destroyers of villages. The bridges know! Ask the bridges!"

A Fehme man held Graber, then, one arm hooked around his throat to silence him.

"Horst Graber," said von Bluckau, "you have been tried by this court of honor on charges of cowardice, treachery and attempted sabotage and you have been found guilty. I find that there are no extenuating circumstances associated with your act of cowardice and treachery in attempting to surrender the town of Lutzin and your act of sabotage in attempting to prevent the demolition of a tactically vital bridge at Torgau. Had you succeeded in your despicable intentions, you would not only have assisted the enemies of the Third Reich in the course of their invasion of our beloved fatherland, but you would also have endangered the security of large formations of our fighting comrades on the

Oder-Neisse front. I have no alternative, therefore, and, I might add, no compunction in so doing, but to sentence you to death. On the rising of this court you will be taken hence to a public highway and there hanged by the neck from the tallest tree so that all who pass may see that the cause of German honor is still sacred to the Fehme."

The blind general looked up as if he were trying to see what manner of a man was this Graber.

"Remove the prisoner," he said.

For a while after Graber had been dragged away struggling and shouting, his ravings echoed crazily in every dark, time-forgotten corner of the dungeons of Schloss Galgenstein.

"The bridges," he kept shouting. "Ask the bridges! The bridges know the traitors."

Over and over again, the ranting litany of his despair rang between the walls of stone. There was a thudding blow, a scream of pain, the clang of a slammed iron door and then silence.

VII
The Girl Who Hated Lilacs

MY GOD, THOUGHT Caroline Brookwood as her name was called. The little Burgermeister might be unbalanced, but by comparison with the men of the court of honor he is entirely sane. Saner, by far, than this blinded general with the death-mask face. Saner than these stupid gutter bullies with the lilac in their lapels. What hope have any of us got before such a tribunal of lunacy?

Staring at the sword and the noose on the plain, rough army blanket on the table between her and the impassive, sightless general, Caroline found herself revolted less by the ritualistic murder trappings of the court before which she stood as an accused than by the pervasive, nostalgic scent of lilac all about her. In the confines of the great cellar it was as rich as the smell of custard hot from the pot.

The lilacs of Germany, growing wild in sweet hedgerows, were something she had never been able to take for granted, least of all on April 26, the day the Russian general and the American general shook hands when the fronts met on the Elbe at Torgau. So far had she come since the time when, with the influence of her father and the Brookwood group of daily newspapers in the Midlands, she had joined the U.S. First Army as an accredited war correspondent. From her first day in Germany she had marveled at the nostalgic fragrance of the lilacs and the prodigal, innocent glory of their blossoms.

Through all the stink of war, though, for it was, as always, an unsanitary, untidy and heedless business, Caroline had still been able to wonder at the scent of the lilacs—the brave flowers of victory or the mocking wreaths of defeat, depending on the uniform in which you had gone to war. Whichever way you looked at it, though, the lilacs were there and you could marvel at the persistence of a natural cycle of creation of beauty that still ran its course, regardless of the men who fought and crouched and crawled across the fields of Germany or died in the open graves of the hidden camps with the oozing putrefaction of their wasted bodies darkening the antiseptic purity of the scattered quicklime. Under skies raveled by the white contrails of Allied bomber formations or fouled with the sacrificial smoke belching briskly from the chimneys of SS crematoriums, the lilacs had still bloomed in the German spring. So beautiful were the scent and sight of the lilacs that she had begun to find something almost obscene about the blooms that burgeoned so while the war engulfed the farms and villages of the Third Reich.

Often, while she had waited for a censor or a phone or a jeep from the motor pool at the press camp, Caroline had begun to wonder about the lilacs. Applying the brittle logic of the London cocktail parties, which had begun to bore her to screaming point before her accreditation to SHAEF as a correspondent, she had assumed that her preoccupation with the lilacs was some kind of sublimation of a neurosis associated with Mike's disappearance in action. She still could not accept the fact that the wedding would never take place. Not just on a mere presumption of Mike's death. People you loved surely died more tidily and definitively than that. Endlessly she had marshaled and remarshaled the only known facts about his disappearance. Hit by heavy flak coming out of the Leipzig target area on the second shuttle raid across Germany in 1944, Mike's B-17, *Old Sour Kraut,* had never reached the briefed base in Russia. Flying as the lead aircraft of the lead squadron from their base in Cambridgeshire, Mike's crew had been bound to get unlucky sooner or later. Most of the other B-17 crews in Mike's wing had watched *Old Sour Kraut* dropping back out of formation that sunny morning with the No. 1 engine stopped and smoking, the airscrew on No. 2 engine idly windmilling and a bright ribbon of fire licking back from the tanks in the port wing. Just before the burning wing exploded and, lifting sharply, broke away, the watching gunners in the other aircraft of Mike's squadron had counted eleven parachutes popping into view like mushrooms below the ragged, drifting smoke-bursts of the flak. The white canopies of the dwindling parachutes were still visible long after the spinning, amputated hulk of *Old Sour Kraut* had erupted in a splash of fire in a forest just east of the Elbe. Including Mike as co-pilot, eleven parachutes accounted for the entire crew, yet nothing had been heard of them since. Alive enough to grab at their rip-cord handles when they jumped from *Old Sour Kraut,* they had vanished entirely into limbo over some of the most peaceful countryside of the Third Reich, clear of any target city and far from any fighting front. The United States Eighth Air Force knew nothing. Nor the RAF. Nor the Air Ministry. Nor the International Red Cross. Mike and his crew had vanished utterly and completely, just as if they had never existed. Obsessed with the circumstances of Mike's disappearance—missing in action, presumed dead—Caroline had induced her father to arrange accreditation for her as a correspondent for the national women's magazine which Brookwood Press had bought just before the war. Ever since her arrival on a captured Luftwaffe airstrip in a creaking C-47, Caroline had remorselessly exploited her privileged position as a war correspondent to carry out an unending search for Mike or at least for confirmation of the time and place of his death. Preoccupied with this private mission of despair, she had unconsciously begun to assimilate something of the strange, almost medieval mystique of this Germany of pines, ranked like endless, austere armies in the gloomy twilight of their domain; this Germany of sullen, arrogant, suspicious, angry, frightened but never repentant faces.

For Caroline, it had been a solemn moment of truth when, in common with all the correspondents and photographers of the press camp, she had realized that, quite suddenly and inevitably, the U.S. First Army was about to link up with the Russians somewhere along the banks of the Elbe. Such a confrontation of two great armies was not so much the occasion for just another rushed story, a hurried dispatch or a formal press release as it was a climactic moment in the struggle for Europe. A little more than a year before, when she had first met Mike after his crew had flown *Old Sour Kraut* into their USAAF base in misted, green-ditched Cambridgeshire and D-Day was still to come, the East Front and the West Front had seemed almost as little likely to meet as the North Pole and the South Pole. To Caroline, in England, the campaigns in the east had always been remote and disembodied, like a struggle for existence between esoteric forms of life on another planet.

Yet, on April 26, the two worlds had met at Torgau on the Elbe in Saxony, and Caroline had been there to see it.

First, though, had come the days of tension, speculation and uncertainty as a million Americans and Russians, allied, yet intrinsically alien, sought to close the gap between the two fronts. Contacts and rumors of contacts were legion. Rumor had succeeded frenzied rumor until on April 25, as day dawned over the tangled wreckage of the bridges which had been blown up at Torgau only a few hours earlier, Caroline had joined the contingent of war correspondents and combat photographers descending excitedly, not only on the headquarters of General Emil F. Reinhardt, commander of the 69th Divison, V Corps, U.S. First Army, at Naunhof, a provincial town in Saxony east of Leipzig, but elsewhere along the line held by the division on the Mulde.

While the minutes ticked by on April 25, tension mounted at Naunhof as reports filtered back to the frustrated press camp that the patrols of the 69th Division were really beginning to get somewhere. Eagerly the press moved forward again to the headquarters of Colonel C. M. Adams, commanding officer of the division's 273rd Infantry Regiment, which was halted at Trebsen on the Mulde. While they waited, questioning and speculating, at the colonel's crowded command post in a villa once comfortably occupied by a wealthy Trebsen burgher, the situation changed hourly, but only to get more confused.

By 11:30 A.M. on April 25, the first contact between the two fronts was made when a bustling jeep patrol led by an eager young Texan, Lieutenant Albert L. Kotzebue, Company G, First Battalion, 273rd Infantry Regiment, met a lonely Russian cavalryman in a farmyard at Leckwitz, a village just a few miles west of the Elbe near Strehla, twenty kilometers southeast of Torgau.

By 4:45 P.M., a patrol led by Major Frederick W. Craig, executive officer of Kotzebue's own battalion, had contacted a troop of horsemen, motorcyclists and bicyclists from the First Guards Zhitomir Cavalry Regiment at Clanzschwitz village, only a few miles from Leckwitz, where Kotzebue had made the first contact of the day during his dash to the Elbe.

Meanwhile, by 4 P.M. that day, 2nd Lieutenant William D.

Robertson, also of the First Battalion, 273rd Infantry Regiment, had reached Torgau on the Elbe with a four-man patrol in a single jeep and crawled across the shattered girders of the castle bridge to shake hands precariously with Russian infantrymen also clinging to the twisted girders after having made their way across the river from the east bank.

Within a few hours, Robertson was triumphantly returning to his battalion's headquarters at Wurzen on the Mulde with four official emissaries of the Red Army—a major, two other officers and an NCO. They were from the 173rd Infantry Regiment of Major General Vladimir Rusakov's 58th Russian Guards Division.

By 8 P.M., Major Conley, commanding officer of Robertson's battalion at Wurzen, was rushing the young lieutenant and his four Russians to Colonel Adams' regimental headquarters at Trebsen, farther south along the Mulde, where Caroline, like most of the other waiting correspondents, sympathized with the colonel in the predicament in which he had found himself all day.

Colonel Adams' announcement that four Red Army emissaries were on their way from Wurzen to the villa at Trebsen created further uproar in his regimental headquarters. By 8:50 P.M, the Russians had arrived, escorted by Major Conley and Lieutenant Robertson. As the press clamored impatiently for interviews and pictures, the Russian visitors were hurried into the map-lined drawing room for discussions with Colonel Adams and his staff. While Caroline shared endless cigarettes and cups of coffee with friends among the waiting pressmen, Colonel Adams had talked with the four representatives of the Russian forces on the division's front—Major Lexinov, Captain Neda, Lieutenant Slaviancko and Sergeant Dnavovich Andnejer. Within seven minutes of the Russians' arrival at his command post, the colonel was telephoning General Reinhardt with the news that the Soviet general, Rusakov, wanted a meeting with the American divisional general at Torgau at 10 A.M. on next day, April 26. After supper, and the inevitable patriotic toasts, the Russians were escorted out of the Trebsen villa at 10:30 P.M., past the crowding pressmen, to Naunhof, where they met General Reinhardt. There, after further talks and still more toasting of the armies now met on the Elbe, Colonel Adams was ordered to attend the 10 A.M. meeting with General Rusakov at Torgau next morning and to arrange for a meeting of the two generals in the afternoon. With the Russians anxious to return to their unit on the east bank of the Elbe, beyond Torgau, Colonel Adams led the party back to his regimental headquarters at about 1 A.M.

After radio messages had been sent warning Major Craig and Lieutenant Kotzebue, still waiting with their mystified and disappointed patrols near Muhlberg, east of the Elbe, to halt any further moves for a Russo-American meeting, the colonel moved out again in the pre-dawn gloom of April 26, leading a column of thirteen jeeps along the lonely road to Torgau. With the four tired Russian emissaries, the column reached Torgau at 5:30 A.M. Rather than waste time crawling across the wreckage of the bridge, members of the patrol were ferried across the river in racing shells from the local Torgau rowing club.

Neither Caroline nor any of her impatient and frustrated colleagues had accompanied the dawn convoy. The first and only pressman to cross the Elbe on this occasion was Jack Thompson, war correspondent for the Chicago *Tribune* and president of the U.S. First Army Press Camp. By 10 A.M., though, as the rising sun broke through the morning mists along the Elbe, Caroline had joined groups of photographers and journalists in a dash to Torgau from Naunhof, Wurzen and Trebsen. Crossing the river by boat, they were in time to take photographs and get interviews as Colonel Adams, commanding officer of the 69th Division's 273rd Infantry Regiment, and Colonel Rogol, commanding officer of the 58th Russian Guards Division's 173rd Infantry Regiment, toasted each other at an early morning banquet set up in a wrecked and rubble-strewn German farmhouse about half a mile from the east bank of the Elbe, opposite Torgau.

With much bustling to and fro, the day had passed until, shortly before 4 P.M., General Reinhardt had arrived at Torgau. Swiftly the 69th Division's 272nd Regimental Combat Team—a battle-tested infantry regiment with a supporting battalion of field artillery—had moved east from its reserve positions at Leipzig to guard the flanks of the road from Eilenburg to Torgau. Since desperate units of the Wehrmacht were known to be still retreating northward toward Berlin from Dresden in the no man's land between the Mulde and the Elbe, the precaution was a soldierly tactic and one welcomed by Caroline, who already had been unable to shake off an inexplicable feeling of impending danger, even as the penultimate climax of the official link-up had loomed closer. Then, exhilarated by the sunshine and the infectious picnic mood of the day's occasion, Caroline had relaxed while she joined the other correspondents to watch General Reinhardt, balanced in one of the narrow-gutted Torgau racing shells, being rowed 175 yards across the deep, fast-flowing Elbe to the East Front by grinning Red Army infantrymen obviously enjoying their duty as oarsmen. Safely ashore—the lighthearted Russian soldiers had been toasting the occasion, too, and still had bottles clenched between their boots as they rowed—General Reinhardt walked up the east bank with his flag-bearing party of staff officers to be greeted more suspiciously than cordially by General Rusakov and members of his own divisional staff. After an exchange of courtesies on the green meadows by the Elbe, the two generals and their staff officers moved to the farmhouse mess of the Russian infantry regiment, where Colonel Adams had already breakfasted, with many toasts in hard liquor, earlier in the day.

While flashbulbs flared, cameras clicked, pencils scribbled and vodka splashed into crystal glasses and dented canteen cups, the two generals toasted the meeting.

For a few hours, Caroline had forgotten her perpetual preoccupation with the circumstances of Mike's disappearance as she marveled at the tangible evidence before her, even as the wild lilacs bloomed in the sunshine outside the farmhouse, that the vast and awesome machinery of the Allied armies in Europe should at last be grinding victoriously toward a long-planned and hard-fought-for conclusion.

From Stalingrad had come Major General Rusakov's 58th Russian Guards Division, a part of the 34th Russian Corps under Major General Balankov, and of the 5th Ukrainian Army under Colonel General Jadov in the Army Group of Marshal Konev.

From Mississippi, U. S. A., over the stormy Atlantic to England and across the winter-bound roads and fields of France, Belgium and Germany had come Major General Emil F. Reinhardt's 69th Division, a part of V Corps under Major General Clarence

F. Huebner and of the U.S. First Army under General Courtney L. Hodges, in the 12th Army Group of General of the Army Omar N. Bradley.

Now, with their dead buried behind them, the two fighting divisions of infantrymen had met face to face on a spring day by a river in Saxony. There were no more rivers to cross.

Mike would have liked to have been here for this, Caroline had thought. Like so many other forgotten B-17s, though, *Old Sour Kraut* had long since flicked and spun out of formation that high and lonely day east of the Elbe, near this same Torgau, shedding a burning, broken wing and the drifting white blossoms of parachute canopies.

While the two generals had exchanged the grave and cautious courtesies of military protocol in the field and the sunshine sparkled on the towers and windows of old Schloss Hartenfels across the Elbe at Torgau, Caroline had mingled with the Russian and American troops as, in their own fashion, they celebrated the fact of the big link-up. While protesting members of the party of about fifty war correspondents and photographers were still clamoring for admittance to the farmhouse banquet where seven tables had been set with looted damask cloths, glass and silverware, Caroline had strolled down to the green meadows by the east bank of the Elbe. Here, where irresolute bands of liberated slave workers and prisoners washed their feet or yawned in the sun while they waited to cross the river, was where she sought the facts which would make the occasion real and immediate to the millions of housewives who would read her magazine column back home in England. Here, where girl camp-followers of the Red Army listened, clapping their hands, as Soviet soldiers sang to the music of accordions looted from a factory in Torgau. Listening, too, were the infantrymen from the U.S. 69th Division, drinking wine, cognac and vodka as they sat pleasurably in the sun with no enemy in front of them, no enemy behind them. Some of the GIs were already wearing high-fitting Russian field boots for which they had exchanged their own GI boots or shoes. Like children at a party, Russian and American soldiers were exchanging weapons and playfully cutting patterns on brick walls with one another's Tommy guns.

Just seventy-five miles south of Berlin, where the besieged

defenders of the encircled capital were still desperately delaying the final hour of certain defeat, the air at Torgau was sweet with the sounds, the sights and the scents of victory.

The lilac was in bloom, thought Caroline, but not for Mike.

Tired suddenly by the excitement of the day's events and exhausted by the tension of the prior days' waiting, Caroline had taken a path away from the river. It led, she could see, to a village crouched at the distant frontier of the plowed fields and the dark, forbidding ramparts of a pine forest away to the east. It was nothing like the rolling, friendly Cotswolds, she thought, but it would do. A walk in the country, any kind of country, might help her face the racket and the hearty extroversion which would surely overwhelm the press camp that night. As a woman alone in a newly captured combat area of central Germany, she would need to walk carefully. This much she knew. The Russians were an unknown quantity, but they were all drinking and singing at the river. The walk across the fields to the distant village seemed worth the slight element of risk she ran without an escort. Behind her, toward the Elbe, the plain had stretched away in warm silence to the west. The scene was serene and high above her some kind of hawk was circling watchfully over the stubble. The war was far away from where she walked. More than that, she knew, the war in Europe was nearly over. This meeting of the fronts, cutting Germany's defenses in half, was the beginning of the end of it all. Strangely, the thought had saddened her, for the imminent end of the war against Germany only seemed to make more undeniable the plain fact that Mike must surely be dead and soon she would be living in a world at peace, alone, without Mike to share its unfulfilled joys.

The day at Torgau had failed her, Caroline thought.

Mike and his crew had been seen to bail out just east of Torgau and to Torgau she had come, eagerly and with hope, seeking news of the living man she had once known and loved. Hour after hour she had sought British and American prisoners crowding into Torgau from liberated camps east of the Elbe, but none had known of Mike. Most had remembered B-17s and B-24s being shot down over the valley of the Elbe during the final phase of the Anglo-American air assaults on targets in central and eastern Germany during 1944, but to them the American airmen had been nothing more than distant little bundles swinging helplessly from the shroud lines of their parachutes before they dropped from view in the forests and fields of Saxony. With a kind of sick frenzy in her heart, Caroline had several times even run after passing GI ex-prisoners making for the Elbe, only to wonder how she could ever have thought the strangers had in any way at first resembled Mike.

Soon, before the sun went down on yet another day of the war in Europe, the generals at the Elbe would be shaking hands for the last time and the meeting at Torgau would have come and gone, a moment in history, and Mike would still be dead. If he did not come now, out of a captivity east of the Elbe, Caroline knew that he would never come to her at all, for in the west there was still no further record of Mike and his crew. That he should have died, Caroline could accept but not the fact of his total disappearance in this gentle Saxony land of fields and pines and quiet villages where idling geese gazed, plump and red-eyed, across the green-scummed waters of their ponds.

Graunitzdorf, when Caroline came to it, was little different from a hundred other German villages through which she had sped in the jeeps of the press camp. West of Graunitzdorf lay the wide, sun-warmed fields which Caroline had crossed on her walk from the Elbe. To the east, like a dark cliff of somber green, ran the edge of the pine forest. In between lay the village street, recently traversed by units of Rusakov's division on their way to the Elbe at Torgau, but silent now, as if a medieval plague had been visited upon the Graunitzdorfers. Uneasy, Caroline had realized that the afternoon shadows were lengthening and she had turned to walk down the street again to return to the open fields and the Elbe. Graunitzdorf or Torgau, neither was a place for an unescorted woman to be left after dark. Then she had seen the German woman weeping in the graveyard, and, hardened yet still sensitive to the face of war as she had known it, Caroline had thought that this could well be the column lead on her story of the link-up at Torgau. The Allied soldiers sharing toasts of victory on the riverbank. The bright flags of success. Across the fields, a German woman weeping in a graveyard alone, with another night soon to fall.

Speaking the courteous but stilted German which she had

learned at school in Sussex, Caroline had asked the woman why she wept.

"I weep for my husband," said the woman, "and I weep for myself. Two soldiers, I think they were British and had been prisoners in the big camp at Muhlberg, helped me bury him this morning. They were good young men, those two. Only boys. But it is no way to see your husband buried. Like a dog under the sky, with no pastor. No friends. No flowers. No Bible."

"Was your husband a soldier, too?" Caroline asked. "Was that how he died?"

The widow of a small, dusty day in history had drawn a shawl closer about her. The wind from the Elbe was cool in the late afternoon.

"He was the postmaster," she said. "A fine postmaster. He had been postmaster of Graunitzdorf for twenty years."

"Was it the Russians?" said Caroline.

The woman had looked angry then.

"It was not the Russians. It was not the fighting. That was soon over in Graunitzdorf. It was murder. And I don't care any more who hears me say it."

The wind from the Elbe had plucked at the accusation of murder and flung it away among the graveled graves and leaning tombstones.

"Murder?" said Caroline. "Why murder? At a time like this?"

"It was murder," said the postmaster's widow. Her voice was dull, almost emotionless, but flat with a kind of utter finality.

"The Fehme did it," she said.

"The Fehme?" said Caroline. "What is the Fehme?"

She was puzzled. Even as a correspondent for a national women's magazine, Caroline had got to know the names and the functions of most of the major formations of the German armed forces and the administrative organizations of the government of the Third Reich. She had never heard of the Fehme.

"The Fehme are bad men," said the little widow in the graveyard of Graunitzdorf, "wicked men. In the old days, after 1918, they were hangmen and executioners and soldiers without uniforms. Then the National Socialists came and there was no more Fehme. Now the National Socialists are kaputt and there is a Fehme again. They murdered my Max."

The woman began to weep again but stopped when she took the cigarette which Caroline offered her.

"Keep the packet," said Caroline. "Please. I have more. But why should these Fehme people kill your husband?"

"I will tell you," said the postmaster's widow, coughing as she smoked and the wind rustled the tall weeds in the graveyard. "A few days ago a telegram came from the Gauleiter telling Max that the Russkis were coming and that everybody was to evacuate Graunitzdorf and to cross the Elbe at Torgau before they blew up the bridge. Max was to see that every house and building in the village was burned down. Nothing was to be left for the Russkis. Max warned the people that the Russkis were coming and that they were to get out of Graunitzdorf and go to Torgau. But he didn't tell them that they were to burn down their houses on the Gauleiter's orders. He said it was too damned silly. He had fought for the Kaiser as a lad in 1914 and he wasn't going to start burning down German villages now. So he burned the Gauleiter's telegram instead."

"Good for Max," said Caroline, wondering at the fierce spirit of integrity which had so moved to defiance a middle-aged postmaster in a forgotten village in rural Saxony.

"That's what I thought," his widow said. "Until after the Russkis came through here yesterday on their way to the Elbe. Max and I were the only people left in the village. He said he wasn't going to desert his post office for Stalin himself. The Russian soldiers didn't even stay in Graunitzdorf, though. They must have been in a hurry to get to Torgau. Last night we came home from the post office thanking God that the Russians had left us alone. There was a sprig of lilac nailed on the front door of our home and there was a note with it. It said that Max had betrayed the German national honor by not carrying out the Gauleiter's order that Graunitzdorf was to be burned to the ground. He was to stand trial as a traitor before a court of honor. Max a traitor! An Iron Cross, First Class, and a plate in his head from the first war! Max just laughed and said it was probably some stupid boys playing a trick. I was worried, though, for my father had told me all about the Fehme and the Freikorps men in Silesia and Prussia after 1918. I begged Max to go away from Graunitzdorf but he wouldn't. He just laughed at me, so we went to bed and I even slept."

The woman paused, watching the tip of her cigarette glowing in the wind.

"Then, in the middle of the night, there was this knocking at the front door. Max made me hide because he thought it might be the Russians looking for women. I heard German voices, though, and then I could hear Max shouting. He was very angry. Then there was a silence and I heard footsteps going away down the street, running hard. I went downstairs and Max was lying there by the front door."

The postmaster's widow stopped and Caroline thought she was going to weep again, but she went on with her story, dry-eyed, and talking as she stared at the rough mound of fresh-turned earth before her.

"He was dead?" said Caroline.

"Not quite," said the widow. "He was choking for breath, but he lived long enough, for a few minutes, to tell me that two Germans from the Fehme had come to take him to the court of honor at Schloss Galgenstein. When he refused and told them he was going to get his shotgun, they threatened him with execution. When he refused again and told them to clear off, one of them took out a water pistol and squirted acid in his face and he fell down and they ran away. He just had time to tell me this when he died. Max died in agony like a rabbit when you gas it in a burrow."

The postmaster's wife held up a crushed sprig of lilac.

"I found this," she said. "They dropped it near Max's body when they ran away. That's all they left behind. That and the smell of crushed almonds. Max said it was prussic acid."

With a sudden gesture of loathing, she threw the lilac away then and began to weep again while Caroline sought to comfort her with an arm around her thin shoulders in the black shawl.

"You had better come back to Torgau with me," Caroline said. "Graunitzdorf is no place for you right now. Not on your own with nobody left in the village."

"I think you are right," said the widow. "There is nothing more I can do for Max now. I have buried him and prayed for him as well I know how. You have been very kind. It has been something just to talk to somebody. The young British prisoners were kind, too, but they spoke bad German. Come back to my house. I will make some coffee and then I will pack some things to take with me. I have a friend in Torgau at least. If she is still there."

Over hot, black acorn coffee in the widow's cottage, in a sunny parlor still companionable with the faint, stale tang of the postmaster's pipe-smoke, the two women had talked, if not like old friends, then at least like acquaintances for whom there was the common bond that, irrespective of their national status, the war in Europe had only brought them grief. When Caroline mentioned the mystery of Mike's disappearance in combat not far from Torgau, the widow had sat forward frowning over her coffee.

"What date was that?" she asked.

When Caroline told her, the widow had just sat there shaking her head.

"You don't recall it?" said Caroline. But, to her surprise, the widow had nodded then, absent-mindedly stirring her coffee.

"I remember it well," she said. "That was one of the first times we had ever seen American bombers flying over this part of Saxony. There had always been English bombers coming over at night, going to Leipzig or Berlin, but the Americans in broad daylight were something new. We were all surprised. We thought it was the Luftwaffe at first. It was like an air show then. Max and I went out into the garden to watch and we saw the flak bursting high up over toward Leipzig. Then we saw this Ami bomber falling behind the others. I remember a little flash and then seeing the wing fall away. It tumbled like a burning branch. Then the bomber began to spin and go crazy and get bigger and Max and I were scared that it might fall on fire into the village here."

Shocked or startled, she knew not which, Caroline had found it difficult to grasp that at last she was face to face with some kind of contact with Mike. She had never really thought it would be as conclusive as this. There was no doubt about it. The date, the time, the place and the circumstances fitted together like the pieces of a jigsaw puzzle.

"Did it crash near here?" Caroline asked.

"Yes," said the widow. "Not near the village. In the forest.

There was a big fire in the pines all that afternoon with fuel tanks exploding and ammunition in the guns popping and crackling. Before it crashed behind the pines, though, we saw the American airmen coming down in their parachutes."

"How many?" said Caroline.

"Eleven," said the German woman promptly. "Max counted them. He was very careful about it. He was a good official. You see he had to make a report on things like that, being the village air raid leader as well as the postmaster."

Eleven, thought Caroline. The whole crew. They all got out, then, like the rest of the crews in the formation had said.

"What happened to the crew?" she asked. The coffee in her cup was cold and untouched.

"They landed in the forest, too," said the widow. "It is very big."

Caroline paused but she knew she could neither deny nor delay the next question to which she was already dreading the answer.

"I mean, what happened to them after they landed," she said. "They were never reported again, dead or alive. Nothing is known of them. Just missing in action, presumed dead, yet their parachutes opened."

The widow then had reached for her hand and as Caroline felt the gentle pressure of the woman's work-roughened fingers on her wrist, she knew that her search was almost over, one way or the other.

"They never came out of the forest," said the widow. "A mob from Torgau went in after them with some Fehme men. Max knew a policeman from Torgau who was there and he said there was nothing he could have done to stop them. In any case, the police had been ordered by the Gauleiter not to interfere with civilians when they caught enemy airmen after a raid. It was the fault of the Fehme men, the policeman said. They kept yelling at the crowd and at the Americans and soon it was all over."

"What was all over?" said Caroline. "What did they do?"

"That's why I was shaking my head," said the widow. "I didn't want to have to tell you. The Fehme men took ropes with them into the forest. They hanged the American airmen."

"The eleven of them?" said Caroline. Suddenly she felt completely devoid of emotion.

"Only ten," said the widow. "One was already dead. I don't know which one. He had died on the way down in his parachute. They say he had been hit by flak before he jumped and bled to death before he got to the ground."

Dear God, Caroline prayed to herself. Please God, I hope that it was Mike who died on the way down under the open sky.

"Pardon?" said the German woman.

"It was nothing," said Caroline. "I was going to marry one of those eleven Americans. I should cry but I can't."

"I know," said the postmaster's widow. "We are both women and we have both lost our men. I could see it in your eyes when I was telling you about it. I did not want to tell you, but you have a right to know. And everybody has a right to know about the Fehme. We did not really believe it existed, even then, for there had never been any real sign of the Fehme in those days. I believe it now, though, good lady."

"So do I," said Caroline, "and I'll never forget it. Let's get out of here before I start making a fool of myself. It's getting late to be on these roads."

It was while the German woman was upstairs packing the pitifully few belongings she was capable of taking away to Torgau with her that Caroline saw the jeep idling slowly down the main street of Graunitzdorf. Subconsciously, at the time, she had thought this odd. In her experience it was unusual for jeeps, particularly those driven by Americans, to do anything but hustle. Suddenly aware of how dark it was getting and fearful of reaching Torgau after the American infantrymen and the press party had returned to the 69th Division's lines back on the Mulde, she had run after the jeep, shouting frantically as she pursued it past the silent, deserted cottages of Graunitzdorf.

To the smiling, surprised padre in the U.S. Army uniform she had shown her identity card, stammered out an almost hysterical story about the Fehme and the murder of the postmaster and the hanging of Mike's crew and then sought transport and safe conduct to Torgau for herself and the woman in the cottage.

Too late, in a last-second recollection that she had seen no chaplains at Torgau and realizing, too, that the jeep had come from out of the east, from the pine forest, Caroline had felt a sick presentiment of fear and dismay when she saw the gay sprigs of lilac pinned in the lapels of the uniforms of the padre and the unwontedly silent GIs riding with him.

That was the last she ever saw of the postmaster's widow at Graunitzdorf. Nor did she herself return to Torgau that night. Instead, under Fehme escort, she came to Schloss Galgenstein and the furtive, echoing cellars below the fire-blackened shell of the great hall of the von Bluckaus.

Had it not been for the bitter thought of Mike's crew and, perhaps, Mike himself, swinging by the neck in the forest and the Graunitzdorf postmaster staggering back at his door with prussic acid splashing into his face, Caroline would have found the trial proceedings against her merely fantastic. Neither the charge of espionage which she faced nor the procedures which she endured bore any resemblance to any system of jurisprudence with which she was familiar. The ritual of the court of honor with its naked sword, its noose and its sprigs of lilac, presided over by the elegantly uniformed figure of the blind general, kept reminding Caroline of the mad hatter's tea party, yet she knew that the madness of the trial in the castle cellars was also invested with the totality of sudden and willful death. Krausnick's presentation of evidence given by Schrader, the young German who had masqueraded as a U.S. Army chaplain, was conclusive and circumstantial but his cross-examination of Caroline had inevitably degenerated into an emotional tirade of denunciation, a harange of hatred. Sustained by a deep and burning sense of outrage at what had been done to Mike's crew, Caroline had answered only in curt monosyllables. Listless and without surprise, she heard the Freischoffen of the jury mumble their agreement of her guilt and then the general, lean fingers settling the dark glasses more easily on his thin nose, was asking her if she had anything to say.

"I have nothing to say to murderers," said Caroline, seeing not the ranks of this macabre court but only a crew of American airmen swinging first from the canopies of their parachutes and then from nooses slung from the trees of the dark forest. "What I have to say will be said only to British, American or Russian intelligence authorities."

The general, she thought, might well have become angry at this rejection of his clandestine jurisdiction, but, instead, he had sat quietly before the sword and the noose on the table, deep in contemplation of what he could not see.

"Caroline Brookwood," he said, with no stumbling over the phonetics of the English names, "this court of honor has convicted you on the charge of espionage and of seeking to compromise the security of the Fehme in Saxony. Since you are a British national and the daughter of a family of considerable rank and influence in England, the sentence of this court is that you be held as hostage, as a Prominente prisoner, pending the final disposition of your case by the higher authorities of the Fehme. You will now be returned to your cell."

Before she turned to walk, sick of heart but calmly erect, to the dark cell from which she had come, Caroline slowly scanned the ranks of faces in the silent court. The entirely unremarkable faces of soldiers and clerks and farmers. The many faces of murder, she thought. The scent of lilacs. I will forget neither.

The general was rapping the sword's hilt on the table.

"Present the next accused," he commanded.

"Call Roland Stolzer," said Krausnick, and a Fehme orderly repeated the name so that it echoed and rang like a chant between the stone walls until the man heard it in his cell and knew that they were coming for him.

VIII
The Man Who Loved Lamp Shades

THERE WAS NO lamp shade in Roland Stolzer's shadowed cell below the dark and deserted great hall of Schloss Galgenstein. The only light was a flickering, uneasy illumination cast by the torches burning in the medieval iron sconces that sprouted like rusty antlers from the dungeon walls beyond the cell. Yet, ironically, had it not been for the lamp shades which he had so recently loved and coveted and in the contemplation of which he had always found endless aesthetic satisfaction, Roland would never have been walking now from his cell to stand before the court of honor that awaited him.

Graduating from his university in Vienna in 1939 with a brilliant degree in anthropology behind him and a world of scientific endeavor before him, Roland had been genuinely dismayed by the Wehrmacht invasion of Poland and the appalling prospect of a general war in Europe. Not only an Austrian but a Viennese to his slim fingertips, Roland was neither a would-be soldier eager for the clash of arms nor a National Socialist with outflung arm ready to salute the new German order. Reared by his mother since her husband's entirely unheroic death during an epidemic of influenza on the Italian front during the First World War, Roland had, as a schoolboy in Vienna, successively announced ambitions to be a composer, a pianist, a violinist and an artist. Watching him studying at night by the lamplight in the library of their elegant if somewhat gloomy apartment overlooking the trees in the Prater, Roland's mother had unceasingly marveled at the sensitivity of her son's profile and thanked the good Lord for the intellect and gay good looks with which He had blessed her only child and son. Guided by his old headmaster, Roland had chosen anthropology as his field of study at the university. Mrs. Stolzer had been privately distressed, if not actually disappointed. Anthropology was something she had always vaguely and distastefully associated with the shrunken heads of unpleasant-looking Indians from the far jungles of Central America. Roland, she thought, had been born for finer things. Even the lamp shades which Roland had fashioned as fond presents for her and with which she had been proud to ornament the lofty rooms of the old apartment seemed far more in keeping with her son's sensitivity and talent. Only Roland's delighted announcement of the discovery that his sketching talents, slight though they might be, would be invaluable in the field as a working anthropologist had conditioned his mother to acceptance of the inevitable. She was glad enough, though, for Roland's graduation as an anthropologist when, at a celebratory party she had given in his honor, a university lecturer in political science—the German National Socialist version—had said there was room in Berlin for young men with her son's qualifications. Beyond the fact that the work would be concerned with an anthropological study of the Eastern European and Slavonic races and that Roland's military service commitments would be set aside so that he could work as a civilian official, Mrs. Stolzer cared to know little more than that her son would not have graduated merely to become uniformed cannon fodder. Roland, when she mentioned it to him, was just as eager for the appointment. The study of the origins of man, not the achievement of his mass destruction, was all that interested him. The university lecturer kept his word.

As an anthropologist in the Berlin headquarters of the SS Institute for Practical Research in Applied Anthropology, Roland found the work absorbing but not unduly onerous. There was still time for parties, of which in 1940, that year of intoxicating triumph for German arms, there was no shortage in Berlin.

Charming, witty and intelligent in the true Viennese tradition, Roland quickly found himself in demand with hostesses already deploring the inroads which even a victorious war was making on the ranks of eligible young German males in Berlin. Roland's lack of uniform, rank or medals was more than counterbalanced not only by his natural charm but also the skill and ingenuity with which he designed elegant and original lamp shades for presentation to his Berlin hostesses and their daughters. Fashioned from materials as diverse and esoteric as medieval music scores on vellum, and silk from the slightly charred parachutes of shot-down enemy airmen, Roland's lamp shades were never mundane. Inevitably they became the pride of his appreciative hostesses.

Not all the lamp shades, though, did Roland give away. Some he added to the growing collection in his own exquisitely furnished Berlin apartment. It was one such lamp shade, in fact, which helped allay his own private fears that he was latently homosexual. Further than this, he had been able to convince himself that sexually he was normally and satisfactorily adjusted. The lamp shade which had figured in this triumph over his suspicions that he might have always been subjected too intensely to his widowed mother's obsessive love, was one which few of his Berlin friends had ever seen.

Arising out of his routine studies of a departmental survey of anti-social criminal attitudes adduced to be an inherent characteristic of the non-Nordic peoples of Poland, Roland had based the inspired design of the shade on a photographic enlargement of the fingerprints of a lovely but syphilitic Polish girl of aristocratic descent who had been hanged as a prostitute and murderess in Warsaw by the SS. An outraged military tribunal had convicted the girl, as unrepentant as she had been wanton, on charges of having strangled in their own disordered beds a succession of comatose and unsuspecting German officers by whom she had first been courteously wined and dined prior to her inevitable seduction. Printed on a thick sheet of photographic safety film, which curved to form the shade of the lamp, the coarsely enlarged whorls of the dead girl's fingerprints, as recorded in her police file, formed an exciting and meaningful pattern in abstract design. Hanging from an accurately scaled-down reproduction, in good German pine, of a field gallows of simple and classic construction, the shade had never been calculated to excite the admiration of Roland's patronesses in their smug and fashionable Berlin homes. Not that this had ever been Roland's intention. The fingerprint shade was his own private pleasure, an academic and mordantly wry tilt at the ways of a world which he increasingly was finding to be more amusing than admirable. Introspectively, though, Roland had become aware of the fact that the lamp shade, glowing starkly with the huge fingerprints of a demonstrably seductive and tempestuous woman, had begun to exercise a psychotic influence upon him which was not without its sexual undertones. Often on the rare occasions when he was not going out and was, instead, spending a night alone in his flat, Reinhardt had fallen to wondering about the hands whose fingerprints whirled and looped around the lamp shade by his divan, the hands which had caressed with such passion and then strangled and killed with such consuming, pathological hatred. Sardonically, he had almost envied the dead German officers their last hours of lust, for he was still a virgin at twenty-three, a charming but uncommitted young man whom his hostesses knew to be no threat to their daughters' virtue. Roland had come, lately, not to relish this role but, instead, to despair for his own inadequacy to cope with what was well known to be in wartime Berlin the simple mechanics of getting into bed with a woman. Basically, he realized, he was just too damned shy. A party boy but no pillow playmate. When it arose, Roland's emancipation from his inhibitions and private fears came about as an accidental circumstance in which the fingerprint lamp shade exercised a curiously catalytic action.

Trudi Muller was five years older than Roland, which, of course, was why he never knew it. At twenty-three, the young Viennese anthropologist only knew that Trudi with the enormous, green thyroidal eyes, the flaxen hair and the husky, sometimes boyishly boisterous laugh, was a woman born to a world he had never known but for which he had often hungered during the fevered and furtive nights of adolescent lustings in his bedroom overlooking the Prater. Although Roland was not to know it, Trudi at twenty-eight was wildly promiscuous, almost an alcoholic and an unfulfilled and frightened woman whose girlhood boy friends, by 1940, had died their heroes' deaths in a variety of laudable and unpleasant ways at the fighting front. Trudi had found no shortage of men to go to bed with her in Berlin, but whenever she had met a man with whom she would have been happy to stand before a fashionable altar, he was either already married or far too busy making the most of a Berlin leave to do anything but roar with laughter at the very thought of marriage.

Obsessed with her desperately amoral pursuit of the unknown man whom she would one day cherish, ravish and nourish as her husband and the father of her children, Trudi had been too busy tumbling into bed with her transient party lovers ever to realize that in Roland, a frequent and favored guest at her mother's Berlin apartment, there was just such a man as she had been seeking. Only a lack of confidence had ever prevented Roland from setting about the realization of his secret dreams for possessing Trudi.

Had it not been for the fortuitous circumstance of an air raid alert sounding while Roland was walking Trudi home from their office building, where she worked most competently as private secretary to a deputy director of the SS headquarters for Racial and Settlement Administration (Eastern Territories), the moment of fulfillment with Trudi might never have come for Roland. Nearing his apartment that evening, he had suggested in all innocence, for he had never seriously regarded himself as a likely contender for Trudi's embrance, that she might care to join him for a drink until the all clear signaled that the fumbling British had finished their pitiful attempts to carry out another air attack on the capital of the Third Reich. Trudi had accepted the invitation so casually and readily that Roland cursed himself for not having had the initiative to think of it long before. Settling down on the divan in the glow of the fingerprint lamp with a bottle of cognac and two glasses in intimate juxtaposition on the low coffee table, Roland had marveled at the fact that not only should this have been the first time he had ever entertained a woman alone in his apartment but that, when it had finally happened, his guest should have been Trudi Muller. For once, Roland found himself at ease in her company. If anything, the distant rumble of sporadic bombing—it sounded as if the industrial suburbs of Reinickendorf or Wedding were getting it—added a companionable spice of shared danger to the fact that just the two of them, out of all the people in Berlin, were alone together in his apartment.

For a while, Roland and Trudi had exchanged the idle small talk of people who happened to work together in the same office. Roland told Trudi that he had been commended for his contributions to the survey of anti-social criminal characteristics of the Polish people. Trudi complained, yawning, that she had been working overtime every night lately, as had everybody else in her department. They had been frantically trying to complete up-to-date lists of death registrations submitted in returns from the commandants of camps at Auschwitz-Birkenau, Delzek, Treblinka and Wolzek. Everybody had been going crazy trying to keep ahead of the work. The coffee in the office canteen was getting worse. SS

Standartenführer Weltzer was rumored to be having an affair with the new girl in the technical library. There was going to be a blitz on smoking during office hours.

"Let's forget the place," said Trudi. "Typing death registrations twelve hours a day is an incredibly dreary occupation. By the end of the week I've been too tired even for parties. Another brandy, darling, and things might begin to look a little rosier."

They had talked about their ambitions and fears and hopes then, and Trudi had relaxed, kicking off her shoes and tucking her slim legs up underneath her as she half sat, half lay against the cushions on the divan.

Contentedly reaching for another balloon of brandy, Trudi had noticed the lamp shade.

"Not one of yours, surely?"

"All my own work," Roland admitted with mock pride.

"It's gorgeous," said Trudi. "In an unhealthy kind of way. You've been holding out on Mother, keeping it for yourself. I'm sure she thinks you're a far better designer of lamp shades than you are an anthropologist."

"I don't think she would really appreciate this one," said Roland.

Trudi looked puzzled, staring at the shade.

"Why not? It looks terribly abstract and traumatically decadent and all that."

Roland then had explained the origins of the design.

"A prostitute?" said Trudi. "A murderess? The actual fingerprints enlarged? How deliciously Freudian of you, Roland. You surprise me. You're quite right, of course. It's not for Mother. I like it, though. I think it's extremely clever of you, darling. Such a seductively sinister approach. Aren't you spoiling the effect, though? Do we need the rest of the lights on?"

Hastily Roland had jumped to his feet and had gone around the apartment flicking off the other lamps, which he had also designed and made. When he came back from the kitchen with another bottle of cognac, Trudi was lying on the divan in the blood-pink glow of the fingerprint lamp. For a moment, he wondered if she had passed out. Then he realized that she had taken off her frock. It lay disheveled on the carpet beside the divan, as negligent as Trudi herself. With the unzipped frock was a pair of silk scantics, brought back from Paris for Trudi by a Ju.52 Luftwaffe transport pilot. From the lamp shade hung her brassiere. The light from the lamp was not so soft that Roland could not see that Trudi was naked except for a sheer silk slip, also a Luftwaffe prize of war. Trudi giggled as she watched Roland staring first at the lamp and the brassiere and then at her.

"Let's get really Freudian, darling," she said. "Just put that bottle down and kiss me. Pretend I'm your passionate little Polish slut. Am I abandoned and drunk enough to be a prostitute? Kiss me, darling."

Without a word, Roland knelt by the divan. Trudi made room for him with a quick, lithe movement of her hips. Then she put her bare arms around his neck and pulled his face down to hers, caressing her soft, moist lips against his. "Right down," she said. With his arms about her body he felt the warm, naked flesh of her beneath the silk. She was trembling. He began to fumble at her thighs, reaching for the lacy hem of the slip. "Not yet," she whispered. "We've got all night, darling." There was need for hurry, though. A great need. It was the first time with a woman for Roland, and in the warm glow of the fingerprint lamp Trudi was unashamed and uninhibited. The moment of climax, when it came for Roland, was a pyrotechnic profusion of proud yet submissive curves of flesh pressed urgently against him, of the scent of perfumed sweat and the fumes of cognac, of the distant, crumping sound of flak and gasped moans of fulfillment from Trudi.

When it was over and they were lying there sharing a lipstick-smeared cigarette and listening to the strident, prolonged howl of the all clear, Trudi had touched Roland's throat gently with her fingertips.

"You weren't scared I was going to strangle you?"

"It would have been a wonderful death," jested Roland. Shifting his weight, he had reached for her again. He had never thought it could be so easy.

"Just a moment," said Trudi and, taking her slip which Roland had put beneath one of the divan cushions, she arranged it over the scarlet glow of the fingerprint lamp.

"That's better. I had the strangest feeling she was watching us, darling."

Looking at Trudi's curve of naked back as she reached out to the lamp, Roland stretched his arm past her and flicked the switch off.

"Now there's just us," he said.

In the darkness, they began to make love again.

In the morning, after breakfasting together in the apartment, Roland walked Trudi to the office, where she telephoned her mother with the explanation that she had stayed the night with a girl friend rather than risk the streets of blacked-out Berlin during the air raid.

Watching Trudi walk away down the corridor to her own office, cool and fresh and lovely, he had wondered at the inscrutable poise with which woman could adapt herself to the pursuit of her desires. By contrast, he had spent an uneasy and conscience-stricken morning listening to Trudi's father, the senior consultant anthropologist to the SS Institute of Practical Research in Applied Anthropology, presiding over a meeting convened to discuss the drawing up of standardized specifications for concentration camp crematories in the eastern occupied territories.

If only he knew where his daughter had spent last night, thought Roland, I'd be going up the chimney myself.

Dr. Muller, however, had been too absorbed in his presentation of a scholarly paper on the historical background of crematory techniques in Western European civilization, as far back as the Vikings, to do more than nod good-naturedly as Roland apologized for having arrived a few minutes late.

Not long after Hitler's Operation Barbarossa had staggered a world unprepared for Germany's invasion of Russia in 1941—an event which Roland toasted so well in captured French champagne at a celebratory party that when he awoke in his apartment next morning he had trouble in remembering Trudi's name as she lay next to him—the young Viennese anthropologist found that he had indeed proved himself a man.

Over black coffee, execrable as usual, in the office canteen later that morning, Trudi had lit a cigarette, exhaled luxuriously and said quite casually, "I'm going to have to give these things up."

Roland had merely yawned. It had been dawn that morning before he had turned off the fingerprint lamp. They had fallen asleep on the divan without getting as far as his bedroom.

"Good idea," he said. "They'll be harder than ever to get now, particularly with this war in Russia. Why the hurry, though, darling?"

"Because I'm pregnant," said Trudi. "Isn't that a patriotic enough reason?"

"Are you sure?' he said. It was a silly question, he knew. Trudi had never been not sure about anything.

"Darling," she said, "it's not a question of being sure. Either I am pregnant or I am not. I can assure you that I very definitely am."

"My God," said Roland. "What are we going to do?"

Trudi smiled and took his hand, pressed it between both hers.

"Darling, you're priceless. The classical cry of the despairing philanderer."

"You don't have to be so damned gay about it," said Roland. "What the hell are we going to do anyway? I know a couple of gynecologists who don't mind helping their friends out."

Trudi shook her head, and for the first time Roland sensed that already there was a different edge to their relationship.

"My," she said, "you are becoming a sophisticate. But that's not for me. I don't want to shock you, darling, but I've had that kind of favor done for me before. This is our baby and I want it. It's one I'm going to have. Even the Führer would agree that it is my patriotic duty."

"You can't have the baby," he said. My God, he thought, what will her parents say? And my mother? There was always the army. He could volunteer for the infantry. Suddenly the front no longer seemed such a terrible place.

"You can't have the baby," he said.

Roland was appalled by the prospect. My God, he thought, and to think I was worried about being sexually maladjusted.

"I can have it," said Trudi, "and I will. Particularly if you marry me.

A brilliant young anesthetist at a table close by who had done some outstanding experimental work on the euthanasia program at Auschwitz and Mauthausen camps waved to Roland, who distractedly returned the casual greeting.

"It's an old-fashioned idea, I know," said Trudi.

To look at her, thought Roland, nobody here would ever know. Not yet. The frank, green, bold eyes. The blond hair, not passionately disordered now, but swept back shining into a prim and so proper bun. The soft and generous lips, almost smiling. Suddenly Roland realized that behind the smile she was trying not to cry. Trudi, the wild one. Trudi, whose name was lettered on the engine cowling of the Me.109 flown by the top-scoring Luftwaffe fighter ace in the legendary Abbeville wing. Trudi, now the conceiver and the bearer of his child and holding back the tears for what might be and what might not be. Compassion and a strange, warm feeling of pride and love had warmed Roland then, and he had reached for her hand.

"Of course we'll get married," he said. "When?"

Dabbing surreptitiously at her eyes with a wisp of handkerchief, Trudi smiled.

"It's a hell of a proposal," she said, "but I accept. As soon as you like. Whatever will your mother say?"

"You're marrying me," said Roland firmly, already proprietorial, "not my mother. The point is, though, what will your people say?"

"Mother adores your lamp shades," said Trudi. "Father thinks you're a very dedicated and promising young anthropologist. What more do you need?"

"It's a start anyway," said Roland. "Then we've got each other, of course."

"And a child on the way."

"And an apartment."

"And a terribly Freudian lamp shade that knows far more than any self-respecting Berlin lamp shade should," added Trudi.

Laughing then and excited, they had gone back to their offices, and at lunchtime Roland had bought a diamond ring for Trudi which, quite unsophisticatedly, she tearfully admired, pridefully twisting it and turning it as they toasted each other in champagne cocktails at an exclusive little bar where she had once played strip poker, and lost, as the bells of Berlin rang in a new year.

Just as soon as Roland's mother had made the rail journey from Vienna and Dr. Muller had concluded a long, tiresome but urgent conference on standardization of specifications with a group of crematory engineers and manufacturers in Westphalia, a large but friendly dinner party was held at the Muller home to celebrate Trudi's betrothal. To Roland's vast relief, the announcement was received happily by everybody concerned with the family gathering. The dinner party was an eminent success once he had succeeded in rescuing his bewildered mother from a puzzling and somewhat disagreeable conversation with Dr. Muller, during which, cigar in one hand and cognac in the other, he had sought to explain to Frau Stolzer that, on the basis of his institute's anthropological survey of all European races, it had been found practicable to arrive at basic dimensions which would permit efficient standardization of crematory specifications throughout the Third Reich and its newly won territories in the east.

"Such an intense man," Frau Stolzer said to her son. "So very German. So serious."

"A fine anthropologist, too," said Roland, "but also a very dedicated public service official."

At Trudi's insistence, for she sought no company of winking, knowing ghosts from the turbulent promiscuity of her past, the wedding was an intimate family affair. After a honeymoon on the Rhine and a visit to Vienna to meet Roland's relatives and friends, they returned to Berlin and the apartment and their respective jobs. They had not been back in Berlin much more than three months when Trudi lost the child. Afterward, when he went to see her in the hospital, Trudi had only nodded apathetically when Roland jokingly said that it was just as well that even the German government could not ration babies. They would have another, he told her. Then she had turned her face to the wall and begun to weep and he had been unable to comfort her, for she had wanted the child more than he had ever thought possible.

The night he brought her home to the apartment and they sat companionably together drinking a cognac with their coffee, Trudi told him that it had been no ordinary miscarriage.

Misunderstanding the implication, Roland had been genuinely shocked, for he, too, had wanted the child.

"You didn't try to get rid of it?" he said, the accusation rising in his voice.

Trudi had shaken her head, the blond hair swirling across her face and the green eyes limpid with tears.

"That's just it," she said. "For the first time in my life that's exactly what I didn't want to do. I wanted our child, Roland. Desperately. On my knees, I tell you."

"What went wrong, then?"

"The old days," said Trudi bitterly. "The gay old party days, that's what went wrong. Too many fashionable abortions. Roland, I have to tell you. I have seen all the specialists, but it's no good. We can never have children, darling."

They had drunk a lot of cognac that night, and many more nights after that, but had found no joy in it. Things had changed. Even Trudi had changed. Not back to her old frenzied, dissolute way of life, for she still loved Roland. Instead, after a time of brooding withdrawal, she had begun to see Roland more as the son she would now never have than as the man she had married. Before the first winter of the war against Russia was over, Trudi had seen to it that her father, as senior consultant anthropologist to the SS Institute for Practical Research in Applied Anthropology, had successfully recommended Roland's appointment as a deputy director of the institute.

Then, at Trudi's insistence and with the weight of Dr. Muller's influence as an SS Gruppenführer, had come Roland's further recommendation for a commission in the SS with the rank of SS Hauptsturmführer, equivalent to the army rank of captain. Roland had at first objected to this move.

Trudi, though, had coaxed him gently but firmly toward a career in the SS.

"It's not just the army, darling. It's the SS. It's an elite corps. They are the leaders of German National Socialism. If the National Socialists want leaders not just now during the war but for afterwards, then I want to be the wife of a leader. Anyway, you'll need the rank and the uniform for where you're going."

When Trudi mentioned to Roland that he would need to be an SS officer where he was going, he had laid down the needle and thread with which he had been sewing a panel for the new shade from the silk escape maps found in the battle-dress pocket of a dead Canadian airman.

"Going where?" said Roland. "You're not sick of me already? You haven't got me a job on the East Front?"

"Not as far as that," said Trudi. "Poland. And I'm coming with you."

Roland grimaced, holding the needle up against the glow of the fingerprint lamp so that he could see the cotton he was threading.

"Poland? Why Poland? Where in Poland?"

Roland pricked his finger and swore softly in the gentle dialect of Vienna.

"Auschwitz."

"Auschwitz? The SS camp? That ghastly, Godforsaken place. Some of the people in our department have been there on surveys and studies. It's at least a hundred and sixty miles from Warsaw, miles from anywhere unless you count Silesia, and smack in the middle of some of the dreariest swampland this side of the Pripet Marshes. The climate in winter is atrocious. Socially the place is a disaster. Darling, you just don't know what you're saying. I'd die if I had to stay there."

Trudi poured black coffee, spiking it with cognac.

"I do know what I'm saying, Roland. Exactly. Father and one of his pals, a professor of anatomy from Strasbourg, have convinced Himmler himself of the necessity of making a collection of skulls of Jewish-Russian commissars for the purpose of scientific racial studies at the Reich University of Strasbourg. It all sounds a little ghoulish to me, but, then, I'm no anthropologist. Himmler is supporting the program. Father has been appointed to lead the study group. Now, the point is, I've persuaded him that you're the right person to lead the field program at Auschwitz."

Roland had demurred. He was enjoying life in Berlin.

"Me?" he said. "The leader of the camp project?"

"Of course," said Trudi. "I admit that you'll look terribly dashing in that black and silver SS officer's uniform, darling, but if you're going to get anywhere in the corps, I think you've got to start taking on leadership responsibilities. Father agrees and the poor old dear is no soldier himself, even though he is the SS equivalent of a lieutenant-general. He's an anthropologist, too, but he admits that the National Socialists, particularly in the SS, are making possible all kinds of practical research programs in their camps."

Roland had thrown his old raincoat onto the divan when he had come from the office and in the blood-glow of the fingerprint lamp he could imagine the runic SS flashes and the gaping, grinning insignia of the death's-head. The Germans, he thought. Disciples of the death-wish. There was, though, he had to admit, a certain élan about the SS which he would get accustomed to sharing once he had begun wearing the uniform of an SS officer at departmental conferences and social gatherings. People would take more notice of him then.

Dr. Muller was delighted when Roland accepted the appointment as leader of the Strasbourg field program at Auschwitz. Genuinely grateful, too, he enthused about the purely scientific benefits which would accrue to Germany from the program.

"As an anthropologist," he told Roland, "you must know that in our better German institutes and universities we do have quite comprehensive collections of the skulls and skeletons of almost every race on earth. However, my anatomist friends and colleagues agree with me that there has always been a dearth of Jewish specimens. Particularly Jewish-Russians. The few we have had at our disposal for scientific studies have not been numerous enough to constitute a sample which would justify our arriving at any very valid conclusions. Maybe the Jews have always been fussy about this sort of thing. Their religion, perhaps. Now, however, it does not matter. With the war on the East Front we have the opportunity to procure all the Jewish-Russian specimens we want. At Auschwitz you will be given every facility for your task of assembling the basic Strasbourg collection."

Academically, as a qualified anthropologist, Roland readily appreciated the potential scientific worth of the program—and, indeed, privately marveled that the Third Reich government was capable of listening to advisers objective enough to counsel a scientific project quite divorced from the logistical demands of the fighting front—but he could not dismiss troubled thoughts about the practical implications of the Strasbourg skull project at Auschwitz. If there was a time to speak his mind, it was now.

"You might as well know," he told Dr. Muller, "but you have a son-in-law who is still somewhat squeamish. Frankly, I don't relish the thought of having to oversee grave digging and body snatching."

Dr. Muller settled back in his swivel chair smiling tolerantly.

"My dear boy," he said, "that is all arranged for you. As an SS Gruppenführer, I have necessarily had to become something of a lobbyist in these matters. In the public service of the Third Reich I have found it absolutely necessary, in fact, to achieve quite limited academic objectives. An SS Headquarters directive, signed by the SS Reichsführer Himmler himself, has been issued to Wehrmacht commanders in the field on the East Front. Jewish commissars of the Soviet, on capture by Wehrmacht units, are to be handed over to the field police, who will in turn inform a particular office attached to our institute here in Berlin of the numbers and locations of these subhuman Jewish-Bolshevik anthropological specimens. On instructions from our institute, they will be transferred for concentration in a particular compound of a new subcamp at Auschwitz. Your compound, in fact."

Now we're getting to it, thought Roland.

"What then?" he said nervously.

"Then the work begins," said Dr. Muller, wagging a playfully admonitory finger at Roland. "You will complete a series of photographs and sketches and collate the anthropologically significant measurements of the specimens. You will support this with relevant details of ancestry, environment, education, date of birth, place of birth and other personal and family particulars with which to complete a file for each specimen."

It all seemed straightforward enough and Roland sighed with obvious relief. His father-in-law, though, held up his hand.

"That's not all. After the subsequently induced death of each specimen in the compound at Auschwitz—during which process the head must not be knocked about—the head will be separated from the trunk. The head of every specimen is then to be placed in preserving fluid in sealed portable containers which have already been designed and manufactured for this purpose. Your responsibility will also be to see that the specimen heads are forwarded to the Reich University at Strasbourg together with the relevant field evaluation files prepared by your unit. It is essential, my dear boy, that specimen heads be clearly tagged and numbered."

Dr. Muller chuckled, sweeping cigar ash from the virginally unblemished blotting pad on his habitually tidy desk.

"We don't, as it were, want to get the right heads on the wrong shoulders, do we?"

Roland nodded, moodily assessing the task before him. Already he was beginning to feel like an undertaker.

"There will be a predictable death rate, then?"

"Quite predictable," said Dr. Muller. "But that is not your concern. Just regard yourself as a staff officer of science estimating the casualties before the battle begins. You are only to be concerned with the clinical aspects of the program. There will be SS people attached to your compound to handle the, ah, terminal aspects of the processing of the live specimens. I suggest you do not need to trouble yourself about that."

"By all means," agreed Roland. "And frankly, I'm glad to hear it. I could find it distracting. As I told you, I still have my squeamish moments."

Dr. Muller nodded benevolently. The white fringe of hair encircling his bald pate was like a halo in the sunshine streaming through the window behind him.

"Naturally," he said. "A little more field work with the SS, my dear boy, and you'll find you develop a higher tolerance to these things. Mind over matter, you know."

A pert stenographer, a pretty little brunette whom Roland had taken to a few parties before that first night of revelation with Trudi, arrived with a tray on which were set some delicate Meissen cups and saucers and a silver pot of herb tea, one of Dr. Muller's milder obsessions. Eagerly he pressed a cup on Roland.

"It clears the head," he said. "Never fails. If I were a commercially minded man I'd have put it on the market years ago and made a fortune."

Over his cup of steaming herb tea, which Roland found to be as repellent as ever, Dr. Muller enthused about the merits of the skull project.

"With the photographs, the sketches, the significant measurements, the life data and the head itself, we can really start getting down to some worthwhile work at Strasbourg," he said. "We can commence anatomical research of a comparative nature, consolidate studies on racial classification, evaluate the form and size of the brain and confirm the subhuman pathological formations of the skulls of these Jewish-Bolshevik commissar classes. I can assure you, Roland, it is an extremely significant project which has the blessing of people in very high places."

Fondly, for he was a great sentimentalist and a devoted family man, Dr. Muller nodded toward a framed photograph of his wife with Trudi as she had been on her confirmation day, a smiling child with a black prayer book clutched devoutly to the bodice of her white dress.

"They'll be proud of us one day, Roland," said Dr. Muller. Walking with him to the door, he put an arm about his shoulder.

"You'll do well, my boy. I have great faith in your ability. This is going to be a great challenge and a great opportunity for you. You're on the way up. No more lukewarm ersatz coffee in crowded staff canteens for you. From now on, at any SS establishment or formation in the land, it's the officers' mess or the civilian executive dining room."

For Roland and Trudi, the transition from their apartment in Berlin to the SS married officers' quarters at Auschwitz was initially an experience which required considerable adjustment. Beyond the guarded perimeter of the vast camp stretched only the bleak swamps and austere pine forests of the Polish plain, a prospect almost lunar in its lonely desolation. Inside the camp, behind the wired fences of the compounds, the very earth itself seemed poisoned and putrescent with the stench of death, disease and defecation. Even the air above the squat, ugly barracks stank with the odors of crowded humanity and, depending on the wind, was rank with the oily stench from the tall chimneys of the crematories where humanity had ceased to be. Intermittently, after long trainloads of trucks had arrived at the railway station at the end of the line, the air was murmurous with shoutings and screamings in the distant compounds and then there would be even more stacks of naked corpses, fouled and ignoble and vile in contorted death, and the smoke would billow faster and faster from the crematory chimneys, streaming out across the marshes and forests of Auschwitz like ragged pennants of despair and degradation signaling to a world unable to intervene. Close to Auschwitz was Birkenau, the other camp of the huge Auschwitz–Birkenau complex. In Birkenau there were no stones to crush, no camp industries to bleed the marrow of life from the working inmates and fatten the paunches of industrialists at home in Germany. Death, and death alone, was, ironically, the life force of Birkenau. Death at Birkenau was a total quota, a triumphant graph, a planned and perfected equation of logistics, not just a hazard. Without quite knowing why, or caring to, Roland and Trudi were glad they had been stationed in their separate little subcamp at Auschwitz instead of at the extermination center in Birkenau.

Not that Trudi at first found anything at all admirable about Auschwitz. Once, and only once, she had visited Roland at his clinic in the Strasbourg compound, which was the area where the skull project was located. Pridefully she had set out to call on her husband, who was quite obviously at home with his status as commanding officer of the Strasbourg unit and still cut a handsome, almost martial figure in his black and silver SS uniform. She had never gone again, though. Thankfully she had returned to their villa in the SS married officers' quarters beyond the electrified fences of the compounds. Here flowers bloomed in little gardens and chirping birds fluffed their feathers, quarreling for crusts of bread tossed to them on the trim lawns. Here was home, where Roland's lamp shades, carefully packed and transported from Berlin, glowed in peaceful elegance, waiting for him to return at evening from another long, hard day at his clinic in the Strasbourg compound.

"I had to have a shower when I came home," Trudi told Roland over dinner, after her visit to his clinic. "I felt as if I had been in a zoo. Or a madhouse. Or a stockyard. Where do all those dreadful people come from? Father's right. They're subhuman, of course. They must be riddled with disease."

"They are," said Roland abstractedly. There was some good Wagner playing on the radio. "They're dying all the time."

Trudi frowned, stirring her coffee. Roland thought that in the blood-pink glow of the fingerprint lamp she looked serenely beautiful, as she had when she had been carrying his child. The little son who would never play hide-and-seek in the Prater. The little girl who would never skip in the sunshine.

"Is there any danger of infection?" Trudi said.

Roland hastily reassured her.

"Good Lord, no. That's why they have the crematories. So long as you can see the smoke from the big chimneys, there's nothing to worry about. The SS people in the camp are crazy about hygiene."

"Thank heavens for that," said Trudi. "More coffee? We got some white sugar in a parcel from Mother today. I don't know how she does it."

Socially, Roland and Trudi found life gay enough at Auschwitz. There was no shortage of servants. They were recruited from among the cleaner, less emaciated inmates of the compounds. Trudi overcame her initial repugnance at having them around the house and the garden once Roland assured her that they had been deloused, showered, medically examined and inoculated and that their striped, pajama-like prison garb was always new and was hygienically and regularly laundered.

With a minimum of household chores to concern them, Roland and Trudi quickly adapted themselves to the round of parties, dances, dinners, coffee-calls and afternoon tea conversations which were the substance of social life in the SS married officers' quarters of the camp. Sometimes there were concerts, provided by surprisingly talented musicians and singers from among the inmates of the main compounds, but these tended to be spasmodic entertainments. As a jovial Munich geneticist on attachment to Auschwitz put it, "One week we've got a magnificent cellist. The next week he's gone up the chimney. It's the same with experimental programs here. The most interesting and worthwhile subjects keep dying. In my humble opinion, it's inefficient and downright wasteful."

Just as quickly as she had adapted herself to the protocol and pleasures of being an SS officer's wife at Auschwitz, so had Trudi, with a sharp eye to the main chance, begun to exploit social contacts at the camp in the interests of Roland's advancement in his career. The young Stolzer couple were welcome additions to the confined social world of the camp staff. There were occasional upsets for Trudi, though. Her major triumph, a fast-ripening friendship with Frau Fischer, the wife of the camp commandant's senior adjutant, had unexpectedly resulted in her having to part with Roland's fingerprint lamp, a possession which had consistently excited the envious admiration of visitors to the Stolzers' villa at Auschwitz.

"The nerve of the damned woman," Trudi had fumed while Roland was yawning, ready for bed. "She was fascinated while I told her the history of the thing and then she practically demanded I give it to her. Not in so many words. It was blackmail just the same. She knew that I knew her husband has to notate your fitness reports and approve any recommendations for promotion. I just had to give it to her, the fat sow. I could have spat in her face."

"I'm glad you didn't," said Roland placatingly. "They're a useful couple to know. If I've got to have a career in the SS, they're the kind of people who can help it along."

"They'd better," said Trudi.

Roland laughed, reaching for her so that she collapsed onto the divan with him.

"I know one thing, Trudi. They won't have as much fun by that lamp's light as we did."

"Don't be disgusting," said Trudi. "We're married now, remember."

"Prude!" retorted Roland. "Let's forget we're married for a while."

In the darkness that night, where the fingerprint lamp glowed no more, it had almost been like the wild, wanton times in Roland's bachelor apartment again.

The loss of the lamp, though, when Trudi awoke next morning, continued to nag at her. To entertain, she needed no special props, but if she had them, she made the most of them, for she was a sophisticated and accomplished hostess. When, quite by chance, she later arrived at the solution of the problem of replacing the fingerprint lamp with something just as socially diverting, Roland at first would not consider it.

"Human skin?" he said. "Good God, Trudi, I'm an anthropologist, not a taxidermist. I think the whole idea is positively barbaric. Worse than that, I think it's vulgar and ostentatious and in the worst of taste."

"There's a woman at Bergen-Belsen has one," Trudi said defensively. "They're quite the thing there, I believe. Shrunken heads, too."

Roland snorted derisively.

"Human skin! Shrunken heads! Trudi, I'm running a serious scientific survey which coincidentally happens to be based upon a study of the skulls of a particular racial group. There's nothing unusual about that. Anthropologists and anatomists all over the world collect, assemble and study human skulls and bones. But I'm not running a circus of shrunken heads and other esoteric trivia to entertain senior SS officers' wives."

It took all of that long, hot summer of 1944 to achieve, but inevitably Trudi prevailed with her demands, seducing Roland's will to refuse with a bewildering onslaught of passionate entreaty, loving submission and wifely devotion to his every want. The human skin was procured, after some modest bribery, with the hesitant connivance of a dull-witted Latvian pathology assistant on the laboratory staff of a medical project experimenting with new and revolutionary techniques in skin grafts. The operational requirements had been specified by the medical branch of the Luftwaffe. The death of the particular subject, aged 28, had been tersely recorded as due to heart failure. There was no official recognition of the fact that much of the group's experimentation had been conducted without benefit of anesthesia, in the clinical interests of evaluating the method for possible use under primitive conditions as an emergency front-line technique.

To Roland's surprise, when he finally capitulated to Trudi and agreed to make the lamp shade, he found that his father-in-law had been right. Just as Dr. Muller had predicted, the level of Roland's tolerance to emotional disturbance had risen appreciably since his arrival at Auschwitz. Pickling the heads of former research subjects in sealed containers for delivery to the new Reich University in historic Strasbourg was enough to toughen anybody's guts, Roland reflected.

Once he had started work on the new lamp shade, Roland had to admit to a certain morbid and fascinated preoccupation with Trudi's latest whimsey. He brooded wryly that he had come a long way since, as a lonely and artistically inclined youngster, he had first begun designing lamp shades for his mother in their old apartment in Vienna. The actual making of the Auschwitz lamp shade was easier than he had thought it would be, once he had overcome the last residual vestiges of instinctive revulsion at the touch and the thought of the material with which he had to work. The skin had been cleverly tanned by the Latvian pathology assistant, who evidently was not as dumb as he looked, and it was easy to cut and sew. There was no tendency to tear or rip. By a freak of good fortune, the skin section had included the subject's prison number, allocated on registration at Auschwitz, and in Roland's final design the tattooed numerals were a curiously compelling and intimate comment on the finality of the fact of one man's death.

"It's positively Grand Guignol," said Trudi when they switched the lamp on for the first time and the tattooed number that once had been a Jew was silhouetted against the opaque parchment of his skin.

"If that doesn't shut that woman's mouth, nothing will," Tudi said, still thinking angrily of her treasured fingerprint lamp shade, now aglow on the bookcase in the villa of the dowdy wife of the commandant's senior adjutant.

With a little more discreet bribery, Trudi procured from a Feldwebel in the records section of the camp Kommandantur the name, place of birth, date of birth and ancestry of the young Jew who had died during the Luftwaffe skin-graft experiments.

"It'll be a topic of conversation," Trudi said to Roland. "God knows we need something to liven up these interminable parties with the same people all the time."

"With a lamp like this," she said, "we'll just have to give a party."

"Naturally," said Roland. "My genius as an interior decorator must not go unheralded. You might say the lamp is representative of my SS period."

"Indeed it is," said Trudi, no less ironically. "Nobody can say that you have not absorbed the cultural traditions of the SS. Seriously, the thing has a most soldierly air. It's the sort of thing they expect an officer to have. A trophy of war. Darling, we must have that party for Solomon."

Roland had had a bad time that day at the clinic in the Strasbourg compound. One of his clerks had stupidly mixed up the numbered metal tags on an entire batch of skull specimens. They had been angrily returned from the Reich University at Strasbourg. The clinic staff had had to reopen the sealed containers and re-identify the heads. Administratively it was unforgivable. Unteroffizier Schwege didn't know it, but he would shortly be returning to front-line service on the Russian front with a Waffen SS punishment battalion.

"Who the hell is Solomon?" said Roland irritably. He doubted if they could really afford a party. Not the way some of the SS gentlemen from the Kommandantur and the compounds drank their liquor.

Trudi couldn't help smiling. When he was irritated, Roland really was like a sulky little boy.

"Who is Solomon?" she said. "The lamp shade, of course. I know all about him. Solomon Prowazacki. A Pole, born in Lublin in 1916. Jewish on both sides of the family. His father was a schoolteacher. His mother's father was a furrier. Solomon was arrested last year as a terrorist. He was a partisan. Before that, though, in 1939, he graduated as a doctor of medicine at Warsaw."

A smile lightened Roland's gloomy mood.

"That's the first good news I've heard today. At least we've got a doctor in the family."

The party was entirely a success. Even the deputy commandant came, although his wife had to take him home early after he had suddenly run vomiting into the back garden behind the neat rows of raspberry bushes. He was a notoriously heavy drinker.

"It's his hypertension," his wife explained to Trudi. "He's driving himself too hard. Berlin has no idea of the problems he's got here in the camp. He says it's almost impossible meeting the quotas they give him." Trudi, though, had not lost her touch as a hostess. After a shower and a bowl of hot chicken noodle soup, the deputy commandant even risked a final brandy nightcap before he left for his own quarters.

"A delightful party," he told Trudi at the front door. "We must see more of you and Roland."

Wait till that lamp-stealing frump of a Frau Fischer hears about this, Trudi thought. Very quickly Frau Fischer did, for the Fischers were also guests, if only for the reason that Trudi had found the man attractive, in a hard-scarred sort of way, and enjoyed flirting discreetly with him.

To Trudi's delight, the skin lamp captivated her guests, who by dawn, as the party reached a state of uproarious disorder, were insisting on being formally introduced to Solomon by their obliging hostess. After dawn, though, as the first yellowing light of day in the east began to pale the night-long glow of fire from the distant crematories, the last of the guests had gone.

"A lovely, lovely party," sighed Trudi, kicking off her shoes and curling up on the divan in the soft light of the skin lamp.

"You saw a lot of Fischer tonight," Roland said. The abruptness was involuntary. He still loved Trudi—more than ever, if that was possible—but secretly he had always feared that one day she would revert to the wild and promiscuous way of life for which she had been notorious in Berlin before he married her.

Trudi smiled, admiring the curve of her leg in the lamplight.

"Not bad for an old married lady! Darling, of course I saw a lot of Fischer. I intended to. I flirted outrageously with him. I hope it makes his frowsy bitch of a wife very jealous. I'll never forgive her for blackmailing me into giving her your fingerprint lamp."

"You certainly made me jealous, anyway," said Roland, nuzzling at her neck with his lips. Women, he thought. The mysterious ways of women. There was nothing to worry about, though, with Fischer. Drowsily, and a little drunkenly, he unzipped the back of her frock.

"Darling," protested Trudi. "In front of Solomon? He's watching us!"

Roland slipped the frock down over Trudi's bare shoulders. She was still brown with the summer's sun, but where she was white she was very white.

"Solomon can watch all he wants," he said, his voice husky. "He might as well have some fun, too."

For Roland and Trudi, then, it was like the first night in his Berlin apartment all over again.

Soon, though, the party was forgotten and with it the last nostalgic days of summer. For the young Stolzers, as for everybody else on the staffs of the camps in the Auschwitz-Birkenau complex, the days and nights of that last winter of the war in Europe began to slip past faster than any they had ever known. Germany's enemies were beginning to tighten a ring of fire around the Third Reich. From the west, early in the new year of 1945, had come disquieting rumors and then confirmed and chilling news. The British and Americans had already begun capturing concentration camps as they advanced into Germany.

Even sworn and dedicated German National Socialists whose indoctrinated fanaticism had sometimes bored their less politically zealous colleagues had begun listening to the German-language programs broadcast from London by the BBC. They sought only news of camps they had known and SS comrades with whom they had served. The news, when it came, was not good. The camps indeed were being captured. The surviving prisoners, who should have been evacuated or liquidated, were being liberated. Alive and talking, too, like the Jewish swine they were, an angry Sturmbannführer told Roland. In some cases, camp staffs had panicked and fled, leaving behind them the crematories and the gassing installations and the silent stacked heaps of the waiting and corrupting dead. Many SS camp officials, even of senior rank, had either surrendered or had been captured.

Night after night the electric lights burned yellow in the Kommandantur at Auschwitz. Conference followed conference as plans were rushed through for evacuation or elimination of the camp's inmates. Because of the march of great events, the weak and wretched prisoners of Auschwitz were daily becoming no longer just a nuisance, another day's death registrations, but a living, speaking, testifying threat to the security and even the lives of their overlords in the black and silver trappings of the SS.

Themselves now driven by fear, never had the staff of Auschwitz worked so hard. Day and night the pellets of Zyklon B rained like crystallized tears into the gas chambers, stifling and choking the screams of the living who only had seconds more to live. Day and night the oven doors of the crematories swung open like an iron hell to gulp into fiery oblivion the never-ending dead and dying whose naked, interlocked bodies came sliding down the chutes or tumbled out of dump trucks. Day and night the mordant plumes of smoke streamed out from the crematory chimneys, drifting across the silent, heedless forests and frozen swamps toward the world beyond. Day and night in the hunted compounds and the diseased and crowded barracks the living waited to die.

Outside the compounds, there was no time any more for parties and coffee chatter in the SS married officers' quarters but only sporadic drinking bouts as the men and their wives sought a desperate, frightened solace in liquor until the bottles were cast aside empty and the morning brought headaches and nausea and fresh, angry fears for the future. Roland saw less and less of Trudi. As the commanding officer of the Strasbourg skull project, he was not involved in the frantic speed-up of operations for the evacuation and liquidation of the Auschwitz-Birkenau installations and prisoners. Strasbourg had been captured and with it the Reich University and the skull collection assembled for Dr. Muller's anthropological study of Jewish-Bolshevik commissar classes. Roland's father-in-law had escaped. From Berlin, indefatigable as ever, he had instructed Roland that he was to continue with his work at Auschwitz until the last possible moment before evacuation.

"We will have to begin our work all over again," Dr. Muller mourned in a personal letter to Roland. "The damned French have not only got Strasbourg. They have also got our magnificent collection. It is too good for them. They are untidy scientists."

Protected by his orders, which still carried the authorization of SS Reichsführer Himmler, and isolated by his duties in the clinic of the Strasbourg compound, as it was still known, Roland remained detached from the chaos and confusion in the main camp area as the SS dynasty at Auschwitz staggered toward the final day of reckoning. With the renewal of his work on the skull project, Roland saw even less of Trudi, for often he worked late into the night. Photographing, sketching, measuring, questioning and completing the files which would accompany the heads sealed in their tins, Roland could not suppress a suspicion which had begun to nag at him more and more ever since the night of the party they had held to show off the lamp shade of Solomon Prowazacki. Trudi lately had formed an inexplicably close and constant friendship with Frau Fischer. Often when she had come home late at night, she would have been at the Fischers. Once she had spent an entire day, a Sunday, at their villa while Roland was working back at his clinic. Quite by chance, he heard later that on this Sunday Frau Fischer had been visiting her brother whose Wehrmacht artillery brigade had withdrawn to take up defensive positions some twenty-five kilometers east of Auschwitz. Sturmbannführer Fischer had not left the camp that day. Sick at heart and not wanting to know the truth, Roland had not questioned Trudi. So long as she did not admit she was having an affair with Fischer, then he did not have to accept the fact of it. Instead, Roland had immersed himself in his clinic's desperate efforts to meet Dr. Muller's renewed demands for Jewish-Bolshevik skull specimens. An isolated unit engaged on academic studies in a remote corner of the subcamp, the Strasbourg compound was left in peace, forgotten and overlooked, while tension mounted in the Kommandantur, the villas and the main compounds as the SS staff listened for the first time to the rumbling of Russian guns somewhere to the east of Auschwitz.

Roland was asleep in his office at the clinic when the Russians arrived at his subcamp. Too exhausted and too despondent about Trudi to care about walking home to the villa, he had dismissed his staff for the night and slept at his desk, his head on his folded arms.

Awakening from a dead sleep, he sensed that at last it had happened. In the compounds outside he could hear prisoners cheering and laughing. This sound, as unprecedented as it was a shock, was enough for him to realize that the climactic moment had come. The Russians were here. The prisoners were free, at least those of them who still lived. The crash of breaking window glass somewhere convinced him. His first thought then had been of Trudi. All he could think of was that neither the Russians nor the camp inmates must get her. There were no more orders. The situation at the camp was now beyond recourse to orders. Only escape was left. Roland paused at the door of the clinic. One look out at the compounds and he knew the prisoners were free. Crawling, stumbling or running, they were free. Croaking, yelling, weeping or laughing, they were free. He had begun to run then, thinking only of reaching Trudi at the villa. Taking a short cut through one of the main compounds, he noticed a skeletal figure in striped and filthy rags lying on the muddy ground. As he ran past, the cadaverous form had raised one bony arm and thrown a stone. By chance, more than by skill, it struck Roland's face, cutting and paining him. Angered, but still running, he wiped at his cheek and saw the red, wet blood on the back of his hand. Like a strange whirlwind then, arising out of the ground itself, other stones had begun to fly at him, a self-generating storm of pain and hatred pursuing him as he ran through the crowded compounds. He was stoned all the way, like some Biblical martyr, until he ran free of the last barbed-wire fence. Shouldering aside excited groups of prisoners impatiently awaiting the arrival of the main force of Russian troops, Roland ran on in the gray, half-light of dawn to where the SS staff villas still clustered together like a tiny garden suburb beyond the stands of pine. As he ran toward his own home, he could see the tender glow of lamplight in the front room where Trudi had so often waited in the evenings with an aperitif ready to relax him. The front door was open now and he felt physically nauseated at the thought that some of the stronger prisoners might have already got to her. Inside, the house stank of liquor and stale cigar smoke and Roland remembered that he had long ago given up smoking. Was he too late after all? He was, but not in the way that he had so feared. In the living room, sprawled on the divan in the mellow parchment illumination of the skin lamp, were Trudi and Fischer, half naked in each other's arms. An empty cognac bottle stood on the coffee table. Two more rolled from the rug onto the polished pine floor, kicked aside as Roland walked toward the divan. Trudi, her mouth smeared with lipstick, still clutched a fine-stemmed glass. She was not dead but asleep, dead-drunk. Beside her, Fischer snored, the lean, scarred face sweating. Except for his drunken snorting, the room was very quiet and Roland could hear, outside and far away, the whine of military vehicles traveling at high speed. If it was the Russians consolidating their capture of the camps, he had very little time left. Knowing what he had to do but not believing that he was actually doing it, Roland went to the rosewood writing desk that Trudi had insisted on bringing from her family's home in Berlin. He unlocked the top drawer. The Luger was still there. It was loaded and ready to fire and now it was in his hand. Looking down at Trudi, disheveled and nearly nude and drunkenly unaware of him as she slept, he wondered that she could be so evil and yet still look so desirable and beautiful. Roland was weeping as he carefully aimed at her heart, for even now he could not bear the thought of disfiguring the face he knew and once had loved so well. The one shot did it. She seemed to bounce, her body jumping, and then she lay quite still. Avoiding the blood which had begun to well onto the bright cushions of the divan from behind her naked back where the bullet had extruded itself, Roland felt her pulse. Trudi was dead. Still warm to touch, but dead. Half awakened by the crash of the shot and stench of cordite, Fischer began to stir, muttering incoherently. With a strangely calm indifference Roland shot him twice in the stomach where the coarse, black pubic hairs began to climb onto his flat, muscular belly. Fischer yelled, clutching at himself and began to thrash about on the divan. So that Fischer would not touch Trudi's body or by his spasms displace it from the divan, soaked and dark now with her blood, Roland put a boot in his back and pushed him off onto the floor, where he lay writhing and clutching and moaning with the agony of his wounds.

"Don't go away, Sturmbannführer," said Roland.

Although he had no car at Auschwitz, Roland had always kept a can of precious gasoline in the little laundry rather than risk its theft from the garage beyond the raspberry bushes, and now he found it and knew what he would have to do with it. Walking back into the living room, be began pouring the gasoline. Over Trudi. Over the divan. Over the rugs. Over the skin lamp. Over the curtains. Over the elegant rosewood writing desk. Finally he returned to Fischer, who had stopped moaning and was just grunting as he writhed in his own blood. The major looked up, eyes bloodshot and glazing like a blinded old dog, as Roland held the can of gasoline over him.

"Have a drink on me, Sturmbannführer," said Roland and poured the rest of the gasoline down onto Fischer's face. It ran down over his neck, his shoulders, his hairy chest and into the bullet wounds of entry in his belly. Fischer's eyes widened in sudden comprehension and fear and he began to whimper, clutching at his groin.

"You always liked your drinks raw," said Roland, "and your women."

Outside the room, Roland took his own SS identity papers and tore and twisted them into a crude torch. Touching a match to it, he waited until the flame was bright and strong and then he went back and tossed the brand onto the gasoline-soaked divan. The violence of the leaping flare of ignition all around the room had surprised and nearly trapped him. It was almost an explosion but not so fast. Curiously, the first thing he saw burning before he had to run was the lamp shade made from the skin of Solomon.

By the time Roland had shed his SS uniform in the garage and changed into civilian gardening clothes, the roof of the villa had collapsed in a storm of flame and sparks, and the glass of the windows was exploding with a sound like the bursting of small grenades. Just before he took to the woods, Roland made himself stand and watch. A funeral pyre, he thought. That's how it all ended. A funeral pyre in a swamp in Poland, and we could both have had so much. As the dark pines of the forest welcomed him to the shadows of their concealing anonymity, Roland realized that Dr. Muller had spoken a great truth. Field experience with the SS had indeed raised his level of emotional tolerance to the sight and sound of pain and death. When he tried to think of Trudi, there was just nothing there any more. He was beyond pity, even for himself. He was free to go.

On the far side of the woods, just by luck, Roland had hailed and ridden with a convoy of Luftwaffe trucks retreating westward toward Silesia. Beyond the Oder, where the tank traps and the bunkers were being dug, Roland had left the convoy and found refuge at Cottbus, where a staging camp had been set up for the despairing columns of German civilian refugees who were still trekking by the tens of thousands into Saxony from Silesia. On the evidence of his original civilian papers which identified him as an Austrian anthropologist with limited qualifications in surgery and medicine, Roland was gratefully retained as an assistant by the elderly local camp doctor, who was attempting to minister to the medical problems of the refugees before they moved on farther to the west.

During the long, lonely nights in his tent at the Cottbus refugee camp, Roland completed the list for which he had taken careful and discreet notes during the last months of madness in Poland when he had feared for his wife's love of him and worried endlessly about their legal status should they ever be hailed before an enemy war crimes tribunal investigating the conditions and practices which had prevailed at Auschwitz. The list was a complete dossier of the names, ranks, numbers, qualifications and duties of the SS staff at the camp. As soon as he could reach the British or American lines in the west, he would surrender himself and hand over the information he had gathered. The cheap, black-covered notebook was his passport to a new life when the war was over and he could go home to Vienna. After that, with luck, there might be an anthropological field appointment in any country except Germany and any continent but Europe.

Roland had had little enough time to complete his list, for soon the East Front was at his heels again as Russian tank columns were reported to be converging on Cottbus, driving hard toward the Elbe. Cossack cavalrymen on horseback had already been seen scouting through the forests ahead of the tanks.

Riding a stolen bicycle, Roland had joined the quietly terror-stricken rush of refugees trekking westward without hope along the road to Torgau and the bridge across the Elbe, beyond which river the Americans were rumored to be advancing to meet the Russians.

Detouring to call at a stalag for British and American prisoners near the Elbe which had been abandoned by its Wehrmacht staff prior to the immiment arrival of the Russians, Roland had halted two armed but friendly Americans.

The meeting had been surprisingly amicable and they had told him that they had crossed the Elbe with an American 69th Division reconnaisance unit to make contact with advancing Russian patrols. When he asked them to take him back to their commanding officer so that he could surrender and then produced the Auschwitz blacklist with its neatly printed names, ranks and numbers, they had silently taken it from him and marched him at gun-point to a waiting jeep. He had not noticed the lilac in their lapels then, but even if he had done so, it would have meant nothing to him, and in any case there was nothing he could have done.

By sunset that day, Roland was lying on the sour straw paillasse in his cell at Schloss Galgenstein. No great moral hero, Roland had still been objective enough to find himself contemptuous of the trial when it came his turn to stand before the blind general and the officers of his dark and furtive court. After Trudi, nothing really seemed to matter any more and Roland knew that in listening unmoved and without fear as the strange jury of stolid Saxon countrymen found him guilty of treason he was not being courageous so much as entirely passive and fatalistic. He had reached the same state of apathetic mental surrender as had the most degraded inmates of the compounds back at Auschwitz. Death now was the reality and life the brief illusion.

When the blind, haughty-faced man in the immaculate uniform of a general of the German army asked him if he had anything to say on his own account, Roland had just shrugged his shoulders without speaking. At this, a dark flush of anger had bruised the taut pallor of von Bluckau's drawn cheeks.

"I am a general of the Wehrmacht," said von Bluckau. "You have deserted your post and your comrades and sought to betray your fellow officers. You have been convicted by a jury of Freischoffen of this court of honor. But, by God, you are still an officer of the SS and still bound by your oath of loyalty to the Führer. You will stand to attention like an officer so that I can hear it and you will answer clearly like a man. I cannot see shrugs or nods or gestures."

Roland stood to attention, clicking the heels of his muddy boots.

The general nodded, his smoked glasses gleaming in the light of the torches on the walls.

"SS Hauptsturmführer Roland Stolzer," said von Bluckau, "the court has found you guilty of the charge of attempted treason. By your intended act of treachery you have degraded and disgraced the good name of German honor. As a sworn servant of the Fehme in Saxony, I consider it my duty and my responsibility to impose the maximum penalty upon you."

The general paused, frowning, as a growl of approving comment stirred the crowded benches of the court.

"Have you anything to say before I so pronounce sentence?"

"No," said Reinhardt, "I have nothing to say except that in 1939 I graduated from a university as a qualified anthropologist so that I might study the origins of man and advance man's knowledge of himself. Instead, man has betrayed me and I have betrayed man. We are all traitors, General. Traitors to our God and traitors to ourselves. Even now you are about to betray yourself and betray me. There is no humanity in us any more. I can see death in your face, General. I have seen enough of it at Auschwitz to know it well. I am familiar with the silly, idiot face of death. Go ahead, General. Play God with me if it pleases you. And your court of honor."

The lilac-scented court was silent. Somewhere in a dark corner a snoring onlooker grunted into wakefulness, conscious of the sudden silence.

The general's hand rested lightly on the jeweled hilt of the sword that lay before him, gentling it as a rider does the neck of his horse. His face was devoid of any expression of emotion. Slowly he nodded.

"SS Hauptsturmführer Roland Stolzer," he said, "you have had your say. I am not impressed. I sentence you, therefore, to death, effective as from the rising of this court."

Holding up his hand, von Bluckau stilled the rising hubbub of comment.

"May God have mercy on your soul," he added. At heart, he was a pious man. A conventional but worthy Christian.

"You will be removed to your cell."

No pretty lamp shades now, thought Roland, waiting with his Fehme escort while the rusted iron door of his cell swung open. Only darkness again, and soon forever. Darkness and peace.

After Roland had been taken away, they called the deserter, the private soldier of the German army whom the Fehme had intercepted and arrested on a country road leading to Torgau. In the hooded silence of the dungeons, his rank and name echoed once more as it had so often on so many brave and bygone parades and roll calls.

"Gefreiter Johann Schwemma! Present Gefreiter Johann Schwemma!"

The name dwindled, echoing. Schwemma. Schwemma. An iron door rang, flung back against stone walls.

Schwemma? thought von Bluckau. I do know that name.

In the old days it had always been the general's pride that he could remember the names of his men. It had been easier when he could see their faces, but with Schwemma now he was certain. He was certain he knew him.

IX
The Wendish Soldier

The general, as usual, was right. On military matters he was rarely wrong. Arms were his profession and his men were like the sinews of his own right arm. He remembered Schwemma, quite suddenly, as he listened to him being marched into the court of honor. It was the weight in the footfalls more than anything else. The evocative sound of Big Johann taking his measured countryman's stride. The Wehrmacht had never cured him of it. Even on ceremonial parades, Big Johann had always looked as if he were still walking behind a plow on his potato farm in Saxony. Thinking about it, as Krausnick got the case under way, von Bluckau wondered how he could have ever not remembered Schwemma immediately he heard his name. Big Johann had been one of his personal drivers in the Panzer Division Elbeland from the day in 1939 when they had moved up from their assembly area in the woods north of Dresden to Silesia and the tense, waiting villages along the Polish border. Schwemma had been his tank driver, his staff car driver, his jeep driver and his groom in the days when there still had been horses for the pleasure of the divisional staff. Until Stalingrad. Schwemma had been with him that final, apocalyptic day in the snow and had found and saddled the straying, shivering white hack from the service corps unit. Schwemma had loped with him through the ice and slush of that last forlorn charge of despair against the Russians, clinging to his stirrup and taking great bounds forward to keep up. Schwemma had been hit by rifle fire and had pitched over backward to lie there in the snow with a stunned but unafraid look of utter astonishment on his big, bony face. Schwemma's face, in fact, had been the last of all the thousands of faces in the Panzer Division Elbeland that von Bluckau had seen close up before he had ridden on into the red blindness which had come so suddenly with the fury of the Russian shells.

In his own strange way, thought von Bluckau, Schwemma was a good soldier. Otherwise, of course, he would not have kept him as a driver. Big Johann had always been the butt of sly jokes in the divisional staff area and a legend and a source of wonderment in the units of the division itself. He was as German as sauerkraut but, more than that, he was a slow and lumbering personification of all the farmers in all the fields of Germany. This was one reason why von Bluckau kept him as his driver and patiently bore the slowness and the strangeness of his ways. Schwemma was a touch of home. He was as reassuring as a familiar oak tree. Like von Bluckau, Big Johann came from Saxony, not very far from Schloss Galgenstein, and each man was at home with the other's district and its ways. Physically a giant of a man, Schwemma was a Wend.

General the Graf von Bluckau, himself a countryman at heart for all his hereditary rank of nobility, knew the Wends well. They, too, had ancestral roots deep in the earth of Saxony. They had been, in fact, the original inhabitants of the great plain stretching eastward from the Elbe to the distant Niemen. Peopling what had been in ancient times a vast and mysterious wasteland of lakes, forests and marshes, the Wendish tribes had spoken their own strange Slavonic language and worshiped heathen gods like the three-headed Triglav and Redigast and Svantovit, whose shrine at Arcona, in Rugen, looked out over the dark and rock-ribbed waters of the Baltic. To this wide and lonely plain beyond the Elbe had come, during the middle ages, the Christian bishops, the noblemen, the farmers and the colonizers of Germany. Beyond the Elbe, they had harried the heathen Wends in their tribal lands. They felled the trees, plowed the fields, drained the marshes, laid the roads and built their churches, their castles and their villages. For the Wends, they brought an often fiery conversion to Christianity, taxes, tithes and feudal bondage. West of the waiting Elbe had run the historic proclamation by Saxony's most noble bishops and princes: "The Slavs are an abominable people, but their land is very rich in flesh, honey, grain, birds and abounding in all produce of fertility of the earth when cultivated, so that none can be compared with it. So say they who know. Wherefore, O Saxons,

Franks, Lotharingians, men of Flanders, most famous, here you can both save your souls and, if it please you, acquire the best of land to live."

Among the soul-saving Saxons who had crossed the Elbe to crusade for Christ against the heathen Wends and, in the process, secure more earthly rewards of rich lands and fine houses had been von Bluckau's own ancestors. Long before its stone battlements had begun to weather and mellow in winter frosts and summer heat, Schloss Galgenstein had withstood the assaults of Wendish tribesmen unwilling to yield either to the faith of the cross or the iron heel of the colonists who came with it across the Elbe from the west. Centuries of Teutonic colonization with the word of God, the sword and the plow inevitably could not forever be denied final victory, and by the time von Bluckau himself came, as a child, to know the Wends in Saxony they were like other Saxons, honoring the same God and loyal to the Hohenzollern crown. Yet, many of them still spoke their ancient Slavonic language and observed many of the ancestral customs of the tribes which had once so stubbornly defended the wild and brooding lands between the Elbe and the Niemen. Proud, courageous and hard-working, they took a lot of knowing, as von Bluckau had learned the hard way with those Wendish peasants who had worked on some of the farms on the estates of Schloss Galgenstein. Johann Schwemma had been no mere peasant but a farmer in his own right near Löbau, between Bautzen and Görlitz in Saxony's Upper Lusatia, where even in 1939 there were Wendish communities still speaking their own language as well as the German of the Third Reich. Often, as a child, Johann had traveled with his parents to Bautzen, the old capital of Upper Lusatia, and there gaped at the proud relics of his racial heritage in the Wendish museum in the Serbski Dom behind the theater in Bautzen's Corn Market.

On a fine summer's day and standing on his own land where the ditches drained into streams that joined the Spree on its marshy, northward meanderings to Berlin, Johann could see the Löbauer Berg, with its mountaintop inn and view tower, standing guard over the distant, clustered town roofs and spires of Löbau, but in the winter when the woods about the farm were stilled and deep with snow, Johann saw little enough even of his own Wendish neighbors. In the long nights by the tiled stove, when the children were asleep, Johann and his wife and his aged mother spoke in the ancient tongue of the Wends. Sometimes, before he went to bed, he would go out in the snow and the moonlight, gun in hand, seeking a marauding fox. When he came to the forest where the dry snow squeaked under his boots and frost racked the clawing branches so that they cracked and groaned, Johann could understand a little why his ancestors had worshiped at the pagan shrines to three-headed Triglav. Once when he had been hunting a fox that had taken three of his fattest young geese in a week, Johann had muttered an angry invocation to Triglav and the full moon had suddenly shone down through a great cleft in the dark clouds of the winter's night. Then it was that he had seen the fox, a slinking shadow against the snow in the clearing, and he had shot it twice so that it fell down, dead and fur-blooded, before the dark clouds again rolled over the bright and watchful face of the moon. The snow had come again, too, with the rolling clouds, and standing there watching it begin to bury the dead fox, Johann had wondered if old Triglav had perhaps heard his pagan prayer.

By the time war came in 1939, Johann had shot a lot of foxes and his farm was prospering. No politician, he knew only that since the National Socialists had come to power in Germany, he had been paid good prices for the crops of his land amid the forests of Upper Lusatia. Then had come his call to service with the Wehrmacht and the Panzer Division Elbeland. Mainly for his giant stature and his patient, unfumbling way with engines and transmissions but also for the deadliness of the rifle-range averages which he had scored with his fox-hunter's eye, Big Johann was chosen by von Bluckau as his personal driver. Before they had soldiered together for very long, the general realized that in Big Johann he also had a magnificent bodyguard. Without actually appearing to do so, the big Wend could move incredibly quickly and at close quarters was more lethal with his big hands than with any spitting, kicking light automatic weapon. Further than that, as both a Wend and a farmer, Big Johann had an instinctive eye for country, an uncanny and intuitive ability for positioning a car, a truck or a tank so that it defied easy stalking and killing. The wind, the weather and the light and shade of the countryside in all seasons were lifelong friends of the Wendish soldier. At the front these things were his allies and his armor, serving his cause with guile and skill as they had once, for so long, comforted his tribal ancestors in their struggles against the German colonists from across the treacherous Elbe.

Had Big Johann not been an indefatigable driver, a patient mechanic, a courageous bodyguard in ambush and a good soldier in the field, General von Bluckau would have never tolerated his periodic eccentricities. Twice a year—once in spring and once at harvest time in the autumn—Big Johann would go home, with or without leave. Never, though, during a time of tactical action when there was any risk of the enemy threatening the person of his general. Always he chose his moment of departure well, when the Panzer Division Elbeland was halted in reserve to rest or refit for the next phase of operations. The first few times it happened, von Bluckau had wondered whether his gentle giant of a driver was quite right in the head. With leave accrued to him and without consulting anybody, Big Johann had suddenly gone home. With no leave pass and no travel authorization, he had evaded the field police behind the front and the railway police behind them and made his way back to Germany and the Schwemma farm in Saxony. Usually he was returned to the division under arrest after voluntarily and placidly reporting to the military travel authorities in Löbau with a polite request for transportation back to the front. Once he even succeeded in rejoining the division after having dodged the field police—first going and then coming back. The explanation, when von Bluckau finally sought it with some asperity, was absurdly uncomplicated. Johann was perpetually worried about his farm. He was unhappy away from it. It had been in the Schwemma family for countless generations. Since Johann had gone into the army, his wife had tried to run the farm with the help of his ailing elder brother, who was finding it difficult enough to manage on his own farm whose fields marched with Johann's.

For most of the fighting year, Johann was always able to sublimate his worries about the farm, but in the spring, when there were young crops to be tended, and in the autumn, when there were harvests to be brought in, his lands called him with an atavistic compulsion that could not be denied. Rather than risk authoritarian denial of the privilege of leave, even if he had earned a furlough entitlement which von Bluckau himself would gladly have granted him, Big Johann would just start for home, a Wend in the thrall of his dark-ages Slav blood.

In campaign after campaign, Big Johann had proved too good a soldier for von Bluckau to lose as his driver and servant-bodyguard. More than that, although the general would not admit it even to himself, he felt safe in the company of Big Johann as might an ordinary soldier of the line pin his faith to a rabbit's foot, a pair of dice, a Bible or a St. Christopher's medallion.

To save Johann Schwemma from trial proceedings which were eventually brought against him by an angry colonel of the field police, von Bluckau had sought the opinion of a psychiatrist attached to the division's medical staff. After studying Johann's exemplary combat record which had already won him the Iron Cross, First and Second Class, and submitting him to a lengthy series of questions and tests, the doctor had reported to von Bluckau's quarters no more enlightened than when he had started.

The doctor had seemed perplexed and downcast by his inability to arrive at any rational psychological explanation for Big Johann's behavior, but von Bluckau had only been tolerantly amused.

"Doctor," he said, "Gefreiter Schwemma is a Wend. In Saxony we know the Wends. We know them well enough to know that we know very little about them. A Wend can smell rain coming. He can hear crops ripening. He can scent a fox over a distance at which you and I would miss him with a gun. I knew a Wend once who could tell you which tree in a forest was going to be struck by lightning during a thunderstorm. A Wend can find mushrooms in the dark. Even if these things are not so, they are the things which I grew up believing. That's why I want you to submit a favorable recommendation, any recommendation, so long as the field police drop these proceedings against Big Johann. He is too good a soldier for that. He belongs out here on the front with me. Until the war is over. Then he belongs to his land."

On his general's insistence, then, on this occasion, Big Johann had escaped trial and certain conviction by a military field tribunal on charges of desertion and had returned to duty with the

Panzer Division as von Bluckau's driver. It was just as well for the general that he did. A week later Big Johann was driving him in a staff car through a birch forest east of the Vistula. The autumn day on the Russian plain had been hot. The general's neck was sunburned and angry. His collar was hurting him. The sweat on his face was streaked with dust. Once inside the birch forest he had relaxed, grateful for the temporary respite of shade and coolness. Then, without warning, Big Johann had savagely braked the staff car, skidded it into a ditch, thrown the general to the ground with his own hands and after hurling a quick succession of grenades at two stacks of trimmed birch logs on either side of the road had cut loose at them with his Schmeisser machine pistol. Only two of the five waiting Russian partisans escaped, leaping and bounding away through the tangled undergrowth with Big Johann's fire showering them with leaves and chopped twigs as they ran.

"How did you know they were there?" von Bluckau had asked, grateful for the ditch mud on his uniform so that by vigorous brushing he could hide the fact that his hands were shaking. He could so easily, and so idiotically, have been dead by then.

"No good farmer would stack logs there," said Big Johann. "Not on low ground like that. A winter's rain and they'd be rotten."

Though wounded and left, literally, for dead in the snow at Stalingrad, Big Johann had somehow succeeded in breaking out through the encircling Russian forces. Playing dead in the snow by day and creeping through the Russian lines at night, he had slowly made his way westward, evading capture and quietly strangling the few Russians unlucky enough to hear and halt him. He left one incautious sentry with his back broken over the breech of his own machine gun. A last contact patrol flung out by a German Panzer division which had been trying to break through to the relief of the German Sixth Army at Stalingrad had picked up Big Johann as he came staggering toward them after nearly a week without food or medical attention and only melted snow to drink. Flown to Germany suffering from blood poisoning, frostbite, exposure and pneumonia, Big Johann had astounded the army doctors in the hospital at Dresden by the speed and surety of his recovery. By the time he was finally discharged, fit again, though, more than a year had passed; the Anglo-Americans had landed in force on the Normandy coast of France and in Saxony there were harvests to be brought in again. This time, to his surprise, Big Johann did not have to dodge the army's watchful police to get back to his farm. Under pressure from the agricultural administrators of Saxony, the Wehrmacht released a quota of local farmers and rural workers who were no longer fit for front-line service but who were still capable of producing crops for a Third Reich already feeling the loss of harvests in occupied territories being sullenly surrendered in the west and in the east.

Among the farmers who thankfully came home to their lands in Saxony was Big Johann, limping a little from the Russian rifle bullet which had knocked him backward into the trampled snow at Stalingrad, but still grateful to see the Löbauer Berg shouldering its way into the quiet sky above the forests of Upper Lusatia as the leave train bore him home from the convalescent depot at Dresden.

For nearly a year, Big Johann asked no more of life than God had given him on the farm to which he had returned. This was the kind of campaigning he knew best. The slow march of the seasons. The tiny green spears of the spring crops. The banners of the blossoms on the fruit trees. The golden ranks of ripening grain. The apples like rosy grenades. Underfoot, no land mines. Just the great, earth-clodded potatoes of Saxony. The only ambush, a sudden frost. The only intruder, a red-eyed forest fox prowling around the chicken run. No grinding tank tracks scarring the shuddering earth, just the rhythmic pattern of a furrowed field. For Big Johann, this was enough. By the new year of 1945, though, the good days were over. He was back in Wehrmacht uniform again. In defeat, the Third Reich was about to reap its final, bitter harvest. Like wheat doomed before the scythe, the armed forces of Germany stood facing the inevitable. With them, in February 1945, stood Big Johann, a giant and unhappy reinforcement rifleman in an infantry division battling against the advancing Americans west of Leipzig.

By April 17, 1945, Big Johann's division was pulling back into Leipzig itself behind the hundreds of 88 mm. flak guns which ringed the shelled and burning city, firing now not at bombers but at tanks. While American artillery shells bounced screaming and clanging from the massive stonework of the Völkerschlachtdenkmal monument commemorating the defeat of Napoleon and from the great columns of the Leipzig railway station, the city became first a dust-shrouded battleground and then, as the Americans encircled it, a trap for the exhausted and shell-dazed German defenders. Gefreiter Schwemma did not stay to put his hands up.

Creeping and running through the flame and smoke and brick dust of burning houses and crashing buildings, Big Johann evaded the wire-cage captivity which claimed most of the survivors of his decimated and disintegrated division after the battle ended on April 19. Big Johann was making his way home again, this time eastbound, heading for the Elbe, which lay between him and his farm. Clearly there was nothing more he could do now as a soldier of the Wehrmacht in surrendered Leipzig. Taking the road from Leipzig to Torgau, Big Johann came to Eilenburg, on the Mulde, the last river before the Elbe, and the war clutched at him again like a drowning man. Here, on April 21, a fanatical young Waffen SS commander was making a last stand against the U.S. 69th Division as it drove on from Leipzig to secure the east bank of the Mulde. Faced with the alternatives of either fighting in sacrificial and useless defense of Eilenburg or dying with an SS bullet in the back of his neck, Big Johann wearily turned to face the enemy once more.

There had been little enough fighting, though. Balked by the last-ditch fanaticism of the Waffen SS, the American commander had refused to risk the lives of his infantrymen for so small a prize so late in the war. Instead, he called up his artillery and for forty-eight hours the American guns poured ten thousand rounds of high explosive and white phosphorous into sleepy, provincial Eilenburg. As the artillery bombardment ended and the American infantry began to move forward, Big Johann had climbed out of his cellar to find that Eilenburg had become little more than a smoking, sulphurous wasteland of broken, charred bricks. The Waffen SS had achieved no more for Germany than the death of just another little city.

For Big Johann, it had been the final insanity. If this was what was happening to towns like Eilenburg, totally unimportant in the grand design of the two converging fronts, now only an easy day's march apart, what was to be the fate of his farm in the forest near Löbau? Where the Americans might think twice, the Russians would just laugh as they watched it burn. Big Johann had seen too much of the war on the East Front to expect anything else. One thing only mattered now. He must get home to his wife and his children and his farm before the Russians. He had taken the road to Torgau, then, turning his back on the phosphorous-streaked brickyard that had been Eilenburg and on the corpses of the Waffen SS men buried under its rubble. Past Sprottau he had trudged; past Doberschültz and Mockrehna and Gräfendorf, where the rolling heathlands to the north were astir with the furtive movement of refugees and Wehrmacht troops moving westward after crossing the Elbe at Torgau.

Just before he came to Torgau, but near enough to see a flight of glinting pigeons wheeling in the sunshine about the towers of Schloss Hartenfels behind the city, on the west bank of the river, Big Johann wondered if they had blown the bridge yet. Or if the Russians had crossed the river already. Leaving the high road to Torgau, Big Johann had moved across country toward a village some five kilometers west of Torgau. Taking the marshy low ground and keeping to the heath when he crossed a rise, Big Johann, a gaunt and haggard giant of a man, came silently to Süptitz. Crouched astride the westward road to Duben and Bitterfeld, the village had no welcome for a stranger. Houses stood empty with front doors open to the wind and sun and the dust. No dogs barked and no children played. Wise in the ways of war as he had known it, Big Johann knew this kind of village. Such a village as Süptitz was populated only by the sad ghosts of happier days. With some surprise, then, Big Johann had heard hammering and had come silently upon two men, German civilians, nailing a notice to a cottage door. Moving lightly, for all the weight of his big, tired bones, he was standing right behind them before he spoke and they knew he was there.

Later he was to reflect sadly that all he needed to have done was to grasp each man's neck and crash one skull against the other. Instead, he had laughed, happy for friendly, human company again after the long, lonely walk from Eilenburg.

"You're not leaving a note for the baker?" he growled. "I doubt if there's a loaf between Leipzig and Torgau."

When the two men spun around, one was holding a knife and the other a water pistol. They relaxed when they saw the torn and dusty Wehrmacht uniform and the big, raw-boned Wendish face.

"No, friend," said one of them. "You're right. The bakery is kaputt. The lilacs are blooming, though."

Puzzled, Big Johann stared at the man, wondering why he should be so lighthearted as to wear a sprig of lilac in times like these. The whole country was going crazy, he thought.

"To hell with the lilacs," said Big Johann. "Are the Russkis at Torgau yet?"

"Not yet, friend," said the man with the knife, "Why?"

Big Johann folded his arms, staring down at the two men. For civilians they were quick with the questions.

"Why? Because I've got to get across the Elbe, that's why. I'm going home. I've got a wife and a family and a farm at Löbau, near Bautzen."

Somewhere an apple tree was in blossom. Big Johann could smell it. Idly, in the sudden silence, he stared at the notice nailed to the door but one of the civilians moved quickly in front of it so that it could not be read.

"Is the bridge at Torgau still up?" said Big Johann.

The man with the knife nodded.

"You needn't worry, though, friend," he said. "You're not crossing it."

"I'm not?" said Big Johann slowly. The knife, he thought. I'll break his arm and use the knife on the other one. They must be looters. Jailbirds. Anything. You just never knew any more.

"Why not?" he said.

"Because you're deserting," said the civilian.

"Deserting from what?" said Big Johann. A slow anger began to overcome his tiredness. "There's nothing left to desert from. What's left of my division is in the American cages at Leipzig. The Waffen SS are still frying in phosphorous at Eilenburg. The Americans are on the east bank of the Mulde. The Russkis will soon be over the Elbe at Torgau, bridge or no bridge. We're in between. I'm going home. That's all that's left. Home."

The man with the water pistol shook his head.

"You're still a deserter. You're coming with us, friend. You're under arrest."

Big Johann frowned. Perhaps they had escaped from a lunatic asylum. There used to be a big one near Dresden.

"Who says so?"

"The Fehme."

"The Fehme? I've never heard of the Fehme."

The man with the knife chuckled.

"You will, friend. You will."

Big Johann undid his leather belt. "Gott Mit Uns" it said on the big buckle. God With Us. He had killed men with it before. Russki partisans in ambush on the East Front. Better men than these crazy civilians. One of them pointed to the garden gate and the silent village street.

"March," he said. "You're coming with us, friend."

The man with the water pistol pointed the toy right at Big Johann's face.

"This is filled with liquid prussic acid," he said. "You're a big fellow and it may take you several minutes to die, but die you will and very unpleasantly. March, friend."

Big Johann was always a man who bided his time when it was better to do so, and on this occasion he just nodded and started walking between the two unshaven, bitter-faced civilians with the lilac gay in their lapels.

Skirting villages, avoiding roads and keeping to the heath and the forests, they came to Schloss Galgenstein that evening but not without Big Johann noting and remembering the way back. Once he saw a fox, a tawny shadow in distant undergrowth, reminding him of the farm near Löbau and it took all of his self-control to remember the liquid prussic acid in the water pistol held by the civilian treading softly behind him. There will come a time, thought Big Johann, there will come a time.

The cell below Schloss Galgenstein did not worry him. After the fatigue and the fury of the fighting at Leipzig, the numbing terror of the bombardment at Eilenburg and the long, lonely escape east toward Torgau, he welcomed the darkness, the silence and the warm, dry straw. Day and night, Big Johann slept and rested in his cell, savoring the hot, ersatz coffee and dry, black bread they thrust at him and husbanding his strength. Without strength he could do nothing. With strength revived, he would find a way. Only death or old three-headed Triglav himself could stand in Big Johann's path now that spring was coming to the farm near Löbau on the far side of the Elbe.

He was as reassured as he was surprised to find that the president of this strange court-martial was none other than his old army boss, General the Graf von Bluckau. More than anything, though, he was puzzled. The general was a gentleman and a fine soldier. What had he in common with these Fehme people, whoever they might be? One thing was certain. They were no good. They were gangsters. They weren't good enough for a von Bluckau. Maybe the Russian shell that had taken the general's sight had taken his mind, too? The enigma confused and concerned Big Johann so much so that he paid little attention to the proceedings against him. Patiently he waited while the man Krausnick questioned and declaimed and ranted about German honor and the disgraceful facts of Gefreiter Schwemma's desertion in the face of the enemy. Patiently Big Johann weathered the accusations and the charges as he might a winter's gale or a blight on his crops at home. His turn, he knew, would come and he would see to it that when God gave him a chance to do what he had to do he would do it well.

For General von Bluckau, the arraignment of Big Johann involved him in a mental agony of doubt and remorse and shame. The gentle giant of a soldier standing before him had known his, von Bluckau's, worst fears and highest hopes in battle, shared the same rations in the field and several times saved his life in ambush. Gefreiter Johann Schwemma was a good soldier. As good a soldier, in his own right, as the general whom he had served so well. Now, thought von Bluckau, Big Johann was standing before him in a clandestine court with no legal jurisdiction but still, in his trusting way, expecting no more and no less than the justice due to a fighting soldier of the Third Reich. Big Johann, though, was on his own. The fact of his having been the general's driver in campaign after campaign only made it more difficult to rise to his defense, for under the terms of his oath as a Freigraf of the Fehme, von Bluckau had sworn to show neither fear nor favor in the execution of his duties as president of the court of honor. Was not his own wife under arraignment before the same court? Unless there was fierce and relentless prosecution by the courts of honor, the Fehme would lose validity as an instrument of punishment and power and the betrayers of Germany would be free to walk in contempt of honor.

For all Krausnick's hectoring and emotional ranting, his spittle-slavered lips and wild eyes, the evidence against Big Johann was plainly undeniable. While the Third Reich was still at war and the Wehrmacht still undisbanded, if largely defeated, Big Johann had been intercepted making his way home from a field of battle at Eilenburg. There was no doubting the intent, and the act, of desertion. Bluntly Big Johann had even announced it to the two Fehme men in Süptitz village. That the last corridor of free Saxony still extant between the converging gunsights of the East Front and the West Front was already harboring thousands of furtive Wehrmacht deserters made Big Johann's crime no less heinous. If anything, it only made his offense all the worse, for these clearly were times when, in the interests of German honor, punishment could only be effective if it were harsh enough to be a deterrent to others.

Plainly this was the view of the Freischoffen of the court's jury, for there was no hesitation or disagreement in their finding that Gefreiter Johann Schwemma was guilty of desertion while still a sworn and serving member of the armed forces of the Third Reich.

For von Bluckau, his hated blindness was suddenly a blessing, a cowardly relief, for it meant that he now did not have to face the bewilderment in Big Johann's eyes as he asked the soldier if he had anything to say before sentence was pronounced.

"No, sir," said Big Johann, conscious only of a feeling of puzzled pity for the blinded general whom he had once admired and respected with an almost feudal intensity of loyalty and pride.

"I have no alternative, then," said von Bluckau. "This court of honor of the Fehme has found you guilty of the charge of desertion. I need hardly say how much this grieves me personally. As not only your commanding general in the Panzer Division Elbeland but as your comrade in arms at the front, I know you to be a good German and a courageous and resourceful soldier. You yourself, however, have not disputed the evidence brought against you by the arresting officers of the Fehme and by the prosecutor of the court. Nor have you sought to appeal against the verdict of the Freischoffen of the jury. You have been found guilty. Yet I would have this court know that I deplore having to pass sentence upon you. I do it only in the name of German honor."

As if in mute appeal for understanding of his dilemma, von Bluckau looked blindly toward the giant soldier, erect in the muddy rags of battle.

Big Johann saw only the thin, set face and the dark glasses over the sightless eyes. The immaculate uniform. The bright ribbons of courage. The gleam of rank. The man he had once known so well and so long as his general.

"Gefreiter Johann Schwemma," said von Bluckau quickly, "it is my duty, my painful duty, to sentence you to death on the rising of this court. May God have mercy on your soul." To himself he had added, "And on mine."

The general had risen then and, standing stiffly to attention, had saluted Big Johann. Not the theatrical, outflung National Socialist greeting but the stiff, soldierly salute of the old German army.

Instinctively Big Johann had returned it and the general had heard his heels click.

"Remove the prisoner," said von Bluckau. "Call the next accused."

Big Johann was not thinking of himself, as the men with the lilac in their lapels escorted him back to his cell. Only of the general, the fighting leader he had once known. He is not only blind, thought Big Johann. He is mad, too. They are all mad here. He was even more sure of their madness when, from behind the iron-barred door of his cell, he heard them calling the next accused. The Gräfin von Bluckau. This could only be madness and he did not believe it, still, until he saw her and recognized her as the Fehme escorted her past his cell. In the old days when the war was going well, he had seen her often at railway stations and on big parades and reviews. There was no mistaking her now. She was still the general's shy and lovely lady. Nor had she changed.

Big Johann, though, was wrong.

Lying there on the straw in his dark cell and already planning his escape from the rat's nest of lunatics encumbering his return to the quiet farm near Löbau, the Wendish soldier was not to know just how much Jutte von Bluckau had changed.

X

The Lady of Galgenstein

JUTTE HAD BEEN drunk since before dawn when the Fehme watchman had clattered down the stone steps from the lookout on top of the Sprengertor and shouted the news that he had seen Russian tanks and cavalry moving along the cleared rides in the Jägerswald only a few kilometers from Schloss Galgenstein itself. Locked by her own hand in the old trophy room below the tower lookout, Jutte had chosen not to join the rest of the castle household in the hidden sanctuary of the dungeons below the great hall, where the Fehme leaders and the staff of the Freikorps Bormann had also set up their clandestine headquarters. The evacuation underground had been painstakingly rehearsed so that within fifteen minutes of a warning the castle could be left apparently forsaken and deserted. The bunker, as the general called the dungeon headquarters, had been victualed and prepared for a lengthy occupation. Once down there with the rest of them, Jutte knew she would have been safe from the Russians or the Americans for an indeterminate period. Access to the bunker had been carefully and cleverly concealed. The key to its security was the Schraubetreppe, the iron stairs that climbed like a corkscrew from the dungeons, encircling the chimneys that soared up from the great hall to the top floor of the Mittelschloss, the central structure of the castle in which were contained the family living quarters.

At the top of its confined spiral, the Schraubetreppe emerged via a concealed and hinged trap door of stone in the floor of the lookout post on the Sprengertor, the highest point of Schloss Galgenstein.

With access to every floor of the Mittelschloss through hinged and spy-holed stone doors which formed the back walls of the tall, open fireplaces, the Schraubetreppe had been forged from good Silesian iron. Sealed off for over a century and knowing only the tiny scamperings of bats and mice and beetles, its iron steps had still rung true when in 1944 the general had ordered it reopened and covertly made ready for use should it ever be needed by the Fehme and the Freikorps Bormann.

For Jutte, the making ready of the Schraubetreppe and the preparations in the dank, medieval dungeon chambers far below had only confirmed her fears that once more the dark forces of evil were abroad in Saxony and that their leadership was in the hands of her own husband. Dietrich she now knew to be morally as well as physically blinded. The man she had once loved and cherished had died in the Russian shellfire which had robbed his pale blue eyes of the power of sight. It was not her Dietrich who had come from Stalingrad. Just the blinded, bemedaled husk of a titled and embittered Junker, a dreamer of dangerous and deathly dreams.

Nightmares, not dreams, had been Jutte's lot during the last few weeks before the Russians came to the lands of Schloss Galgenstein; living nightmares which she endured alone behind the locked door of the old trophy room of a long-dead, hunting von Bluckau. There had been no more riding and no more furtive adulteries with frightened, lusting men on the von Bluckau estates. The familiar countryside had become no place for Jutte, dissolute in her drunkenness and careless in her unhappy adulteries. Confined by threat of battle in the great castle of which she was still the mistress, as a Gräfin von Bluckau, Jutte had been alone with the thoughts and fears that plagued her, for her own husband and son were too immersed in the secretive affairs of the Fehme to spare her time, much less love or tenderness. Already Dietrich and Siegfried were more than father and son. They were comrades in arms, concerned only with the struggle that was to come. So Jutte had retreated to the lonely quiet of the old and almost forgotten trophy room in the Sprengertor. Eating, drinking and sleeping there, she had waited out the days and nights, wondering if she really were going mad and whether soon, in some delirium of sorrow and dissolution, she, too, would spring to her death from the high tower. It would be in the soldierly von Bluckau tradition, she thought bitterly. Not for the same reason, though. The only enemy from whom she would be escaping would be herself.

Sometimes, glass in hand, she would stand at the narrow, embrasured window looking down at the cobblestoned courtyard far below or staring out at the distant sweep of fields and forest and marsh, a tranquil and pastoral perspective which had changed little since Martin Luther's angry voice had first rung loud in the awed churches of his native Saxony.

For a little while, then, Jutte would know peace of heart and mind but not for long. Something, perhaps a purple plume of early lilac blossom in a faraway hedge or the crouched figure of a speeding motorcycle rider, would remind her of the Fehme and the festering hate and terror which it soon would distill like a pestilence from the headquarters in the dungeons below Schloss Galgenstein. Jutte would seek a drunken forgetfulness then with one of the bottles stored in the gun cupboard of the old trophy room. Soon after that she would be sprawled unconscious on the leather couch which was her bed, oblivious to the timeless and unblinking stares of the mounted heads of boar and bear and deer.

After such a night of oblivion, Jutte had awakened to the sound of the Fehme watchman shouting warning of the Russians and pausing in his retreat below only to fire the three shots which were the signal for evacuation of the castle and occupation of the bunker in the dungeons.

Standing at her window, Jutte had toasted the approaching Russians in contempt and neat brandy until the sound of shattering glass in a window below the trophy room, followed by a crackle of rifle fire, surprised her in the realization that the Russkis were not only here but shooting at the castle. Only after short, staccato bursts of machine-gun fire had lashed across the face of the Sprengertor, chipping the old stone and startling the nodding pigeons into swooping flight, had Jutte moved aside. Exhilarated both by the brandy and the shock of being under enemy fire, Jutte had realized what she must do.

Her destiny would not be to stumble blindly down the ringing iron steps of the Schraubetreppe, scurrying underground with the menfolk to hide and wait and plot while the sprigs of Fehme lilac wilted and faded in their caps and lapels. The old way of life in Saxony was going, her own included, and she no longer cared. The past would soon be where it belonged and she with it. There was still time for a gesture, though, and she knew what it must be.

Jutte, the Gräfin von Bluckau, the lady of Schloss Galgenstein, would go downstairs—past the armor and the paintings on the walls, over the landings still flung with rich rugs, across the great hall hung with tapestries—and throw open the oaken splendor of the outer doors. Standing alone on the worn but massive steps that rose from the terrace, she would await the arrival of the Russians. If the East Front had come to Schloss Galgenstein, she wanted to meet it face to face. She had had enough of retreat. There was still time, though, for one more dinner party at Schloss Galgenstein. One more man. One more night of wine and brandy and laughter. After that it would be the high climb to the Sprengertor and then the waters of the Schwarzesee far below could have her bones, her breath, her life.

The guests would be the Russians.

When they came to Schloss Galgenstein, no tanks crossed the narrow stone bridge which spanned the dark and reedy depths of the encircling Schwarzesee. Only infantry, moving cautiously and sullenly, with their searching eyes raised to the silent windows of the castle and their rifles and Tommy guns held cocked and ready against German ambush.

Watching them come as she stood with one hand trembling on the carved stone balustrade that confined the sweep of the steps up to the oaken doors of the castle, Jutte wondered briefly if they would casually take her and rape her as was said to be their Mongol custom.

The Russian soldiers looked different, certainly, but hardly barbaric; stockier than Germans but quite young and, like all infantrymen, tired-looking and burdened by their equipment. There was an air of peasantry about the smocklike tunics, the bagged and shapeless breeches and the clumsy knee boots; only the red-starred caps pushed back on their shaven heads, the tinkling medals and the earth-brown color of their uniforms were martial reminders that these men, and millions more like them, had driven the once-mighty Wehrmacht back into the very heartlands of Germany itself.

Jutte was glad when she saw that the troops were led by an

officer, who, when he saw her, halted his men on the terrace and mounted the steps alone to salute her and greet her in passable, if accented, German. With her own half-remembered Russian, acquired at her university in Leipzig, Jutte found the encounter easy enough, though curiously formal.

"I am Colonel Alexander Yuriev," he said stiffly, "Commanding officer of the One Hundred Ninety-third Infantry Regiment of the Fifty-eighth Russian Guards Division under Major General Rusakov."

So young to be a colonel, thought Jutte. He could not be more than thirty.

The colonel smelled of eau de cologne and cigar smoke, but he was clean-shaven and clear-eyed.

"I am the Gräfin von Bluckau," she said, "the wife of the owner of this estate, General the Graf von Bluckau."

"General?" said Colonel Yuriev. The magic word, Jutte thought wearily. In any language, in any army. He actually looks impressed. Soldiers are all the same. They instinctively revere the system.

"The general is retired," said Jutte. "He was wounded at Stalingrad. He has no staff. He is not in the castle. The castle is empty. There are no troops here."

Half-lies, she thought, half-truths. One as base as the other.

The Russian stood there, hands on hips, evaluating the situation. His high-collared tunic was tailored from good, olive-green whipcord. The breeches were cut smartly and flared like a cavalryman's. The quality of the brown leather jack boots was obvious even under the dust of a morning's march. The sun glinted on the scarlet and silver of the flat shoulder epauletes of his rank. He was a good-looking young officer with a thin, intelligent face and eyes capable of much warmth.

"I have my regimental staff and a reconnaissance patrol with me," he said. "With your permission, we will billet for the night here in the castle."

"You are my guests," said Jutte, astounded by the courtesy with which the request had been made. "I assumed you would do as you wished."

The colonel shrugged, the thin, sensitive lips mobile as he smiled slightly.

"There are several millions of us Russians in the Red Army," he said. "Not all of us are necessarily Asiatic barbarians as Dr. Goebbels would have you believe. There are, presumably, even German SS men who are not sadists and murderers. I doubt it, but I like to think it is possible. I am just a soldier of the line."

After the Russian infantrymen had searched the castle, without detecting or suspecting the existence of the Schraubetreppe and the bunker underground in the dungeons, sentries were posted around the castle and the colonel set up his command post in the great hall.

By late afternoon when the Russian signalers and the regimental staff had finished with the traffic of orders and reports on their radios and the colonel had folded his maps and was sitting back yawning with an unlit cigar in his hand, Jutte had held a match for him while she suggested that he and his staff might like to join her at dinner.

"There is food and liquor in our kitchens," she said. "If you have cooks, then I will play hostess for the last time."

Crinkling his eyes against the cigar smoke, the young colonel had regarded her thoughtfully.

"That is very kind of you. On behalf of my staff, I accept." Quizzically he added, "We are unused to such German courtesy. Why? And why the note of final doom? Are we Russians so terrifying a disaster? Perhaps you are planning to blow us all up at dinner."

"Only with explosive cigars," said Jutte demurely.

Yuriev had laughed, white teeth flashing, and had repeated the joke in Russian for the enjoyment of those of his officers who spoke little German.

"We will take the chance," he said. "My adjutant, Captain Kuznir, will see to the cooks. Tonight I will be a Russian baron in his German castle. It's been a long war."

More than that, thought Jutte. You with the bright gold filling that gleams when you smile. You can be the last man I will have. Thank God you are young and strong and quite good-looking, even if you are a Russian and use more eau de cologne than you do soap and water. There are no frontiers in a bed. I am beginning to lust for you, young Colonel Yuriev of the narrow hips and the strong arms with the blond, bleached fuzz on the sinews of your sunburned arms. You will strip well and I will delight in you, dishonoring the noble name I bear and despise, and degrading the national honor of this Germany which has taken from me everything I ever loved.

Jutte had gone back upstairs to her old bedroom, not to the trophy room. Bathed and powdered and perfumed, she had changed into the low-cut gown she had last worn at a valedictory dinner party for Dietrich's commanders and their wives before the Panzer Division Elbeland had returned to the East Front for the final assault on Stalingrad.

The dinner party began when she came down the staircase into the great hall, where Yuriev and a score of his officers were already standing with drinks by the blazing warmth of the fireplace with the von Bluckau arms glittering above it and, beyond the flames, the concealed stone door that gave access at this level to the iron rungs of the Schraubetreppe and the dungeons bunker. Stimulated by the vodka pressed upon her and excited by the restrained yet sensual admiration of the group of officers in Red Army olive-brown, Jutte had begun to flirt cynically but agreeably with Yuriev. The mood of the night was already upon her in the light of the open fire and the silver candelabra ranged along the bare, polished table where so many von Bluckaus had dined with their ladies and their guests.

As they sat down to dinner, the colonel at one end of the long table set with silver and crystal and Jutte at the other, and three grinning Russian infantrymen began to play a wistful medley of tzigane airs on a balalaika, a harmonica and an accordion, Jutte felt as if she were dining with Czarist, not Communist, Russians.

Kuznir, the colonel's adjutant, sat on Jutte's right hand. Although he spoke tolerable German and attended her with a clumsy, heavy-handed courtesy, she was both resentful of his proximity and uneasy in his company. A squat, barrel-chested ape of a man with an enigmatic, flattened Slavonic face and a shaven head, Kuznir was a poor substitute for the lean, almost elegant Yuriev, who from time to time, beyond the far perspective of the dinner table, raised his glass in smiling salute to his hostess.

The dinner was a lavish affair. The wines and the rest of the liquor came from the cellars of Schloss Galgenstein, and some of the food. The greater portion of the food was ostensibly supplied by the Russians, but, except for the fresh, sour-tasting bread baked in their field kitchen, the victuals were commandeered from German farms. With the grease from a roasted suckling pig glistening on his chin, Kuznir explained that his division in its pursuit of the Wehrmacht to the Elbe had outrun its supply units and necessarily had had to live off the land to supplement combat rations.

"Not that I mind," he said, belching and reaching for a crystal goblet of red Rhine wine. "You have good farmers here in Saxony. Not since before the war have I seen such cattle and poultry. Spoils to the victors!"

Laughing so that the candlelight glistened yellow on his decayed teeth, Kuznir had laid his hand on Jutte's leg below the table. Wincing inwardly, she had smiled politely.

"Just the same, Captain, it would be wise not to kill the goose that lays the golden egg."

Kuznir took his hand away from Jutte's thigh to pour more wine.

"Only tonight do we live so well. Tomorrow we move on. The Czechs are waiting for us in Prague."

Then had come the toasts. To Jutte's relief they were at least not given in any political or nationalistic context. These men were not demagogues but soldiers enjoying good wine and food in the company of a woman of beauty and intelligence in surroundings far from the fear and the sweat and the dusty discomfort of regimental duty. After they had toasted their regiment, their division and their Red Army, they raised their glasses again to their wives and sweethearts, their mothers and their children. Abruptly, after the last of the toasts, Kuznir had turned and hurled his glass into the fireplace. Cheering, and staggering on their feet, the other officers emptied their own crystal glasses and they, too, crashed and splintered in the fire. All except Yuriev, who carefully set his glass down, made his way toward Jutte and, bowing stiffly, asked her to dance with him. Waltzing to the surprisingly effective music of the three infantrymen, Jutte realized that with the smashing of the glasses there had come a change in the mood of the dinner party, a shift toward boisterous and unpredictable bad manners. If the night had begun already with the tinkling of shattered crystal, how would it end? Jutte was glad suddenly that Yuriev, and not Kuznir, was the commanding officer. The colonel danced well for a while and then led her back to the table, apologizing for having stumbled through the last waltz.

"I am not accustomed to so much good wine," he said. "The fighting has been hard this spring. I am very tired. My officers will be happy to dance with you."

Clutched in Kuznir's bearlike embrace and with her face turned aside from the stench of wine, garlic and rotten teeth, Jutte had, herself, at first begun to feel faint and confused. Then the wine, the heat of the fire and the speculative looks in the eyes of the Russian officers with whom she danced conspired only to have her crave more drink so that she might forget her fears for the future and her regrets for the days and nights already gone.

Soon there were no more gentle, graceful waltzes but only the wild, tempestuous music of Russian folk songs with Yuriev's officers competing against one another in high-kicking, fast-stamping dances that brought the sweat coursing down their reddened necks and faces. Pleading she had had enough, Jutte returned to her high-backed chair, carved with the von Bluckau arms, to find Kuznir waiting with more wine for her. When she saw that Yuriev at the far end of the long table had fallen asleep, face-down in a pool of wine spilled from his glass, Kuznir had grinned and then shrugged his burly shoulders.

"Even Red Army infantry colonels get tired," he said, "As his adjutant, I am now in charge."

Clenching his hairy-backed fist he brought it crashing down on the table. The wine bottles and the glasses shivered and rang together.

"Now," said Kuznir, "you will show us how you German women can dance."

Pushing back his chair so that it tumbled over, he grasped Jutte around the waist and swung her up onto the table.

Signaling for more music, he stood there, hands on hips.

"Dance, German lady, dance."

As the rest of the officers, except the comatose Yuriev, crowded around, cheering and clapping, Jutte began to dance. Desperately and with fear, she began to whirl and stamp to the music of the steppes. Around and around went the great hall, the fire, the grinning Russian officers, the olive-brown uniforms, the cigar smoke, the flickering candelabra, the clapping hands and the sly, sensual eyes.

Kuznir reached for her first, grasping at the twirling lace skirt of the gown so that it ripped as she spun in the dance. She stopped then, but they shouted for her to go on. Kuznir was holding a gun, a German Luger, like Dietrich's.

What a swine he is, she thought. They are all swine. This is all they ever wanted. Maybe it's all I ever deserved.

Soon, from both sides of the long table, all the hands were reaching at her, ripping at the flying remnants of the gown and then her flimsy underclothes, pawing and clutching at her flesh. When she was naked and still dancing for the grinning, shouting Russians, she no longer cared. They are only degrading themselves, she thought, not me. If this is what you want to see, then take a good look at me and lust for me and never forget me when you go home to your stinking peasant women in Russia.

When two of the younger Russian officers began brawling, she sensed, correctly, that the dispute was over the matter of which of them was going to have her first. They were still struggling and grunting, awkward in their drunkenness, when the music stopped at a signal from Kuznir.

A helmeted American army officer was standing on the staircase overlooking the great hall.

Slowly he walked on down the marble stairs and crossed the expanse of floor, his heels ringing on the parquet, until he came to the table.

"Russki?" he said.

"Ja," said Kuznir. "Amerikanischer?"

The American nodded and put out his hand.

"I've come east from the Mulde with a reconnaissance patrol," he said in German. "We've been trying to make contact with you boys all along the Elbe."

He glanced at Jutte, still standing naked on the table, but she could not look at him, ashamed to be discovered like this by an American. The Russians did not count. They were animals.

"I see you're fraternizing already," the American said to Kuznir.

The adjutant laughed, buttoning up the high, red-starred tunic collar over his hairy, sweating throat.

"Just soldiers' fun," he said. "It can wait. You must drink a toast with us to this meeting."

As the Russian officers gathered excitedly around the American, clinking glasses with him and slapping his back in drunken good humor, Kuznir swung Jutte down off the table. He bent her backward, one hand on her breast and the other twisting her disheveled hair so that her face was jerked back.

"You will dance for us again later, German lady," he said and pushed her away so that she stumbled and fell to the bearskin rug which a nineteenth-century von Bluckau kinsman had brought back from the Carpathians. Crouched there, shivering in the firelight, Jutte had reached for the gown which had been torn from her and flung aside. Kuznir's boot came down on her hand. Reaching past her, he flung the torn, once-costly fabric into the fire.

"You won't need that tonight," he said.

Naked in the light of the fire, Jutte had still crouched there waiting while the Russians and their American visitor from beyond the Mulde toasted the imminent defeat of Nazi Germany and the victory of Allied arms well met along the line of the Elbe. Then, after some good-humored argument and laughing protestations by the American officer, the Russians were guffawing and clapping in cadenced slow-time as he walked steadily across the great hall, past the disordered and wine-stained table where Yuriev still slept, until he came to the fireplace before which Jutte lay. Over one arm he was carrying his overcoat with the bold divisional flash on the shoulders, but Jutte saw only the muddy, tight-laced combat boots, for she still did not want to look up. The boots halted and she wondered what was to come next. Not the American, too, she thought. Are they all the same?

"You will not appear to recognize me," a quiet voice was saying then. "You will do exactly as I say. Otherwise, Gräfin von Bluckau, I will kill you. Immediately."

Looking up, Jutte saw the Fehme lilac in the lapel of the American uniform and, then, below the helmet, the face of Schrader. It occurred to her that he must have entered an upper floor of the Mittelschloss by the Schraubetreppe from the dungeons. That would be why he appeared on the staircase.

"Take my hand," he said.

When she was standing and he was still holding her hand, he said, "Turn around, Gräfin."

As she turned, hot now in the heat of the fire, she sensed Schrader's eyes coveting her body.

"You're as beautiful as I always thought you would be," he said softly. "I am going to get you out of here. In the interests of Allied good will, your drunken Russian friends have offered to let me, as an American, take you first. They wanted me to take you here by the fire while they watched. As a man I would like to. As a German I would not degrade even you before these pigs. Instead, I told them I would take you upstairs in your own bed while they drank some more of your husband's wine. They said they would wait. Having watched you while you were dancing I am staggered both by their restraint and their generosity."

Quickly Schrader slapped her buttock, as he would have the body of the peasant girl Helga with whom Jutte had surprised him that day long ago in the fields of Schloss Galgenstein. The thought of it stung her more than the open-handed blow itself.

Then he slipped his overcoat around her shoulders.

"Let's see how you dance in bed," he said loudly for the benefit of the grinning Russians.

Picking her up, enfolded in the overcoat, he carried her to the staircase while the Russians whistled and clapped.

With a foot on the first marble step, he paused and swung around with Jutte in his arms.

"Thank you," he called to Kuznir. "I will warm her up for you, comrades."

They cheered again, then, and as he climbed the stairs, Jutte could hear the crash of glass in the great hall. They were opening magnums of champagne, smashing the slender, green-glassed necks against the edge of the oaken table.

In the darkness of the first floor landing at the top of the staircase, Schrader put her down, waited to make sure that no Russians had followed and then led her quickly into the library. In a darkness relieved only by moonlight shafting through the narrow windows, he cautiously swung back the fireplace door that opened into the Schraubetreppe.

"What now?" said Jutte.

With the rough warmth of the army overcoat against her skin, she felt like a member of the human race again, not like an animal.

"The court of honor," said Schrader. "You have hardly enriched the traditional concept of the ideals of German womanhood this evening, Gräfin. There were those of us who were in the Schaubetreppe, behind the fireplace in the great hall, who watched you tonight and are prepared to testify to that."

In the darkness on the dark iron corkscrew of the hidden way to the dungeons, Jutte began to sob. She was still sobbing when they put her in the cell to await arraignment before her husband. She had not wept next morning, though, when they told her that Yuriev's officers, drunkenly enraged by her disappearance, had wrecked the great hall—slashing at portraits of powdered and wigged von Bluckaus and their womenfolk, blasting with their revolvers at the gilded Meissen chinaware chandeliers and setting fire to medieval tapestries which had once hung on the palace walls of the royal house of Saxony. Jutte's only regret, by then, was that she had not thrown herself from the top of the Sprengertor while she had still been free to do so.

There were no tears left in her the day they escorted her from the cell to the waiting court of honor and to the stiff seated figure of her husband with the brilliant, bemedaled uniform of his rank and the thin, white mask of a face that was as bereft of expression or emotion as the smoked glasses over his sightless eyes.

Krausnick and his Fehme informers had worked hard on the presentment of charges against the Gräfin von Bluckau. Listening to the sordid recital of her many adulteries, her many offenses against the honor of her husband, his family and of German womanhood, Jutte realized that the Fehme must have been busy long before the Russians came. Its spies and informers had missed little. The Polish woodcutter. The French gardener. The British soldier who had been so good with horses. They were all there, and more. The frightened but eager men of her anarchic and amoral embraces. The sorry, shoddy story of deranged infidelities and compulsive assignations. Then there was the dinner party for Colonel Yuriev and his officers. For Krausnick, mouth frothing as he shrieked his accusations, it was what he described as the last disgusting stab in the back. Leading Schrader through the evidence of what he had seen through the spy-hole of the Schraubetreppe behind the immense fireplace in the great hall, the prosecutor could barely contain his paranoiac fury as the Freikorps leader coldly but accurately described how the drunken Russian officers had begun to strip their dancing hostess on the great table of Schloss Galgenstein.

When Schrader had finished his evidence and stepped down, Krausnick had whirled on his feet, pointing at von Bluckau.

"There he sits," Krausnick shouted at the stolid Freischoffen of the jury. "The husband of this very same woman, if God will pardon me for so defaming the name of womanhood. The president of this court. A general of the Wehrmacht. A nobleman of Saxony. A hero of Stalingrad. Blinded by Russian fire in the cause of National Socialism and the defense of the Third Reich. The father, God help him, of her son, who is himself a young comrade of the Fehme and a servant of this court. This is the man, the president of this very court of honor, whom she betrayed. In him, she betrayed me and you and all of Germany."

Listening to the shrill voice ranting its hate, Jutte knew beyond all doubt that she no longer wanted to live. If there had been doubt before, any element of histrionic neurosis in her urge to destroy herself, there was none now. Standing before her husband, with their pink-cheeked and round-eyed son at his side, Jutte knew that she was already spiritually dead. The physical fact of its accomplishment was now only a formality. For her son, Siegfried, she felt only a strange, dispassionate pity that he should have been born to her and lived to see this day. Already he was a stranger to her. For Dietrich, the stern and outward aristocrat and hero, she bore, strangely, a sudden tenderness that she would have expected to have felt for their son. Dietrich, she realized, was still the dreamer, the lonely boy in the great castle towering over the marshes between the Elbe and the Mulde. Always Dietrich had dreamed. Dreams of glory. Dreams of patriotism. Dreams of a rebirth of German pride, nurtured and sustained by the Fehme. Now she had darkened his dreams as the Russian shells had darkened his vision of the world he had always known so proudly. Dietrich had never really grown up and now it no longer mattered.

There was much she could, and should, have had to tell Dietrich and their son about the reasons for her retreat from decency, her flight to debauchery and adultery and fraternization, even with the Russians. There was the fact of the gun that Kuznir held while she danced but it was all too late for words from her. The other words were too strong, the words spat out by Krausnick, obscenities over which she could see the Freischoffen nodding.

Krausnick was pointing at her and ranting again, the blood vessels at his temples distended like blue worms.

"With all deference to our president, and Freiherr of the Fehme, General the Graf von Bluckau," he shouted, "I ask this jury to weigh the evidence against the accused, to consider the vileness of her infidelities, the degradation of her behavior with captives of the Third Reich and the debauchery and treachery of her fraternization, above our very heads and in the ancestral home of her husband, with the Communist defilers of our homeland. I ask this jury of the Fehme to consider all these things. And then to find her guilty on all counts of this vile indictment. Then, as the prosecutor to this court of honor, I demand the maximum penalty. I demand death."

God, let them be quick, thought Jutte. The quicker the better. Let me die. Let me die.

She had not long to wait for the verdict.

On the facts presented by Schrader and the other Fehme informants testifying as to the particulars of the charges against her, the jury had needed no further haranguing from Krausnick to arrive at a finding.

The foreman of the jury, a miller from Zorndauf village, stood awkwardly to attention, embarrassed and ill at ease as he addressed von Bluckau.

"Mr. President," he said, "the jury is unanimous. I regret to have to inform you that we find the accused guilty on all charges. I have been asked to tender our sympathy to the general."

The foreman's boots creaked as he shifted uneasily on his feet.

On the general's face there was no visible change of expression and for a while he seemed not to have heard the verdict. With his right hand lying inert on the hilt of the sword before him, he had remained seated, bead bowed, as if he were undecided as to what he should do.

Then he nodded and stood up, erect and shoulders squared back, as if about to take the salute at a divisional parade.

"Jutte von Bluckau," he said, his voice clipped and staccato, "you have been found guilty on charges which amount to scandalous and treacherous conduct profaning the honor of our German race during the darkest hours of our glorious Third Reich. As the court is well aware, I am your husband. You are the mother of my son. Nevertheless, as a Freiherr of the Fehme and as the president of this court of honor in the jurisdiction of Saxony, I am also the sworn servant of this court. I have no alternative, therefore, but to impose upon you the sentence appropriate to the nature of the offenses of which you have been convicted. That penalty is death. I order, therefore, that upon the rising of this court, you be put to death."

The court was silent then, more silent than it had yet been. Though no man spoke, the general held up his hand, waiting for complete silence before he spoke again. The narrow mouth and the thin, firm jaw were set hard, a tautened mask of resolution and iron will, but behind the dark glasses tears glistened.

"I have further decided," he said, "that, with the court's indulgence, I myself will carry out the sentence of execution."

Uncertain in his blindness, von Bluckau faced toward his wife.

"Jutte," he said, "I loved you once. I wish I had loved you more. May God have mercy on our souls."

Quietly yet resonantly, as the Fehme orderlies silently began to escort Jutte toward her cell, a voice intoned, "Amen."

It was the voice of the next, and last, accused to appear at the sitting: a thin and balding pastor, barefoot in the filthy, striped rags of a concentration camp.

XI

The Pastor in Rags

BEHIND HER, as she walked to the cell to begin the lonely wait for a time of execution, Jutte left an emotional vacuum which seemed momentarily to have exhausted and halted the proceedings of the court, inhibiting thought and stifling speech.

To most of those present at the court, Jutte had long been well known as the lady of Galgenstein and had commanded the simple, unthinking respect always accorded the feudal title of a Gräfin von Bluckau. Now she had failed them. The rank and file of the Fehme, mainly villagers and farmers and tradesmen of the district, had been shocked by the revelations of the Gräfin's promiscuous and casual adulteries with prisoners of war who had labored on her husband's estates; they had been angered by the profligate aid and comfort which she had tendered the Russian officers who had dined as her guests at Schloss Galgenstein in the sacked great hall above the very dungeon chambers in which they now were gathered.

Further than the wanton destruction of old values based upon the influences traditionally wielded by such patrician Saxony households as the von Bluckau family, the men of the Fehme also resented the humiliation and the anguish which Jutte's arraignment before the court and its president had thrust upon the thin shoulders of the Graf von Bluckau himself.

Respecting his moral fortitude and admiring his stern adherence to the obligations of his sworn oath to the Fehme, they deplored the fact of his having been so put upon the rack by the folly and the treachery of his wife. Such an affront to the hereditary master of Schloss Galgenstein was in itself a blow to the sensibilities of the farmers and villagers whose families had for generations plowed the fields and reaped the harvests of the lands of the von Bluckaus. The humbling of such a feudal patriarch as the Graf von Bluckau had brought no pleasure to any except the now silent and contemptuously aloof Major Schrader.

Standing again and speaking, for once, in a hushed voice,

Krausnick had addressed the motionless, erectly seated figure of the general.

"Mr. President," he said, "in view of the circumstances of the preceding case it might be that you would prefer to adjourn these proceedings until such time as you so feel disposed?"

The general had shaken his head, the dark glasses glinting impersonally in the shadowy illumination from the torches on the walls. He looked less than human.

"No, Mr. Prosecutor. I believe the next case is the last of this session. We have little enough time to spare. We will proceed."

"As you wish, sir," said Krausnick. "The next accused is already present."

He turned toward the tall, bald-headed man, a barefoot scarecrow of a figure in the dirty, ragged remnants of the striped garb of the concentration camps.

"You are Otto Schillinger?" he said.

"I am," said the ragged man.

"What is your occupation?"

"I am an ordained pastor of the Lutheran Church of Germany."

"Where was your parish?"

The pastor smiled gently, the face furrowed deep with lines and the eyes severe and steady behind the cracked lenses of the steel-rimmed spectacles.

"My parish was, and still is, at least in the eyes of God, in the village of Kotzdorf."

"Thank you," said Krausnick, a measure of ironic courtesy in his voice. "You have already pleaded not guilty to having committed seditious acts in the parish of Kotzdorf between April twentieth and April twenty-third? This very month, in fact?"

"That is so," said the pastor. "However, if it pleases the court, I am prepared to plead guilty to a charge of having lawfully preached the word of God."

"Pastor," said Krausnick, unwontedly patient, "it does not so please the court. You will be quiet now and you will not speak until you are spoken to. You are no longer standing in your pulpit."

The prosecutor turned to face von Bluckau.

"Mr. President, I propose to call a witness who will testify as to the circumstances of the acts of sedition which resulted in the arrest of this accused by the Fehme."

The general nodded curtly, almost with impatience.

"You may proceed, Herr Prosecutor. I am relieved to hear that you can call evidence which is germane to this case. This is no ordinary prisoner who stands before us."

The witness called by Krausnick was Martin Moyzisch, a stooped and knuckle-handed carpenter from Kotzdorf. Nervously pulling a graying bristle of clipped mustache in the Hitler tradition, Moyzisch awaited the prosecutor's questions without once looking at the pastor.

"You know the accused?" said Krausnick.

"I do."

"How long have you known him?"

"Twenty years. At least twenty years."

"After his absence over the last six months of 1944 and the first few months of this year, did the accused return to Kotzdorf?"

"He did."

"When was this?"

"A few days ago," said Moyzisch. "On April twentieth."

"In your own words, witness, I want you to tell the court what then transpired. As you remember it."

Moyzisch cleared his throat, his eyes shifting uneasily as he still avoided looking at the pastor. A solitary man, the carpenter had no liking for speaking out in public.

"He just walked back into the village," said Moyzisch. "We were surprised to see him. We knew he had been arrested after the July twentieth plot against the Führer last year. We had also heard that he had been found guilty of sedition at the People's Court in Berlin. There had been no Lutheran pastor in Kotzdorf after that. When he came back to the village, he was dressed like he is now. The same prisoner's rags. He was barefoot even though it was still cold and muddy."

"Just so," Krausnick interrupted. "What did the accused do after he came back to the village?"

"He preached," said Moyzisch.

"In the church?"

"No. The church had been damaged. In February, American fighter-bombers had attacked a troop train at the railway station. One plane was shot down by the flak guns on the train and it crashed and exploded in the village. The fighter's motor bounced away and hit the church. There was a fire and the church was burned out. It was a small church but very old."

"Quite so," said Krausnick irritably. "A lot of old churches have been burned down in Germany lately. There will probably be a lot more. Where, then, did the accused preach?"

"Anywhere," said Moyzisch. "In the streets. At the railway station. At the crossroads. In the fields. He said that it had been good enough for the Son of God to preach under the open sky and so it was good enough for him, too."

The prosecutor frowned, nodding impatiently.

"No doubt, but what did the accused preach about?"

"National Socialism," said Moyzisch, "and the war. He said we should rise up and unite to destroy the Nazis before they destroyed us. He said the Nazis were evil. The forces of the devil. The satraps of the Antichrist. He said that if we did not destroy them and the Führer, then we were as guilty and as wicked as they were."

"Did the people listen to him?"

"They did. They couldn't help it. He has always had a loud voice."

"What do you think they thought about it?"

"I don't know. I can only speak for myself."

Krausnick sighed, mopping at his mouth with a handkerchief. "Well, what did you think?"

"I thought he was mad. I knew he had been in prison and in a camp. To have walked all the way back to Kotzdorf, barefoot and in rags, he must have been crazy. He looked crazy."

"Where did he sleep?"

"Anywhere. In the forest. In barns, In haystacks."

"Did anybody take him into their homes?"

"No."

"Why not?"

"I think they were too frightened."

"Frightened?" said Krausnick, his voice incredulous and light with amusement. "Frightened of a ranting old man with dirty feet and wearing only his prisoner's rags?"

"They were frightened of everything and everyone, by then," said Moyzisch. "Frightened of the pastor and what he said. Frightened of the police. Frightened of the war. Frightened of the Russians. The Wehrmacht had gone, by then, and the Russians had come to the district."

"So," said Krausnick, "the Russians were there and while the Wehrmacht was still fighting elsewhere in the defense of Germany, the accused was preaching open sedition and urging the villagers of Kotzdorf to rise and overthrow the government of the Third Reich in its most critical hours? A futile enterprise, I might add, but a dangerous sentiment."

"Not just Kotzdorf," said Moyzisch. "He meant all the people of all the villages of Germany. He said it was still not too late to come to grips with the beast that was National Socialism and to save our own souls even if we could not save Germany. Forgive me, Mr. Prosecutor, but I am only repeating what he said."

"We do not doubt your patriotism, witness," said Krausnick. "Otherwise you would not be here. When did the accused stop his preaching?"

"Not until two Fehme men came to the village. They arrested him and took him away one night. The next time I saw him was here, today."

"Thank you," said Krausnick.

Negligently he spoke to the pastor.

"Otto Schillinger, you have heard the evidence given against you. Do you wish to cross-examine the witness?"

"I do not," said the pastor. "According to his lights, he has spoken the truth. I would dispute his interpretation of my state of mind as to sanity, but I would not quarrel with his statement of the facts as he knew and saw them."

Krausnick pursed his lips, seemingly surprised.

"You wish to put no questions, then?"

"None that the witness is competent to answer," said the pastor.

After Moyzisch had stumbled back to the anonymity of his seat on one of the crowded benches in the shadows of the court, there came more witnesses from Kotzdorf, corroborating the evidence of the carpenter and confirming the fact of the pastor having preached sedition. As he had with Moyzisch, the pastor calmly declined to put any questions to the later witnesses and after Krausnick had formally concluded the presentation of evidence, the Freischoffen of the jury began a mumbling deliberation. It was not prolonged. Reluctantly almost, the foreman stood once more and announced that the jury was agreed upon its verdict. The accused, Pastor Otto Schillinger, was guilty of the charges of sedition on all counts.

"With the court's indulgence," the foreman added, "most of us here know the accused and are familiar with the facts of his long years of service as pastor to the village and district of Kotzdorf prior to his arrest after the July twentieth plot. Having regard to this record of service to his parish and bearing in mind the possibility of his having returned to the village in a deranged state of mind, we would like to add a recommendation of mercy."

Sitting stiffly upright with his hands spread flat on the rough blanket of the table, either side of the jeweled hilt of the ceremonial sword, von Bluckau inclined hs head in an almost imperceptible nod.

"Thank you," he said. "I will bear your recommendation in mind."

The blade of the sword glittered, a razor-edged frontier between life and death.

"Pastor Schillinger," said von Bluckau, "you have been convicted of the charges laid against you by the Fehme. Before I pronounce sentence do you have anything you wish to say to the court in mitigation of these offenses?"

The pastor folded his arms as he had so often done, standing in the pulpit of his church on the Sundays before it had been consumed by the reckless fires of war.

"Thank you, Mr. President," he said. "Do I have your permission to speak now?"

"You do."

"In that case," said the pastor, "with the indulgence of the court, there are certain things which I would like to say. Firstly, I cannot accept the jury's recommendation of mercy since I cannot agree that the simple act of preaching the word of God constitutes being in a state of mental derangement. Concerning the witness Martin Moyzisch, I would say that his statements were substantially correct. He had indeed known me for a long time. He had good reason to know me. I married him to his wife. I christened his children. I brought him and his family the word of God. This I did for many people in Kotzdorf over the years of my time in the village. I preached the word of God, even after 1933, when National Socialism began to put the clock back in Germany."

Imperiously, with raised hand, von Bluckau stilled the sudden murmur of comment in the court.

Unperturbed, the pastor continued, speaking quietly with a clear resonance that all could not but hear.

"After the National Socialists came to power, I still preached the word of God at Kotzdorf. I will concede that no Gauleiter sought to stop me, but this was because I was already sinning. I was myself walking the very brink of hell itself, treading warily between truth and lies, good and evil, love and hate. I compromised with God. I compromised with the devil. I told myself that if I did more, if I spoke louder against the new tyrants of the devil in Germany, then I would be forbidden to preach any more. Possibly, even, I would die as a martyr and this would have achieved nothing, for, God knows, there were already enough martyrs in the camps and prisons of the Third Reich. So I took the middle way, the easiest way. I took the hand of God and I took the hand of Satan. When the war came, I was still the Lutheran pastor at Kotzdorf. Then, in the autumn of last year, the Gestapo came to our village and they took away my old friend, Father Josephus, a Roman Catholic and a Jesuit but a good man who had served God in his own way and in the true spirit of his own faith at Kotzdorf. They tried Father Josephus before Judge Freisler in the People's Court at Berlin. They convicted him of high treason and they sentenced him to death. There was no stay of execution. They hanged him by a noose of piano wire from a meathook on a steel rail in a cellar of the prison at Berlin-Plötzensee."

The pastor looked at the faces ranked in the shadows of the dungeons.

"Now, my fine and noble patriots of this court of German honor, why do you think Father Josephus died like that?"

The court was silent. Many of the sullen-faced Fehme men on their benches and stools, even the Protestants among them, had respected the Catholic priest of Kotzdorf as much as they had revered Pastor Schillinger.

"I will tell you why," said the pastor. "Father Josephus was strung up by the neck from a butcher's hook in the cellars of a Berlin jail because he had refused to betray the seal of confession under which a conspirator in the July twentieth plot against the life of Adolf Hitler had confided his complicity and his intentions and had sought forgiveness from God. When the Gestapo finished their interrogation of Father Josephus, they had broken his body but not his spirit, his mind, his soul or his faith. Not even the executioner could do that. Father Josephus died as a martyr, not a traitor, to his faith."

The pastor halted, pushing his glasses up onto his forehead and rubbing at his eyes so that they were sore and red when he spoke again.

"When I knew what they had done to my good friend Father Josephus, I knew what I myself had to do. I had to cry out, in God's name, against the people who in the name of German law and order could do such a thing to such a man. I had spoken of this for only one Sunday at my church in Kotzdorf when I, too, was arrested and taken to Berlin. Like Father Josephus, I was also convicted of high treason and the same Judge Freisler sentenced me to death. I was sent to the concentration camp at Flossenburg to await execution, and there I suffered gladly for my sins of omission as a pastor of my church who had for too long turned his back on his God."

The pastor held out his cracked spectacles.

"They broke these at Flossenburg as they whipped us in through the front gate. There are many places like Flossenburg in Germany. You know the names. You have heard them whispered. Belsen and Dachau. Buchenwald and Ravensbruck. Oranienburg and Sachsenhausen. For every one you know and name, there are always more. They are not just death camps. They are the garrisons of the godless, monuments to man's inhumanity to man, vile cancers corrupting the soul of our German nation. Yet, when I walked out of Flossenburg, a free man, after the Anglo-Americans captured it on April ninth, before my set date of execution, and when I came back to Kotzdorf to cry out to God at what I saw all about me, your Fehme arrested me and charged me before your court in the name of German honor. In God's name, my children, what honor? I see that I have had company, that other prisoners have stood here before you to answer for their crimes against your code of German honor. I suggest that there is another court in a far higher jurisdiction than any to which you could aspire, a court with a judge who alone is competent to preside over the souls of us all. I commend you all to His mercy. Amen."

Head bowed and eyes closed, the general nodded.

"Amen," he said.

The court was silent, awaiting the sentence.

"Pastor," said von Bluckau, "we may or we may not be in need of your prayers. As a von Bluckau and as a parishioner of the Lutheran church at Galgenstein, I was taught to respect the principles and ideals for which you stand. On the other hand, Pastor, these are strange and perilous times for our beloved Germany, times that call for stern, even violent, measures. We of the Fehme, for instance, are gathered here like thieves in a cave. As a general of the Wehrmacht, I do not relish the role of partisan, the trade of terrorist, the fate of a fugitive. By nature, I am a proud man. Nor do I relish having to sit in judgment on such a man as yourself. Yet, as a Freigraf and a member of the Fehme, sworn to lead Saxony's fight for the preservation of German honor in these days of despair and disaster, I must so sit in judgment. This is no time for treachery, sedition and subversion. You have been convicted of these things and the penalty is death, so, in the name of German honor if not in the name of the Lord, you must be punished. It would serve our cause poorly, however, if I were to unwittingly canonize you as a saint and a martyr. I do not for one moment doubt that you have the faith to possess the courage to accept, if not welcome, such a destiny. I must, therefore, carefully consider the verdict of the jury and arrive at such a sentence as the circumstances warrant."

Immobile in his rags and with his feet bare upon the cold stone floor, Pastor Schillinger waited.

"Mr. Prosecutor," said von Bluckau, "the prisoner is remanded for sentence on the rising of this court tomorrow. It now well past midnight and I must have time to think. The court is adjourned until sunset tomorrow."

The next evening, while the lengthening shadows of Schloss Galgenstein stretched like gigantic fingers across the moated waters of the Schwarzesee, there was a solemnity and a new tension in the air as the court reassembled for the sentencing of Pastor Schillinger. Momentous tidings that day had been flashed from Berlin to the Werewolfsender radio station on the deserted airfield at Falkewitz and relayed to the Freikorps Bormann communication center in the old medieval armory beyond the cells.

"Gentlemen," said von Bluckau, speaking slowly as if in quiet pain, "Germany's time of destiny is at hand. This is our darkest hour. I have to tell you that the Führer is dead. He has died a soldier's death at the Führer headquarters in Berlin."

Abruptly the general pushed back his chair and stood before the blanket-covered table with the sword and the noose.

In the hushed silence of the underground court, a man was sobbing.

"We will stand to attention, gentlemen," von Bluckau commanded. "In the name of all Germany, we will observe a minute's silence as a mark of respect to the memory of Adolf Hitler."

The benches and the stools scraped. Boots rang out on the stone floor. In the silence, as the seconds ticked away, a man still sobbed. In the cells, the prisoners were alone with their thoughts. Emboldened by the silence, a rat crept forward out of the shadows, its eyes red in the torchlight. Time was running out for what might have been the thousand-year Reich.

With the minute gone, sixty seconds of memories of the past and fears for the future, the general reached for his cap, setting the peak over one eye in the jaunty, arrogant cavalry fashion once proudly emulated by every officer and man of the Panzer Division Elbeland.

"Heil Hitler," shouted von Bluckau, his gloved right hand outflung in the last Nazi salute that he would ever give.

"Heil Hitler," responded the men of the Fehme, their voices thunderous with the echoes of the dungeons. Startled, the questing rat fled back down the grating from whence it had crawled.

The general laid the cap down on his table, pulling the chair forward as he sat.

"This court is now in session," he said briskly. "Mr. Prosecutor, bring in the prisoner Pastor Otto Schillinger for sentence."

The pastor came slowly on naked feet, towering above the booted Fehme escorts. Slowly heads turned and voices whispered as they brought him to the table to face von Bluckau across the noose and the sword.

"Pastor Otto Schillinger," said the general, "the Führer, as we now know, is dead. It is God's will. Sane or insane, there is now no longer any reason or cause for you to preach the overthrow of the Führer and of German National Socialism. Your words would fall unheard and unheeded on the empty air. There is no reason for me to detain you. There is no reason for me to punish you. You have lost your parish and your church and your cause. You may even have lost your reason. There are Russians all around us now, Pastor. The strategic and tactical situation, in a military sense, is desperate. Already our Christian Saxony is prostrate under the clumsy heel of the heathen Slav, the barbaric Bolshevik from out of the east. You wanted to preach, Pastor. Now is your chance. You are free to, with our blessings. The forces of evil are waiting out there for you. Go preach to the Russians, Pastor. Go preach to the Russians."

Heads nodded approvingly, and somewhere in the court a Fehme man guffawed.

"General," said the pastor, "in all humbleness, and before God, I accept this challenge which you make in your pride."

The guffawing man was silent then as Pastor Schillinger slowly raised both his hands and clenched them above his head.

"I will go back to Kotzdorf," he said, "and with these hands I will build my church again. Stone by stone and beam by beam. When this is done, I will preach there again. If the Russians are in sin, I will preach against them."

Smiling, haggard-eyed, he looked about him at the silent, watching faces.

"If you are truly concerned with German honor," he said, "if you do have hearts of courage and a will to fight for a Germany in which God and all His works are not to be denied, then you will come to Kotzdorf and hear me. It is not far across the fields. I will be waiting, my brothers, I will be waiting. And so will God."

Strangely, there were at first a few men of the Fehme, then

many, who rose to their feet and stood in quietness as Pastor Schillinger was escorted from the court, a thin old man in rags with bare, blackened feet.

The Fehme guard, a railwayman from Kranszchau village, who took him up the winding iron steps of the Schraubetreppe and led him out into the fire-blackened great hall through the hinged door in the fireplace, watched him go.

Standing there alone on the top of the castle steps, the railwayman shook his head, for the sun had set and there was no moon and it seemed that the ragged pastor from Kotzdorf was walking away into a world of infinite darkness.

BOOK THREE

THE COURT RISES

I

The Briefing

WITH THE GOING of Pastor Schillinger, General the Graf von Bluckau had waited until the court was still again. Then he had taken the ceremonial sword and, holding it upright as would a cavalryman on parade, had rapped the jeweled hilt on the table before him.

"The proceedings of this session of the court of honor of the Fehme in the Freistuhle of Saxony are now completed," he said. "We now have other business before us. Following upon the death of the Führer, we have had radio instructions from Berlin that Phase Two of Operation Lilac will come into force as from midnight. Major Schrader, as the commanding officer of the Freikorps Bormann, will brief you and his commanders on the operational details of your tasks and will assume tactical command of the operation. Under these circumstances, then, it is essential that these proceedings, and all actions necessarily arising from them, should be terminated speedily. It is my ruling, therefore, that the sentences of death imposed by me as president of the court are to be carried out at midnight."

The general paused, a martial and almost knightly figure with the sword held so that the burnished steel of its blade glittered like a silver taper in the torchlight.

"With the authority vested in me as a Freigraf of the Fehme and as the president of this court of honor, I now confirm one particular ruling which I have already made."

There was no discernible expression of emotion on his thin face, proud above the high, oak-leaved collar of his rank.

"I myself," said von Bluckau, "will carry out the execution of the prisoner, Jutte von Bluckau."

Even through the blanket, the wood of the table rang as the general brought the sword hilt down upon it. No man spoke. There was nothing to say.

"This court is now risen," said the general.

For Major Schrader, it was none too soon. Already there was a quickening tempor of activity in the underground bunker which housed the command post and the communications center for the Freikorps Bormann. Even as he stood, on the rising of the court, an orderly handed him another radio message. It was from Bormann, in Berlin. Hastily he pushed his way through the crowd of Fehme men who were standing respectfully around von Bluckau.

Saluting, he handed the general the signal.

"This has just come in, sir."

"Major," said von Bluckau, "you will have to read it to me."

Flushing with embarrassment that he should have made a fool of himself by forgetting that the general was blind, Schrader read the message aloud:

"The lilacs will fall at midnight on May eight. In interests of total security of operation, the court of honor will delay all executions, hold all prisoners and cease all further proceedings pending my arrival after sunset on May eight to assume overall command of Operation Lilac. You will proceed with Phase Two effective from your acknowledgment of this order. Signed, Barbarossa."

"Barbarossa?" said von Bluckau.

"Bormann," Schrader prompted. "His operational call sign, as laid down, if you remember, sir."

"Of course," said von Bluckau, conscious of the fact that he was mentally confused by the sudden realization of the circumstance that Jutte had been reprieved, if only for less than a week.

"This is it, then," he said. "You will have to move fast, Major. It is the first of May today. When will you brief your people?"

"Tonight, sir," said Schrader. "Just as soon as my battalion commanders and their company commanders arrive. If you will excuse me, sir, I will start calling them by radio now."

Waiting for his subordinate commanders out in the woods, the farms and the barns to answer and acknowledge the radio call summoning them from their hiding places to the bunker in Schloss Galgenstein, Schrader was warmed by an inner sense of excitement and pride. His time was coming at last. In Bormann, he had chosen the right star to follow. As Bormann had predicted would happen, the Führer was dead. With him now would die German National Socialism, withering on the branch, but in its place would rise the Fehme Front Party with Bormann as the Führer of the new Fourth Reich. There would be a new SS, too; the Fehme Korps and the elite Leibstandarte Bormann, both commanded by Major Schrader. Not for long will it be in the rank of major, thought Schrader. Not after we have launched Operation Lilac and the Anglo-Americans and the Russkis are at each other's throats. If only von Bluckau knew, thought Schrader. He'll be saluting me soon, the blinded half-pay general with that gorgeous slut of a wife of his. Acknowledge, you damned fools, acknowledge. What are you doing out there in the woods?

Schrader waited by the radio, fretting and cursing, until the operator was able to confirm that all subordinate commanders had acknowledged the order to report to the command post that night in the castle bunker.

Suddenly jovial, Schrader slapped the operator on the back.

"Good work, Feldwebel," he said. "Keep those big ears open. There's going to be a lot of traffic relayed to and from Berlin through Werewolfsender. Anything signed Barbarossa is secret and urgent. See I get it—quick and first."

It was midnight again before Schrader was able to begin his briefing for Operation Lilac. Waiting at the head of the table which had served its somber judicial purpose during the proceedings of the court of honor, the major stood by the enlargement of the district map mounted on its blackboard easel and studied the seated men waiting to hear him. On his right, in U.S. Army uniform, was Hauptmann Ketteler, commanding Battalion Ost, with his five commanders of Companies A, B, C, D and E. On Schrader's left was Hauptmann Polke, commanding Battalion West, and his own five company commanders, all wearing Russian uniforms. Their heads were bent as they studied the small briefing maps prepared for each of them by Hencke, the major's adjutant. They were good men, thought Schrader. The best he knew. Hard, fit, disciplined, self-reliant and ruthless. If they couldn't carry out Operation Lilac with the thousand handpicked troops who were at their disposal, then Operation Lilac was a bad plan. Beyond them, at the far end of the table and isolated in his blindness, sat von Bluckau, the general who could no longer read a signal or study a map.

"Gentlemen," said Schrader, "our months of planning and rehearsing and our days and nights of hiding and hoping are over. You are here tonight because this day I received orders from Barbarossa that Operation Lilac is to be carried out at twenty-four hundred hours on May eighth."

The major paused, sensing and evaluating the reactions of his operational commanders. The lifted heads. The nods. The narrowed eyes. The quick sighs of relief. They were ready to go. He had chosen well, he thought. With men like this he could make history.

"We have, many times, been through the detailed planning," he continued. "For that reason, and for the sake of security in the field, no printed operational orders will be issued. You are already familiar, in detail, with your tasks. All you need to know to put them into action is Z-hour for the operation. You now have that. Z-hour, I repeat, is twenty-four hundred hours on May eighth. You will simply implement your operational duties as planned. However, with General von Bluckau's permission, I will refresh your minds, listen to any suggestions and answer any questions. This, gentlemen, will be our last opportunity to do so before you go into action. We all have much to do and we will not meet again until after Operation Lilac."

Schrader fingered the sprig of lilac in a buttonhole of his U.S. Army padre's uniform and noted with satisfaction, that, in conformity with the standing security instructions for the Freikorps Bormann, lilac also adorned the bogus Russian and American uniforms of the two battalion commanders and the ten company commanders.

"Gentlemen," said the major, "Phase One of Operation Lilac is now complete. A thousand men of the FkB have been concentrated in the Galgenstein area and successfully hidden in tactical dispositions of battalions and companies. Security has been maintained at all times and the Freikorps Bormann is now trained, equipped and briefed, ready for operations. Gentlemen, I compliment you. Before I review planning for Phase Two and Three, I want to know if we have any deficiencies or problems capable of immediate solution. Captain Ketteler, what is the operational status of Battalion Ost?"

This battalion, which would move east to storm the Russian positions near the pontoon bridge at Torgau, was battleworthy.

American uniforms, weapons and ammunition had been issued to the 500 officers and men of the battalion. All the captured American motor transport, smuggled into the district prior to the arrival of the Red Army on the line of the Elbe, was fueled and ready to go. There were ten men on the sick list, but they would be fit for combat. Two men had deserted. They had, however, been recaptured and would be shot as the battalion moved out to take up its forward positions under the planning for Phase 2.

"You have done well, Ketteler," said the major. "Captain Polke? How does Battalion West stand?"

Polke's battalion, which would attack the divisional headquarters of the U.S. 69th Division at Naunhof, west of the Mulde, was also in a state of combat readiness. Russian uniforms, weapons and ammunition had been issued to the battalion's 500 men and the captured Red Army motor transport was also fueled and ready to move. One company had three men on the sick list, but they were fit enough to fight. One man had deserted but had been shot while resisting recapture.

"You, too, Captain Polke, are to be congratulated, as are the company commanders of both battalions."

Schrader smiled, still toying with the sprig of lilac in his buttonhole.

"I think we should all be grateful to the Americans and the Russians for the prodigality with which in the past they have abandoned arms and equipment on the field of battle. Their generosity was much appreciated by our FkB quartermaster and his salvage company, whose responsibility it has for so long been to equip our forces for Operation Lilac. Now, gentlemen, the task ahead of us is our only concern. As I said earlier, I will take this last opportunity to refresh our minds on the order of battle and the sequence of operations."

He pointed to the big district map on its easel. On the Perspex overlay, red arrows for Battalion Ost, and blue arrows for Battalion West swerved and wriggled in stealthy convolutions of infiltration that converged respectively on Torgau and Naunhof.

"You will recognize this as the operational plan for Phase Two of Operation Lilac. It is effective as of twenty-four hundred hours today. At midnight, gentlemen, you will move out. Taking

Battalion West first, Phase Two calls for you to have your five companies in their assault positions by sunset on May eight, ready to reach and attack the American divisional headquarters at Naunhof at midnight on that day. Battalion West's five companies will take up assault positions in or near the following villages: Company A, Polenz; Company B, Ammelshain; Company C, Staudnitz; Company D, Gretchen; Company E. Rohrbach."

Schrader paused, but neither Hauptmann Polke nor any of his five company commanders had any questions.

The major pointed to the red arrows snaking eastward on the map from Galgenstein to Torgau.

"Similarly," he resumed, "the plan for Phase Two also calls for Battalion Ost to have its five companies in assault positions by sunset on May eighth. They, likewise, must be ready to reach and attack the Russian positions at Torgau on the west bank of the Elbe by midnight. The pontoon bridge is to be destroyed. Companies of Battalion Ost will occupy assault positions at or near the following villages: Company A, Neiden; Company B, Zinna; Company C, Süptitz; Company D, Klitzschen; Company E, Staupitz. Are there any questions or suggestions, gentlemen, as to the route of march for either battalion? Are there any reports of local dispositions of enemy forces which alter the plan?"

Conferring quickly with the officers commanding the companies, Hauptmann Ketteler and Hauptmann Polke agreed that, as they stood, the planned lines of march to the Elbe and across the Mulde were still valid.

"We are fortunate," said Schrader. "Just the same, we must be prepared to be flexible. Depending on the tactical situation, company commanders can vary their assault point locations at the discretion of their battalion commanders, without reference to me."

Turning away from the map, Schrader faced his commanders in their uniforms of the enemies of Germany.

"Gentlemen," he said, "I cannot impress upon you too strongly that the sole and ultimate objective of Operation Lilac is to create a major international incident designed to trigger off a situation which could result in the development of a state of armed conflict between the Americans and the Russians. The stage is already set for us. Already we have ample evidence that a state of considerable political tension is now already in existence along the line of the junction of the East Front and the West Front. There is tension in Washington and Moscow. The situation needs only a spark to set it aflame, to turn distrust and suspicion into fear and anger. Operation Lilac will provide that spark. The success of the operation, as you know, rests upon the Americans concluding that they have been attacked by the Russians at Naunhof and, conversely, the Russians assuming that they have been stabbed in the back by the Americans at Torgau. To ensure this, there must be evidence as well as action."

Schrader studied the lean, wind-burned faces that had so often faced death with him in the uniform of the Waffen SS.

"Let us be frank, gentlemen," he said. "There must be evidence left at the scene of both actions. Circumstantial and conclusive evidence. Some of us and many of our men may be that evidence if we die. This is why we carry the identity discs and the documentation of dead Americans and Russians. By the grace of God and the fortunes of war, it might be that no man of the Freikorps Bormann does, in fact, fall in action. For this reason, therefore, I stress the fact that, between twenty-four hundred hours tonight and sunset on May eighth, each company of Battalion Ost must capture a liberated American prisoner in this area and each company of Battalion West must similarly capture a liberated Russian prisoner."

Frowning, Schrader slapped angrily at his leg with the pointer he had used for the briefing.

"This should not be a difficult task," he said. "We all know that liberated prisoners of war of every enemy nationality are infesting Saxony like a plague of lice. During the course of the attack at Naunhof, each Battalion West company will shoot its own Russian prisoner. Likewise, at Torgau, each Battalion Ost company will leave a dead, genuine American prisoner at the scene of the assault. Thus, whatever happens, there will be five dead actual Russians left at Naunhof and five dead actual Americans at Torgau. Additionally, a percentage of Russian and American weapons are to be left behind, respectively, at Naunhof and Torgau. Are there any questions or comments at this stage?"

At the far end of the table, General von Bluckau leaned forward.

"Yes, Major. I have a comment. On the face of it, there would appear to be a remarkable and arresting coincidence in the discovery of five dead Americans at Torgau and five dead Russians at Naunhof. In the interests of complete credibility, why not have a minor variance?"

"Thank you, sir," said Schrader, mildly annoyed that he had not thought of this himself. "There are almost certain to be FkB dead, as well, to vary the totals but I agree with you. We cannot count on that. In the interests of saving time, then, we will subtract one American."

The general smiled, a thin and secret smile.

"He'll never know how lucky he was."

Returning to the briefing map again, Schrader pointed to a concentration of green-ringed names east and west of both the Elbe and the Mulde.

"These are Wehrmacht prisoner-of-war camps," he said. "They have all by now been captured, either by the Russians or the Americans. They have a tactical significance in the planning for Phase Three of Operation Lilac. As you already know, there will be no further orders issued after you leave here tonight. You will be committed to the operation. Without further instructions, you will carry out your respective assaults at twenty-four hundred hours on May eighth. The hands of your watches will issue the order to attack. By oh one hundred hours on May ninth, Battalion Ost will have withdrawn from Torgau and Battalion West will have disengaged at Naunhof. No wounded survivors of the FkB will be left behind to face interrogation. If they cannot be moved, it is their company commander's responsibility to see that they are not left there alive. This is a risk and a sacrifice to which every one of us is committed, regardless of rank."

To Schrader's satisfaction, there was no comment from his commanders, so he continued.

"Since the Freikorps Bormann is to remain a force in being for further Fehme actions, survival is the prime requirement after action has been broken off. Every company of each battalion, therefore, has been allocated a liberated Wehrmacht prisoner-of-war camp to which it can withdraw. Our friends of the Fehme assure us that conditions of chaos, confusion and lack of discipline exist in these camps. Many prisoners of various nationalities—British, American, French, Dutch, Czech, Polish, Italian and Russian—are still quartered in their camps. With the Wehrmacht administrations gone from these places, there is no organization and no system. I am assured, gentlemen, that any one of these camps is an excellent holding place for no more than a hundred apparent Russians or Americans who could pose as a group of liberated prisoners of war from some other camp."

On Schrader's left, Hauptmann Polke stirred.

"What about our weapons?"

"They should be hidden before entering the camps," said Schrader. "Guards will be left with the weapons. In the camps there will probably be minor language embarrassments, but there are enough English and Russian linguists in the FkB companies to take care of this problem. It can be overcome by a few nods, a tight mouth and some discretion and quick thinking. In any case, the liberated enemy prisoners in this district are too busy looting and pillaging and worrying about getting home to bother asking other people too many questions. Are there any further comments at this point?"

The general spoke again, the smoked glasses like black holes in his thin, white face.

"Major, will there still be an action to cover the withdrawal of the battalions from Naunhof and Torgau?"

"Yes, sir," said Schrader. Having the damned general sitting there and listening made him nervous and forgetful, he thought. "I will leave the bunker here at midnight on May eight with the FkB headquarters company and a force of Fehme men in German civilian clothes. They know the district particularly well. By oh one hundred hours on May ninth we will have taken up positions along the Torgau-Eilenburg road between the Elbe and the Mulde. We will ambush and harass any military traffic, Russian or American, trying to move between the Operation Lilac assault points on the two rivers. This should provide enough confusion and distraction to cover Captain Ketteler's withdrawal from Torgau and Captain Polke's withdrawal from Naunhof. I will be back here in the castle bunker and command post, with the headquarters company, before dawn."

"During the assault," said Polke, "I take it our function is to shoot to kill not to capture prisoners, even if I could bring back the American general, Reinhardt, and his divisional staff?"

Schrader nodded. "No prisoners," he said. "They would only be a nuisance."

"What about communications?" said Hauptmann Ketteler. "With our pack radios we will be out of range of the command post transmitter here at Schloss Galgenstein once we move into our assault positions."

"There are no problems there," said the major. "We have arranged for the Werewolf organization in Saxony to supply two runners to each company. They are all Hitler Youth boys and, as such, can move freely about the countryside without suspicion. They will be at the disposal of the company commanders until radio contact can be resumed with the command post here during the reassembly after Operation Lilac is completed."

"On the subject of communications, Major," said von Bluckau. "I take it that the radio call signs are as originally agreed?"

"They are, sir," said Schrader. "They will stand. As a final check, I repeat them: Oberstuhlherrführer Bormann, originally Rossbach, now Barbarossa; General the Graf von Bluckau, Elbeland; the FkB command post here at Schloss Galgenstein, Fehme; myself, as FkB field commander, Tannenberg; Captain Ketteler, commanding Battalion Ost, Roosevelt; Captain Polke, commanding Battalion West, Stalin. There are, of course, in case of enemy monitoring, certain obvious and advantageous implications in using Roosevelt as a call sign before the attack on the Russians at Torgau and Stalin during the assault on the American divisional headquarters at Naunhof."

One of the young company commanders raised his hand.

"What about us, Major?"

"Companies will use numerals with the battalion prefix," said Schrader. "For example, Company A of Battalion Ost will be Roosevelt One. Company D of Battalion West will be Stalin Four. The Werewolfsender radio station at the Falkewitz airfield has been notified of these call signs should there be any need for radio traffic between Werewolfsender and FkB units in the field during Operation Lilac. Incidentally, you will, of course, be unlikely to have any success in contacting Werewolfsender after dawn on May ninth. The station will be broadcasting sabotage instructions to the Werewolf organization and resistance propaganda to the people of Saxony. Appropriately, Werewolfsender's call sign is a recorded wolf howl. Whatever else you may think about it, you will certainly be unable to mistake it."

Smiling, Schrader beckoned to a Fehme orderly, who came forward with a tray of glasses and a bottle of cognac.

"If there are no more questions, gentlemen, that concludes the briefing. You are, of course, responsible for your own detailed briefings at company level. For the last time, are there any more questions or suggestions?"

The lean, attentive men who would lead Operation Lilac were silent.

"Good," said Schrader. "With the general's permission, I will propose a toast. In fine cognac, I might add, from the cellars of Schloss Galgenstein, thanks to the general. There is no need, I think, for me to make brave speeches. You would not be here tonight nor would your men be waiting out there in the woods and the barns and the farms unless you were ready and willing to fight and, if necessary, die for the greater glory of our beloved Germany. The time for brave words is past. The hour for cold steel and action is at hand. The operation in which we are taking part could set the Russians and the Americans tearing at each other's throats like wild dogs. Even in these days of victory for our enemies, a thousand patriotic Germans of the Freikorps Bormann could still change the course of history."

The glasses were filled and Schrader raised his own high in the torchlight of the dungeons.

"I give you a toast, gentlemen. To the success of our arms. To the damnation of our enemies. To the beginning, if you like, of the Third World War. To the greater glory and honor of the Germany we love. Gentlemen, in the name of the Fehme and the Freikorps Bormann, let us be upstanding like loyal German officers. I give you—Operation Lilac!"

The responding voices rang, resonant and with confidence, so that in the cells the waiting prisoners heard them and wondered uneasily at the sound.

"Operation Lilac!" said the voices. "Operation Lilac!" And the echoing walls gave back the words, distorted yet fierce with pride.

In his blindness, General the Graf von Bluckau spoke and heard the words of the toast with no pride at all, for he knew he would not be marching and fighting with these hard and desperate men of the Freikorps Bormann. His battle station, instead, would be at the command post and communications center in the bunker below Schloss Galgenstein, waiting with Bormann for news of failure or success. Mellow as its year was, the cognac was bitter in von Bluckau's mouth.

For ex-SS Sturmbannführer Schrader, it was a proud moment of destiny fulfilled. A blond and Nordic figure, he still looked like a German officer in the U.S. Army padre's uniform. The fighting, killing years with the death's-head units of the Waffen SS had left their mark on the petulantly boyish face. On this night, more than on any other which had gone before, he was conscious of the fact that as the fighting leader of a clandestine German nationalist party, he was standing at the very threshold of a new life. He had no doubts and no fears. Had not the great Nazi leaders of the Third Reich begun this way? Even the greatest of them all, the Führer himself, had known the furtive underground times, hiding and planning and waiting for the time of ultimate triumph. Even as a prisoner in Landsberg jail, the Führer had not lost heart. It had happened before and it could happen again, thought Schrader. He was ready for it.

Standing alone in the moonlight at the top of the stone steps below the great doors of the silent, deserted Mittelschloss of the castle, the major watched his two battalion commanders and their company commanders slipping away into the dark, secret shadows of the Jägerswald beyond the bridge over the moat of the Schwarzesee.

Except for the distant rumble of massed Russian artillery still thunderously closing the ring of death and destruction around Berlin, sixty miles northward, and the thin, lonely rattle of a solitary machine gun amid the trees of the Jägerswald between the castle and the Elbe, the night was silent and foreboding.

"The lilacs will fall," Schrader whispered to himself. "The lilacs will fall."

Shivering suddenly in the night air, the major turned and walked quickly back up the moonlit steps.

There was still much to be done before midnight on May 8.

II
The Waiting

THE WAITING THAT WEEK was worst for the prisoners. They knew little but they surmised much. Even in the dark loneliness of their medieval cells below Schloss Galgenstein, they sensed the militant urgency of the preparations for the final phase of Operation Lilac, the onset of tension which was beginning to claw at nerves already raw with too long a captive exposure to the perpetual half-light of the torches on the dungeon walls. As the days and nights ticked by, undefined by any sunrise or sunset, the prisoners came to know the voices if not the faces of Operation Lilac; the squealing and muttering of the command post radio when the volume was high, the metallic clink of weapons slung over the shoulders of waiting men, the comings and goings of men who walked quickly but quietly, the rattle and tinkle of plates and knives and forks as men conferred over meals or interrogated other men who brought them news of a Saxony staggering toward anarchy. To most of the prisoners, alone with their thoughts behind the rusted iron bars of their cell doors, it seemed incredible that the Fehme men whom they could hear, and sometimes see, should be quietly and methodically getting ready to light the fuse of an explosive situation designed to bring about a collision of arms between the Russians and the Americans and the plunging of Europe into yet another state of war.

For Major Bruno von Kleist-Schulenhorst, waiting to die at the hands of an executioner carrying out the sentence of a court with no jurisdiction other than that of terror, the waiting was a time of great sadness rather than fear. Death was no stranger to Bruno. In the Luftwaffe, he had learned to live with the presence of it. Then, though, it had been different. Death had been the thump of a close flak-burst, spent fragments of enemy steel rattling like hail on the metal skin of the wings of his Me.109. Death had been many things and it had many faces. The shock of seeing a Spitfire or a Mustang suddenly large and intimate in detail in the unexpected sun. The whining, puzzled dog that suddenly began to get on the other pilots' nerves as it waited for a master who would never come back. An empty bottle, a hang-over and the fast-blurring memories of a squadron comrade last seen as a pool of burning gasoline in the Thames Estuary. A chalked name rubbed off the battle-order blackboard and a statistic in the intelligence summaries. Even the smiling, eager, stupid face of a young replacement pilot was the face of death if you had known and flown with the man who had gone before him. Always, though, death in the air had only ever been an adversary, an enemy to be outwitted and outfought. There was always something you could do about it. You could turn tighter, fly better, shoot straighter, dive faster, climb quicker or, as a final resort, drink harder. Death in those innocent days had never been like this: just an executioner patiently waiting for you to walk out of your cell for the last time. In the Luftwaffe days, too, there had always been a reason for death. Never a reason any more logical than the stupid waste of war itself, but at least it was a reason with some elemental kind of logic to it.

To die like this, thought Bruno, at the hands of such deranged and misguided fanatics as the men of the Fehme, was a bitter prospect to contemplate. If his executioner were to have been a Russian or an Englishman or an American, it would have been different, for they were the enemy, but to die, as a German, at the hands of other Germans was a tragic and a foolish thing.

If he had loved Germany less, Bruno reflected, he would not now be waiting to die. Because he had cherished Germany more, he had been adjudged a traitor by other Germans capable of destroying the very nation for which they were so ready to kill and be killed. What great dishonors are done in the name of honor, he thought. Always in Germany there is somebody who will come riding out of the dark woods of these Teutonic lands on a white horse with a raised sword and a banner bearing a strange device. Not for long, though, does he ride alone. Always, too, there are Germans who will march with him, eager for a cause which they can enshrine and worship. After Hitler, was there now to be yet another Pied Piper of Hameln to rid Germany of the rats infesting its hours of defeat and then, in return, claim the nation's soul?

Major Bruno von Kleist-Schulenhorst turned on his side on the rustling straw of the crude paillasse beneath him and once more sought the brief oblivion of a troubled sleep.

He was very tired.

It was the evening of May 7, 1945.

In a little more than twenty-four hours, the Fehme would have carried out the executions and the Freikorps Bormann would be crouched in its assault positions around Torgau and Naunhof, waiting for midnight and the launching of Operation Lilac.

Like Bruno von Kleist-Schulenhorst, the other prisoners in the dungeon cells of Schloss Galgenstein were also waiting, each in his own way.

"Rita!" said Technical Sergeant George Abraham Kowalski, standing by the door of his cell.

"Hayworth!" responded Dermott Duncan's voice from the door of the next cell. "But we've had her before."

"I guess I'm running out of names," said Kowalski.

They had been playing this game for days, the American soldier and the expatriate American writer, ever since they had discovered that it was possible to talk at their cell doors without any objections except from the more officious of the Fehme guards. Dermott would have been just as happy to lie on his back on the miserable straw paillasse they had given him. Already, during the past few months in Germany, he had walked much farther than the total distance he would ever have covered on foot as a journalist and author during the last five years before the war. Walking, then, had been no way to meet a Fleet Street deadline or the demands of a publisher's list. Brooding in his cell, Dermott had suspected that in the immediate future, if he ever got away from the Fehme, he would still have a lot more walking to do. He was going to need all the rest he could get. Apart from that, there was "The Well of Death." Now that he had had time to think about it in depth, waiting for sleep to come grudgingly to him in his cell, he knew that "The Well of Death" was more than a chapter in *Kreuzenberg*, more than just a coded testimony to the sordid guilt of some shabby provincial Nazi war criminals. Done properly, it was a book in itself, a book which he was already writing feverishly in his mind without recourse to a typewriter.

He had not talked to Kowalski long, though, both standing at the grilles of their cell doors, before he realized that the young American was concerned only with the fact of his having been sentenced to death by that cold fish of a German general who had presided over the medieval rituals of the court of honor. Nor could Dermott blame Kowalski for worrying. Although he still could not himself believe that the Fehme was really going to carry out the sentence of death on Kowalski, Dermott realized that this was only because he did not want to believe it. There was also the fact that it was Kowalski who had been sentenced to death and not Dermott Duncan. It made a difference, even if the Fehme were only bluffing or even if they were going to kill everybody. With people like this, thought Dermott, how would you know?

In any case, as a war correspondent, Dermott had seen enough of men under the strain of threat of death to recognize the sound of it again in Kowalski's voice. The least he could do would be to try and help keep him sane. So long as the young American soldier stayed alive and did not try anything silly, there was always the chance of a lucky break, a twist in the fortunes of war. So Dermott had begun to talk with him, interminably, about anything and everything. That was when they had begun to play the movie game. Kowalski was no Harvard graduate, but there was one subject he knew backwards, frontwards and sideways: the movies. They took it in turn to call the Christian names of the stars, and most of the time Kowalski was ahead on the game. It was a major tragedy now that they had run out of names. It could be Kowalski's last night to live to see a new day and he knew he would not sleep. With the long and desolate hours still to be passed, Dermott suddenly realized that they had only played the game with the names of women movie star. They had forgotten about the men.

"What about the men?" he said. "We forgot about them."

"You're damned right," said Kowalski gratefully. "I'll start. Let's see now. Here's an easy one. Clark!"

"Gable," said Dermott.

"That's it," said Kowalski. "Your turn."

Dermott thought for a moment.

"Noel," he said.

For some minutes there was silence in the cell next door and hopefully Dermott wondered if the American had at last dozed off to sleep.

"You got me there, old buddy," said Kowalski.

"Coward," said Dermott. "Noel Coward. A British actor and playwright."

"Never heard of the guy," said Kowalski. "You sure you're not kidding?"

To himself, Dermott groaned. Already he was tired and it was obviously going to be another long night, if the last.

Ulrike Engelhöffer and Johann Schwemma occupied adjoining cells and they, too, talked to each other at the iron-barred doors but not casually and openly like Dermott and the GI. Ulrike and Big Johann on this night were talking softly of escape. It had begun when Schwemma heard her weeping during their first night in the cells after the rising of the court of honor. Although with his bare hands Big Johann could break a man's arm like a stick of rhubarb, he was by nature gently inclined and the sound of a woman crying always made him feel angry. Although there had never been any luxurious living to be enjoyed on his farm near Löbau, the giant Wendish soldier had never heard his own wife weep. With their children and the crops of their land they had always lived in happiness if not in wealth. There had been the bad times as well as the good times, but the land had always relented and Frau Schwemma prayed regularly to her God, thanking Him for the goodness of life with her husband.

When Big Johann called to Ulrike from his cell door, and spoke to her and learned that her two children, if they were lucky, were still being cared for by friends in a strange and largely deserted village, he knew why she wept. He could not bear the thought that his own children might also be so placed. It was bad enough that only his wife stood between his own children and the Russians or any other intruders who might visit his farm to rape and loot and pillage. The thought of this had haunted him less since, after long deliberation, he had decided that he would break out of the dungeons of Schloss Galgenstein and make his way home to the farm near Löbau.

As for him submitting to execution at the hands of the Fehme, the idea was outlandish. If the Russians had already tried without success to kill him on the East Front, then no fellow German was going to succeed where the Ivans had failed. Nobody, not even General von Bluckau, was going to stop him going home. The general had been a good man once, an officer to respect. That was long ago. Big Johann now knew that if it became necessary in the interests of saving his life and regaining the freedom of the open fields, he would kill von Bluckau as swiftly and easily as he would a fox in the woods of Löbau. There was no doubt in his mind that he would escape. Having come to this decision and chosen his time, Big Johann had slept soundly, night after night, as if he had been plowing all day on his own land. Yet Ulrike's plight, and the implications of what might be in store for her two children without her, had worried him. Like most men who earn their bread by pitting themselves against the elemental forces and cycles of nature, Big Johann was an intensely religious man. Not in any formal sense. Churches stifled him and their dogma and ritual he found meaningless and sterile, even though he saw to it that his children were taught the meaning of the word of God. Over the years he had formulated his own interpretation of the Ten Commandments, like the farmer who plants the right seed in his own fashion but in the way that he alone knows is best for his own land.

Having comforted Ulrike as best he could during their talks through the barrier of the cold iron bars of their cell doors, Big Johann realized that he would be unable to live with his conscience if he escaped and left the woman behind at Schloss Galgenstein. True, she had not been sentenced to death as had he. The general had sentenced her and her children to banishment as exiles from Saxony on release from the jurisdiction of the court. Big Johann, though, had seen enough of how the SS, and even the regular German army, had handled trapped Russian partisans on the East Front to have any illusions about what the Russians in Saxony would do to the Fehme if they found the bunker headquarters below Schloss Galgenstein. There would be no time or opportunity to explain to a patrol of drunken front-line Russian infantrymen that you were a German but a prisoner, not a blood brother, of the Fehme men. Then again, there were the ex-SS troops of the Freikorps Bormann. Big Johann also had seen what the SS were capable of doing to their fellow Germans in the name of the greater glory of the Third Reich. You could not reason with mad dogs. There could be no question of leaving Ulrike Engelhöffer behind when he escaped.

"You will come to Löbau with me," he told her. "My wife would be happy to have you. You could help us on the farm. Our children would be happy, too, having your Günther and Gerda staying with them."

Unexpectedly, Ulrike had wept a little then, marveling that there should be so much goodness and gentleness in the heart of the big, shambling Wendish farmer turned soldier of the Reich. There had been no thought of refusing his offer. Where Günther and Gerda were concerned, she was, in her own fashion, prepared to stop at nothing so that she might return to them and never let them go again. God only knew what things might be like for them in Kotzdorf. What if anything had happened to her friends there? The thought of her children left alone in the ransacked village was insupportable. Only the prospect of escaping with the Wendish soldier had kept her from the brink of hysteria. The prospect, also, of finding a measure of security, however rough, with the household at the Schwemma farm gave her a promise of such joy as she had never had before in her days of bourgeois peace and prosperity in Elsterwalde. Willi would do what I am doing, she thought. Prayers and tears and ideals are no longer enough. I can still hear Willi saying it the day before the Fehme killed him in the barn at Kotzdorf:

"They have burned our books. Soon they will burn us. In the name of God, we must fight fire with fire. First, though, we must stay alive and with our children, for the children of Germany are Germany's only hope for the future."

So Ulrike had whispered her thanks to Big Johann, her face pressed against the cold bars of the cell door, and he had told her not to worry. There would be a way, he said. Always there was a way, but he would have to think about it first, because he was a soldier of the line, not a general; a farmer, not a genius.

Big Johann had thought long and he had thought well, quietly observing the routine of the guards while he stood there at the bars of his door watching the Fehme men as if they were foxes skulking in the woods beyond his mustard field. Sometimes he even joked with them and yarned amiably when they brought his rations for the day.

On this, the last night before Operation Lilac, Schwemma had rattled his spoon lightly on the bars, signaling Ulrike, and she had come forward to her own door.

"You will stay awake now," Big Johann said softly. "When you hear my spoon rattling on the bars again, call for the guard. He is a little drunk and he will be alone. They are having a party in the command post in the bunker. Soon there will be noise. Not too much, but enough. Some laughing and talking and a little singing. When you call the guard tell him that you think I have hanged myself. He will open my door and come into my cell to make sure before he dares report it to Sturmbannführer Schrader. Or to the general. Schrader would be very annoyed if I hanged myself, for it would be against the orders of the court. When the guard comes into my cell, I will look as if I am hanging by my neck from my belt. Once he is close enough I will break his neck and take his keys. I will let you out of your cell then, and we will go quietly up the iron stairs. There are no FkB men on patrol outside the castle. Only the civilians of the Fehme. If they keep out of our way, they will live. There is an old battle-axe on the wall out there. It is rusty but it is still heavy and sharp. I will take it with me. Do you still want to come, Frau Engelhöffer?"

Trembling, not with fear but an intense excitement, and seeing only the sad, heroic faces of little Günther and Gerda, Ulrike had wanted only to kiss the rough hands of the big Wendish soldier, for her eyes were burning with tears of gratitude.

"Of course," she said. "I'll be waiting, Johann."

How strange, she thought. Ulrike Engelhöffer, mother of Günther and Gerda and widow of Willi Engelhöffer, respected proprietor and editor of the *Elsterwalder Kreisblatt,* waiting for the sound of a spoon tapping on prison bars and then the surprised grunt of a guard having his neck broken by a prisoner supposed to have hanged himself.

"O God," she said quietly in the darkness, "it is only for the children that I condone this."

For Tommy Dart, the most curious discovery which he had made during the long days and nights of intermittent talking with

Horst Graber at the doors of their adjoining cells was that, as the British man-of-confidence of Stalag IV J, Hohenleipisch, he had virtually been the mayor of a far larger population than had Graber as the Burgermeister of Lutzin. Certainly, the population for which Warrant Officer Dart, RAF, had been responsible at Hohenleipsich was all male and entirely captive, but the two men, the Englishman and the German, still had had much in common. Not that this was immediately apparent. At first, because of his wife's death during the American machine-gunning of the refugee train on its way back to Torgau, Graber had refused to talk to Tommy, whom, as a British airman, he assumed to have been a Terrorflieger and a Luftgangster like the train-strafing Americans. Not until Tommy, during an acrimonious exchange of words, pointed out that as an air gunner in the rear turret of a British bomber, he himself had been entirely liable to machine-gunning by German night-fighters—which was how he came to be in Germany—did Graber calm down long enough to listen to Tommy's reasoning.

"Look at it this way," Tommy said. "You've been in action. You've lost an arm. You know what it's like when complete strangers are likely to start firing real bullets right at you. Take the pilot of one of those American fighter-bombers. He's over enemy territory in the middle of Germany. He sees a train. It could be full of troops for all he knows. It's probably carrying flak guns. There may be German fighter planes in the area. There may be German flak in the woods along the railway line. His formation leader says they'll take the train. So over and down he goes. He makes a pass and his guns are firing. He's doing maybe three hundred miles an hour on the way down. He's moving at five hundred feet a second, at least. How the hell can he find out whether the passengers are soldiers or civilians?"

Surprisingly, Graber had conceded the point and then, when Tommy mentioned that the prisoners of Stalag IV J had themselves been strafed by random pairs of P-51 Mustangs and had accepted it as an unpleasant but inevitable risk of involvement in total war, the German had begun to ask Tommy about conditions which had existed in the camp. As a Burgermeister, Graber had had to familiarize himself with the problems of local government in wartime Germany and he was intrigued by Tommy's function as Vertrauensmann, or man-of-confidence, at Stalag IV J.

"Did it work?" Graber asked.

"In some ways," said Tommy. "I was responsible, as man-of-confidence, to the German commandant. The British camp leader was responsible to me. The compound leaders were responsible to him. The barracks commanders were responsible to the compound leaders. In every barracks there were section leaders responsible to the barracks commander. Within the sections in each barracks, a man could remain an individual or team up with friends in a combine for drawing and sharing rations and rotating fatigues."

"It was very thorough," said Graber grudgingly. He was a thorough man himself, with an ingrained respect for law and order. He had never thought of the British as being particularly thorough or orderly.

"It had to be," said Tommy. "Right down to the rationing of the last potato and the last slice of black bread to every single man."

"You had your Red Cross parcels," said Graber.

"Not all the time," said Tommy. "Not in the early days. Not for very long after D-Day. We wouldn't have survived another winter like the last one on Wehrmacht rations. We were getting like the poor bloody Russians. They'd been dying like flies for years. That's why I was heading for Torgau. There are still a lot of sick men in the camp at Hohenleipisch. I've got to get them across the Elbe somehow and the Russians haven't been any help so far. Damn their orders to stay where we were."

"I know," said Graber. "There comes a time when orders are not enough. They cease to mean anything. That was how it was at Lutzin when I wanted to save the bridge and surrender the town. I didn't like doing it. I'd been a soldier myself. But sometimes the man on the spot just has to make his own decisions."

Even now, waiting out his last night of life before execution by the Fehme, Graber did not regret having tried to save Lutzin, the town he loved, from useless destruction.

"I'd do it again," he told Tommy. "So help me God, I would."

"I know what you mean," said the Englishman. "I'd like to think that if I had been in your shoes I would have done the same as you did. Don't worry about tomorrow night, though. Something could happen before then."

Horst Graber bit gently on the false tooth in his lower jaw. Not even his wife had known about it. The metallic taste gave him a feeling of security. "I'm not worried," he said. "I can sleep forever if I have to."

Few others of the prisoners of Schloss Galgenstein could look forward to such a blessing that night as the solace of untroubled sleep.

Since his conviction before the court of honor and his return to the tomblike silence of the darkened cell, Roland Stolzer had slept for no longer than an hour at any time and every such hour had been peopled with nightmarish images that always woke him, sweating and trembling with fear. The nightmares were not so much concerned with his impending execution as with lamp shades that danced and writhed and shrieked and burned in strange and obscene fantasies of horror. Sometimes when he reached out to touch the shade of such a lamp while it was still beautiful, he would find that it was Trudi's skin, or his mother's, stitched or stretched so that it was as tight as a drum's and translucently pale as medieval parchment; sometimes he would be back with Trudi again, kissing and caressing her and then, without warning, her head would shrink to the size of a wrinkled apple, grotesque and hideous on her beautiful body, and he would wake up shouting but making no sound in the silent cell. Once he dreamed that he had been sewing the skin of Solomon, the Jew from Auschwitz, to make a lamp shade for the Graf von Bluckau, when suddenly the dream changed and he found that with needle and thread he was instead stitching the living skin of Trudi and she was struggling and screaming to him to stop. When he awoke, himself screaming aloud, he realized that it had not been Trudi screaming but one of the women in the cells near him.

The recurring nightmare, though, was the worst; the one in which he was always trying to put out the fire that was consuming the naked bodies of Trudi and Sturmbannführer Fischer in his old married officers' villa at Auschwitz. Every time he threw a bucket of water onto the flames, he realized, too late, that it was not water but gasoline. More and more, as his day of execution drew closer, this one nightmare had returned to haunt and horrify him and it was for this reason that SS Haupsturmführer Roland Stolzer, half-crazed by the exhaustion of insomnia, now sat staring into the darkness of his cell and talking incoherently to himself so that he might not fall asleep on this last night before the dawn of the day that would end in his death and the launching of Operation Lilac.

Strangely, it was Roland's frenzied shouting, as he struggled back to consciousness after the nightmare in which he kept trying to douse the fire with buckets of gasoline, that had brought Caroline Brookwood together with the Gräfin Jutte von Bluckau at the doors of their adjacent cells. For days there had been no communication between the two women until Caroline, unable to bear the sound of Roland Stolzer's ravings any longer, had screamed to him to stop. It was then that Jutte spoke to her as they both stood at the iron bars of their cell doors.

"A remarkable sound, that," said Jutte. "I never thought I would live to hear it. An SS officer screaming. They can bleed, too, it seems."

"Wasn't he a doctor of some kind?" said Caroline.

Jutte laughed, without joy and without pity.

"A doctor of death, perhaps. He was from the camp at Auschwitz, in Poland. You have not heard of Auschwitz yet. If you survive at the hands of these fools of the Fehme, you will hear about it one day. You and all the world. They had many kinds of doctors at Auschwitz, but they all had one thing in common. The Hippocratic oath was all Greek to them."

Caroline was silent.

"That's not very funny, is it?" Jutte apologized. "A clumsy German pun, but then what would you expect from me?"

"You speak English well," said Caroline.

"I should," said Jutte. "I was not always the mistress of Schloss Galgenstein. Or of any man I could lay my pretty little hands on. My father was a publisher in Leipzig. Until he committed suicide. Even before I went to university, I spoke fluent French, English and Italian. I traveled a lot with my father and we had friends in many countries. They would often visit us in Leipzig. They were good days. You might have known my father's firm. The Wittenberg Press. He had a great respect for old Luther. As an individualist, more than anything else. We published in Leipzig, of course. Wittenberg was just the name of the publishing house."

As it happened, both as a newspaper proprietor's daughter and a university graduate, Caroline did know the Wittenberg Press and its books. She could remember many Wittenberg titles that had stood on the shelves in the study of her father's home in the Cotswolds.

"There were different series of English-language pocket books," she recalled. "Elbe Books and Mulde Books and Elster Books. We had a lot of them at home."

"They were named after rivers in Saxony," said Jutte. "My father loved rivers. He used to say that a river was like the life of man, only far more logical."

"He must have been a good man," said Caroline. "I remember my father talking about him when he died. Father said that there was not much future for a country that drove men like your father to their deaths."

"He was perfectly correct, of course," said Jutte. "Take a look around you now. We are living in the dark ages again. My father was a good man, as you say. I'm glad he's not here with me now, though, to see how his little Jutte turned out. Like a lot of intellectuals and humanists, he was a nonconformist and a rebel and the status quo never impressed him. Yet he was delighted when I married Dietrich and became the Gräfin von Bluckau. He said that if he had to have a noblewoman in the family, he was glad that it was his favorite daughter. Actually, he loved it. He had never had the time to become a snob before that and he used to love coming out here to the castle. The poor dear wouldn't have liked what he would have seen and heard if he had visited us during the past few years. Evidently I had quite a reputation. You must have heard Herr Krausnick summing me up for the benefit of his precious court of honor. Even from here. Alcoholic! Adulteress! Nymphomaniac! Traitoress!"

Jutte sighed and rested her forehead against the cold bars.

"I hate to have to admit it, but they were right. Sooner or later it had to come down to something like this. You must be shocked, Caroline."

"Not shocked," said Caroline. "Saddened, perhaps, but not shocked. When I think about it, I no longer feel so sorry for myself."

Jutte had sounded surprised.

"You? Sorry for yourself? The cool, elegant English girl. The home in the Cotswolds. I remember them well. Your life, I would have thought, must have been like one of my father's rivers. Smooth and flowing and untroubled."

"It was," conceded Caroline, "until I met an American pilot. His name was Mike. I could have been happy for the rest of my life with Mike. I know it."

"What happened to Mike?" said Jutte.

Caroline told her then. Missing in action, presumed. The opened parachutes swaying down after the B-17 had spun and burned. The bland, smiling countryside of Saxony drifting behind, far below, as the rest of the formation roared on to fight its way back to Cambridgeshire with the report that Mike and his crew had bailed out. After that, nothing. Only an official presumption of death. Then Caroline's chance to come to Germany as an accredited war correspondent and the compulsive preoccupation with the circumstances of Mike's disappearance after bailing out. Finally, the meeting at Torgau, as the generals shook hands, and the lonely walk to the village by the woods where the postmaster's widow wept alone in the graveyard.

"I've tried to forget what she told me," Caroline said, "but I can't. Yet, at the same time, I can't believe that that was how it all ended up for Mike and his crew. Just lynched in the woods like that. By ordinary Germans. Townspeople and villagers. It's incredible."

Jutte did not find it so incredible.

"There are no longer any ordinary Germans left," she said. "Not after twelve years of Nazi government. Not after five years of a war that started in triumph and is ending in disaster. So far as the lynching was concerned, there were also the Fehme men, remember. They were there in the woods urging the townspeople on to hunt for the Americans. Even here at Galgenstein, we heard about what happened to the American airmen in the woods, that day. The whole district knew. I could have told you myself. Tomorrow night the Fehme will do the same thing to me and a few other unfortunates who will die for the sake of German honor. I hate to have to tell you, Caroline, that you came to Germany for the truth and in Germany you found the truth. You don't like the truth you have found and I don't like the truth I have found. We both have one great consolation, though. After the truth, there is nothing more. No more lies. No more cheating. No more self-deception.

Nothing except, perhaps, death. That is the final truth we must all face sooner or later."

Beyond their cells, the Fehme guard for the night was tipsily lighting a cigar.

"My time has come earlier than I had expected," said Jutte. "That is all. I suppose it is always a shock. You know something, Caroline? I think I will even shock the Lord Himself tonight. I have almost forgotten how to pray, but I think I will pray to Him tonight."

The cell block was silent. On his stool, the Fehme guard was dozing, forgetful of his cigar. For once, even Roland Stolzer was quiet, merely muttering to himself.

"I will pray, too," said Caroline.

"Thank you," said Jutte. "I will not feel so alone then. I am not a brave woman. Good night, fräulein. I think I will pray now."

While the untidy straw of the paillasses rustled beneath the restless prisoners and the Freikorps Bormann men began to toast the success of Operation Lilac and the cell guard began to snore drunkenly at his post, the two women began their prayers; the one in English and the other in German.

Alone in her cell, the Gräfin Jutte von Bluckau found that she had not, after all, forgotten how to pray.

III
The Shooting

FOR ALL THE DEW SPARKLING on the night's spider webs, bees were already busy amid the fragrant lilac on the terraces of Schloss Galgenstein as dawn broke over Saxony on May 8, 1945, and Sturmbannführer Schrader yawned contentedly in the bright benevolence of the early sunshine as he reached for his binoculars and checked the safety catch on his U.S. Army carbine.

The view from the Sprengertor, high above the battlements and towers and chimneys of the castle, was remarkable not so much for the sweep of Saxony countryside which it embraced, from the Elbe to the Mulde, as for the fact that it was seemingly innocent of the traffic of war. Southward, along the line of the Elbe, toward Belgern, Mühlberg, Strehla, Riesa, Meissen and Dresden, nothing seemed to be moving at any greater pace than the waters of the great river itself, swollen with the spring thaws of the high snows of the Erz Gebirge. To the east, the drab pines of the dark forest beyond the Elbe, at Torgau, still stood somberly on guard over the crude, shallow graves of the American airmen who had parachuted not to safety but the encircling approach of angry strangers with noosed ropes swinging in their hands. In the west, where Leipzig had so often endured its fire storms of Anglo-American bombing and, finally, the drum roll of American shelling, a shimmer of smoke still rose skyward above the city from the last of the smoldering fires of battle. To the north, where the Russians were tightening their iron-fisted grip on the very guts of Berlin itself, the distant, pulsating rumble of massed artillery beat gently at Schrader's ears as he listened, head cocked and with the rising sun warm on his unshaven face. He had taken the last watch on the final night before Operation Lilac not because he could not trust the men of the Freikorps Bormann, nor the Fehme, but because he knew he could have neither slept nor rested in the climate of tension which had begun to invest the claustrophobic silence of the bunker down in the dungeons below Schloss Galgenstein. As the field commander for Operation Lilac, too, he had to be sure personally that there was no breach in security and that no enemy troops, Russian or American, were moving in to surround and storm the FkB headquarters below the castle.

Daylight, though, when it had come on that morning of May 8, brought no sudden perils, no massive Russian or American troop movements to upset the planned pattern for Phase 3 of Operation Lilac.

For two tranquil hours after dawn, Schrader had remained engrossed in a giddying, high-amplification, binocular study of every field, every road, every hedge, every farm and every stretch of woods which he could observe from his post on the watchtower of the Sprengertor.

As the sun rose higher, the countryside around Galgenstein had begun to stir with life, but there was no menace in it, no threat to the success of Operation Lilac. A curiously intimate and revealing world with the binoculars, a pastoral and timeless landscape without peril. A group of liberated British prisoners of war trudged wearily along the road from Dommitzsch. A Russian supply truck loaded with trimmed pine logs raised an early morning cloud of dust as it headed for Torgau and, presumably, the pontoon bridge which the Red Army engineers had completed there. Two German children were leading a limping cow toward the barn on their farm. An old lady was breaking twigs from a hedge for a brief fire to warm her morning pot of ersatz coffee. A lone Russian soldier was riding a bicycle without tires toward Galgenstein village. Even from high up on the Sprengertor, Schrader could hear the metal rims of the bicycle's wheels grinding on the stones of the country road. In some of the furrowed von Bluckau fields, Schrader could just distinguish the shy, green blades of spring crops reaching timidly toward the sun. They, at least, would survive whatever destiny was in store for Germany, he thought.

Satisfied by his careful surveillance of the countryside, Schrader reflected that it might well have been a day for a picnic or some hunting with a shotgun hooked over your arm or perhaps a parade with buttons glinting and regimental banners all bright against the proud, blue sky. Regretfully, he decided it was time to go back down to the command post in the dungeons. He would send a good man up to the Sprengertor and then spend the morning going over the disposition of his FkB forces, trying to anticipate the tactical problems and emergencies which might arise with the launching of Operation Lilac at midnight.

General von Bluckau was waiting as he returned to the bunker, shivering a little in the underground chill and grateful for the hot ersatz coffee which a Fehme orderly brought him.

"All quiet up there?" said von Bluckau.

Schrader sipped at the bitter, black brew, regretting that they had drunk the last of the Graf's cognac the night before.

"You can almost hear the mice in the haystacks," he said.

"It's a pity we can't say the same down here," said the general.

Momentarily Schrader was more puzzled than alarmed. Although Battalion West had moved into its assault positions near Naunhof and Battalion Ost had reported that all companies were successfully deployed and hidden in their positions near Torgau, Schrader had steeled himself to be ready for interceptions of the two FkB forces by American or Russian patrols. The last place he had anticipated encountering trouble was in the brooding quiet of the FkB headquarters deep below the ancient foundations of Schloss Galgenstein.

Still mindful of von Bluckau's rank as a general of the Wehrmacht, he had restrained his impatience and annoyance.

"What's happened, sir?"

The general told him. Gefreiter Schwemma, the big Wendish soldier, had escaped during the night. He had taken with him the woman, Ulrike Engelhöffer, the editor's widow from Elsterwalde.

Frowning, Schrader considered the implications of the escape. The obvious risk was that the security of the FkB and the Fehme, even of Operation Lilac, had been compromised and was now in hazard. The general, though, did not agree.

"I know Big Johann," he said. "We marched a lot of miles together at the front, Big Johann and I. It's spring, you see. He just wanted to go home to his farm. In the spring, he always did. He was a Wend, remember. The woman Engelhöffer would only have wanted to get back to her children in Kotzdorf. You have no worries there. Anyway, by the time your men picked Big Johann up again, we'd have launched Operation Lilac. And God only knows what kind of a situation we may be in by then. And, if I know Big Johann, your men would never find him now if he had decided to go to earth."

"I'll still want to see the cell guard," said Schrader. The fair, boyish face was flushed red and swollen with anger. "He must answer for this."

"You'll get no answers from him," said von Bluckau. "He's dead. Big Johann broke his neck."

"There was a Fehme guard on patrol, in civilian clothes, outside the castle," said Schrader. "What happened to him?"

"Ah," said von Bluckau, "he was more alert. Too alert for his own good. He challenged Big Johann. The big Wend nearly took his scalp off with a clout from an old battle-axe from the wall outside his cell. In fact, the axe belonged to my great-great-great-grandfather. Anyway, Big Johann then pitched the Fehme man into the Schwarzesee moat. He's lucky just to be alive. There is also one other corpse, though. Horst Graber. The Burgermeister from Lutzin, on the Neisse. Apparently he had a false tooth with a poison capsule in it. After we found the dead Fehme guard in Schwemma's cell and discovered that Big Johann and Frau Engelhöffer had escaped, we immediately checked the other prisoners. We thought that Graber was asleep. Instead, he was dead. A very effective poison, apparently. Both men were already buried before you came down off watch from the Sprengertor."

"That's something anyway," said Schrader, "but it's not a very good start to Operation Lilac, sir, is it?"

"I've seen better starts to operations," conceded von Bluckau, "and I've seen worse. In battle, it's the end result that counts, Major. You must have seen this at the front. Even in the Waffen SS. As an old campaigner, Schrader, I suggest you make the regular noon radio check with the battalions, confirm their companies' tactical dispositions and then crawl into a bunk and try and get some sleep for the rest of this afternoon. You're not going to get much after midnight tonight."

On this day, which was to culminate in the blood and fury of Operation Lilac, the noon radio reports from the battalions were reassuring enough, apart from some minor redispositions at company level. Battalion West, using the code name Stalin, reported that Company C, Stalin 3, had had to move out of Staudnitz because the American forces in the area had begun concentrating Russian slave workers in the village prior to their repatriation eastward across the Mulde and the Elbe. In their Russian uniforms, Company C's FkB men would have been risking too eager and friendly a fraternization from the scarecrow Russian workers and their American liberators. Similarly, Battalion Ost, reporting as Roosevelt, warned that Company D, Roosevelt 4, had had to vacate Klitzschen, in their U.S. Army uniforms, after a column of liberated American prisoners had staggered into the village on their way west to the Mulde.

Apart from these tactical readjustments, the FkB force which would carry out Operation Lilac was in position to make its dual attacks, east and west, at midnight.

In both Torgau and Naunhof, the young Werewolf runners reported, the new day was no different from any other that had gone before since the arrival of, respectively, the Russians and the Americans.

After a final study of the arrows and times on the big situation map in the command-post bunker, Schrader realized that he had been given good advice by General von Bluckau. He might as well get some sleep while he still had the chance.

"I'll take over responsibility for the radio watch," said von Bluckau. "I might not be able to see but at least I can still hear and think and make decisions. Your adjutant can keep an eye on the situation map for me. Unless there is a major crisis, I won't call you until just before midnight. There's nothing more you and I can do before then. It's up to the troops out there now. Just try and get some sleep. You're going to need all your wits about you tonight, Major."

When Schrader awoke, still heavy with sleep, it was half an hour to midnight by his watch and von Bluckau was shaking him. The general was holding a wireless transmission message.

Apart from the plain-language call signs, "Barbarossa to Fehme for information to Elbeland and Tannenberg," the signal was in code. Struggling back to wakefulness with the bitter, furry taste of tobacco in his mouth, Schrader remembered that Barbarossa was Bormann, Elbeland was von Bluckau and Tannenberg was himself.

"What's it all about?" he said, fumbling for a cigarette in the pocket of his U.S. Army padre's uniform. The rank smoke stung his eyes and he felt more exhausted than before he had gone to sleep.

The general repeated the decoded message spoken to him by the sergeant radio operator.

"Bormann is landing at Falkewitz at midnight," he said, "by Ju.-fifty-two."

"Good," said Schrader. "I'll have time to brief my own men before he gets here."

Calling for his adjutant to assemble the FkB headquarters company, which, with the Fehme men, would carry out the diversionary action along the Torgau-Eilenburg road under his own command, Schrader waited by the situation map. Scanning it, he thoughtfully reviewed the plans which would erupt into sudden fury at Naunhof and Torgau at midnight. Whatever happened, he thought with grim satisfaction, there would be some very surprised Ivans and Amis before the sun came up.

"There was just one more thing," said von Bluckau. "They are typing the signal for you now." Blindly but expertly, the general was checking the oiled action of the Luger which he had carried with him since 1939.

"The executions," he said. "Bormann confirmed that they were to be carried out at midnight."

Schrader studied the lean, long-nosed face. The haughty curl of the thin mouth. The scarred jaw. The decorations on the green tunic. The bright, twisted braid of rank on the epaulets. The smoked glasses, enigmatic as they were dark.

"I'm sorry, sir," said Schrader. "Do you still want to do it?"

"She is still my wife," said von Bluckau. "This much, at least, I owe her. We had our happy days. What time is it now, Major?"

Schrader checked his watch. He wondered if it had stopped, time was going so slowly now.

"Fifteen minutes to midnight, sir."

"There's not too much time left then," said the general. "I can't keep the Gräfin waiting. On such an occasion as this, to be late would be the ultimate in discourtesy."

Watching him go, tapping with a cane at the dungeon walls, Schrader recognized for the first time the extent of the pitiless, terrifying lengths to which the old-guard officers of von Bluckau's class, background and training were prepared to go in the name of

German honor. In their own way, he now knew, they were as hard and inflexible as their successors, the SS. The products of generations of Junker tradition and Prussian discipline, their paths of duty were as undeviating as those of any medieval monastic order. The sword, though, not the cross, was their emblem.

Neither the Luftwaffe major, von Kleist-Schulenhorst, nor the American soldier, Kowalski, were to be executed until after Jutte von Bluckau had died, a small concession to her husband's sensibilities and although Schrader was listening for the crack of the general's Luger, it still shocked him when it came.

Even as a battle-experienced veteran of the fighting Waffen SS, Sturmbannführer Schrader still found it incredible that he should just have heard the sound of a German aristocrat, and general of the Wehrmacht, shooting his own wife.

Reluctant to carry out his prearranged duty as witness to the executions, Schrader had still not moved when he heard the second shot and then the anguished cry of anger and pain from the cell guard.

Grabbing up his American carbine, Schrader ran through the echoing dungeons. The iron-bound door of the cell which had held Jutte von Bluckau captive was wide open. Inside, the General the Graf von Bluckau lay spread-eagled on his back on the stone floor. In the flickering light from the torches on the walls outside the cell, the yellow straw beneath the general was dark and glistening with the sheen of blood that still flooded from the back of his head. He was dead, but, without the smoked glasses he had habitually worn, the general's eyes were open and blue and staring. He looked curiously alive. The dank air of the cell was heavy with the stench of cordite.

Outside the cell, the Fehme guard was doubled up on the lower steps of the Schraubetreppe, clutching at his arm with a hand that was also wet with bright blood.

So much for the Fehme, raged Schrader. Amateurs, civilians, potato-diggers, farmers and fools.

"What happened?" he demanded.

In his pain, the Fehme man was cursing and grimacing.

"I opened the Gräfin's cell for the general," he said. "I knew it was time for the executions. He told me to come back to my post here. He said the Gräfin was going to be released. Then he went into the cell and talked for a while with her. I couldn't see properly but I could hear them talking. Then I heard the shot. The Gräfin came running out. She was crying and carrying his Luger. When I went to stop her, she said that the general had shot himself through the mouth. Then she shot me in the arm and ran up the Schraubetreppe. It all happened so fast."

Sweating with the pain of his wound, the guard was still gasping out excuses when he realized that the formidable Sturmbannführer Schrader, of the pink face and the flaxen hair, had gone, bounding up the iron steps of the Schraubetreppe so that his boots rang like hammers beating quickly on an anvil.

The bitch, Schrader was thinking. The beautiful, willful, aristocratic bitch. Far above him he could hear the iron echoes of her footfalls as she climbed the Schraubetreppe. If she gets away now, he thought, she'll compromise the entire operation tonight and put the whole Fehme organization in hazard. I should have shot her the night I took her away from the Russians in the great hall.

Pursuing her up the dark spiral of the Schraubetreppe, he was puzzled by the fact that she had not fled through the fireplace exits on any of the floors of the Mittelschloss immediately above the level of the dungeons. Yet this was what he would have expected her to do in a bid to reach the open country.

Just below the last twist of iron stairs up to the watch post on the top of the Sprengertor, Schrader realized that the total darkness about him was relieved by a narrow slit of light from the escape door in the back of the fireplace in the old trophy room, the topmost chamber of the Sprengertor. If that was where she had gone, then the chase was over.

The hinges of the heavy old door, cast in sturdy Silesian iron, squealed under the balanced weight of the metal-framed stonework as Schrader pushed it open, but Jutte von Bluckau, standing there in the light of a candle by her bed, made no attempt to pick up von Bluckau's Luger which lay on the pillow. Instead, she raised the glass of cognac which she had just poured.

She smiled ironically.

"As the Americans and the English say, Major. Just one for the road."

Schrader settled the M-1 comfortably under his arm, snicking off the safety catch as he pointed the barrel at her.

"You're not traveling any road tonight, Gräfin."

"There's no need for that, Major," said Jutte. "It doesn't go very well with your American chaplain's uniform. I can save you the trouble. I have my late husband's Luger. I know how to use it. Pour yourself a drink, Major, before you go."

A fine cognac, thought Schrader appreciatively. And a remarkable woman, even if she was a bitch. Few women he had known were capable of even picking up a gun, much less thinking about shooting themselves. Speculatively, he looked at her and realized that she must have changed into a summer frock for her execution. She would, he thought. The sheath of silk fitted tightly and the pattern of dark, purple lilacs on the cool, white material clung sleekly to the firm, swelling lines of her thighs and breasts. Flushed either by the cognac or her flight up the ringing iron steps of the Schraubetreppe, she looked red-lipped and much younger in the candlelight and in no way debauched or dissipated. Indeed, she was disturbingly beautiful, even arrogantly so, as she had been that summer day long ago when she had been out riding and had come contemptuously upon him having a harvest tumble in the warm and drowsy cornfield with poor, foolish Helga, How different the Gräfin had looked, though, when he watched her dancing naked for the Russians on the long table in the great hall of Galgenstein. She had been no haughty aristocrat then. Just a drunken, wanton, frightened woman who had gone too far and was suddenly naked to any man's touch.

Remembering how he had himself lusted for her that night, Schrader moved closer. She was fragrant with perfume and the scented warmth of her body stirred a familiar longing in him, a fever of sexual wanting and longing.

"You are very beautiful tonight, Gräfin," he said. His voice was husky with the excitement of his reawakened desire for her.

Jutte von Bluckau stared at him, swirling the cognac in its stemmed, breastlike glass. The night breeze stirred the muslin curtains at the open window of the trophy room and the Gräfin smiled, full-lipped, her face soft in the candlelight. It was a night and a place for seduction.

"You never give up do you, butcher-boy?" she said, smiling.

Then she flung the cognac in his face.

Before she could reach for the Luger on the pillow, Schrader was upon her and had thrown her to the bed. Ripping at her frock, he had stripped her naked to the slim, rounded waist and with one hand cupped brutally on her breast was forcing her thighs apart, when Jutte, whom he had thought to be lying quiescent, swung one outstretched arm back toward him. Too late, he saw the cognac bottle which she had grasped in the attitude of surrender and now swung at him like a club. Abruptly the night burst about his head in an explosion of blood, pain, cognac, shock and breaking glass and he reeled back, lurching from the bed to the floor. Still conscious, he began crawling after Jutte as she backed away from him.

"Siegfried!" she screamed suddenly. Over and over again she screamed her son's name as she moved away from Schrader, who had unsteadily regained his feet and was now staggering after her, clutching at her nakedness. Then she was standing at the window, trapped and with no further line of retreat, so that Schrader paused to wipe away the hot blood running into his eyes but exulting in his embattled yet imminent moment of mastery over the body of the Gräfin von Bluckau.

He had not, though, reckoned with her will.

Even as he put his hands out for her flesh, it was already too late. Only the muslin curtains were there, mocking him in the night wind. Jutte had jumped from the window. He was alone in the silent room.

Clutching at his cut and bleeding head and nauseated by the raw pain of his wounds, Schrader stumbled to the window. The night air was cool and somewhere in a distant barn a foolish rooster was crowing at the moon. Far below the Sprengertor, hundreds of feet down, great rings of concentric ripples were retreating across the black waters of the Schwarzesee from a point directly below the high, lonely window of the trophy room. Staring down giddily at the center of turbulence, Schrader thought he saw something splashing feebly. Then it was gone and the Schwarzesee was calm and silent again except for the uneasy croakings of wild fowl in the reeds of its marshy shores.

Only in death had Jutte, the Gräfin von Bluckau, found the solace that had for so long evaded her in life. For her, the Sprengertor had again fulfilled its legendary role as a final way of escape for a von Bluckau.

Alone in the lookout post on the very top of the Sprengertor, Siegfried von Bluckau had been keeping the midnight watch, alternating his sweep of surveillance from distant Naunhof in the west to Torgau, not so far away in the east. Soon, he knew, Operation Lilac would startle and shock the unsuspecting night and he would be his father's eyes, monitoring the distant flash and flame of action as both battalions of the Freikorps Bormann went into the attack in the uniforms of their enemies' allies.

There had been little to report so far.

Even the small column of Russian tanks which had bivouacked that morning under the pines on the other side of the wide, reedy moat of the Schwarzesee was without threat.

During the long day, the Russian crews had swum and frolicked with gusty, peasant humor in the murky waters of the Schwarzesee and then, after some maintenance on their tanks, they had slept until evening, casually unaware that they were under observation from the empty castle. Since sunset, they had stirred again, moving about between their campfires and eating and drinking and singing to the music of harmonicas and accordions. Studying the tank lager under the pines and watching the Russians at their pleasures, Siegfried had been grateful for the night's duty. He was as far away as he could be, at Schloss Galgenstein, from the dungeons and the place of his mother's imminent death at the hands of his father. Alone under the moon and the stars and the dark, drifting clouds, Siegfried had wept for he knew not what: his father who was about to kill his mother; his mother who, they said, deserved to die; himself, who had loved both his mother and his father. Siegfried had never felt more lonely and afraid than he did now, yet he could think of nothing he had done to deserve what was happening to him, to be living in a world of waking nightmares. The only reality was the cold metal of the anti-tank Panzerfaust weapon which he held propped and chocked on the parapet of the lookout. In itself, death was, at least, something certain in an uncertain world. Death was the Panzerfaust, a rocket-sped bomb screaming toward its target; a magnificent toy no longer just to be enviously admired in the *Völkischer Beobachter* newspaper photographs of heroic fighters at the front.

Wondering how it would be when he first fired the Panzerfaust and hoping that its fiery tail would not burn him, Siegfried could not believe that it was his mother's voice calling his name. Had they not already told him she would be dead by now and that his stern duty as a von Bluckau was to be a brave German and to put the thought behind him?

Yet certainly it was her voice and she was not calling to him but screaming. Just his name: "Siegfried, Siegfried, Siegfried." Over and over again, until he had to hold his hands over his ears. Fright chilled the boy then, for he had never heard terror in his mother's voice; not until now as she screamed his name, the familiar name which he had only ever heard her use in a voice that spoke of love and tenderness and security.

Trying hard not to be frightened, and finding it hard, for he himself had never known real terror before in all his childhood at Schloss Galgenstein, Siegfried ran down the stone steps of the Sprengertor to his mother's secret place, the trophy room of his hunting ancestors. She was not there as he came into the room. Only Sturmbannführer Schrader was there, the man his father always called a major. Schrader was holding his hands against his face. Blood was running from between his fingers.

"Where's my mother?" said Siegfried.

Without knowing why, he was walking quietly toward Schrader on the balls of his feet and tensed with one hand on the water pistol in his pocket.

"She's gone," said Schrader.

"Gone where?" said the boy. "She was here just now. I heard her. She was screaming. Screaming for me."

"The window," said Schrader. "She jumped out of the window. She's in the Schwarzesee. She's dead."

In the flickering, darting light of the candle, Siegfried stared at the tumbled bed, the broken cognac bottle, the shattered glasses, the blood on the carpet, the idle swirl of curtains in the open window and, finally, at Schrader.

"You made her jump," he said. "You killed her."

Tears were running down Siegfried's cheeks as he took out the water pistol and walked toward Schrader, who dropped his hands away from his face. It was a grotesque mask of oozing blood and mangled flesh. A sliver of glass was stuck like a broken tooth in his lip.

When Schrader saw that the boy was holding the water pistol, the SS man put out one blood-smeared hand in front of his face. "Don't be silly," he said.

"You killed my mother," said Siegfried. The boy stated it as a matter of fact, without emotion. Yet, he was weeping when he quite slowly raised the pistol, aimed it carefully at the major's slashed, gory face and gently squeezed the trigger.

The liquid prussic acid made tiny splashing sounds as it splattered over Schrader's eyes, mouth and nostrils. He uttered no sound other than a surprised grunt. Then briefly he staggered blindly toward Siegfried before he fell choking and gasping and snorting to the floor. He died very quickly, within minutes. Quicker than any fish Siegfried had ever caught in the Schwarzesee. There was a strong and sickly smell of almonds.

Wondering what to do next, the boy jumped involuntarily as a bright flash suddenly lit the sky outside and the blast of an explosion beat at the window, rattling the wooden storm shutters on their hinges.

Dropping the water pistol, Siegfried ran back up the steps to the watch post. His first thought was that his Panzerfaust must have exploded.

Instead, back at his post, it seemed to Siegfried that all Saxony had erupted in flame and sound.

Shocked by his mother's death and shaking still with the quiet horror of his encounter with the blond and bloody-faced major, Siegfried gripped the rough masonry of the parapet of the Sprengertor lookout and stared about him awestruck.

The dark and familiar countryside had gone mad. The night sky was streaked by curling chains of colored tracer arching into the air, and the flaring muzzle flashes of big guns were silhouetting the stark, photographic outlines of the trees and barns and houses which had hidden them. Like some demonic thunderstorm, an orchestration of sound was sweeping across the fields and forests. Guns boomed. Grenades cracked. Machine guns chattered insanely and savagely. Flares hissed upward, blossomed in their rainbow colors and died falling.

The Fehme had been right about Operation Lilac, thought Siegfried. It certainly has started something. Then he ducked hastily, blinded by the muzzle flash from the snouting gun of one of the Russian tanks under the pines on the other side of the Schwarzesee. Whispering and sighing, the shell fled through the night, sailing high over Schloss Galgenstein.

Standing at the parapet, Siegfried nervously sighted the Panzerfaust at one of the tanks, enormously squat and black and ominous in the light of the Russians' campfires. Steadily Siegfried squeezed the trigger. A gout of fire, a gigantic hiss and then the Panzerfaust missile was gone, streaking through the darkness like a falling star. It dropped short, exploding as it bounded through the pines and felling a tree, which began to smolder halfheartedly.

Before Siegfried had had time to reload the Panzerfaust, the Russian tanks were firing point-blank across the moated Schwarzesee at the towering bulk of Schloss Galgenstein. In rapid succession, a storm of high-velocity shells began slamming into the Sprengertor. Siegfried did not hear the thunder of the last one. It blew the top right off the Sprengertor and, with it, Siegfried. He was dead long before his spinning, cartwheeling body splashed into the Schwarzesee—lifeless as the lichened stone and smoldering timber that hurtled down with him. As the thin, bruised young body slowly sank, fire was already licking at the curtains of the window in the trophy room in the shattered stump of the Sprengertor. Only the bright, dead eys of the antlered heads still mounted on the wall saw the first flames dancing over the U.S. Army chaplain's uniform of the bloody-faced figure sprawled dead on the floor.

Simultaneously with the explosions of the tank shells, which continued to crash and boom against the high walls of Schloss Galgenstein, the sergeant radio operator in the Fehme command-post bunker, far below the Sprengertor, suddenly shouted for Major Hencke, Schrader's adjutant and deputy.

The adjutant, then, had just clattered down the iron steps of the Schraubetreppe, back into the dungeons. He had found Schrader's body in the blazing trophy room near the top of the Sprengertor, but there had been nothing more he could do. The Sturmbannführer was dead and the Russian tanks beyond the Schwarzesee were taking no more chances, pounding at the windows of Schloss Galgenstein with frenzied speed and ruthless accuracy. Schrader's body was already charred and seared by fire. Hurtling masonry and debris were whipping the surprised waters of the Schwarzesee moat into a spouting, leaping boil of foam, and the Sprengertor itself was a caldron of fragmented steel and stone, an inferno of flame and smoke and dust. Hencke had retreated rapidly back down the Schraubetreppe to the deep dungeons.

Heedless of the thunder of the tank bombardment, the operator was crouched over his set, hands pressing the headset to his ears.

"It's Barbarossa," he said, "calling Tannenberg. He'll be landing at Falkewitz soon."

"The Sturmbannführer is dead," said Hencke. "I'm his deputy. I'll talk to Barbarossa."

Events were moving so fast, and so catastrophically, that Major Hencke did not find it strange to be speaking by radio-telephone to the Führer's faithful shadow, Martin Bormann himself.

"Barbarossa, this is Tannenberg Two," he called, articulating carefully, as if he were still at the front with the Waffen SS. "Tannenberg is dead, repeat dead. This is his deputy speaking. I have assumed command of Operation Lilac in his place."

Out of the squeal and roar of static came the thin, lonely voice of Bormann.

"Tannenberg Two, this is Barbarossa. I understand your message. Tannenberg is dead. You are in command as his deputy. Now, stand by. Listen carefully to what I have to say."

Except for the constant growl and screech of the static, there was silence then, and Hencke looked inquiringly at the operator, but radio contact had not been lost with the aircraft, for Bormann's voice was coming through again, speaking slowly.

"Tannenberg Two, this is Barbarossa."

There was another pause, a static-buffeted silence.

"The war is over. I say again, the war is over. Germany has surrendered unconditionally to the Anglo-Americans and the Russians. The surrender became effective at midnight, twenty-four hundred hours on May eighth. It has now been in force, therefore, for twenty-seven minutes. Confirm this message."

Staggered by the news, Hencke and the operator looked at each other.

"My God," said the operator. "It doesn't sound like it outside." Inexplicably, he began to laugh.

"Tannenberg Two confirming," said Hencke. He was finding it hard to concentrate. Never had he thought it would all really end like this—not in abject and total surrender.

Bormanns' voice, thin but insistent, was whispering again in his ears.

"On orders from Moscow, all units of the Red Army are now expending live ammunition in celebration of the end of the war."

Poor little Siegfried, thought Hencke. He didn't know.

"Tannenberg Two, this is Barbarossa. The surrender has been confirmed by official announcements broadcast on Anglo-American radio and from Hamburg. I am still airborne. The aircraft is a Junkers Ju.fifty-two. We will be landing at the designated airfield within about twenty minutes. These, now, are your orders. They will not be repeated."

As broadcast from the lone Ju.52 circling quietly over the darkened and devastated airfield complex at Falkewitz, the orders were both unforeseen and explicit. Operation Lilac was abandoned and with it the Freikorps Bormann troops who had already gone into action at midnight as scheduled. The diversionary action along the Eilenburg-Torgau road to cover the withdrawal of the FkB forces from Torgau and Naunhof was canceled. Battalion Ost and Battalion West were now on their own. Major Bruno von Kleist-Schulenhorst, the prisoner, was under no circumstances to be executed. He was to be escorted by Major Hencke and armed guards to the airfield to take over from the Ju.52 pilot. He had been seriously wounded by Russian light flak during the take-off from the autobahn west of Berlin, behind the Russian forces encircling the city. Bormann, who had been perilously picked up and flown out from a rubble-strewn Berlin street in a Fieseler Storch and transferred to the waiting Ju.52 on the autobahn, had radically changed his own plans. Instead of coming to Schloss Galgenstein from the airfield, he was flying on to Warsaw from Falkewitz to negotiate secretly with the Russians for the premiership of what would now become Russian-occcupied East Germany, including Saxony. In return, he would limit all future Fehme operations to the German territories occupied by the British, the French and the Americans.

The surviving prisoners of the Fehme at Schloss Galgenstein, whether or not sentenced to death, were to be escorted under guard to the airfield at Falkewitz and flown to Warsaw, with Bormann, as airborne hostages to ensure Major von Kleist-Schulenhorst's strict adherence to the flight plan.

The Fehme organization in Saxony was to be disbanded and its members dispersed to their homes.

Operation Lilac was irrevocably canceled and all documentation relating to it was to be destroyed.

Finally, the Fehme headquarters in the dungeons of Schloss Galgenstein were to be blown up.

Hencke acknowledged the instructions and hung the headset on the hook by the side of the radio.

"Kaputt?" said the operator, looking up.

The major nodded. He was still only a little less staggered than he had been earlier.

"Everything," he said. "When we move out, just pour a can of gasoline over your signal logs and equipment and then wire up a demolition charge. After that, you're free to go home, Feldwebel. I wish you well. You've been a good soldier."

They shook hands and Hencke moved off to the underground command post, calling for his infantry NCOs. There were two Feldwebels and four corporals. Quickly he briefed them. Within ten minutes, the preset demolition charges in the dungeons of the castle had been checked and activated, ready for detonation. Blinking their eyes in the light of the torches still flaring in their iron sconces on the walls, the prisoners were lined up outside their cells, ready to move out. Hencke checked them.

He was ready to go.

The escape route would be through the old seepage tunnel under the Schwarzesee where the black waters narrowed to the conventional span of a medieval moat. With him would go the surviving prisoners, as hostages. The Luftwaffe pilot, Major von Kleist-Schulenhorst. The English airman Dart. The American author Duncan. The American private Kowalski. The English woman journalist Caroline Brookwood.

"Where is Stolzer?" said Hencke, realizing that he was missing from the line-up.

The Feldwebel tapped his head.

"Crazy," he said, "like a lunatic. He keeps setting fire to the straw in his cell. He's got a cigarette lighter but we can't find it. He hides it every time we go into the cell. When we told him he was going to Warsaw, he started screaming and yelling about Auschwitz and the Russians. Now he's got hold of a grenade and he says he's going to stay in the cell and kill himself rather than have the Russians get him. He keeps saying they'll skin him alive. He's got the grenade wired up so that it will explode if you open the cell door."

Hencke was skeptical.

"Where would he get a grenade from?"

"He's got one all right, sir," said the Feldwebel firmly. "One of the Fehme men here was Jewish. Nobody knew. He deserted last night. Before he cleared out, he gave the grenade to Stolzer. For the Jewish New Year, he said."

"Some joke," said Hencke sourly. "Just for once, though, I'm on the side of the Jews. Stolzer would be no loss to anybody. There's no time now to fool around with him. Bormann will be landing any time now, as soon as the pilot can pull himself together long enough to get the aircraft down onto the ground in one piece. There are some Werewolf boys waiting for us at the Elbe with a boat. It's not far. They have a couple of FkB jeeps on the other side, on the east bank, to take us to the airfield. We can't waste time with Stolzer. Just lock him up and leave him there with his grenade. I hope he has a happy Jewish New Year. The whole place is going up with a bang soon, anyway."

Stolzer began to scream and weep, begging Trudi to forgive him, as they locked the door of his cell. He was still raving and trying to set fire to the straw on the floor as Hencke and his NCOs herded the remaining five prisoners and hostages into the tunnel. The rest of the Fehme men and the FkB troops of the disbanded headquarters company had already left the castle by way of the Schraubetreppe. Hencke had ordered them to cross the Schwarzesee by the moat bridge and create a diversion near Galgenstein village. This was planned to cover the airfield party's withdrawal through the woods toward the nearby Elbe from the tunnel exit on the eastern shore of the Schwarzesee.

"Smell that gasoline," muttered Tommy Dart. "They're pulling out, all right."

The prisoners were hurrying through the tunnel, stumbling in the yellow glare of their escorts' flashlights and splashing in the water that streamed down the slimed brick walls of the narrow tunnel.

"They've got enough high explosive connected up back there to blow the whole goddam castle clear over the Elbe," said Kowalski. "I sure as hell hope we get clear of this tunnel first."

"I'll say this for them," grunted Dermott Duncan, "they're certainly not wasting any time." He was gasping for breath. At first the tunnel had descended. Now it was climbing again.

"It smells like a public lavatory," he wheezed.

"Some dirty son of a bitch has been crapping in here, that's why," said Kowalski.

A sharp and resonant boom of sound raced after them along the narrow tunnel. A pressure wave of blast smashed suddenly at their ears.

Caroline Brookwood slipped in the slime and fell, grazing her knees on the wet, rough bricks.

"God," she said to Dermott as he helped her up, "we're like rats in a sewer. What a way to die."

"It was just a grenade," said von Kleist-Schulenhorst. "I think the gallant SS officer from Auschwitz just changed his mind and tried to blow open the door of his cell. They told me he did not want to come to Warsaw with us. Too close to Auschwitz, I imagine."

"Grenade or no grenade," gasped Kowalski, "it still scared the living Jesus out of me. If the flash had kicked off those demolition charges or that gasoline, we'd have had it by now."

Silently and desperately, the prisoners stumbled on. They needed no urging from their guards. The tunnel boomed and rang with vast, distorted echoes of labored breathing, splashing feet and the clink of slung guns knocking against the narrow, embracing walls.

When they came at last to a steep flight of stone steps, Hencke ordered them up, one at a time.

"No talking," he said, swinging a Schmeisser machine pistol in the light of his torch. "No tricks. I'll be right behind you with this."

After the fetid, echoing confinement of the tunnel, the night air was sweet with the smell of pine and grass and moss. They were standing near a pump house in an overgrown quarry which faced the Schwarzesee and Schloss Galgenstein. The Russian tanks had stopped firing at the castle. High above it, the tall, shattered stump of the Sprengertor was burning like a beacon. Somewhere inside it, burned the body of Sturmbannführer Schrader. The Mittelschloss was also ablaze. The windows of the great hall were square-cut rubies of flame. Sparks and burning debris hissed down into the black waters of the Schwarzesee where the bodies of the Gräfin Jutte von Bluckau and her son drifted under the reeds.

Major Hencke knelt by the plunger which one of his Feldwebels had carried all the way from the command-post bunker while the other had paid out the wires that ran back through the tunnel like thin, black umbilical cords.

The night wind sang mournfully in the waiting pines.

"Here goes five hundred years of history," said the major, his voice bitter. "Stand clear of the door to the tunnel. Since the Russkis started expending live ammunition all over Saxony tonight to celebrate victory, they might get a laugh out of this."

With both hands and all his weight, he suddenly pushed down on the plunger.

The result was apocalyptic.

Prisoners and escorts alike were aghast, awed by the spectacle of violent destruction.

They saw first an enormous and blinding flash of light that flickered on and on, eerily, like the transient play of sheet lightning on a hot summer's night. Then, beneath their feet, the rocky ground shuddered and shook so that pine cones and twigs rained down from the trees about them. Toward their shore, a shock wave of concussion shivered across the black waters of the Schwarzesee. For a stark, sharp-etched moment, Schloss Galgenstein still proudly stood, burning but unbroken. Then, fantastically, the great castle began to change its shape as if it were sand and had suddenly been flooded by a rising tide.

As the roar of the demolition charges smote at the affronted night, Schloss Galgenstein began sliding down into the girdling Schwarzesee in a rumbling, thundering cataract of stone, fire and smoke, all half obscured by a climbing wall of steam and spray and dust. In the abysmal darkness which followed the flashes of the explosions, the landslide stopped as suddenly and inevitably as it had begun.

Schloss Galgenstein was visible only as a gigantic mound of rubble and smashed stone.

Against the debris of its destruction surged the shocked waters of the Schwarzesee.

The night was raucous with the lonely, frightened cries of wild fowl and the beating of their wings as they took flight.

In the quarry, smoke was pouring from the tunnel exit, an exhalation foul as a dragon's breath with the sulphurous stench of explosives and the stench of stagnant water and slime. The iron door had been blown from its hinges, cutting a swath through the pines. There was no way back. There was no longer a Schloss Galgenstein.

"March," said Major Hencke. "Single file and quietly. No talking and no foolish attempts to escape."

After the urgent and labored flight through the tunnel under the Schwarzesee, the night march through the silent woods was, somehow, a less ominous enterprise. Even the drifting passage of the wide, swift waters of the Elbe brought no challenging shots from patrolling Russians alerted by the furtive squeal of oars in the river skiff's oarlocks. For the Fehme's prisoners, crouched miserably together on the wet thwarts, interception by the Russians would almost certainly have brought not liberation but death, if only by drowning; there would have been neither time nor opportunity to prove their strange status to the Russians. With relief, they felt the boat's keel rasp noisily onto a spit of sand and gravel below the east bank of the Elbe. They were safely across. The sense of deliverance from the risks of the river crossing was short-lived, though. Even in the darkest hours of Germany's surrender, there had been no breakdown in the local field organization of the Fehme and the Werewolf organization. Two husky, quietly-spoken youths were waiting to hand over two spare FkB jeeps parked under the willows that hung down over the rough track along the riverbank.

"This is it," Kowalski whispered to Tommy Dart as they were hustled toward the leading jeep with the Luftwaffe major, von Kleist-Schulenhorst. "This is just about as far as I go with these goons. Let me sit on the outside, old buddy."

"Don't be a clot," the English airman said, his voice low and strained. "We've only got one Feldwebel as a driver but the major and the other Feldwebel will be riding behind us in the second jeep with Duncan and Miss Brookwood. Hencke will cut you to pieces if you jump."

Kowalski, though, got his way. He was sitting in the back of the jeep, on the right-hand side, as it turned cautiously onto a ditch-lined road that slanted away between the plowed fields from the Elbe toward the heights of Falkewitz and the air base. The other jeep was close behind. They were both traveling quite fast without headlights, for the rising moon was bright on the open country, bright enough for Tommy to see, in a single glance over his shoulder, that Major Hencke was riding with his Schmeisser propped ready on his knee.

Tommy was sitting crushed between the Luftwaffe major and Kowalski in the back of the jeep so he felt the quick slide of feet and tensing of muscles as the American crouched ready.

As, no doubt, had Major Hencke, Kowalski waited until the jeep ran into the dark cover of the woods that camouflaged the dispersal bays of the airfield at Falkewitz. Suddenly, with a scraping of boots on metal, Kowalski was gone, arms outflung like a man jumping for a lifeline. Below his line of fall dropped a grassy embankment which led the road across a marshy tributary of the Elbe.

Above the lurching squeal of brakes and skidding tires, Tommy heard the sharp, spiteful rip of the Schmeisser. Kowalski was hit even before his body began bouncing down the embankment toward the marsh like a great, clumsy rag doll.

Leaping and sliding down the embankment after him, Hencke came to Kowalski's body, sprawled in the moonlight between the pines, and turned it over slowly with his boot. Then, with infinite care, he fired two single shots from the Schmeisser. With each shot, Kowalski appeared to jerk and shake his head. Then he lay still.

Dragging the American's body to the edge of the marsh, Hencke rolled it into a black pool of slimy water. There was barely a splash and soon the body had sunk. The major had learned his trade with the Waffen SS, but he was still a prudent officer. With the war over, even by barely an hour, there was even more reason not to be careless about evidence of murder.

Back on the road again, Hencke paused by the leading jeep and spoke to von Kleist-Schulenhorst still sitting silently alongside Tommy.

"He wants to know if there are any more volunteers for suicide," said the Luftwaffe pilot.

As the jeep rolled eastward again, Bruno shook his head and patted Tommy's knee.

"Don't try to be a hero," he said. "The war ended at midnight. Only fools die now. There are no more medals."

Falkewitz airfield, when they came to it, was seemingly deserted. No flarepath sparkled. Only moonlight illuminated the wide, empty runways. Blindly, flak guns poked their cold barrels at the scornful stars. Bombed, strafed and sabotaged aircraft sprawled awkwardly at their dispersals, wings twisted at grotesque angles. The shattered hangars were vast caverns of shadowed destruction. In the high, stilt-legged control tower, though, where the radio transmitter for Werewolfsender had howled its hymns of hate, there was quick movement as the two jeeps swung to a halt on the wide and windy tarmac area. A man was clattering down the steel ladders, his boots ringing on the rungs, so that Caroline Brookwood was reminded of the Schraubetreppe back at Schloss Galgenstein. As the man joined the group waiting by the jeeps and saluted smartly to Hencke, she could see the sprig of lilac in his lapel, deathly white in the light of the moon. She could not hear what he was saying to the major, for by then she was watching the dark shape of an aircraft circling the airfield.

"What is it?" said Dermott Duncan.

Tommy waited until the aircraft banked in triple-snouted outline against a mass of cloud shining in the moonlight.

"A Ju.fifty-two," he said.

"That's Bormann's," said the Luftwaffe major. "Next stop, Warsaw."

"This is damned ridiculous," said Dermott angrily.

While they had been waiting to enter the escape tunnel under the Schwarzesee at Schloss Galgenstein, Bruno had told them of the orders from Bormann. The flight to Warsaw with himself, von Kleist-Schulenhorst, as pilot, and the role of the other prisoners as hostages for his enforced allegiance to the secret flight plan. Dermott Duncan had been fiercely unable to believe it or accept it then, nor was he now, even on the tarmac at Falkewitz.

Somberly Caroline watched the circling Ju.52. It was dropping lower over the black pinewoods beyond the end of the main runway. Caroline was trying to remember everything of whatever she had read or heard about Martin Bormann. All she could recall was that he had a sinister reputation of facelessness. The Führer's shadow, she thought, like Cerberus, the hound of hell, guarding the gates of the underworld and preventing both the good and the evil from escaping to the world above. What would he be like? How strange that he should be up there with his fugitive staff in that dark, lumbering bat of a plane, peering down at where she stood in the moonlight. The desperate, hunted satrap of Adolf Hitler himself. Soon, though, they would know his face, for the Ju.52 was dropping still lower.

"He's landing," said Tommy Dart. "He's coming in."

Even after so many years of not flying, Tommy was once more experiencing the tightening of the stomach muscles which he had invariably suffered before take-off for a German target. Always he had returned to base ravenously hungry because he had never been able to eat before flying on operations. The thought of being killed with undigested food in his guts had always disgusted and nauseated him. After the prolonged, disintegrated horror of the night when he had been shot down with his crew, Tommy had sworn that he would never fly again. Yet, here he was, standing on an airfield and waiting to board a German aircraft which was about to make a clandestine flight 300 miles east over Russian-occupied territory to Warsaw. Every fiber of Tommy's instinct for self-preservation was registering only one thought in his anxious mind. The flight was going to be a cock-up. He just knew it. And in Tommy's long experience as an operational airman, a cock-up in the air invariably resulted in disaster. If Tommy had eaten a meal during that long day and night he would have been vomiting on the grass.

"How are the mighty fallen," said Dermott Duncan. Martin Bormann himself, he thought. A fugitive in his own Third Reich. As a foreign correspondent in Germany before the war, Dermott had reported day by day the ruthless rise to power of the Nazi party. So many names and so many places. Hitler, Göring, Goebbels, Himmler, Hess, Ley, Frank, Streicher, von Ribbentrop and von Schirach and the rest of them—a whole high-priesthood of infamy. Berlin, Berchtesgaden, Innsbruck, Vienna, Hamburg, Munich, Nuremberg and all the other garlanded altars of National Socialism where the barbaric banners flew and the marching boots shook the supine streets.

The sights and the sounds beat at his memory like the roll of distant drums, yet, strangely, he had no really cogent recollection of Martin Bormann.

That he, Dermott Duncan, should be waiting now to keep even such an unbelievably insane appointment as this with the living man, not the enigmatic legend, filled him with a savage exultancy. Despite the hazards, real or imagined, which might attend the secret flight to Warsaw, Dermott knew that he would not change places with any journalist in the Western world. If he survived this journey as a hostage, it would have been worth it if only for the meeting with Bormann, the only self-effacing man of mystery in an overtly evil hierarchy of strutting extroverts, the medaled Caesars of the Third Reich.

O Lord, prayed Dermott, deliver this evil man into mine hands. Deliver him unto me and I will rend him with the truth of my words so that all the world may read and revile.

Until this moment, Dermott Duncan had not prayed for years.

"He's going to make it," said von Kleist-Schulenhorst. He meant the pilot, not Bormann. In the moonlight, the Ju.52 was sailing in on final approach over the woods toward the runway. The great black wing of the Junkers, sagging with flap, was reaching for the earth. Not bad, thought Bruno. He had overheard Hencke talking with the Fehme man before he returned to the control tower. Bormann's pilot had been wounded badly by the Russian light flak. It had shattered his windscreen and lashed him with singing shards of hot, splintered steel. Since then, the pilot had been slowly bleeding to death as he flew and was barely conscious. That had been the last coherent report to the tower at Falkewitz. He was probably still bleeding even as the aircraft sank toward the runway.

Bruno watched critically, with professional detachment. The poor bastard, he thought, and wondered if it was a pilot he may have known. He would be checking back on the stick now for the flare-out from the approach. Throttles back. Power off. The last few sinking moments of flight. The agonized waiting for the rumble of landing gear that would tell the dying pilot that his ordeal was over.

The Ju.52 touched down awkwardly on one wheel. Then it straightened and ran fast and true. Any time now, thought Bruno.

He can't possibly miss the mines. That had been the final phase of the evacuation plans for Falkewitz, as he remembered them. The long, black bitumen runways; so empty and so inviting but sown with a mathematically computed pattern of mines. No Russian aircraft, though, had bothered to land at Falkewitz. Ironically, Bormann's Ju.52 was the first aircraft to land since the demolitions and the evacuation from which Bruno had escaped in Leipzig.

For a few seconds, Bruno wondered if the final surge forward of the Russians into Saxony had overrun Falkewitz before the runways could have been mined by the cursing armorers. He had been too busy with his plans for desertion to the Americans to have worried about the mining of the runways.

Then, instantly, there was no doubt.

Beneath the Ju.52, still rolling fast, as if its braking system had been shot up, the runway was erupting in wicked gouts of flame as if the aircraft were being pursued by rapid and accurate bursts of shellfire. A severed main landing wheel bounded away as the Ju.52 suddenly ground-looped, dug in a wing and cartwheeled grotesquely down the runway, detonating more mines, until it flicked over onto its back.

At first there was no sign of fire in the dark and twisted shape of wreckage. After the staccato reverberations of the detonated mines and the thin, high screech of sliding metal, the silence was immense.

Slowly then, almost innocently, like an enormous pink bubble, the fuel tanks exploded.

The hollow, echoing boom of the detonation galvanized Major Hencke out of the stupefied state of inertia which had gripped him since the landing had first thundered into disaster.

"My God," he said. "They'll be trapped."

With his two sergeants, he ran for a jeep. Throwing turf from its tires, the vehicle lurched as Hencke spun it around, bouncing across the airfield toward the roaring column of fire that was already devouring the wreckage on the runway.

"They'll be too late, of course," said Tommy. "People always are when an aircraft prangs on landing and burns. The crew and the passengers have had it." Tommy had seen it all before on flarepaths back in England. Too many times.

"I'd rather not watch," said Caroline.

Inconsequentially, and to nobody in particular, she added, "I think I might be sick."

Dermott fumbled for a cigarette. As usual, he didn't have one. Right then, he would have swapped his typewriter for a pack of Chesterfields. He swore savagely and with feeling.

"There goes my Martin Bormann story," he said.

Nobody was listening, least of all Caroline.

Dermott took her by the elbow.

"On the grass," he said gently. "Not on the concrete. That way, it won't splash."

There was still the Kreuzenberg book and the dossier on "The Well of Death," he thought. Thank God for that.

Major Bruno von Kleist-Schulenhorst was standing by the remaining jeep. He held up an ignition key so that it glinted briefly in the moonlight.

"Let them put out their own fires," he said in his pedantic, slightly sing-song English. "They'll have lit enough for other people to burn in. The war is over. I am going home. Is anybody else coming?"

They waited while Caroline washed her face and rinsed her mouth at the gush of a fire hydrant and then drove quickly away from the airfield, and nobody spoke until Bruno halted the jeep where the road back westward to Torgau mounted a ridge that overlooked the airfield at Falkewitz, behind and below them. Like ancient temples, huge and desecrated, the wrecked hangars of the base were silhouetted against the funeral pyre that still blazed on the treacherous perspective of runway.

Major von Kleist-Schulenhorst shook his head.

"A hero's death," he said. "I hope Herr Bormann dies happy. Now he'll know what it's really like."

Again, nobody spoke or looked back as he drove on. Enough, at last, was enough.

Near Torgau, Tommy Dart recognized a village he knew and had the Luftwaffe major halt the jeep. Dermott looked over at the little English air gunner, the slightly pathetic man-of-confidence.

"For God's sake, Tommy. We're in a hurry. What's up, now?"

"I'm going back to Hohenleipisch," said Tommy. "There's a road to there out of this village."

"Whatever for?" said Caroline, grateful for the warmth of big Dermott's arm against the chill of the night wind.

"The war may be over, but I'm still the man-of-confidence at Stalag IV J," said Tommy. "Somebody's got to organize repatriation from the camp. I'm going back to see Kravchenkov, the Russian commandant."

"For Christ's sake," said Dermott. "Now I've heard everything. Haven't you had enough?"

He said no more, though, and, instead, held out his hand to shake Tommy's.

The sparrow-like little figure in the battle dress, shabby now, was still standing at the village crossroads in the moonlight and waving as they drove on.

"A good soldier," said Bruno. "In the end they win the wars. Only the generals lose them."

In the great woods near Torgau where the Fehme men had urged the running townspeople on to hunt and lynch the crew of the American bomber that lay burning in the forest, the German stopped the jeep again. It was a bad moment for Caroline. Somewhere behind the dark ramparts of pines along the road, Mike and his crew still lay in unmarked graves with broken necks. She wanted to get out and run away.

"Do you drive?" the German asked Dermott.

The big man with the shaggy, unkempt hair nodded. "Well enough."

Bruno climbed down out of the jeep. Stripping off his Luftwaffe jacket he threw it into the ditch by the side of the road.

"I won't need that any more," he said.

Bowing slightly, with the faintest suggestion of a click of heels, Bruno held out his hand.

"Good-bye," he said. "Good luck. Just keep going west. You'll come to the Elbe soon enough."

Quickly, then, he was gone, stooping below the undergrowth between the pines. It was as if he had never existed. Already, thought Caroline, Major von Kleist-Schulenhorst was just part of the memory of an old nightmare to be evoked only, perhaps years later, by some psychological catalyst as trivial as the fragrance of lilacs in the spring.

Dermott had a little trouble with the jeep's gears but not for long. Caroline, it seemed, knew more about driving jeeps than he did. Soon they were out of the bitter, brooding forest and the tires were singing on a moonlit road that swept them on toward Torgau and the Elbe.

Beyond them, the sweeping bends of Saxony's greatest river still lay spilled like molten metal in the moonlight. It was strange to think that to these peaceful banks the Russian and the American armies had fought to close the gap between the East Front and the West Front.

"There she is," said Dermott, "the Elbe. After that, there's only the Mulde. Then we're in the American zone of occupation. I might have a chance to trade you for a carton of Chesterfields."

Caroline put her hand on Dermott's as he reached for the gear-shift.

"Just one more river to cross?" she said.

Dermott laughed out loud, teeth white against the dark, piratical beard. "Yes," he said, "and I don't think we'll even have to get our feet wet."

Their heads were close together, almost like lovers, as Dermott drove quite slowly toward Torgau and the Russian bridge which Operation Lilac had failed, after all, to destroy.

There was no need to hurry any more.

The road to the west was clear.